T0089037

Praise for Sofi Oksanen's

WHEN *the* DOVES DISAPPEARED

"Vivid. . . . A tense, politically relevant novel. . . . Weave[s] an intrigue that builds to moments of shocking revelation."   *—Financial Times*

"A thrilling page-turner. . . . A shattering family drama and an unsparing deconstruction of history. . . . Renewed Russian-sabre-rattling in the Baltics makes this a perfect time to read this superb writer."
                              —The Independent (London)

"A superb novel. . . . Over it hangs a Graham Greene–like atmosphere of human wretchedness and compromised political faith." *—The Daily Telegraph* (London)

"Astonishing. . . . No one in these pages is predictable, because survival in this period, Oksanen so beautifully reveals, meant learning to love only from the part of the heart that knows how to betray."   *—Toronto Star*

"Brilliant. . . . [A] great historical thriller. . . . [Oksanen] has woven a story of betrayal, lies, political deceit and modern history."   *—The Globe and Mail* (Toronto)

"Engaging. . . . Suspenseful. . . . Gorgeousness jumps off the page when least expected."

—*Winnipeg Free Press*

"Powerful fiction that stirs history, war crimes, and psychology into a compelling mix. . . . Oksanen captures both the futility of the citizens of a tiny country who yearn for freedom and the dark heart of an opportunist who would sell out his own family in order to survive."

—*Booklist*

"Oksanen depicts civilian life in wartime and under communist oppression in rich historical detail, skillfully manipulating chronology and threading clues subtly throughout the narrative as suspense builds. . . . Highly recommended." —*Library Journal* (starred)

Sofi Oksanen

WHEN *the* DOVES DISAPPEARED

Sofi Oksanen is a Finnish-Estonian novelist and play-wright. She has received numerous prizes for her work, including the Swedish Academy Nordic Prize, the Prix Femina, the Budapest Grand Prize, the European Book Prize, and the Nordic Council Literature Prize. She lives in Helsinki.

www.sofioksanen.com
Twitter: @SofiOksanen
www.facebook.com/sofioksanen

ALSO BY SOFI OKSANEN

Purge

WHEN *the* DOVES
DISAPPEARED

WHEN *the* DOVES DISAPPEARED

A Novel

Sofi Oksanen

Translated from the Finnish by Lola Rogers

VINTAGE BOOKS

A Division of Penguin Random House LLC

New York

FIRST VINTAGE BOOKS EDITION, FEBRUARY 2016

Translation copyright © 2015 by Lola Rogers

All rights reserved. Published in the United States by Vintage Books,
a division of Penguin Random House LLC, New York.
Originally published in Finland as *Kun kyyhkyset katosivat*
by Like Kustannus Oy, Helsinki, in 2012. Copyright © 2012
by Sofi Oksanen. This translation originally published in hardcover
in the United States by Alfred A. Knopf, a division of
Penguin Random House LLC, New York, in 2015.

Vintage and colophon are registered trademarks of
Penguin Random House LLC.

This is a work of fiction. Names, characters, places, and incidents
either are the product of the author's imagination or are used
fictitiously. Any resemblance to actual persons, living or dead, events,
or locales is entirely coincidental.

The Library of Congress has cataloged the Knopf edition as follows:
Oksanen, Sofi, 1977–
[Kum kyyhkyset katosivat. English]
When the doves disappeared : a novel / Sofi Oksanen.
p. cm.
1. War stories.   I. Title.
PH356.O37 K8613 2015   894'.54134—DC23   2014034970

Vintage Books Trade Paperback ISBN: 978-0-345-80590-4
eBook ISBN: 978-0-385-35018-1

Map by Martin Lubikowski, ML Design, London, United Kingdom

Book design by Cassandra J. Pappas

www.vintagebooks.com

146122990

Propaganda is the collapse of language.

—*Lev Rubinstein, Warsaw, 2014*

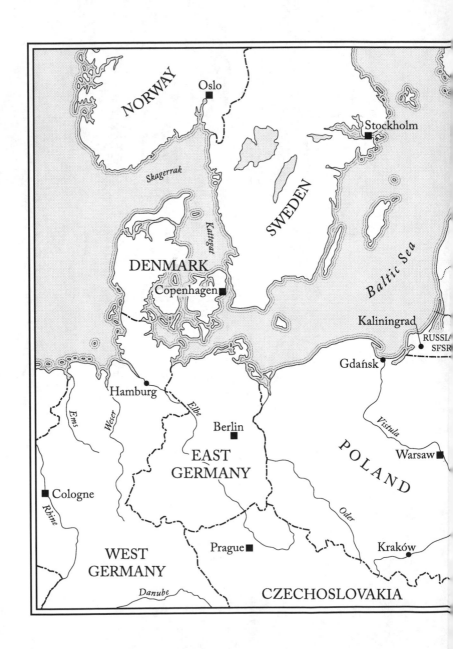

FINLAND

Helsinki

Gulf of Finland

Leningrad

Tallinn
(Reval)

Narva

**ESTONIAN
SSR**

Tartu
(Dorpat)

Lovat

Volga

Moscow

**LATVIAN
SSR**

Riga

Dvina

RUSSIAN SFSR

LITHUANIAN
SSR

Vilnius

Neman

Minsk

**BELORUSSIAN
SSR**

Kiev

Dnieper

UKRAINIAN SSR

Bug

**Soviet Occupation of Estonia,
1940–1941, 1944–1991
*(German National Socialist
Occupation, 1941–1944)***

0   1   200   300 kilometers

PROLOGUE

Western Estonia,
Estonian Soviet Socialist Republic,
Soviet Union

WE WENT TO Rosalie's grave one last time and placed some wildflowers on the grassy moonlit mound. We were silent for a moment with the blooms between us. I didn't want to let Juudit go, which is why I said out loud what a person shouldn't say in that situation:

"We'll never see each other again."

I could hear the gravel in my voice, and it brought a gleam of water to her eyes, that gleam that had often knocked me off balance, welling up and sending my rational mind lightly afloat, like a bark boat. Rocking on a stream that flowed from her eyes. Maybe I spoke bluntly to dull my own pain, maybe I just wanted to be cruel so that when she'd left she could curse me and my callousness, or maybe I yearned for some final declaration, for her to say she didn't want to leave. I was still uncertain of the movements of her heart, even after all we'd been through together.

"You regret bringing me here," Juudit whispered.

I was startled by her perceptiveness, rubbed my neck in embarrassment. She'd given me a haircut just that evening, and it itched where the hair had fallen down inside my collar.

"It's all right. I understand," she said.

I could have contradicted her, but I didn't, although she hadn't been a burden. The men had insinuated otherwise. But I had to bring her to the safety of the forest when I heard that she'd had to flee from Tallinn. The Armses' farm wasn't a safe place for us with the Russians advancing. The forest was better. She'd been like an injured bird in the palm of my hand, weakened, her nerves feverish for weeks. When our medic was killed in combat, the men finally let Mrs. Vaik come to help us, us and Juudit. I had succeeded in rescuing her one more time, but once she stepped out onto the road that loomed ahead of us, I wouldn't be able to protect her anymore. The men were right, though—women and children belonged at home. Juudit had to go back to town. The noose around us was tightening and the safety of the forest was melting away. I watched her face out of the corner of my eye. Her gaze had turned to the road that she would leave by; her mouth was open, she was gulping the air with all her strength, and the feel of her breath threatened to undermine my resolve.

"It's best this way," I said. "Best for all of us. Go back to the life you left behind."

"It's not the same anymore. It never will be."

PART ONE

Then Mark, the guard, came and took them one at a time to the edge of the ditch and executed them with his pistol.

—K. Lemmick and E. Martinson, *12,000: Testimony in the Case of the Mass Murderers Juhan Jüriste, Karl Linnas, and Ervin Viks, Tartu, January 16–20, 1962*, Estonian State Publishing House, 1962

Northern Estonia,
Estonian Soviet Socialist Republic,
Soviet Union

THE HUM FROM beyond the trees was growing louder—I knew what was coming. I looked at my hands. They were steady. In a moment I would be running toward the oncoming column of vehicles. I would forget about Edgar and his nerves. I could see him from the corner of my eye fiddling with his trousers with trembling hands, his face the wrong color for battle. We had just come from training in Finland, where I'd worried whether he would be all right, as if he were a child, but now that we were in combat the situation had changed. We had a job to do. Soon. Now. I took off running, my grenades whacking against my leg, my hand ready to tug one loose from the side of my boot, my fingers already feeling its spin through the air. The Finnish army shirt I'd put on when we were training on Staffan Island still felt new; it gave strength to my legs. Soon all the men would wear only Estonian gear, nobody else's, not the occupiers', not the allies', only our own. That was our aim, to take our country back.

I could hear the others coming behind me, the ground groaning with our power, and I ran still harder toward the hum of the engines. I could smell the enemy's sweat, could almost taste the rage and metal in my mouth. It was someone else running in my boots, the same emotionless warrior who in the last battle had leapt over a ditch to throw grenades at the destruction battalion—cap . . . cord . . . throw, cap . . . cord . . . throw. It was someone else—cap . . . cord . . . throw—and that someone was sprinting toward the column. There were more of them than we'd thought. There was no end to the destruction battalions—Russians, and men who looked like Estonians—no end to their vehicles and machine guns. But we weren't scared. Let them be scared. We had hate running through us, running with such force that our opponents halted, the tires of the Mootor bus spinning in place, our hatred nailing them to the moment when we opened fire. I charged with the others toward the bus and we killed them all.

MY ARMS WERE trembling from the bullets I fired, my wrists heavy from the weight of the grenades I threw, but gradually I realized the fight was over. When my feet adjusted to staying in one place and the shells stopped raining onto the ground, I noticed that the end of the battle didn't bring silence. It brought noise. Greedy maggots making their way out of the earth toward the bodies, the eager rustle of death's minions hurrying toward fresh blood. And it stunk the stink of feces, the reek of vomited bile. My eyes were blinded, the gunpowder smoke was starting to disperse, and it was as if a bright golden chariot had appeared at the edge of the clouds, ready to gather up the fallen—not just our men, but also the destruction battalion men, Russians and Estonians. I squinted. My ears were ringing. I saw men gasping, wiping their brows, swaying like trees where they stood. I tried to keep my eye on the sky, the shining chariot, but I couldn't just stand there leaning against the battered side of the Mootor. The quickest ones were already moving like shoppers at a market. The weapons had to be collected from the dead. The guns and pocket cartridge belts—nothing else. We waded through body parts, twitching limbs. I had just taken an ammunition belt from an enemy soldier when something on the ground grabbed my ankle. The grip was surprisingly strong, pulling me down toward a murmuring mouth. Before I could take aim, my knees gave way and I slid down next to the dying man—as helpless as he was, sure that my moment had come. But he wasn't looking at me. His words were directed at someone else, someone beloved. I didn't understand what he was saying, he was speaking Russian, but his voice was the kind a man uses only when speaking to his bride. I would have known even if I hadn't seen the photograph in his stained hand, the white skirt in the picture. The photo was red with a bridegroom's blood now, a finger covering the woman's face. I wrenched my leg free and the life disappeared from his eyes, eyes where I had just seen myself. I forced myself to stand. I had to keep moving.

When the weapons were collected, there was a rattle of engines again from farther off and Sergeant Allik gave the order to retreat. We guessed that the destruction battalion would wait for reinforcements before making another attack or searching for the camps, but we knew they would come. The machine gunners had already made it as far as the edge of the forest when I saw a familiar figure bent over a still flailing body: Mart. His feet had already crushed the skull—brains mixed with mud—but still he hit and hit with his rifle butt, as if he wanted to put it all the way through the body and into the ground. I ran over and skidded into him hard, which made him lose his grip on the rifle. He bucked blindly, not recognizing me, roaring at an invisible enemy and thrashing the air, but I got hold of him, took my belt off, wrapped it around him, and led him to the dressing station, where the men were hurriedly piling up the things they'd found. I whispered that this man needed looking after, tapping my temple, and the medic glanced at Mart—who was gasping, frothing at the mouth—and nodded. Sergeant Allik hustled the men onward, snatched a pocket flask from someone's hand, and shouted that an Estonian doesn't fight drunk like a Russky does. I started to look for my cousin Edgar, suspecting that he had run away, but he was perched on a rock with his hand over his mouth, his face wet with sweat. I grabbed his shoulder, and when I let go he started to rub his coat with a filthy handkerchief on the spot where I'd touched him with my bloody fingers.

"I can't do this, Roland. Don't be angry."

A sudden disgust sloshed in my chest, and an image flashed through my mind of my mother hiding coffee, brewing it secretly for Edgar and no one else. I shook my head. I had to concentrate, forget about the coffee, forget about Mart, how I'd recognized what I saw in his addled eyes, a man like the one who had run into battle in my boots. I had to forget the enemy soldier who had grabbed my leg, how I'd recognized myself in his gaze, too, and I had to forget that I hadn't seen myself in Sergeant Allik's face. Or the medic's. This was my third battle since coming back from Finland, and I was still alive, the enemy's blood on my hands. So where did this sudden doubt come from? Why didn't I recognize myself in the faces of the men that I knew would survive to see peace come with their own eyes?

"Do you plan to look for more of our men, or stay here and fight?" Edgar asked.

I turned toward the trees. We had a job to do: weaken the

Red Army, which was occupying Estonia, and relay information of their progress to our allies in Finland. I still remembered how glad we had been to dress ourselves in our new Finnish gear and form ranks in the evenings, singing, *Saa vabaks Eesti meri, saa vabaks Eesti pind*—Be free, Estonian sea; be free, Estonian land. When we got back to Estonia, my unit only managed to cut a few phone lines; then our radios stopped working and we decided we'd be more useful if we joined up with the other fighters. Sergeant Allik had proved himself a brave man—the Forest Brothers were advancing at a breakneck pace.

"The refugees may need our protection," Edgar whispered. He was right. The crowds escaping through the cover of the forest were accompanied by several good men, but they were moving slowly because they were surrounded—the only way out was through the swamp. We'd fought like maniacs to give them time, holding the enemy back, but would our victory give them enough of a head start? Edgar sensed my thoughts. He added, "Who knows what's happening at home? We haven't heard anything from Rosalie."

Before I had a chance to think, I was already nodding and on my way to report that we were leaving, going to protect the refugees, even though I was sure Edgar had suggested it only to avoid another attack, to save his own skin. My cousin knew my weaknesses. We had all left our fiancées and wives at home. I was the only one using a woman as an excuse to leave the fight. Still, I told myself that my choice was completely honorable, even wise.

The captain thought it was a good idea for us to leave. Nevertheless, my mood was strangely detached. Maybe it was because the hearing in my left ear hadn't returned yet, or because the words of that dying soldier still echoed in my head. It felt as if nothing that had happened was real, and I couldn't get the stink of death off my hands, even though I washed them over and over when we found a stream. The lines on my palms—the life line, the heart, the head—still stood out in dried blood stamped deep into my flesh, and I walked onward hand in hand with the dead. I kept remembering how my feet had run into battle, how my hands hadn't hesitated to make my machine gun sing, how when the bullets ran out I grabbed my pistol, and after that some rocks I found on the ground, until in the end I was pounding a Red soldier's head against the mudguard from the Mootor. But that wasn't me, it was that other man.

I'd lost my compass in the fight, and we were slogging through unfamiliar forest, but I kept on as if I knew where we were going, and cheered up a bit when I heard a bird singing. It wasn't long before Edgar noticed that I wasn't sure of our direction, but he was hardly going to complain. We were safer if we kept our distance from the refugees the destruction battalion was looking for. There was no need for him to say it out loud. A few times he tried to suggest that we should just wait patiently for the Germans to arrive, that anything else we did would be a waste of time, and why take risks at this point? I didn't listen, I just kept going. I was going to the Armses' place to protect Rosalie and her family, and to check on Simson Farm—my own family's place—and if the fighting continued, I would look for a brother I could trust, and join his troop. Edgar followed me, just like he'd followed me over the Gulf of Finland for training. The water seeping up through cracks in the sea ice had turned his cheek pale and he'd wanted to turn back. When our skis froze up, I had hacked the chunks of ice away for him, and we'd kept going, me in front, Edgar behind, just like now. This time, though, I wanted to keep a good distance between us, let his panting fade into the rustling of the trees. My fingers trembled when I took out my tobacco pouch; I didn't want him to see that. The look on the face of the man who'd grabbed my leg came back into my mind again and again. I quickened my pace. My knapsack weighed me down, but still I went faster, I wanted to leave that face behind, the face of a man who may have died from my bullet, a man whose bride would never know where her bridegroom fell, or that his last thought was *I love you.*

There were other reasons that I'd left so willingly, left the others to prepare for the next attack. I already had my doubts about our German allies. They'd sent us to attack the rear of the Red Army with a few grenades and pistols and a radio that didn't work. Nothing more. We hadn't even been given a decent map of Estonia. We'd been sent there to die, I was sure of it. But I followed orders and kept my mouth shut. As if the last few centuries hadn't taught us anything, all the times the German barons of the Baltic had flayed the skin off our backs.

Before I went to Finland, I had planned to join the Forest Brothers, had even imagined leading an act of sabotage. My plans changed when I was invited to join the training organized by the Finns. The sea had just then frozen over, making the passage to Finland easy. I thought it was a good omen. In the ranks of the Forest Brothers there had been a kind of bluster and carelessness that wasn't going to win any wars or drive away our foes or bring anyone back from Siberia or reclaim our homes. I thought the Green Captain took unnecessary risks with his troops. In his shirt pocket he carried a notebook where he wrote down all the information about the men he provisioned and sketched out precise plans for attacks and tunnels. My fears were confirmed by Mart's daughter. She told me that the destruction battalion had found the food records her mother kept, with careful lists of who came to their house to eat, and when. The Green Captain had promised that she would eventually be repaid for

the food and the trouble. But now Mart's house was a smoking ruin, Mart himself had lost his mind, and his daughter was
among the crowds of refugees somewhere ahead of us. Some of
the Brothers mentioned in her mother's provision records had
already been executed.

I knew that once Estonia was free again, people of good
conscience would want to examine these years, and there would
have to be evidence that we acted according to the law. But such
thorough record keeping was a risk we couldn't afford. The acts
of the Bolsheviks had already proved that our country and our
homes were under the control of barbarians. But I didn't criticize
the captain openly. As an educated man and a hero of the War
of Independence, he knew more about fighting than I did, and
there was a lot of wisdom in his leadership. He had trained the
troops, taught them how to shoot, how to use Morse code, made
them spend time every day practicing their running, the most
important skill in the forest. I might have stayed in Estonia with
his group if it hadn't been for his habit of taking notes. And the
camera. I'd been with the Forest Brothers for some time when
one morning they started talking about taking a group photo. I
slipped away, said I shouldn't be in it since I wasn't really part
of the gang. The boys posed in front of the dugout leaning on
each other's shoulders, their hand grenades hanging from their
belts, one of them with his head stuck into the horn of a por-
table gramophone as a joke. The photo included a proudly dis-
played knapsack full of communist money taken from the town
hall. The Green Captain had given it out in bundles. Take your
fair share, he'd told them. This is a repayment for the cash the
Soviet Union confiscated from the people.

The captain was a legend, but I didn't want to be that kind of
hero. Was it weakness? Was I any better than Edgar?

Rosalie would have been proud to have pictures of my

training on Staffan Island or my time with the Green Captain's group of Forest Brothers, but I didn't intend to make
the same mistake the captain did. I even tore up Rosalie's
picture, though my fingers didn't want to do it. Her gaze
had comforted me at many hopeless moments. I would need
that comfort if my life were flowing out of my veins into the
earth. I needed it now, as we trekked over the stones and moss,
now that I'd left our fighting brothers behind. I needed that
look in her eyes. Edgar, clomping along behind me, had never
carried a photo of his wife. When he showed up at the cabin
where I was waiting to leave for Finland, he made it clear that
I shouldn't say a word to anyone about his being back in his
home province. An understandable worry for a deserter, and
he knew how fragile Mother's nerves were. Still, I couldn't
imagine doing such a thing myself, not giving Rosalie any
sign that I was alive. I could hear Edgar huffing and puffing behind me and I couldn't fathom why he wanted to let
his wife believe he was still a conscript in the Red Army.
I was in a mad rush to get to Rosalie's house, and Edgar hadn't
said a word about seeing his own wife. I half suspected that
he was planning to leave her, that he'd found a new girl,
maybe in Helsinki. He'd often been out and about by himself
there, traipsing off to the Klaus Kurki restaurant. But he never
seemed to let a woman cloud his vision, and he didn't go in
for drinking like the other men did, you could tell by the
freshness of his breath when he came back to our quarters.
He also wore the same free clothes that I did, although he
had puckered up his mouth when he saw the cut and the fabric. You couldn't take a girl out for a stroll in those clothes,
and you couldn't amuse her on twenty marks a day, let alone
sample Helsinki's brothels. It was just enough money for
tobacco, socks, the bare necessities.

The other men had taken one look at Edgar and decided he was different, and I was afraid he'd be sent away from the island as unfit to fight. I really had to work on him after he split his forehead open with the kick of his rifle butt and turned even more gun-shy. I wondered how he'd managed in the Red Army. And where had he gotten so soft around the middle? Red Army provisions were hardly pure lard and white bread. On Staffan Island his belly had disappeared, since everything in Finland was rationed.

Edgar had been forgiven a lot because he was a talker. When members of the Finnish command became instructors, they let him give a lecture about Red Army insignia, smoothly churning out the Russian words. He even tried to teach the other men to parachute, although he'd never once done it himself. He spent the evenings mastering the falsification of papers for when we went back to Estonia, whispering to me about his plans for an elite group made up of men from the island. I let him blather. I'd grown up with him, I was used to his overactive imagination. But the other men pricked up their ears at his nonsense.

We had plenty of free time, moments when most of the men would gawk at every skirt they saw like she was the original Eve. I passed the time thinking about Rosalie and the spring sowing. That June we'd learned about the deportations. No one had heard from my father since his arrest the year before. At the time my mother had wept, said he should have known to take off his hat and sing when "The Internationale" played, keep his mouth shut about the potato association, not say anything against the nationalization, but I knew my father was incapable of that. And that was why his house was taken, his son was in the forest, and he was in prison. The Bolsheviks wanted to make an example of him. Then they told people that their land wouldn't be taken away—but who could believe them?

Edgar, on the other hand, wasn't upset about Simson Farm, even though it was the farm that had paid for his school, the student days in Tartu that he had so many stories about. There were a lot of students on the island, not as many men from the countryside. Edgar and the other university boys hadn't seen much of life. You could hear it in the way they laughed at anyone who struck them as simpler than they were. For them, "uneducated" was an insult, and they judged a person by whether he'd made it to the third grade, or higher. Sometimes they sounded like they'd been reading too many English spy novels. They got carried away fantasizing about the secret agents they were going to send out from the island, about how the Reds' days were numbered. And Edgar was right out in front, preaching the gospel. I wrote some of the men off as adventurers, but there weren't any cowards among them, which gave me some confidence. And we mastered the basics. We were all trained on the radio and in Morse code, and although Edgar was clumsy at loading his gun, his supple fingers were well suited to the telegraph. He'd gotten his speed up to a hundred strokes per minute. My clumsy mitts were made for farmwork. At least we agreed about the most important things; we both had the same politics, the same pro-English position.

I had my own plans: where I used to carry Rosalie's photo I now kept loose-leaf notebook paper—carrying the entire notebook would have been foolhardy. I'd also bought a bound diary. I wanted to collect evidence of the destruction wreaked by the Bolsheviks. When peace came, I would turn the documents over to someone who was good with words, someone who could write the history of our fight for freedom. The importance of this task gave me strength whenever I doubted that I'd be a part of these grand plans, whenever I felt like a coward for choosing a course of action that avoided combat, because I knew I was doing my part, something that I could be proud of. I had no intention of writing anything that would put anyone at risk or reveal too many identifiable details. I wouldn't use names; I might not even mention locations. I planned to get a camera, but I wouldn't be taking any group photos. Spies' eyes glittered everywhere, greedy for the gold of dead Estonians' dust.

Tallinn,
Estonian Soviet Socialist Republic,
Soviet Union

THE GRAIN WAREHOUSES were burning, the sky grew columns of smoke. Buses, trucks, and cars filled the roads, their worn tires screaming like the people were, screaming to get away. And then an explosion. Shrapnel. Shards of glass like a shower of rain. Juudit stood with her mouth open in a corner of her mother's kitchen. Her mother had escaped to the countryside, to her sister Liia's house, and left Juudit on her own to wait for the bomb, the bomb that would end everything. The roads from Tallinn to Narva had for some time been clogged with trucks full of evacuees' possessions, and there were rumors about the evacuation commissariat, rumors that they'd set up commissariats for cattle evacuation, grain evacuation, lentil evacuation—a commissariat for anything they could get their hands on. The Bolsheviks intended to take it all with them, every last crumb, down to the smallest piece of potato. They weren't going to leave anything for the Germans—or the

Estonians. The army had ordered its men to empty the fields, and all of it was headed to Narva or to the harbors. Another explosion.

Juudit put her hands over her ears and pressed hard. She had already accepted that the town would be destroyed before the Germans could get there; she only hoped that her time wouldn't come until some more ordinary day, that the last sound she heard would be the clink of a spoon on a saucer, the jangle of hairpins in a box, the hollow ring of a milk pitcher set down on a table. Birds! Birds singing! But the Luftwaffe and the antiaircraft guns had devoured the birds, she would never hear them again. No dogs. No cats meowing, no crows cawing, no clatter from upstairs, no sounds of children downstairs, no errand boys running, no squeak of pushcarts, no clank against the door frame as the woman downstairs bumped her bucket coming into the building. Juudit had tried it, too, balancing the washbasin on her head, secretly, in front of the mirror, and wondered why the milliners didn't design a hat that you could balance a little washbasin or bucket on. It would be a guaranteed success. Women were so childish, so foolish. A bucket hat was just the kind of crazy idea they needed right now. But that clank of tin, that ordinary life, was a thing of the past. Those buckets had been a mark of defeat, tainted by the Bolshevik occupation, but an ordinary thing nevertheless, with an ordinary sound.

HER BROTHER JOHAN had taken her to her mother's house on Valge Laeva Street in case anything happened, but the days had just continued. He and his wife had been taken away in June and Juudit hadn't heard from them since, and strangers had moved into his house, important people from the commissariat. Juudit's husband had been mobilized by the Red Army a long time ago. The woman who lived in the basement had been convicted of counterrevolutionary activity—accused of knowing that her renter was planning to leave the country. Juudit had been interrogated about it, too. And yet the days continued, even after that, and as they continued they became ordinary days, and even those days were better than these days of destruction. Out in the country, at Aunt Leonida's house, Rosalie went right on milking the cows, even as her fiancé's family was terrorized. The Simsons' farm had been taken away; Roland's father had been arrested and his mother, Anna, had moved to the Armses' place so Rosalie could take care of her. Juudit was grateful to Rosalie for that. She wouldn't have been able to cope with Anna Simson, not even in an emergency. She didn't have Rosalie's patience. If Juudit's husband knew about it, he would have one more thing to complain about, would say that Anna didn't deserve such an uncaring attitude from her favorite nephew's wife. Maybe not, but Rosalie could fuss over Anna better than Juudit could, and Rosalie would fill the house with little darlings soon enough to make her happy. That was something that Juudit would never see happen.

She tried to think of a sound from the past, something to be the last thing she thought of before the end. Maybe a day in her childhood, the ordinary noises of Rosalie in the kitchen, the sounds of a morning like all the other mornings of that peaceful time, when you knew that today would be just like yesterday, a day when the plywood of her mother's Luther chair scraped across the floor under the window with that annoying grate, a day when there was nothing very important in her own head, when the most insignificant irritation could make her cross. Or maybe before she died she'd like to think about a day when she was still unmarried, a young lady, a time when there was nothing more exciting than a dress, wrapped in tissue paper, in a box, a dress for her future suitors. Under no circumstances would she think about her husband. She bit her lip. She couldn't keep her husband out of her mind even if she tried. If that last flash of explosion had hit the house, her marriage would have been the last thing she thought about. Another round of fire made her muscles twitch, but she couldn't hear anything, didn't double over.

The idea of staying behind, of going down with the rest of Tallinn, had come to her the day before her mother left, and it had stuck, as if it were the only thing she'd ever wanted. She liked Tallinn, after all, and she didn't like her husband's aunt Anna. Anna was staying at the Armses' place now, with Aunt Leonida and Rosalie taking care of her. Juudit's mother had tried to get Juudit to go there, too. At times like these it was good to be among loved ones.

"Thank the Lord your father isn't here to see this. We're just extra mouths to feed now, one sister taking me in, one taking you in. But it's just for a little while. And, Juudit, you could at least try to get along with Anna."

Juudit had pretended to agree so her mother would leave. She wasn't going to go to Leonida's house. Juudit wasn't as confident as her mother about their chances for victory, but she was grateful in a way for the pneumonia that had taken her father when everything was still going well in the country. He wouldn't have been able to bear it, watching the Bolsheviks' progress, Johan's disappearance. The Soviet Union had an endless supply of men—why were things changing now? Why hadn't they changed before the deportations in June? Why not before her brother was arrested? The din of battle rolled onward, the heavy, muddy wheels of the gun trucks that would kill them all. Juudit closed her eyes. The room lit up. The bursts of light in the air reminded her of the fireworks at Pirita Shore

Club at midsummer, back when she had been married for only a year. Her ears were working then, and she'd had other things to worry about, a dull longing for her husband, or rather for the husband she'd imagined he would be. And on Midsummer Night in Pirita she had hoped, hoped so much. She saw herself deep in the Pirita darkness, focused on the flaming barrels of tar that served as torches, the forest sighing with contentment like a hedgehog just awakened to summer. She could taste a bit of lipstick on her tongue, smeared, but she didn't care, it showed that her mouth was a mouth that had been kissed. The musicians were giving their all, in a song like a fleeting dream of youth, about deer drinking from a stream, unafraid, and the night was full of twittering girls hunting for fern flowers, double entendres said with a hint of a smile, as Juudit's unmarried friends giggled and shook their bobbed hair defiantly—they had everything ahead of them, and midsummer magic made anything possible. Juudit felt her marriage flow over the flesh of her cheeks, the suppleness of her flesh, the lightness of her breath—these things that were no longer objects of pursuit—and pretended to be more experienced than the other girls, a little better, a little wiser, holding her husband's hand with the relaxed air of a married woman, trying to drive away the seed of bitter envy, envy of her friends who hadn't yet chosen anyone, who hadn't yet been led to the altar. And then her husband swept her onto the dance floor and sang along with the song about his little missus, small as a pocket watch, and the tenderness in his voice carried her far away from the others, and the orchestra started another song, and the carefree deer were forgotten, and Juudit remembered why she had married him. Tonight. Tonight would be the night.

Juudit's eyes snapped open. She was thinking about her husband again. She could see the sun rising over the Gulf of Finland. But it wasn't dawn yet; those were the flames of Soviet ships, what was left of Red Tallinn escaping over the sea, their horns shouting like panicked birds. The sound of retreat. Juudit stumbled across the floor, made it to the other side of the room, and leaned against the wall. She couldn't believe the Bolsheviks were leaving. Light flashed in a corner of the bedroom and she realized that the Luftwaffe's planes weren't interested in Tallinn, only in the fleeing ships, but the knowledge didn't feel like anything. Her twitching legs remembered too well what the sound of a plane meant: run for the bushes, for shelter, run anywhere, like the time in the country helping Rosalie and her aunt with the distilling when the enemy appeared in the sky without any warning and made her aunt kick the kettle over and they bolted under the trees and stood panting and staring at the low-flying plane with its belly, thankfully, emptied.

Juudit pressed her back against the wall, her feet firmly on the floor, readying herself for another explosion. Although the air was heavy with the stench of war, not all the familiar smells were gone. The wallpaper still gave off the smell of an old person's home, of something safe—and gone. Juudit pushed her nose up against the wallpaper. The pattern was the same, old-fashioned, like the one in the room in Johan's house where she and her husband had lived while they waited for their own house to be finished. The house was never finished. She would never furnish it. She would never see the new water-lily wallpaper she'd chosen from Fr. Martinson's after changing her mind several times and fretting over every floral pattern one after the other with her husband and brother, and her sister-in-law, who at least understood how important it was to choose the right wallpaper. When she'd finally made her decision and walked out of the shop, it was a relief to be through with examining samples, comparing them at home, then back at Martinson's, then at home again. She had gleefully taken a taxi to bring the good news to her husband, who was also relieved to have solved the wallpaper dilemma, and she had announced her decision to her sister-in-law at the Nõmme restaurant, and she'd gotten cream from her pastry on her nose, a nose silky and glowing because she scrubbed her face every night with sugar. Imagine, sugar! Had they drunk cocktails? Had they danced that evening? Had her husband joined them later, and had she thought again, *This is it, tonight's the night?* Had she thought that, like she had so many times before?

THE END JUUDIT WAS EXPECTING didn't come. The town shook, burned, smoked, but it was still standing, and she was still alive, and the Red Army was gone. Happy shouts from outside made her crawl to the window, its panes crisscrossed with paper tape to keep them from shattering, and open it, not caring about the broken glass. The Wehrmacht with their helmets and bicycles filled the street like locusts, a multitude without number, gas-mask canisters waving, the soldiers covered in a downpour of flowers. Juudit stretched her arm out. Smiles sparkled in the air like bubbles in fresh soda, arms waved and sent a breeze sweet with the scent of girls toward the liberators, girls with their hands fluttering like leaves on summer trees, shifting and shimmering. Some of the hands were tearing down the Communist Party posters, the photos honoring communist leaders, tearing their mouths in two, ripping their heads in half, cutting them off at the neck, heels grinding into the leaders' eyes, rubbing them into the ground, cramming the dust of rage into their paper mouths, the shreds of paper floating into the wind like confetti, the broken glass crunching underfoot like new-fallen snow. The wind slammed the window shut, and Juudit winced.

This wasn't how it was supposed to happen. Where was the

end she'd been expecting? She was disappointed. The solution hadn't arrived. She breathed in the air of a free Tallinn from the window. Doubtful. Wary. As if the wrong kind of breath could take the peace away again, or cause a woman who didn't believe in the German victory and the Soviet retreat to be punished. She didn't dare run into the street—her restlessly squirming legs were hiding inappropriate thoughts, thoughts that rushed in when the neighbor's little girl ran into the yard and yelled that Daddy was coming home. The little girl's words made Juudit remember her situation and she had to hold on to the chair for support, like an old woman.

Soon the shops, stripped bare by the Red Army, would be full and would open their doors again, with salesgirls behind the counters to wrap your purchases in paper. The water treatment plant would be repaired, the bridges would rise again, everything that had been plundered, destroyed, and butchered would wind back to how it was before, like a film played backward. Tallinn was still wounded, sucked bare, the streets groaning under horse carcasses and the corpses of Red soldiers swarming with beetles, but soon that would all be gone. The wharves would be rebuilt. The train tracks would be mended. The gashes torn in the roads by the bombs would be patched. Peace would rise from the ruins, plaster would cover the cracks in the walls of the buildings. Journeys would no longer be halted by broken roads. The candles could be taken off the tables and put back in their boxes, the electric lights would come on behind the blackout curtains, maybe the ones who'd been deported would come back, Johan could come home, no one would be taken away anymore, no one would disappear, the knocks at the door in the night wouldn't come, and the Germans would win the war. Could there be anything better? Things would be ordinary again. But even though that is what Juudit had just been hoping for, the idea of it changed, in the blink of an eye, to something unbearable, and the indifference she'd felt a moment before changed to panic about the future. The ordinary life she would get wasn't the ordinary life she wanted. Outside the window a Tallinn emptied of Bolsheviks was waiting; the first Estonians were already returning home, their boots already turning the roads to dust. Soon the town would be filled with an assortment of Estonian, Russian, and Latvian uniform jackets new and old, and the girls would swirl around them—maidens, fiancées, widows, daughters, mothers, sisters, an endless horde of clucking, sniffling, dancing females.

JUUDIT DIDN'T WANT to face those women, talking about their husbands coming home, or the women whose fiancés, fathers, and brothers had already come out of the woods or wandered home from fighting in the Red Army in Estonia or on the Gulf of Finland. She wouldn't have anything to say to them. She hadn't sent her husband a single letter. She had certainly tried, had gotten out paper and ink, sat down at the table, but her hand couldn't form any words. Just writing the first letter of his name had been too difficult, thinking what to say in the first sentence impossible. She couldn't write her husband a letter from a wife who missed him, and that was the only kind of letter to send to the front. All the nights she'd tried and failed, and the nights when she didn't even try, ate into her memory. All the times she'd tried to lower her neckline a little more, to make him take some notice of her breasts. She remembered vividly how embarrassed she would feel afterward, remembered how it felt when she realized that everything she had imagined about him, everything that had charmed her about him, had been wrong. The memory of how her newly wed husband would push away the breasts she offered him, push her to the other side of the bed like spoiled food shoved away at the table.

JUUDIT'S HUSBAND HAD LEFT in the first phase of Bolshevik rule, along with all the other men who fled conscription to hide in the attics of houses and summer cottages, and she had been relieved. She had the bed all to herself. But she remembered, of course, to knit her brow like she should, to pretend to be a wife who was worried about her husband. When he'd been picked up on his way to get food by Chekists in a black ZIS, Juudit had managed to darken her gray eyes with tears, because that was what she was supposed to do. Even then, she was already hoping that it would be his last trip, that's what those black cars had meant for so many people, and she was afraid of her own wish, afraid of the wild joy in the possibilities the war had brought her. There were no divorced women in her family. Widowhood was her only option if she wanted her freedom back. But her husband's auntie got news from the commissariat that he'd been sent to the front, and once again Juudit clutched her handkerchief for the sake of custom. She couldn't tell anyone how much she enjoyed her bed without her husband. She would have liked to have a lover, but where would she get one? It was wrong to even think such a thing. But she did read *Madame Bovary* and *Anna Karenina* several times, and although the women in the books didn't suffer quite the same marital problems that she did, she'd felt a great spiritual kinship with them, because she knew what it was to yearn.

Before Juudit's wedding, her mother had slipped in some advice between the lines about marriage and its potential problems, but the problems Juudit had weren't in her mother's repertoire. She'd had her doubts even during her engagement, and had told her mother in a roundabout way that, contrary to what she seemed to think, Juudit's fiancé hadn't made any physical advances at all. Her girlfriends had a quite different experience with their husbands-to-be, who couldn't wait to get to the altar. Rosalie, for instance, was constantly hinting at the fiery nature of her dark-browed Roland. Juudit's mother had smiled at her daughter's worries, said it was a mark of respect, told her that her father had been just as gentlemanly. Everything would work itself out once they started living together.

So Juudit concluded that she was silly to find it strange. It was a sign of a great love, and she hurried impatiently toward her wedding day, and a room for the honeymoon was reserved at the Shore Hotel in Haapsalu. But putting a wedding ring on her finger hadn't changed anything. The wedding night was awkward. Her husband entered her, and then something happened. He withdrew, went behind a screen, and Juudit could hear water pouring into a basin, and frenzied washing. Then he settled himself into the other side of the bed, as far from his wife as possible. She pretended to sleep. The next night wasn't any better. The night after that, he fell asleep on the sofa, and in the morning he acted as if everything was normal. In the daytime they promenaded on Africa Beach and in the evenings they danced at the Shore Hall like a normal, happy couple on their honeymoon. When they got back to Tallinn, he went to work as an assistant in Johan's notary office and Juudit concentrated on building a home and feverishly contemplating what to do.

In public he behaved like a model husband, offering her his arm, often kissing her on the hand, and even on the mouth when he was in a playful mood, but his behavior changed as soon as they were alone together. If he didn't feel any attraction to her, then why had he proposed? Had it all been a lie from the very beginning? Rosalie had introduced Juudit to the Simson family after she got engaged, and at first Juudit hadn't taken any notice of Roland's bookish cousin, not until Rosalie told her that he wasn't quite as bloodless as he seemed at first glance. He was going to be a pilot. Juudit had read *The Red Baron*, and everything she asked him about or wondered over excited the boy in a way that charmed her, and they had many ardent discussions about Manfred von Richthofen. There was something so strange and passionate in his enthusiasm, and Juudit didn't doubt her choice at all, didn't doubt that her place was in the stands as he executed an Immelmann turn in the air show. Rosalie praised the match, and Juudit praised Rosalie's. They considered themselves lucky. In his letters, Juudit's betrothed promised to fly her to Paris and London. They both wanted to travel, to see the world. The idea of nothing but air under her feet frightened her, but it was worth it to see the expressions on her girlfriends' faces when she told them she was going to be a pilot's wife, a woman of the world, going to buy her gloves in Paris, where the salesgirls shook powder into them before they tried them on your hands. One day her husband might even be in a newsreel, and the audience would sit there thrilled, sighing, some of the women's hearts skipping a beat. Sometimes it baffled her that a man with such an exciting future was interested in her, of all people, and when they became engaged, he kissed her on the forehead, and she felt a heat inside her so intense that she couldn't imagine ever having relations with anyone else. And then there were no relations.

Finally she worked up the courage to ask her married girlfriends about intimate matters. She didn't dare ask Rosalie. Rosalie was still collecting her trousseau and the Simsons were preparing for the young bride to arrive. In spite of the sparks that flew between Roland and Rosalie, the two weren't in a hurry to walk down the aisle. They wanted everything to be just right. But once Juudit was married, her heart wasn't in it anymore when Rosalie wanted to talk about her wedding plans. The two of them used to always be talking about wedding hairdos and bridal bouquets, pondering the time when they would both be wives, their letters flying between the Armses' farm and Juudit's apartment in Tallinn. Juudit made Rosalie swear that they would take their husbands to Haapsalu and take mud baths together at the spa and try to coax the two men into getting along better—not that there was any trouble between them, but it would be nice if the two of them were friends. After all, they grew up together, so why couldn't they be just as close as Juudit and Rosalie? At first Rosalie thought that taking a Singer sewing class would be more suitable for a housewife, but then she agreed that maybe she could pay someone to take care of the house for a couple of days, long enough to take a trip, and they could spend time together as two couples. There was always so much work to do in the countryside, you never had time to just visit. Rosalie finally decided that Juudit's scheme was a good one, but after her honeymoon, Juudit gave up the idea. She was sure Rosalie would see right through her, see that her marriage was a lie, and Juudit didn't know how to explain it to her. How could she tell Rosalie that marriage had marked her as inadequate? Rosalie wouldn't understand. She wouldn't believe it. No one would.

Juudit didn't know where to turn. She searched the *Housewife's Handbook* she'd been given as a wedding gift. Under "marriage," there was a reference to difficulties that occurred during sexual intercourse. Under *S,* she also found "sexual frigidity," and an explanation that it usually happened for personal reasons—fear of pain, disgust toward one's partner, or painful memories. She could tell that the passage wasn't talking about men, just women. So it was her fault. Many of her married friends said that their husbands seemed to never get enough. One of them talked about tightness. Another said that her husband wouldn't leave her in peace even when it was time for her woman's troubles, which was terribly unhygienic, and even dangerous, and another suspected that her husband had a venereal disease. Juudit's situation was unusual, but she had finally figured it out: gonorrhea, syphilis, chancre. Of course! That had to be it! Her husband was just too ashamed to tell her! She had to get him to a doctor, but how? She couldn't tell him that she thought he was carrying a disease.

She put down the book. The photograph of the foot of an infant with hereditary syphilis brought back a memory from her childhood—a woman she'd seen once when she and her mother were out walking. Her mother had slowed her steps as soon as she saw the woman, steered Juudit down a different street, and said they could go to the import shop some other time. The woman had a trouble that bad women get, maybe from using the same dishes that a sick person has used. Her mother had been right about that—the *Housewife's Handbook* said the same thing—but then wouldn't Juudit have symptoms, too? She could still remember the woman's face. It was clean, no signs of illness or cocainism, even though when they had been to visit the family doctor he had whispered, "The medical association claims that cocaine sickness in the country has decreased, but the number of psychopaths and neurotics hasn't decreased, and those are the very people who are carriers. One can only imagine how many of them there must be. . . ."

The *Housewife's Handbook* didn't tell her whether the sickness would affect her husband's capabilities. She couldn't bring herself to think any more about it. Syphilis, the most serious and frightening of the venereal diseases. She couldn't have such terrible luck. She must be wrong. Her husband's eyes weren't red and he didn't have sores in his mouth or on his legs, or any deformities. And anyway, how could she be sure he had it, that he had kissed bad women, or maybe even done something worse; and if he had, what did that mean? And how could she know whether he'd been to a doctor?

Juudit started examining herself, checking her tongue, her limbs, every day, panicking at a bug bite, the swelling that followed, a pimple on her chin, a callus on her foot, wondering if she'd had sores she hadn't noticed, if she was in the symptomless phase that the *Housewife's Handbook* talked about. Everyone had already started dropping hints about a little bundle that was on its way, had started to wonder about it, because they'd interpreted her hurry to get married as a sign that she was in a family way—Anna Simson in particular had whispered about it, knowingly, reproachfully. Finally Juudit got up her courage. She had to know for sure. The doctor was friendly, the visit awkward, even agonizing. It ended with him telling her she had nothing physically wrong with her, no disease.

"My dear," he said, "you were created to give birth."

Western Estonia,
Estland General Region,
Reichskommissariat Ostland

WE TRAVELED FOR a week through woods blighted with fighting, made our way around seething horse carcasses and bloated corpses, avoiding bombed bridges, trying to interpret the rumble of the destruction battalion bombers. Eventually the forest started to look familiar, restored to health as my longing for home was soothed and we came upon the road to our old mail drop. I left Edgar shivering at the edge of the woods as lookout and approached the house warily, but the dog recognized us from a long way off and ran to meet me. I could tell by the way it scampered around that there was no danger, so I relaxed and, accompanied by the dog, went to the window and gave the knock we'd agreed on. The woman we called "the mail girl" opened the door immediately, smiled broadly, and told me the news: The Bolsheviks were still in retreat, the eastern front was crumbling, and the Finns and Germans were hunting them down at Lake Ladoga. The Russians had doused the woods with oil and set them on fire, but a burning forest wasn't going to stop the Finnish-German troops! The Andrusson brothers came to the door behind her, and Edgar trotted over when I shouted that everything was all right.

Within a moment the cabin was filled with fun, everyone laughing and talking over each other. It felt far away to me, like I was watching them from a distance. Later that evening we heard yet more promising news, but even though I was gradually beginning to believe my ears, there was still no pounding drum of joy in my chest. I looked at the lines on my hands every so often, and scrubbed them for a long time in the sauna with the Andrusson boys, but still they looked bloody to me sometimes, clean other times. My cousin was already a new man, his posture straightened, the flow of his talk opening up like an uncorked cask, full of stories of his time in flight school, speculation that he might teach there after the war, and assurances to Karl, the youngest of the brothers, that he could be a pilot, too—never mind the broken ankle, Mrs. Vaik's skill with splints is well known. The sky's the limit! The Andrussons warmed to these dreams of the future and Edgar got carried away reminiscing about building the seaplane hangar. I didn't say anything about his sudden manhood, a milk mustache still warm from the cow. I let him rhapsodize. I also didn't mention that when they built the seaplane hangar he wasn't even born yet. "Think about it. This border area was already an important defense point for the Russians, even back then," Edgar said with a flourish. I felt my breast pocket, the loose-leaf paper. The time would come soon. I had already started making a record of events, but every word I wrote felt wrong, like a desecration of my fallen brothers, pitiful whining compared to the deeds I'd witnessed on the front. The things I'd seen resisted being put into words. I could smell the swamp in my boots, see the red lines on my hands. The mark of my pen wasn't pure enough.

The mail girl told us more news whenever she could get a

word in through the constant hum of Edgar's stories. In Vil-jandi, at least, the people who had owned farms before the Bolshevik land reforms were cutting the rye, and they were supposed to sell the grain for thirty kopeks to the tenants the Reds had given their property to. In return, the new tenants were supposed to help the original owners with the work, and weren't allowed to cut any timber except to take the bark off the trees they'd already felled. The managers of the sovkhoz farms had their careers cut short; the manager of the nationalized Kase linen factory had run off with the Red Army and the for-mer owner was running the factory again. Anyone who needed a tractor from the tractor stations could sign up for one. They had started rebuilding the houses that were burned down by the communists, and you could get assistance for it. The mail was running again. There was good news everywhere, it seemed. I picked up the thin newspapers filled with minutely detailed instructions, adjusted the heart of the lamp's flame larger. Visi-tors from farther away had brought several issues of *Sakala* with more decrees concerning the cutting of rye. I wasn't ready to think about what condition our house and fields were in, or who was harvesting the grain. I became engrossed in the other laws of the new overlords: All tenants were ordered to regis-ter. Homeowners were forbidden to rent rooms to anyone who wasn't registered. All Jews, arrestees, refugees, and communists were to register with their local administrator immediately; all other renters and homeowners were to go there as well to declare their assets. Those who'd come from the Soviet Union were to register at the offices of the local commandant within three days. All Jews were to wear the Star of David. Enforcing this order was the responsibility of the police and police auxil-iary. Listening to Russian or anti-German radio was prohibited.

All of this meant that we had gotten rid of the Bolsheviks. I put down the copies of *Sakala* and picked up *Järva Teataja*. An announcement bordered in mourning on the front page made me raise my hand to my temple, although my hat was already on the table. "In memory of all who fell for Estonian freedom, with deepest sorrow . . ." In the newspaper, freedom had a black border. In my mind, it dripped red blood. I let the others rattle on and suddenly I realized that they were already living in a free country. As if the war had never happened. As if peace were already here. Edgar had stepped into the new era in a moment. Could it really be over? The hiding, the living in the woods, could it all be behind us? Did they already believe the promise that soon our houses would be given back to us, that I could go and get my girl with the smiling eyes, that we would soon be married? Would we be sowing vetch for the cows by next year, stacking the timothy hay? Would I be walking the Simson family fields with the harrow again, my feet bare, the rich dirt between my toes, my gelding balking at the job like he always did? The grass was a long way off when you were harrowing, so the gelding had never liked the job, but he was always lively when he pulled the hay stackers to the barn or hauled the sheaves of rye to the threshing, and in the evening my smiling-eyed girl would make me some real coffee, and take off her apron, and it would have a bit of hay stuck to it, and her eyes would be as bright as vetch blossoms. Edgar would finally leave, and he'd build his own home and take care of his wife, and I wouldn't have to listen to his endless chatter anymore. Maybe the people who'd been sent to Siberia would be able to come home, maybe the Soviet Union could be forced to let them come. Maybe my father could come home.

I'd made a record of every smoking ruin and unburied body I'd encountered, with either a house or a cross, even if I couldn't find words for all those lifeless eyes, those corpses swarming with maggots. I would find people who could use my notes, and then my own paltry contribution to freeing the country wouldn't bother me anymore. It wouldn't matter that I wasn't with the Green Captain's troops or Captain Talpak's company when they freed Tartu and Tallinn. Soon it would be time to rebuild the country. This was the beginning. I was about to ask the mail girl what officials I should contact to give them my information about the destruction wrought by the Bolsheviks. And at that moment, I realized my foolishness. The German army would nab me immediately to fight in their ranks, and Edgar, too, though judging by the stories he was telling he didn't seem to understand the situation. The war wasn't over. I wouldn't be sowing vetch next summer, wouldn't hear the ripple of Rosalie's laughter in the evening. The Bolsheviks' retreat had blinded me, made me as shortsighted as a child. I cursed myself. I watched the mail girl jump up and dance with the older Andrusson boy while Karl played the accordion, and I had a sinking feeling. I was sure that the old Russian draft announcements pasted to the walls would soon be replaced by German ones.

Reval, Estland General Region, Reichskommissariat Ostland

W HEN JUUDIT FINALLY dared to leave the apartment, she stopped at the front door first, to listen. The sounds of war had vanished, they really had. She adjusted her collar and bent her arm at a right angle to hold her purse, her glove hiding the tension in her clenched fist. Her first steps over the cobblestones were tentative, broken glass still crunched underfoot. She couldn't seem to find the right way to walk down the streets of the capital, as if she'd left it behind in the world that had vanished. The town rushed toward her at the first street corner in a flood of baby carriages, stray dogs that seemed to have appeared from nowhere, laughing ladies, German soldiers playing harmonicas and winking at her. She caught her breath and blushed, but she'd hardly had a chance to recover from the embarrassment when the hum from the post office spilled over her, bank doors opening, delivery boys running down the street, and as she was stopped in her tracks with astonishment, a young scamp selling pictures of the Führer grabbed her by the sleeve and she couldn't see any way to get rid of him because the proceeds went to people whose houses had burned down, and of course the young lady wanted to help homeless families, and she stuffed the picture into her purse and bent her arm again as she walked past the movie theater. Suddenly she heard a bang, a truck going by carrying a load of bricks, and she jumped, bent over double, but it was the sound of rebuilding, not war. An urchin at the corner laughed at the lady who was frightened by a truck, and Juudit, red-faced, straightened her hat. Tallinn was blooming with Estonian and German flags tangling in the wind. The Palace Theater was being quickly rebuilt, a crowd of kids already gathered to marvel at the movie posters, even the adults stopping to look at them as they passed, and Juudit got a glimpse of the little red smile of a German actress and Mari Möldre's long eyelashes. The merriness of the crowd played around Juudit's ankles and she felt like she'd stepped into a movie herself. It wasn't real. Still, she would have liked to join in, keep walking with no destination and never go home. Why not? Why couldn't she? Why couldn't she participate in the joy? You couldn't smell the smoke from the fires anymore—at least not here; it was still coming in the windows of her apartment—and she sniffed the air, which carried a smell like freshly baked buns, until she was dizzy. The town wasn't destroyed at all. The Russians must have been so busy burning the warehouses and factories and blowing up the Kopli armored train that they didn't get around to the homes. She kept walking, looking for new evidence of peace, and passed the Soldatenheim, where young soldiers stood casually chatting, and their eyes fastened on her lips, and she sped up, averting her eyes from a woman putting up a big poster of "Hitler, the Liberator" in the window of the button shop. Juudit looked around for something more, greedy to see more people who seemed to have forgotten the last several years. Tallinn was suddenly flooded with young men. It annoyed her. There were too many men. She wished she were home, had a sudden, pressing desire to get back there. She quickly bought a newspaper and also snapped up a copy of *Otepää Teataja* that someone had used as a lunch wrapper, and she stared for a moment into a café where she had once known the buffet girl by name. Had they already gone back to work, or did the café have a new owner and new employees? She had sometimes gone there in the past to enjoy a pastry, meet her friends, but now her wedding ring was tight around her finger under her glove. Near the hospital, Wehrmacht soldiers were snaring pigeons. One of them noticed her and smiled, the others urged him to keep working. "Dinner's on its way!"

JUUDIT COULD SEE a crowd of boys from far off gathered in front of her building marveling at a DKW with a plywood chassis parked on the street. The boys weren't a problem—they wouldn't ask her about her husband—but next to them stood her talkative neighbor. Walking past her might be awkward. The woman grabbed Juudit's arm and clucked, "Are they going to make all the cars from plywood now? What's next?" Juudit nodded politely but the woman wouldn't let go, wanted to share her astonishment at rail lines being fitted for steam engines, the coal generators. "Can you imagine? Trams that run on wood! The Germans think of everything!" All the way to the courtyard Juudit could hear shreds of the woman's talk behind her, gradually shifting to talk of her husband's return. She had to pull herself away rather rudely. She hurried up the stairs. She could hear the phone ringing from the hallway. It was still ringing when she came into the kitchen, but she didn't answer it, just as she hadn't answered it the day before. She hadn't dared. She hadn't opened her door, either, although there was a knock. Instead she'd peered out the window at the blue will-o'-the-wisps of German flashlights, frightened by the strange shadows, the clack of wooden shoe soles, the dimmed car headlights swerving, shouts in German. There was no doubt of the Germans' final victory. The papers said that Lenin's remains had even been evacuated from Moscow. Juudit spread the newspapers over the table, made some grain coffee, and lit one of her last paperossis to brace herself for the news, but there was still no mention of anyone returning home. Instead the papers encouraged readers to send in jokes about the days of tyranny, and published lists of all the new grocery prices. Emmental cheese, 1.45–1.60 Reichsmarks; Edam, 1.20–1.40 Reichsmarks; Tilsit, 0.80–1.50 Reichsmarks. Yoghurt, 0.14 Reichsmarks. A grade 2 goose without giblets, head, wings, or feet, 0.55 Reichsmarks/kg. She should go get some food coupons tomorrow, register for them at the nearest shop, stand in line, tugging at shoulder pads that would never stay put, just like she used to. Her neighbor had been lodging some relatives from Tartu with a flock of children, their noise seeping through the walls and reminding her of the family life she didn't have and never would have. Her ruined life was reverting inexorably to the way it had been before her husband left. All that was missing was his return.

Gradually Juudit began to realize she was being foolish. The men wouldn't all be sent home until the war was over. They were needed at the front. They wouldn't come running home in one day. Only the deserters who had been stationed in Estonia and nearby areas had returned. If she had answered her phone, opened her door, or talked with her acquaintances, she would have known that. The war had taken away her ability to reason. She'd just seen it in her mind, her husband at the door, a husband she ought to be even more understanding with than before, because you had to be understanding with men who'd been to war. The anxious waiting could go on forever. There was no telling how far away he was. And what if he had disappeared? How long would Juudit have to wait before she could respectably start a new life? Maybe she should have done what the downstairs tenant did, the crime that got her neighbor convicted of counterrevolutionary activities—sign on to work in a ship's kitchen, sail away, to another country, leave everything, start over, look for a new man in a new place, forget she was ever married. But then Rosalie, or her mother, or someone else in her family, might suffer the same fate as her neighbor.

WHEN THE LISTS of the names of those returning began to appear in the papers, her neighbor put a bottle of wine on the sideboard to wait for her husband's return. The phone rang morning and night and eventually Juudit had to answer it because she knew her mother would be trying to reach her— and it was her mother, demanding news, saying she'd been asking the men returning if they knew Edgar or Johan, and Juudit couldn't stop her from calling, but she jumped every time the phone rang, every ring threatening to sentence her to the life she had lived before. But she still had to arrange her days, figure out what she was going to live on. She was stopped many times on the street and asked for food, even just a piece of bread. Out in the country there was always plenty of food. In the country they made moonshine. You could smuggle all kinds of things from the country into town, start up a business. It was her only option, even her mother said so, told her to go to visit Rosalie at slaughtering time, or even better, to stay there. Juudit had to go, even though she knew she'd have to listen to Anna worrying over whether a young wife like her could manage alone in town, and talking about Edgar, her favorite, telling her how special he was, decreeing what they should cook for him when he came home. Anna wouldn't talk about her own husband. Juudit was almost sure he would never return—Rosalie had told her that the mice had come back to the farm in June, and mice never lie.

ALTHOUGH MOST of the train traffic was transporting soldiers, now and then the boys would pick up ordinary travelers along the way. That was why Juudit dressed up more than was necessary for the difficult journey. The soldiers' whistles as they helped her onto the train put roses in her cheeks. She had a black-market travel permit in the pocket of her muff, and she smoked her last paperossis even though she was in a public place. The whole way there she worried that Anna would see through her, see right through to her traitor's heart. Hadn't she pretended to be a happy wife at the beginning of her marriage? Hadn't she done her best to look like a normal newlywed? She had, in fact, only fought with her husband once, after a year of marriage and just two attempts at sexual activity of any kind. Juudit had thought for a long time about how to ask him if he'd been to a doctor or even a healer. The words fell with a thud onto the dinner table, in the middle of their cutlets. He was dumbstruck, put down his fork, then his knife, but kept chewing. The silence trembled in the gravy dish. He switched to his dessert spoon. "Why would I?" he said. "There's nothing wrong with me."

"You're not normal!"

Her chair fell over, the plywood scraping across the floor-boards, and Juudit ran to the bedroom, closed the door behind her, pushed a chair under the latch. Their medicines were kept in a box in the washstand, but all she could find there was some Hufeland's powder. She poured all of it into her mouth, grateful that Johan and his wife were away visiting relatives.

Her husband knocked on the door.

"Open up, darling. Let's straighten this out."

"Come with me to the doctor."

"Is something troubling you?"

"You're not a man!"

"Darling, you sound hysterical."

His voice was patient. He spoke slowly, told her he was going to get her a glass of sugar water, like his auntie had always made when he was little and woke up from a nightmare. It would calm her down. Then they could talk about taking her to a nerve doctor.

JUUDIT MADE an appointment at the Greiffenhagen private clinic. Doctor Otto Greiffenhagen was known for his competence with men's diseases and his clinic was definitely the most modern one in town. If he couldn't help her, no one could. At the appointment, Juudit's voice cracked as she sputtered out her problem.

The doctor sighed. "Maybe you should both come in. Together. Or your husband could come alone, as well."

Juudit got up to leave.

"Ma'am, there are various preparations you could try. A dose of Testoviron might help, for instance. But first I would have to examine your husband."

But Juudit couldn't get her husband to come to the clinic. There would be no Testoviron, no treatment of any kind. She would never fly in an airplane. Not long after that she stopped going to her English conversation group and abandoned the daily French practice she had taken up during her engagement, back when she'd thought that a pilot's wife needed to be cosmopolitan and keep up her language skills.

Taara Village,
Estland General Region,
Reichskommissariat Ostland

WE COULD HEAR the rush and crackle of the sleigh from far off. My cousin Edgar was returning with great fanfare from his excursion to town. As soon as the sleigh came to a stop at the cabin, the flood of German stories would start. I knew that, and shut my mouth tight. That morning I had suggested in passing that we go to Rosalie's. I had been there to help with the hog butchering, and I knew there would be fricadelle soup, which Edgar was fond of, but Mother had obviously already told him who else would be there. Edgar turned the offer down and went his own way. And his attitude toward his wife wasn't the only reason I was angry. He didn't know a thing about horses, so I went out to meet him, knowing he would leave it to me to take off the harness. My gelding was tired, his nostrils steaming. It was obvious he'd been driven too hard. Edgar had forgotten the oats, as usual—there were a couple of liters left in the feed bag, but at least some of the field hay I'd put in the sleigh the night before had been eaten. I left his excited greeting unanswered. He halted his steps halfway, the snow squeaking uncertainly under his feet. I didn't care, I just led the gelding to the stable to get the packed snow out of his hooves and give him a firm brushing on his flanks—the spot they call "the hunger pit," his favorite spot for a rub. Edgar followed me, stomping his felt boots to get my attention. Clearly he had something he wanted to talk about. Whatever it was, it was hardly likely to have anything to do with the hay, so I didn't care. The situation looked bad. Leonida had promised there would be enough hay for the winter, twenty bales' worth, but already we were having to mix it with straw, although my gelding always poked around until he found the timothy hay. Things weren't any better in the Armses' stable. The Germans' big horses had eaten everything, till the village animals were skin and bones, and I could hardly expect Edgar to fetch more feed on his trips unless I got Mother on my side. But she simply wouldn't ask Edgar for anything. As soon as we'd reached our home province, I had seen how Edgar started pining for his auntie's house. Mother's smile had shone like a greased skillet when we arrived, and Edgar seemed relieved to find her in Rosalie's good hands. He managed to get Leonida and Mother on his side about keeping his return a secret, too. They still hadn't told their houseguests he was back—not even Edgar's wife. Mother said Edgar could be arrested as a communist if he was seen in the village, which baffled me, since no communist would have suffered the kinds of misfortunes that we had at Simson Farm under the Soviets. I could understand why he'd wanted to hide his desertion when the Reds were still in charge, but what was the point now? Other men who'd left the Red Army were walking around the village, and those of us who'd been on Staffan Island had fought against the Bolsheviks. Mother, of course, didn't want either of us to go to the front. She had weak nerves, and I couldn't bring myself to contradict her when she was teary-eyed with fear. She was always so happy when Edgar came to look in on her. She would immediately fry up some salted meat for consommé or find some other delicacy to put on the table. Still, I knew Edgar must be up to something. He'd given himself a new name, Fürst, which was appropriately German, fine as a rayon shirt. I called him Wurst. I pressed him again about what he had to hide. Rosalie talked about sending a message to his wife, but Edgar forbade it, and Mother forbade it, and Leonida followed suit. The more time that passed, the harder it would be to tell Juudit he was back.

EDGAR WAS STILL stomping his feet behind me. I was in no hurry, patting my horse's side, grown thick and shaggy with winter, in the dimness of the stable.

"Aren't you going to ask the news?" he said, rustling some newspapers he had taken out of his bag. He couldn't wait until we went into the house; he started reading them aloud in the stable, straining to see in the light of the hurricane lantern. Two hundred and six political prisoners had been freed in Tallinn, as a Christmas present from the Commissar General for Estonia to the innocent wives and children who had fallen into difficulties because their family providers were imprisoned. Edgar's voice was full of portent, his pale eyes taking on color.

"Are you listening? How many men would treat the families of their enemies so mercifully? Or are you still thinking about your tobacco field?"

I grunted in agreement before remembering that I'd intended to avoid talking about it with Edgar, who, in spite of all his shuttling back and forth, didn't seem to have done much to promote the family's interests. We hadn't heard from my father, and our fields were still in the wrong hands. I couldn't plant any potatoes even though three years' worth of clover had put plenty of nitrogen in the soil, which was good for potatoes. The Germans had banned the growing of tobacco and even Rosalie couldn't get any seedlings, but the bunglers the Bolsheviks had put on the Armses' farm had been evicted and the section of land the Reds had confiscated belonged to the Armses again. I'd gone over to spray their fruit trees with Estoleum, which I'd advised them to buy early, just in case. Aksel was thankful for the tip. I was like a son to him, not just a future son-in-law. I'd told him that Estoleum was better than Paris green, that he'd get apples good enough to sell at the market, but that was all I managed to do for my bride—for my own home at Simson Farm, I couldn't manage even that. This bothered me. Edgar had never learned a thing about farmwork, though he did know that cream fresh from the morning milking was good for weak lungs.

He continued reading the paper as I did the stable work. The war hadn't changed him a bit. " 'We all still remember how the Bolshevik propaganda painted the German National Socialists, and especially their Leader, as savages. They were hardly considered human.' " Edgar's voice had risen, he wanted me to listen. " 'The aim of National Socialism is to unite all levels of society into one element, to strengthen the well-being of the people. The incitement of violent class resentment, this shocking bloodletting of one's own people, is completely foreign to our movement. We strive to keep peace among the classes, and all are given the same right to life. . . . For our small nation, every individual is indeed as precious as every other.' " The gelding's ears twitched.

"Stop it," I said. "You're frightening the horse."

"Roland, don't you see? The Commissar General has found just the words that the nation needs."

I didn't answer. Anger was hardening me into a pillar of salt. I could tell that my cousin had his own reasons for burnishing the Germans' image. Maybe he wanted me in on some venture of his. But what did he need me for? I remembered how he had huddled in the cabin right after the Reds retreated, when the areas they had left were swarming with men from the destruction battalions, hiding out in fear for their lives, and Germans chasing them down. The special units had broken off from the Omakaitse—running like rabbits with everyone else, and the woods were filled with the smoke of gunpowder. Then I'd spotted two men nosing around our cabin. I recognized them. They had been with the Chekists who had surrounded the Green Captain's troops. I remembered them because I was on watch at the time, had stared them straight in the face, would never forget them. They'd gotten away from me once, but they weren't going to do it again. Edgar clapped a hand over his mouth when he saw the puddles spreading beneath their bodies in the yard. He looked exactly like he had as a boy the first time he saw the hogs slaughtered. He'd just come to live with us then. His mother, my mother's sister Alviine, had sent him to our house in the countryside to toughen him up after his father died of diphtheria. She was worried about his anemia. He fainted. My father and I were sure that a sissy like that would never manage on a farm. But we were wrong. He managed very well, hanging on to my mother's skirts. She had always wanted another child to keep her company, and the two of them took to each other. They were both supposedly sickly. We had another word for it: lazy.

When Edgar recovered from the sight of two dead bodies, he showed surprising initiative and said he would dispose of them. I doubted he could accomplish such a thing, but I helped him get the corpses into the cart and he hauled them away somewhere. The next day he came back looking shifty, with a poorly hidden grin on his face. He wasn't in any hurry anymore to get to town until the fighting in the woods died down. I could tell he had invented some story about the bodies so that we'd be left in peace. Sooner or later the Germans would have started to wonder what Finland-trained spies like us were doing lurking around in a cabin in the woods if he hadn't made some kind of deal with them, convinced them that they had nothing to fear from us. Maybe now was the time to ask what was going on between him and the Germans, but I couldn't bring myself to talk to him about it. He would be so pleased if I showed some interest in his affairs, and I didn't want to see the flattered look on his face. I saw that there was a knot in the reins, untied it, and went into the house to look for an awl and some waxed thread to splice it together. I felt the Hungarian leather, thought I ought to grease the harnesses, and the thought made me homesick for the fields, and frustrated. If the Germans weren't able to return the land that the Russians took or bring back the people, they were of no use to me, no matter what my cousin said. I thought again about the tobacco field that some Bolshevik bastard had dumped night soil on to grow who knows what, and a horse with a hunger pit so deep that I couldn't see how it managed to pull the wagon. Edgar didn't notice things like that. When we were standing by the spoiled field, all he did was wonder at the smell. That field had once been our land, the Simson land, and that horse had once been my horse, a horse who'd worn a blue ribbon next to his ear at the agricultural fair year after year. I would have recognized that horse anywhere, and he recognized me, but we had to let the field be and let the horse go on his way.

Edgar followed me to the cabin, lit a lamp after rubbing the soot off its hood a bit, and continued reading aloud where he'd left off. Did he want me to approve of what he was doing? He wanted something from me, but what?

"You're not listening," he said.

"What do you want?"

"I want us to start planning our lives, of course."

"And what does the Commissar General have to do with it?"

"You have to get new identity papers, just like everybody else. They've given orders about it. I can help you."

"I don't need any advice from Mr. Wurst."

"Auntie Anna wouldn't like it if I didn't look out for you."

The idea made me laugh. Edgar was getting cheeky.

"You're well suited for the police force," he said. "You ought to apply now. They're in serious need of new men."

"That's not for me."

"Roland, all the Bolsheviks have been cleared out. The work is easy and you wouldn't have to join the German army. Isn't that why you're still sitting here? What is it you're hoping for?"

Finally I sensed what he was getting at. Now that the time for muscle and gunpowder had passed and the ranks of the police needed filling, he saw his opportunity. I looked at him and saw a glitter of greed in his eyes: the Baltic barons were gone, and so were the Bolsheviks and the leaders of the republic. Empty leadership positions, just waiting for him. That's why he'd been acting so important, that's what he'd been holding in. My cousin had always considered the German gentry superior, admired the bicycles imported from Berlin, gone crazy over their video-telephones. He even arranged his sentences sometimes in German word order. But I didn't understand why he was telling me about his schemes. What did it have to do with me? He'd been sent to the *gymnasium* in Tartu and to the university, he had plenty of opportunities without me. I remembered how cocky he used to be, strutting around the yard during his vacations. He was always able to get some money from Mother when he wanted to order books about aviation from Berlin, pictures of airplanes and German flying aces, and while everyone else was making hay, Mother would lie around the house complaining of faintness and Edgar would sit by her bed and tell her stories about Ernst Udet's aerial tricks, even though in the country that kind of behavior was considered very strange. They were so alike, Mother and Edgar. Neither one of them paid any attention to my advice, but I had to take care of the two of them anyway. I started hoping that Edgar would leave, start his own career, take care of himself.

"So go join the police. What do you need me for?"

"I want you with me. For the sake of all we've been through together. I want you to have a good situation, a new beginning."

"Mr. Wurst is awfully concerned about my affairs, but why isn't he with his wife? Or have you found yourself some lady friend to aid you in your maneuvers?"

"I thought I should get my life in order first. That way Juudit can jump right in. Into a life ready-made. She's always been so demanding."

I started to laugh. Edgar's voice grew tense but he bit through his anger, his Adam's apple bobbing up and down until it finally settled. He turned his face away and said:

"I wish you would come with me. For friendship's sake."

"Have you talked to Mother about your plans?" I asked.

"Not until everything's certain. I don't want to get her hopes up unnecessarily." He raised his voice again. "We can't stay here in Leonida's cabin forever. And I've already told them that I know of a well-trained man qualified for the police force. You. You're needed. Estonia needs you!"

I decided to go back to the stable to water the horse. I hoped

Edgar wouldn't follow me. I didn't lack for plans of my own, whatever my cousin might think. I had collected all my notes and arranged them, and I had gathered more information whenever I happened upon more of our men, not to mention the facts I'd deduced from Edgar's stories. I already had plans to go work at the harbor at Tallinn or the railway in Tartu—I might even get enough pay to send some back home. Edgar hadn't brought Mother a bean, and the Armses had been sharing their meat with his citified wife. I had to provide for them, and hunting and guarding the moonshine wasn't enough. Leonida's back was bent because Mother wasn't any help and Aksel was missing a leg. The harbor was the more tempting option because Tallinn was closer to Rosalie and I could also avoid the German army. I had already falsified the birth date on my papers, in case they should ever get the men from the harbor into their files. But if Edgar had promised me to the police force, the Germans might already know too much about my past. I wouldn't be allowed to work at the harbor for long unless Edgar made me new papers under a new name—but if he did, could I trust him not to tell the Germans about it?

Taara Village,
Estland General Region,
Reichskommissariat Ostland

WHEN JUUDIT ARRIVED in the countryside, no one said anything about her husband. Anna's knitting needles clicked swiftly in her hands and a sock grew, a child's sock, and somehow Juudit was certain that she wasn't knitting it for Rosalie and Roland's future little ones. Anna had always fussed over Edgar, but not over her own son. They said Roland was staying at Leonida's cabin and came over now and then to help with the work. They didn't mention it again, although Juudit kept waiting to hear more. But no, Rosalie just mentioned that Roland was staying in hiding, said it in passing, and her face didn't shine with the happiness that Juudit expected. After all, her fiancé had come home in one piece. It felt strange that they didn't talk about the homecomings like everyone else did. There was no shortage of talk on other subjects. First there was the lament over how the railway inspectors—they called them "the wolves"—confiscated passengers' food supplies for their own use, and advice about how Juudit should behave if she had

an inspection on her way home. They said it was a good thing
her train hadn't had to stop for any air raids. Later in the evening their talk focused on the village manor. It had been empty
after Hitler invited the Baltic Germans into Germany, and now
it was occupied by the Germans for use as the local headquarters, and they'd rigged a dove trap on the terrace above the
main entrance. Apparently the Germans ate pigeons; this made
the women laugh. The Germans had brought in bathtubs, too.
They were very clean people, and the officers were so easygoing. The gardeners who'd stayed on at the manor and the
women at the washhouse said the Germans gave the children
candy, and there was only one soldier on guard at a time. But
whenever Juudit caught Anna's or Leonida's eye in the midst of
this chatter, either woman would quickly freeze her mouth into
a smile. Something wasn't right. Juudit had expected Anna to be
having one of her sick spells, what with her favorite boy on the
road somewhere, his whereabouts unknown. She expected her
to insist that Juudit stay with them in the countryside, but Anna
didn't seem worried about Juudit living in Tallinn alone, even
smiled to herself, admiring the sock heel she'd just turned. The
mere fact that Roland had survived couldn't account for such
cheerfulness. Was it because they had gotten the Bolsheviks'
tenants off their land? But the farm was still in such bad condition that they couldn't manage the work without help. That was
no cause for rejoicing.

Rosalie fell asleep before Juudit had a chance to talk with
her alone, although they'd always used to talk after the lamp
was extinguished. The next morning Juudit began to wonder if
Rosalie had just been pretending to sleep. Her smile was tight as
a sheet stretched on a laundry line, and she was in a great hurry.
At the end of the day's work, the blockade of Leningrad slipped
out of Anna's mouth, as if by accident:

"I heard that under the blockade you can only buy half a

liter of water a day, for two rubles. Ten thousand people dying every day. They've eaten the horses. But could the men surrounding them be any better off?"

Leonida asked Juudit to help her break up the salt. Juudit picked up the mallet. There was a curl at the corner of Anna's mouth, although the blockade shouldn't give her any reason to smile. Maybe she was getting senile, or maybe she just didn't know how to respond to Juudit's dry eyes. Should Juudit have burst into tears at the thought that her husband might be in the blockaded city? Should she pretend to be sad and hopeful? Juudit's mother had heard that someone had seen Edgar among the troops that were transferred to Leningrad, but who knew if any of those rumors were true? Anna didn't mention it, in any case. The talk was starting to weigh on Juudit's chest. She wanted to get away, go back to Tallinn. The watchful eyes of Anna and Leonida pecked at her face, and it stung. It was impossible to talk with Rosalie alone—Anna and Leonida kept buzzing around, poking their heads in the door just when Juudit thought they'd gone to the barn, jumping in behind her when she tried to go with Rosalie to give the chickens their mash. Rosalie didn't seem to notice anything, constantly busying herself with something, fingering the worn spot on her barn jacket where her favorite cow always licked her, avoiding Juudit's gaze. Then she grabbed a lantern to go out to the barn, and Juudit was left to deal with Anna's jabs alone. It started off innocently enough. Anna expressed concern about whether Juudit would find any buyers for the lard in Tallinn. It was easy in the countryside. The Germans were going from house to house chanting *"ein Eier, eine Butter, ein Eier, eine Butter."* They sounded so desperate, it made Anna feel sorry for them.

"The children in Germany are dying from hunger. A lot of these men have children. You don't understand it yet, but you will once you have your own kids hanging on your skirt."

Her eyes fastened on Juudit's middle. Juudit lifted her hand
to her waist and cast a glance at the china cabinet, the row of
empty tins for the soldiers waiting on the shelf—they couldn't
send their families their own provisions, but other food was
allowed. There was a scurry at the edge of the room and Juudit saw a mouse run behind her suitcase and another one follow right after it. She pressed harder against her belly and Anna
continued her lament as she pulled open cabinet drawers filled
with chocolate for the soldiers. Leonida had been bringing
chocolate, along with a five-liter churn of hot soup wrapped in
a wool scarf, to the guards shivering on the antiaircraft platform
they'd built on the roof of the school. The guards were more
alert once they'd had a little chocolate.

"Those soldier boys don't have anything to give in return, a
few ostmarks perhaps. I'll get by all right, but those children!"

If Juudit hadn't desperately needed the supplies, she would
have gone right back to Tallinn. Everything Anna said seemed
to point to Juudit's worthlessness. She decided not to care. She
wouldn't come back—but then what would she sell? She had
to find some other way to make a living. Her stenography and
German weren't enough, there were too many girls whose fingers knew their way around a typewriter better than hers did,
too many young women looking for work. But nobody made
moonshine in town. When she left Johan's house, she'd left
behind all of her husband's things, and she regretted it now. But
there was no point in hankering after his brand-new overshoes
and winter coat. Her mother had said that she would reclaim
Johan's house when they returned to Tallinn. She couldn't do
anything with the place now, the house had suffered too much
damage from the Bolsheviks, and no one knew where Johan had
stashed the ownership documents. But Juudit had to think of
something. Something other than tins of lard and moonshine.
Because she wasn't coming back here, and she couldn't survive

on German aid packages alone. Juudit still held her arm to her middle. Anna's furtive glances at her waist made her want to protect it, although there was nothing to protect. What was going to happen when her husband came back? Juudit was sure he would insist that Anna live under the same roof with them, always watching her, making sure she made his fricadelle soup the right way. In town, you could make it practically every week, after all.

The tension created by Anna's pointed comments broke when Aksel came to fetch his slaughtering knife and toss his work gloves on the stove to dry. The scent of wet wool spread through the kitchen, the lamp's flame flickered. The hog had been hung up in the shed the day before and Aksel had slept there all night with one eye open for thieves. Rosalie came in from the cowshed, and when the others went to get the meat, Juudit took her hand and wouldn't let go.

"Has something happened that I don't know about?" Juudit asked. "You're all acting so strange."

Rosalie tugged away, but Juudit wouldn't let her go. It was just the two of them in the yard—Leonida had gone to tell the others what size pieces of meat she wanted. They could hear her voice from the shed, pushing its way between them. Juudit's chapped lips were tight.

"No," Rosalie said. "It's just that Roland has come home, and it feels so bad to be able to see him when your husband's still at the front. It isn't right. Nothing's right."

Rosalie freed her hand.

"I'm not the only woman with a husband at the front, Rosalie. You don't need to worry about me. If you only knew . . ."

She didn't continue. She didn't want to talk about it with Rosalie. Not now. "Are you having trouble with Anna?" she asked.

Rosalie's shoulders relaxed at the change of subject.

"Not at all. She does housework and small chores, washes the cheesecloth, all the sorts of things children usually do. It's a great help. Roland has one less thing to worry about, knowing that his mother's well taken care of. Come on, they're waiting for us."

Rosalie hurried into the shed. Juudit took a breath. The evening was quiet. Too quiet. She followed Rosalie. Soon she would get away from here and the train would be jostling her bony knees. She just had to wait a little longer, long enough to fill her tins with lard and hide a bottle or two on a moonshine belt under her skirt. Juudit didn't try to talk to Rosalie anymore, just laid the pieces of meat in a row on the block. Leonida and Anna carefully picked out the best pieces for the bottom of the salt barrel—for summer—then the side meat for gravy, the back meat for frying, the leg meat for Easter, the tail to be packed a little closer to the top, for sauerkraut soup in the winter. The women made so much noise recounting all the village news that no one took any notice of Rosalie and Juudit's silence.

Reval,
Estland General Region,
Reichskommissariat Ostland

THE MURMUR FROM the Town Hall Square carried into the room in the Hotel Centrum, car horns and the shouts of newsboys framing Edgar's erect posture as he stood in his dark suit in front of the wardrobe mirror. Fervent but controlled, he raised his arm, counted to three, let it fall, then repeated the gesture again, counting to five, then to seven, checking the angle of his arm, making sure that it was straight enough and that his voice was energetic enough. Would he remember to leave enough space between them for the salute? He hadn't been using the German salute when meeting his contacts; they were unofficial meetings and meant to be inconspicuous. This situation was new, he was unfamiliar with the protocol. His arm might cramp, or tremble. He'd secretly practiced a little in the woods, too, when he had the chance, taking care to remember from the outset that Eggert Fürst was left-handed. It was inevitable that it would make his salute a little more uncertain, a little slower

to rise from the shoulder. The name had sprung into his mind
back on Staffan Island when he was getting ready to return to
Bolshevik-controlled Estonia and he'd had to hastily make
some Soviet identification papers for the boys. He'd remembered a man named Eggert Fürst from Petrograd, born into an
Estonian family, a childhood friend of one of his old colleagues
in the Commissariat for Internal Affairs. Edgar couldn't have
found a better identity for his purposes: Eggert's background
couldn't be investigated on the other side of the border, and
he wasn't likely to run into the man's family on the street. All
he had to worry about was keeping his own family quiet—and
if he did ever respond to the name Edgar, it was close enough
to Eggert that he could always say he had misheard. The original Eggert Fürst, a stranger to him, might not have been so
distinct in his mind except that a colleague in the commissariat
had taken the man's death from tuberculosis particularly hard,
and Edgar had spent many nights keeping him company, going
through old letters and childhood memories. It was easy to copy
the curve and slope of Eggert Fürst's handwriting. And as far
as forcing himself to use his left hand instead of his right, he'd
known how to do that since he was in *gymnasium*. As he calmed
his tense nerves with some cream-filled *biskvii* from room service, he was thankful for his old schoolmate Voldemar, who had
needed so much help with his homework. He still remembered
the boy's expressions and gestures, his clumsiness with a fork,
the bulky mitten tied to his left hand to stop him from using it in
secret. They'd made up more than one song to tease him about
it. It wasn't absolutely necessary for Edgar to use his left hand,
but the key to success was in the details. When he'd signed in
at the hotel registry, he had even picked up the pen with his left
hand first, then switched to his right and laughingly said something about old habits to the hotel clerk, and made a couple of

jokes about left-handers for good measure, and when the porter brought him his freshly steam-pressed suit, Edgar gave him a generous tip with his left hand.

Edgar licked bits of frosting from the fingers of his left hand and continued practicing in front of the mirror. He was starting to feel satisfied with his new self—he'd aged just the right amount in the past few years; he wasn't a young pup anymore. One of the men who'd been with him on Staffan Island was already working in the office of the mayor of Tallinn, and several others were building their reputations in other countries. Edgar didn't intend to settle for less. Quite the opposite.

He practiced a little longer, then sat down at the desk and went through the papers he was planning to bring to German security police headquarters in Tõnismägi. Edgar's list of communists who had written for the newspaper *Noorte Hääl* was perfect, and that had taken a bit of work. They'd found the bodies in the prisons and the cellars of the People's Commissariat without any help from him, but SS-Untersturmführer Mentzel had been tremendously pleased with the information Edgar handed over about less obvious locations where the executed had been buried. And Edgar had already given Mentzel a catalogue of his former colleagues at the Commissariat for Internal Affairs back when they'd met in Helsinki.

IT HAD BEEN at the Klaus Kurki Hotel, when Edgar was on leave from his training on Staffan Island, which was why he was nervous now, in spite of all his preparations. Although it was to be expected that the backgrounds of the men who trained at Staffan would come to light sooner or later, the appearance of the SS-Untersturmführer, who knew too much, thoroughly frightened him at first. But Mentzel had given his blessing to

Edgar's new, elegantly invented identity, and given his word that he would keep the matter to himself. They'd become fast friends, and Germany wouldn't want to lose a good man. Edgar had been satisfied with that. He understood these sorts of transactions. Mentzel obviously thought the information he provided was useful, but still Edgar wondered what the man had in mind for him. He must have a plan of some sort, and Edgar didn't know how long his supply of information would last.

HIS NERVOUSNESS ABOUT making the salute properly proved needless. No one at headquarters burst out laughing, there wasn't a trace of mockery on their faces. Mentzel waved Edgar to a chair across from an unknown Berliner in civilian clothes whose manner somehow indicated he had just arrived here in far-flung Ostland. Maybe it was the way he examined the office, and Edgar, or the way he settled into his chair as if he wasn't sure that a place in the Dienststelle postal zone would even have proper office furniture.

"It's been quite a long time, Herr Fürst," Mentzel said. "The Klaus Kurki was such a pleasant place."

"The pleasure was all mine," Edgar answered.

"I'll get right to the point. We're hoping for a solution to the Jewish question. We already have an abundance of material, of course, but you have more local knowledge. What's your estimation of how conscious the Balts are of the dangers presented by the Jews here?"

It was an awkward moment. Edgar's mouth went dry. He'd prepared for the meeting all wrong, that was clear. He'd gone over numerous possible subjects that might come up, but he hadn't anticipated anything like this. The man in civilian clothes was waiting for his answer. He hadn't even introduced himself.

Edgar thought he must be wondering why he was wasting his time listening to some dimwit's report, wishing Edgar would just hand them the briefcase and get it over with. Mentzel sat examining his impeccable cuticles—Edgar would get no help from him.

"First it must be said that I'm not really informed about the situation in Latvia and Lithuania," Edgar said haltingly. "Estonians are very different from Latvians and Lithuanians. In that sense, the Baltic designation can be misleading."

"Is that so? Haven't the Estonians mixed with the Eastern Balts as well as the Nordic races?" the unknown German asked.

Mentzel spoke up. "You may have noticed that the Estonians have noticeably fairer coloring. So the Nordic race is dominant. A quarter of all Estonians are of pure Nordic stock."

"And there are more blue eyes, yes, we have noted this positive aspect," the civilian agreed. The conversation was interrupted then by another German, apparently an old acquaintance of the Berliner's, who came into the room unexpectedly. Edgar was forgotten for a moment and he tried to use that to his advantage, to think of what to say, what to do. Lists of Bolsheviks weren't going to be enough, although that's exactly what Mentzel had been interested in when they were in Helsinki. Edgar had miscalculated. He would never be invited here again. His career would go nowhere. His focus on the difficulties of his own past had blinded him, made him imagine that all he needed was the identification card under the name Eggert Fürst in his pocket. The racial characteristics of the Baltikum and the basic tenets of Reichsminister Rosenberg's works on the significance of heredity flitted through the conversation and Edgar tried to think of something to say. He had at least had the foresight to commit the names of Rosenberg's works to memory: *Die Spur des Juden im Wandel der Zeiten* and *Der Mythus des 20. Jahrhunderts.* But just as he was beginning to fear that he would be asked a question about their contents, Mentzel clearly started to tire of his guests. Edgar hid his relief. He might not have made it through a discussion of complex racial issues. Now he just needed to keep a cool head. He would prepare better for their next meeting, look for people who knew Reichsminister Rosenberg—schoolmates, relatives, old neighbors on Vana-Posti Street, his colleagues from the Gustav Adolf Gymnasium in Tallinn. He would track down someone who would know what kind of person Alfred Rosenberg was, and what plans he had for the land of his birth. Once he'd learned to think like Rosenberg, Edgar would know what kind of information the Germans expected from him, what would interest them. His mind was already clicking feverishly, searching the archives of his brain for the right people, people who knew or might have known Jews who came to Estonia to escape the German pogroms or Baltic Germans who had fled to Germany and returned once the Soviets had withdrawn. There weren't very many of them.

Mentzel started to move toward the door to indicate that the visit had ended.

"If I may trouble you for one more minute," he said, gesturing for Edgar to follow him.

As they walked down the hallway, Mentzel gave a sigh. "Herr Fürst, did you succeed in obtaining the information I requested? I've been eagerly expecting your list."

Edgar's relief was so great that he didn't realize until he'd stepped into the office that he was holding his briefcase in the wrong hand, his right hand. Mentzel didn't seem to notice his embarrassment—he was focused on the list Edgar had handed him. Edgar parted his lips, trying to get enough oxygen.

"Congratulations, Herr Fürst. We need people of your caliber outside of Tallinn, and the political police B4 section is an excellent post. There's a lot of work to be done in the Haapsalu Aussenstelle. First report to the B4 Referentur's office at Patarei. You'll receive further instructions from them."

"Herr SS-Untersturmführer . . . ," Edgar stammered, "may I ask to what I owe such an honor?"

"The most obvious Bolshevik cells have already been cleaned up, but I'm sure you know how important a thorough disinfection is when it comes to stubborn vermin. And you, Mr. Fürst, have an excellent understanding of vermin."

Then Mentzel turned on his heel and went back into his office, leaving Edgar standing in the hallway. He had succeeded after all.

AS HE STEPPED inside the prison walls of Patarei, Edgar felt dizzy. He was alive when many others weren't. He would begin familiarizing himself with the Jewish question that very evening. These walls, meters thick, had silenced the screams of thousands of executions. They breathed death, death past and death to come, death that didn't distinguish between nationalities or leaders or centuries. But his steps rang through the hallways, advancing purposefully toward life. He was well received at the B4 bureau, where he filled out the forms with Eggert's information, in Eggert's handwriting, and didn't see any familiar faces. He felt like he was in the right place. He even got permission to visit Auntie Anna before he started his job in the Haapsalu office. He was told to be prepared for long hours, and that suited him, though he didn't know yet how to explain the situation to Roland. It would be good to have his cousin along, because his background was so trustworthy, and because Edgar needed to keep an eye on him. What better way to do that than to keep him as close as possible? Besides, you should never go into a fight without a wingman. Roland was a closemouthed, reliable type. Edgar knew that Roland wouldn't blow his cover. Roland didn't ask a lot of questions. Like when Edgar showed up at his place after he left the Commissariat for Internal Affairs. Getting caught in that bribe had been amateurish. Edgar knew that, and it upset him. But Roland hadn't pried, he just brought Edgar with him to Finland. He'd had that same weary look on his face that he had when Edgar got caught selling border passes at the Estonian border guard post, where they were both fulfilling their military service requirement. Roland had lied for him, said they'd been told that you had to pay for the pass, and Edgar had avoided going to jail. Roland had felt that Edgar's discharge from the army would be punishment enough, and he was right. All in all, the risks he'd taken for Roland had proved useful. Without Roland, without his recommendations, without the time in Finland, Edgar wouldn't have such a trustworthy background, and he would never have met Mentzel. He knew he could count on the family. Rosalie's mother obeyed Rosalie, Rosalie obeyed Roland, Roland obeyed Auntie Anna—and Anna obeyed Edgar. Auntie Anna had learned his new name so quickly, without asking any questions. It was enough for her to look into Edgar's eyes and see that he was serious. She was just happy that her nephew, her favorite boy, had returned home alive from the gates of death. All he had to do was assure her that everything was fine and he had a job. Life was good for Eggert Fürst. He would think of a way to get Roland on board. If Roland wouldn't listen, Anna would find the right words, or she could talk with Rosalie. After all, she wanted a bright future for Roland, too.

Taara Village,
Estland General Region,
Reichskommissariat Ostland

M Y COUSIN EDGAR WAS standing in the cabin doorway and his mouth was moving. He was saying something about Rosalie, his hands gesticulating, but I didn't understand why he was talking about my beloved. The wind blew in through the open door. My shirt flapped. The floor was dark with rain.

"Are you listening? Do you understand what I said?"

His shouting seemed to come from far away. The glass jar on the table crashed to the floor; there were buttercups in it. The wind whirled the flowers against the wall next to the mousetrap. I stared at them. Rosalie had picked them, with fingers that had just recently clasped mine. I was trembling like a tobacco leaf hung to dry, hot as tobacco in a sweating barrel. After the heat, a coldness started to spread from my chest down to my stomach. I couldn't feel my arms or legs. Edgar's mouth kept clapping open and shut.

"Did you hear what I said? She's already been buried."

"Shut the door now, Wurst."

"Roland, you have to accept Leonida and Anna's decision. The burial had to be done at night. There was a mark on her neck."

"Be quiet, Wurst."

I looked at the mousetrap. It was empty.

"What do you mean, a mark?" I shouted.

"There was a mark! Women have fragile minds. There's no way of knowing what drove her to such a sin."

I was already on my way to harness the gelding.

I DIDN'T GET any answers, but it was true: Rosalie was gone. Mother and Leonida treated me like a stranger; Leonida knotted her scarf tighter like she was trying to squeeze her face to nothingness and continued mixing the mash. I wasn't wanted. Mother's mouth hung open like a stuck door, without any words. I tried to pry some hint out of them about what had happened and why, who had been there and when, the names of the soldiers who'd come for lard and eggs. I didn't believe my cousin's filthy innuendos, didn't believe she would have done herself harm. Mother's eyes danced away from my shouts, told me to leave. I wanted to shake her. My hands were twitching. I would have hit her, but I remembered my father. He'd taken a worthless woman as his wife and it was a cross he bore without complaint, without argument. I'd become my father, in the sense that love had made me weak, but I didn't want him to come home to a place where his son had raised a hand against his mother, not even if it was for love. I lowered my fist.

"The girl has brought shame on this house with her sin," my mother whispered.

"Shame? What do you mean, shame? What exactly are you saying?" I yelled.

Aksel came in from the pantry and sat down to take off his

muck boot—his other leg was a wooden one he'd gotten in the War of Independence. He didn't look in my direction, didn't say anything. How could these people carry on as if nothing had happened?

"Why didn't you let me see her? What are you hiding?"

"There was nothing to see. We never would have thought it of her, never believed she could do such a thing," Mother said, tucking her handkerchief into her sleeve. The corners of her eyes were dry. "Be sensible, Roland. Talk with Edgar, will you?"

I ran through the house. The threshold of the back room stopped me in my tracks. I saw Rosalie's scarf on the chair. I rushed out of the house. The people living there had become strangers to me. I never wanted to see them again.

IN MY DESPERATION all I could think of was to go to Lydia Bartels's spirit session and ask for her help. Venturing into town was risky, but I needed some sign from Rosalie, a sign of where she was now, something to help me find the culprit, which no one else seemed to be interested in doing. I made my way to town on foot, taking the old cattle paths, the forest trails, ducking into the brush when a motorcycle approached or I heard the rattle of a cart or the clopping of hooves. I gave a wide berth to the manor house occupied by German headquarters and made my way to Lydia's house through the deep shade. The village dogs were alert as soon as they noticed a stranger at the edges of their property, so I avoided the footpaths and walked in the middle of the road, ready to spring into the bushes if I heard anyone coming. From the road I could make out the outline of telegraph poles and a house, hear the clatter of dishes from the kitchen, the pounding of a hammer, a cat's meow. The sounds of people who have a home. The sounds of people who have someone with them as they do their evening chores. All that had been taken from me. Anguish shriveled the outer reaches of my body like a piece of paper burned at the edges, but I had to let it go.

I headed for the graveyard before going to the Bartelses' place. I could see the spot, or what I thought was the right spot. I went around the fence, stumbling into gravestones and dodging crosses. If there was any place where I might hear her voice, it would be here. This church was where our wedding would have been, where I would have seen my bride at the altar in the veil she had been so happy about, the hint of a shy smile peeping out beneath it. The night was bright with stars and when I came to a heap of dirt, I started to look for a recently dug grave. I found it easily, the only one unmarked by a cross or flowers. A dog would have been given a better place to rest in the earth. I pounded my fists against the stone wall until the moss fell away, got on my knees, and prayed for a sign from my beloved so that I wouldn't need to go to Lydia Bartels, a sign to tell me that she had found peace, a sign that I could turn back. I didn't know why Rosalie had left the farm, who she had gone with, who had found her, or where. Why was she buried behind the churchyard? What priest had allowed that? Had there even been a priest? Rosalie wouldn't have taken her own life, although that's what they had been implying, and the way she'd been buried seemed to suggest it. But it couldn't have happened that way. I was ashamed that I hadn't been with her, hadn't prevented this. How could we have been so far away from each other that I didn't know she was in danger? It was unfathomable that all this had happened while I was sleeping or stoking the fire, going about my everyday chores. *Why didn't your thoughts turn to me? Why couldn't I protect you?* It was important to know what I'd been doing at the exact moment when Rosalie had departed this world. If I knew that, I would know how to search that moment for some kind of sign.

No sign came, no answer—Rosalie was resolute. I spit on the church steps and took out my pocket watch. It was striking midnight; the spirit hour was beginning. It was time to go to Lydia Bartels's house. I didn't know anything about the woman except that she held her séances on Thursdays, and that she had inherited the Seventh Book of Moses from her mother on her deathbed. Leonida strongly disapproved of Lydia Bartels's un-Christian activities, her folk beliefs, but Rosalie's girlfriends had been to see her to ask about parents who'd disappeared or been sent to Siberia. They always went in pairs, not daring to go alone. I didn't have anyone to ask to come with me, so I just had to strengthen myself with the Lord's Prayer, although I knew that the sign of the cross or images of God weren't allowed in Lydia's house. I stood in the main street and pulled my hat tighter around my ears. I hadn't shaved off the beard I'd grown in the woods, and I looked like an old man, so I didn't think I would be recognized. I had considered getting a German uniform. The mail girl had told me that several Jews had bought them, and some even joined the service—there was no better way to hide. She'd laughed when she said that, her laugh dripping with fear like the rim of an overflowing bucket. I knew she was also talking about her own fiancé.

THERE WAS ONE CANDLE burning in Lydia Bartels's room. There was a plate on the floor with a line drawn across it. A large piece of paper with the words "Yes" and "No" written on it was placed under the plate. Under the paper was some kind of shiny fabric. Lydia Bartels sat on the floor with her palms upward, her eyes closed. Mrs. Vaik, who opened the door, asked who I wanted summoned. I had taken off my hat, turning its brim in my hands, and had just begun to speak when she interrupted me:

"I don't need to know any more than that. Unless your errand concerns gold."

"It doesn't."

"There are so many asking after gold coins, people looking for caches taken from their families, but the spirits aren't interested in that sort of thing. Frivolous requests are tiresome to Her," she said, nodding toward the darkened room. I went in and sat down in the circle with the others, my limbs numb, nervous sighs heavy in the air, a faint draft from the curtains, and then Lydia Bartels asked if a fair-haired man's daughter was in the room. I heard a horrified gasp from my left. The plate moved. The circle breathed, hearts fluttered, barely contained hopes pounded, and I could smell the bitter scent of sweat, the sour smell of fear. The plate moved to the affirmative.

The woman on my left started to cry.

"She's already left . . . there's another here . . . Rosalie? Rosalie, are you here?"

The plate moved back and forth on the paper as if it didn't know which way to go. It stopped at the word "Yes."

"Are you all right, Rosalie?"

The plate moved. *No.*

"Did you come to a violent end?"

The plate moved. *Yes, yes.*

"You didn't do anything to yourself, did you?"

The plate moved. *No.*

"Do you know who did this to you?"

The plate moved. *Yes.*

"Do you know where he is?"

The plate remained motionless.

"Rosalie, are you still there?"

The plate didn't move in either direction, just stirred a little.

Mrs. Vaik came over and whispered that I could present my question. Before I had a chance to open my mouth, someone on my right got up quickly and backed toward the door, trembling and chanting the Lord's Prayer. Lydia Bartels sagged toward the floor.

"No!" The shout came out of my mouth. "Rosalie, come back!"

Mrs. Vaik sprang to her feet and pushed the trembling creature out of the room. The door slammed, a lamp was lit. Lydia Bartels had opened her eyes. She pulled her shawl tighter around her and stood up, only to sit down again in a chair. Mrs. Vaik started to shoo the people out of the room. I was so shaken I didn't care that everyone in the circle was staring at me. Some of them looked disappointed that the séance had been interrupted before their turns had come; others' expressions told me that even those who didn't know Rosalie would be talking about her after this. I stayed at the back of the group, leaning against the wall, where shadows from the lamp were dancing, then slid down to sit on the floor. I blinked and noticed myself staring at a forbidden photograph of former president Päts, shoved behind the bureau.

"You have to go now," Mrs. Vaik said.

"Bring Rosalie back."

"It won't work now. Come again next Thursday."

"Bring her back now!"

I had to know more. Someone had told me that a tramp had been seen following the women in the village. I didn't believe it, or the talk about Russian prisoners of war who served as laborers in the homes there. There weren't any at the Armses' place; it would have sent my mother around the bend to see Russians around or hear their language, although I had tried to convince them to take some on. The farm needed workers; the man of the house had a wooden leg, and I wasn't enough help on my own. But the prisoners were watched by guards. The Germans weren't.

"Listen to me, young man. These sessions are very difficult. The spirits suck away all Her energy, because they have no energy of their own. It's impossible to hold a séance like this more than once a week. Can't you see how tired she is? Come into the kitchen, I'll get you something hot to drink."

Mrs. Vaik brewed some grain coffee and poured half a glass of pungent liquor. I knew that she worked as a midwife, even for the bastards, and that she had bound the wounds of the men who went into the forest. If I couldn't get help from her, I would be lost.

"I'll pay you to bring Rosalie back. I'll pay anything."

"We don't summon the spirits for money. Come back next Thursday."

"I can't come here again—I've been seen. I have to find out who did this. Otherwise I'll have no peace. And neither will Rosalie."

"Then you'll have to find him yourself."

Mrs. Vaik's gaze was as firm as a knot in a gut cord. I stared at the mousetrap in the corner of the kitchen. My hands, accustomed to activity, twitched under the table. I gulped from the glass so frantically that I knocked my teeth against the rim. The pain in my head sharpened, but I couldn't shake the fear that I wouldn't be able to contact Rosalie again and these women could. I'd also acted against Rosalie's wishes. She said that you shouldn't summon spirits into this world, that they should be left in their own realm. But I didn't care. I'd left the ways of the church behind, they weren't my ways anymore. The church hadn't accepted Rosalie as one of its own.

Mrs. Vaik went to look at the mousetrap by the cupboard, took a mouse out, and threw it into the slop bucket.

"Was it any relief to learn that Rosalie wasn't at peace?" she asked.

"No."

"And yet you wanted to know. Otherwise you wouldn't have come here. We're only intermediaries. What comes of the knowledge, what it has to give, is not our responsibility. You didn't want to know anything about your father, though."

I stared at her. She slowly shook her head, looking me straight in the eye.

"On the train. He was an elderly man. It happened the moment he got on the train to Siberia. But you probably already guessed that."

I didn't say anything. She was right. Rosalie had mentioned that a mouse had run under Mother's bed in June, but I didn't want to listen. Mrs. Vaik's daughter Marta lumbered into the kitchen and started puttering at the stove. I didn't need any extra ears listening, but at that moment I didn't care.

"Your bride came to a session with a friend," Mrs. Vaik said. "Marta remembers the night well. There were too many people because some Germans had come unexpectedly and we couldn't send them away."

"Rosalie was worried about your father and her friend asked about her brother, and also asked about her husband," Marta continued. "Only your father appeared." She swept the scarf off her head and I couldn't bear the sympathy in her eyes.

"Rosalie never told me about that. She didn't approve of summoning spirits."

"She wanted to know," Mrs. Vaik said. "And once she did know, she decided that it was better for you to have hope."

I drank another glass of the liquor, but I didn't feel drunk. A mouse floated in the slop bucket. I had a plan, and Juudit could help me.

AT THE CABIN, I started making preparations—packing my knapsack, cleaning my Walther, hardening my heart for what was to come and against what had already happened. The whole time, I could feel Rosalie's little hand on the back of my neck, where she had laid it the last time we saw each other. No one had mentioned her name for a long time and the silence around her was losing its weight. People started to talk briskly about lands and soils and flowering borders as soon as they saw me, leaving no space between sentences for me to barge in with my uncomfortable words. Had the deportations in June made them so timid that they were all willing to shut their mouths as long as the Germans kept the Russians away? The Armses were happy that no one had been taken from them, that only my father and Juudit's brother had been caught in the Russians' net, but were they so happy that they would keep quiet even at the cost of their daughter's life? Were they frightened that it would make the Germans nervous if they pestered them about Simson Farm? Had they decided that Juudit was an unsuitable daughter-in-law because of her brother, because her mother was trying to get Johan's house back? Had Edgar used his mysterious comings and goings with the Germans to buy Mother protection at the Armses' place? How far were these people willing to go? I didn't know them anymore. I could grieve for my father later, continue my work documenting the depredations of the Bolsheviks to honor his memory, but first I would find the people responsible for Rosalie's death. It was time for action. The time for waiting was over.

"What are you up to? You're not thinking of doing something stupid, are you?"

Edgar stood in the doorway like a harbinger of doom, the wind fluttering his coat like black wings. I already regretted telling him what I'd heard on my way to the cabin: the neighbor's brat had seen a German coming from the direction of the Armses' place the night that Rosalie left. Or at least a man in a German uniform—it had been dark and the boy hadn't seen his face. Was it a stranger after Leonida's tins of lard? I didn't think so.

"Whoever it is, he's running free and all you can think about is your business schemes."

"There was talk of a tramp in the village," Edgar said. "There's no telling where he'd be by now."

"You know very well that's complete nonsense."

"You're blaming all Germans for something that some lunatic did. It's clouding your reason, making you act like a lunatic yourself."

Edgar's voice grated in my ears. I had to stand up, put some wood on the fire, bang the stove door.

"And what good would it have done if Leonida had gone to the police? It wouldn't have brought Rosalie back."

Edgar ladled some porridge into his bowl, first with his right hand, then his left. His words squished with the rhythm of his shuttling spoon, his mouth smacking with disapproval as lumps of porridge fell on the table.

"Think about it. What if Leonida had gone and claimed that some unknown German had done something to Rosalie? Where would Anna and Leonida get their extra income if the soldiers started avoiding the farm? They desperately need the money. And you can be sure the soldiers would start to avoid them if these kinds of baseless rumors were coming from their house."

When he finished speaking, Edgar drew his mouth into a disapproving pout, deepening the curve of his frown.

"Look at yourself," he said. "And look at me, at Leonida, Anna, our friends. Our lives will go on, and yours should, too. You could at least shave off your beard."

There was impudence in his words. He was always a little more obnoxious when he got back from one of his outings. Often he would stay out in the yard striding back and forth as if he were having a conversation with someone, some new acquaintance or whoever it was he went to meet in town. I had told him he should try to find out what had happened to Rosalie, listen for rumors. Somebody must know something. You can't keep secrets in a small town. I waited for news, but he would always just shake his head when he got back. In the end I stopped believing he was doing anything about it. I couldn't go to Leonida and Mother's place, I was afraid of what I might do. Edgar looked in on Mother now and then, and if there was anyone she would talk to, it was Edgar, but he wouldn't try to coax her into telling him about it, wouldn't ask for names, for details about who had come to the house, no matter how much I pleaded.

"What if it wasn't a German? What if you're making a false accusation?"

"What are you getting at?"

"What if your girl had another suitor . . ."

Edgar was lying on the floor. The bowl of porridge was shattered. When he opened his mouth, his teeth were bloody. I stood there shaking. Edgar crawled toward the door. I guessed that he was headed for the stable. I stepped in front of him. He didn't look at me. Fighting had always terrified him. I was afraid I would hit him again, afraid I might beat him to death. I stepped away from the door, lifted the latch.

"Get out of here."

Edgar crawled out into the yard. I closed the door and went out the back to the paddock and stood watching the stable. Edgar had taken the bicycle. He pushed it toward the road, then stopped. He must have guessed I was watching him from behind the bushes.

"Your girl had a reputation," he shouted.

He took off at a run, didn't try to get on the bike—I must have hit him pretty hard.

"Don't you remember her girlfriend at the distillery?" he added. "The distillery at the manor house? Rosalie started sneaking over there whenever no one was looking. What do you think she was doing there? She had suitors. Germans as well as local boys!"

I almost went after him, but I tensed my muscles and forced them to hold me still. My heart was full of dark thoughts, blacker than nightmares. I was like a tree blown to bits by artillery fire, limbless, wounded, and the landscape around me was the same. Rosalie, my Rosalie was gone. I would never hear the ripple of her smiling-eyed laughter, never walk with her along the fields, never again plan our future. It wouldn't fit in my skull, even though the cover of my notebook was filled with crosses for my fallen brothers. They had died in battle. This was different.

ONCE I HAD SENT Edgar away, I left, too. I took the forged rubber stamps that Edgar had made so cleverly, which I was sure I would find a use for. I hid the gelding in the Armses' barn. He felt like my only friend now, but I couldn't bring him with me. I wasn't going to stop until I got to Tallinn, to the gate of the apartment house on Valge Laeva Street.

———

I DIDN'T KNOW if Juudit had already heard, and if she had, what she'd been told. My slicker dripped and in my mind I went through that moment again when Edgar stood in the doorway and Rosalie's buttercups were scattered across the floor.

When Juudit's thin form appeared at the street door, I stepped in front of her. I hardly recognized her. She jumped like a nimble bird and I felt a kick in my chest, because every light-footed woman reminded me of my beloved.

"Roland! What are you doing here?"

"Let's go inside."

It wasn't any easier to say it once we were indoors. I fortified my courage by remembering that I may have been a man who'd lost everything, but I was also a man with a plan: to look for the killer and give Rosalie peace. I couldn't get our fields back, or my father, or Rosalie, but I could blow a hole under my enemy's feet.

"How did you get here?" Juudit asked.

"I just came."

"How was the trip?"

"Good."

"Has something happened?"

I stared into the entryway. A wet ring was growing around my slicker, which I'd tossed over a chair. The words were so heavy that I couldn't push them out. I sat down at the kitchen table. I had to get her to go along with my plan. It was strange to sit there like that, my hands limp. Talking would have been easier if I'd had a pen to fiddle with or a harness to grease. I rubbed my stubbly chin, ran my hands through my bristling hair. I wasn't fit for a city lady's table. Those were the kinds of thoughts that went through my mind—trivialities, so I wouldn't have to think about the thing itself.

The silence grew heavy. Juudit made a restless movement and although I could tell she wanted to ask me more, she didn't speak. She started to tidy the already tidy kitchen, moved a box of lard off the table, said that Leonida had brought it for her when she came to sell some at the market in town, to the Germans, to send home to their families.

"You can get anything you want for it. I got two pairs of stockings for two tins. And some egg powder."

I opened my mouth to tell her to be quiet. But I didn't know of anyone better than Juudit for the task I had in mind. I closed my lips tight.

"You have a fever, Roland."

She held out a handkerchief. I didn't take it. A cupboard door slammed and she came up beside me with a dropper, squeezed a drop of iodine into a glass of water, and held it out to me. I didn't want it. She left the dropper and the glass in front of me and started to fuss with a basket of compresses, was already spreading out Billroth batiste and flannel. Her hands smelled of Nivea cream.

"You look sick," she said.

"I have something I need to talk about. With you. I need you to get some information from the Germans. Nothing dangerous. Nothing too difficult. Just a few things."

"Roland, what are you talking about? I'm not going to get mixed up in any foolishness."

"Rosalie . . ."

Juudit's hands froze.

"My girl is buried in the ground. Outside the churchyard. No cross to mark the grave."

"Rosalie?"

"The Germans."

"What do you mean?"

"The Germans did it."

"Did what? Do you mean that Rosalie . . ."

I stood up. My forehead was burning like brimstone. I couldn't get any more words out. Her lack of emotion was like ice-cold well water dashed in my face.

"Roland, please, sit down and tell me what happened."

"Rosalie is gone. There is no Rosalie, except in the heart of the earth. And in my heart."

Juudit was quiet. Her eyelids fluttered, a sound like birds' wings on the surface of a lake. Circles of tears spread across my eyes.

"She was buried outside the graveyard. The Germans did it."

"Stop harping on the Germans."

"I have something I want you to do, and you're going to do it. I'll come back when everything's ready," I said, and I left. Juudit was still muttering. I had reached the ground floor when I heard a slam from upstairs and she ran after me.

"Roland. Tell me everything. You have to."

"Not here."

We went back inside and I told her what I knew.

Juudit's basket tumbled to the floor, the bandages unwinding like a shroud.

PART TWO

Our purpose is to expose the overseas fascists' organized efforts to rehabilitate the Hitlerists and their stooges.

—*The Estonian State and People in the Second World War,*
    Kodumaa Homeland Publishers, 1964

Tallinn,
Estonian Soviet Socialist Republic,
Soviet Union

THE CEILING CREAKED under footsteps on the floor above. A creak of steps to the upstairs washstand, from the washstand to the window, from the window to the wardrobe, and from the wardrobe back to the washstand. Comrade Parts's tight, dry eyes swept over the ceiling. Now and then he could hear his wife sit down in a chair, the leg of the chair stabbing the floor with a sound like a stab to his forehead. He pressed his fingers against his moist temples, his pounding veins, but his wife's slippers didn't stop, her foot just kept tapping in place with a knock that dug into the floor, straining the thick, light-brown paint, testing its cracks, creating an unbearable noise that prevented him from concentrating on his work.

When the pendulum clock struck eleven, the springs on the bed above screeched, then faded to a rasp. Then silence.

Comrade Parts listened. The ceiling didn't sag, the cornice along its edge held firm, the furtive sway of the light fixture subsided.

The silence continued.

This was the moment he'd waited for all day, waited patiently, sometimes trembling with rage. But the waiting was seasoned with excitement, a giddiness that he rarely experienced.

The typewriter sat ready. The light from the overhead fixture glimmered softly on the Optima's metal case, its glittering keys. Comrade Parts adjusted his cardigan, relaxed his wrists, and curved his hands into the correct position, as if he were preparing to perform a concert, a sold-out performance. The piece would be a success, everything would work itself out. Still, he had to admit that when he sat down at his desk his collar always tightened to one size smaller.

On the roller was a half-written page from the day before with its carbon copy. Parts's wrists were already poised over the keys, but he pulled them back and laid them on the carefully pressed creases of his pants. His gaze focused on the words typed on the page. He read through them several times, murmuring under his breath, tasting them, approving them. The narrative still felt fresh, and his collar started to feel a little looser. Cheered, he seized the first page of the manuscript, walked to the middle of the room, imagined an audience, and quietly read the first paragraph:

> *"What unbelievable acts the Estonian evildoers are capable of, what horrifying crimes! The pages of this investigation will reveal fascist conspiracies and chilling acts of murder. You will read evidence of bestial forms of torture that the Hitlerists gleefully seized upon, with pleasure, and without shame. This investigation will cry out for justice and leave no stone unturned in exposing crimes intended to exterminate the Soviet people."*

When he got to the end of the paragraph, he was as breathless as the text itself. He thought this was a good sign. The beginning was always the most important; it had to be expressive, to cast a spell on the reader. This paragraph did, and it was also written according to Office guidelines. The text had to distinguish itself from previous books dealing with the Hitlerist occupation. He had three years—that was how long the Office had given him to research and write the book. It was an unusual gesture of confidence. He had even been given the new Optima to take home, to his own desk, but this time he wasn't writing a small piece of counterpropaganda or a reader for young people about the friendship of nations or a didactic fairy tale for children, but a work that would change the world—a work about the greater fatherland and the West. The beginning ought to take your breath away.

It was Comrade Porkov's idea, and Comrade Porkov was a practical man. He liked books. He liked making use of them. And book buyers paid the costs of operations. He liked films for the same reasons. And his words still warmed Parts in his moments of doubt, although Parts knew that Porkov had just been flattering him. He had said that he'd recommended Parts because he knew of no greater magician with words.

The revelation of the project had been a great moment. They'd been sitting in the safe house that they used for their weekly meetings, going over the situation with Parts's network of correspondents, and Parts had had no idea that Porkov had any other plans up his sleeve, that in a single moment Parts's priority would no longer be his wide correspondence with the West, but something completely different. In the middle of the meeting Porkov simply said that now was the time. When Parts confusedly asked what he was talking about, Porkov answered:

"You, Comrade Parts, are going to be an author."

HE WAS OFFERED a large advance—three thousand rubles. Half the money would belong to Porkov because of the work he'd done on Parts's behalf, and because he'd chosen the materials the work would be based on. The documents were now locked in Parts's cabinet—two briefcases filled with books about the Hitlerist occupation, as well as publications from Western countries that had never been seen by Soviet eyes. Parts had gone through the material quickly and deduced what general direction he should take. The book would have to show that the Soviet Union was exceedingly interested in solving the crimes of the Hitlerists, in fact more interested than the Western countries were. It was clear that a different idea had been propagated in the West. The instructions to use adjectives like "just" and "democratic" to describe the Soviet Union as often as possible made it evident that this was not how the West saw them.

It was also clear that another main target would be Estonians abroad. A great deal of the material he'd been given was from the impressively productive pens of refugees. The Politburo was obviously alarmed by their stridence and their opinions about the Soviet Union. They painted the homeland with a black brush. And because Moscow was nervous, it was time to spring into action and make a retaliatory strike—to present Estonians abroad in a light that would make them unreliable in Western eyes. Parts couldn't have thought of a better method himself. Once the fascistic nature of Estonian nationalism was revealed, the Soviet Union would have all the traitors handed back to it on a silver platter, since no one in the West would protect Hitlerists. Criminals had to be brought to justice. No one would listen to Estonian emigrants' complaints and pleas anymore, no one would dare to publicly support them. That would be interpreted as support for fascism, and the Estonian government in exile would be seen as being in league with the dregs of humanity. He wouldn't even need any evidence; sowing doubt would suffice. Nothing more than a hint, a whisper.

"Of course, your own experience will give the book its piquancy," Porkov added when he told him about the new project. They had never discussed Parts's past before, but Parts took the hint. He had no need to try to hide the reasons he'd been sent to the Siberian camps. Those reasons were now to his credit. Every step he'd taken on Staffan Island was to his benefit, a mark of his expertise.

"We wouldn't have succeeded in destroying the nationalists as well as we did without your help," Porkov continued. "A thing like that isn't forgotten, Comrade Parts."

Parts swallowed. Although Porkov had made it understood that he could speak freely about the matter, Parts preferred not to discuss his peculiar secret, because it could also compromise him. But Porkov saw fit to continue, and Parts twisted his mouth into a smile.

"Between you and me, I'm assured that no one has given the Directorate of State Security more complete information on the activities of Estonia's anti-Soviets—all of their collaborators, English spies, forest bandits—and their addresses. Remarkable work, Comrade Parts. Without you we never would have learned about the fascist Linnas's escape route to the West, not to mention the identities of all the Estonian expatriate traitors who aided him, which you helped to uncover."

Parts felt naked. Porkov only mentioned these things to show that he knew everything about him. Parts had not imagined otherwise, but speaking out loud about such things was a show of strength. It was a method familiar to him. He forced his hand to remain still, fighting the urge to raise it to his breast pocket to make sure his passport was still there. He kept his feet motionless, looked straight at Porkov, and smiled.

"When I fought on the German front, I was able to acquaint myself with the activities of the Estonian nationalists, and I'm very familiar with the subject. I would venture to say that I'm an expert on the nationalists."

EESTI RAAMAT WOULD BE his publisher. Porkov would make sure that the project would go forward without complications. Parts could expect a signed contract, a celebration. He could order champagne and napoleon cake, carnations for his wife. There would be translations, lots of them. Medals. There would be numerous reprintings. At antifascist celebrations, he would be given a place of honor.

He could give up his cover position at the Norma factory guard booth. The advance and the brown envelopes from the Office would be enough to live on very well.

He could get gas heat.

He honestly couldn't believe his luck.

The only problem was that the peace he needed for his work was nonexistent at home. He'd hinted that he would require an office for his research, but there had been no progress in the matter, and he couldn't reveal the nature of his work to his wife. There was no point in hoping that its importance would calm her nervous attacks. He went back to his desk and unbuttoned his collar. He had to get started. Porkov was already waiting for a taste, the first few chapters, and so much was at stake—the whole rest of his life.

ВИ.ЛЕНИН
4 коп
1963

Tallinn,
Estonian Soviet Socialist Republic,
Soviet Union

T HE WIND FROM the cellar of the Pagari building hit Comrade Parts hundreds of meters before he reached the metal
doors of the entrance. The same peculiar wind had swept his
ankles when he was a young man visiting the building in the first
Soviet occupation, before the Germans came. He'd been there
to meet his colleague Ervin Viks on matters of the People's
Commissariat of Internal Affairs. He remembered how Viks
had stepped out of the door to the cellar just as Parts stopped
to shake the snow from his overcoat. There were bloodstains
on Viks's cuffs. His shoes left red tracks on the white tile floor.
There were all kinds of rumors going around at the time about
a decompression chamber located in that cellar. For Parts, that
wind was the worst thing about the place. He recognized it now,
guiding him with a certainty from the street to the entrance. The
Directorate of State Security was the same from one decade to
the next. There wasn't a wind like that anywhere else. It fol-

lowed you into the elevator and up the stairs, blew straight into Porkov's office and across the parquet floor, and shook Parts's carefully constructed confidence as he stepped in front of the captain. Parts could feel the floor, its every contour, through the soles of his feet, as if his new shoes had been switched for the ones he wore in his youth, the ones with steel toe taps and soles so thin that the sand got in and chafed his toes.

Porkov smiled from beneath a picture of the leaders. He was sitting behind his desk with his elbows on top of a folder he'd closed purposefully slowly, slowly enough that Parts had time to get a glimpse of his own picture inside. They spent a moment admiring the charming view from Porkov's office window onto Lai Street. You could even see the Baltic, and the steeple of St. Olaf's Church, according to Porkov. Parts squinted. He could just barely make out the tip of St. Olaf's tower. For a fleeting moment he imagined what it would be like if someday he had an office like this one, his own department, here where the corridors felt like corridors of power, and the wind from the cellar blew on someone else's ankles, not his. He would let the office workers use the old servants' elevator and use only the main elevator himself. He would have keys to all the offices, the communications center, the film archives, and the cellars. The messages spitting out of the telex tapping through the night would be his messages. The goings-on of all the citizens. Every telephone conversation. Every letter. Every business. Every relationship. Every career. Every life.

A draft fluttered his pant leg. Porkov cleared his throat. Parts sat up straighter, adjusted his shoulders. The invitation to Porkov's bright office was a mark of esteem, and he should behave accordingly, and pay attention. A crystal carafe sparkled in the last rays of the setting sun. Porkov poured drinks into Czech crystal glasses, turned on the milk glass ceiling light, and pronounced himself very satisfied. Parts swallowed—they had looked at his pages. Porkov was in a benevolent mood. The honey of Porkov's praise put Parts momentarily into a sticky state of mind; first he was blushing speechlessly, then stuttering and struggling to make some response.

After a drink he had to pinch himself, remind himself that he must use this to his advantage. He had passed the Glavlit censorship offices at Pärnu Highway 10 on his way home many times and looked up at the windows on the highest floors, wishing, as any man would, that he could go inside to show the progress of his manuscript to the staff there, who would understand its significance, its accuracy. The dream was enough. He wouldn't actually ever do it, wouldn't ever see the censors he was supposed to impress. Instead he should try to get in to talk to the publisher located in the same building, and soon after that, the publisher would owe him some money. But these things would happen in their own time—it was wisest to wait until later to remind the people there about the advance. First he had to keep Porkov happy, to earn his trust. Best not to disturb the Comrade Captain's mood, not sound impertinent when he made his request—he wanted more archive materials to broaden his research.

Porkov was getting tipsy. The bottle was already half-emptied, and as he poured more liquor into it their chat started to skate along doubly well. At first Porkov pretended not to understand Parts's roundabout question—the flicker of surprise in his eyes was sharp enough that Parts guessed he was exaggerating his drunkenness, just as Parts was. But Parts, too, could put brash behavior down to drunkenness if need be, and with that in mind he forced himself to present his request directly. He let an offended expression show through, mumbled that he was certain he would recognize more dregs of humanity in the archives, that he would be able to identify them. Porkov laughed, slapped him on the back, and said: We'll see. Have another drink. We'll see.

As he poured more vodka, Porkov glanced at him again from behind his drunken face, and Parts dried his eyes, let his posture sink into a tipsy softness, pretended to set his glass down and miss the table, and restrained his hand from brushing the dandruff from his shoulder.

"You've already been given an abundance of material for your work. It ought to be enough. We have our instructions, Comrade Parts."

Parts hastened to express his gratitude for their confidence in him and added, "I'm quite certain that the Comrade Captain would be considered a hero in Moscow, should the final manuscript exceed expectations."

These words brought Porkov to a halt in front of him.

"Of course, you might find something in the materials that no one else has."

"Exactly. I was, after all, an eyewitness to the crimes of the fascist scum, and would have lost my life if the Red Army hadn't liberated the Klooga camp. I've dedicated my life completely to recording those heroic events and laying bare the crimes of the Hitlerist cancer. I might even recognize the names of the guards. Many of them were nationalists who later became bandits."

Porkov burst into laughter again, drops of his spit landing in Parts's glass, and Parts joined in, flavoring his cackle with a touch of shared understanding. Every man in the Comrade Captain's position hoped for a promotion, and Porkov's operation was well up to speed. Could he resist a gold-paved road to Moscow? There had been numerous recent books about the escapades of the Hitlerists, and they'd been distributed so widely abroad that Parts knew the operation was considered important.

For whatever reason, the Politburo placed an emphasis on these things in Estonia. And that was always a spur to competition.

Porkov filled their glasses again.

"I'm hosting a little evening party at my summer place. Come with your wife. I want to meet her. It's time we started planning your future. The Estonians are hiding the nationalists, and they don't realize the danger they're in. The problem is one of morals. The morals of the nation have to be improved, and it's clear that you have the talents needed to do it."

COMRADE PARTS'S STOMACH started to gnaw at him while he was still on the bus. It wasn't because of the drinks. It was because he was going home and Porkov's invitation worried him. The Comrade Captain had seemed inclined to grant his archive request, but could he stay in his favor if he refused the invitation? The bright kitchens and clink of dinner dishes in the passing houses depressed him. Two doors down they made fricadelle soup on Wednesdays and macaroni with milk for the children on Thursdays, with meat for the man of the house. They made jam. Parts had a cold stove and a pot of potatoes covered in lukewarm water on the burner waiting for him at home. There were no more cutlets like in their early married years, not since he came back from Siberia, or any berries from the bushes in the yard—his wife hadn't once spread ashes under them.

But a surprise greeted him at the front steps—sheets on the clothesline, flapping in the wind. He stood for a moment admiring the fluttering linens, the most charming thing he'd seen in a long time, although they ought to have been brought in by this time of day. Still, his wife had done the laundry, at home! Suddenly even her coy habit of hiding her underwear beneath the sheets to dry didn't annoy him, or the fact that his bath had been empty that morning, or the fact that soaking the linens for hours in Fermenta was by no means good for them, or that their fight about using the common laundry was about to begin again (he could tell the sheets had been washed in the machines, and they were edged with Auntie Anna's handmade lace, after all). But what of these small details? Perhaps the situation wasn't hopeless. Perhaps things were changing for the better. Perhaps they could accept Porkov's invitation.

Parts approached the front door. Liszt came barreling out of his wife's record player all the way to the yard. At the front steps, the railing trembled under his hand as he took hold of it for support. Hope and the suspicion that he would be disappointed battled in his mind as he took his keys out of his pocket, clicked open the lock, and stepped over the threshold without turning on the light. There was a whining sound from the living room, a light through the glass in the door. A wailing that rose and fell, sometimes fumbling out in words. Still, Parts hoped that the living room door would open and his wife would come to meet him, that it would all be a cheerful lark, but disappointment was hatching like a worm in an onion, the twinge of hope brought on by the laundry in the yard was stubbed out in the overflowing ashtray on the telephone table. He put his Moroccan leather briefcase down beside the trumeau, hung his coat on the rack, and changed his shoes for his slippers. Only then did he feel ready to push open the door, which stood ajar, and face the state his wife was in.

She was rocking back and forth in the beam of orange light from the ceiling fixture, the hem of her coatdress lifted to her waist, her underslip stained, her bloated face hidden by her tangled hair, the record player pounding. A lit cigarette smoked in the ashtray, its tip glowing, a bottle of Beliy Aist cognac was half empty, a mass of striped men's handkerchiefs wet with weeping lay heaped under the table. Parts closed the door quietly and went into the kitchen. His steps were heavy. The sheets could wait. The smooth meeting at the Pagari building had lulled him into a ridiculous feeling of optimism. He had just hoped, hoped so strongly, that they could go to the party together, as a couple. How stupid he was.

Years ago it had been different. Parts had received a letter in Siberia from Auntie Anna that said his wife was well, was in her care. The knowledge that his wife was all right didn't stir any emotion in him, although the message was the first of its kind in years. He didn't know what she'd been doing before the German withdrawal. He himself had been tried and put on a train to Siberia quite soon afterward, and news of his wife hadn't been uppermost in his mind. But when he'd finally made it to the last leg of his journey back to Estonia, it felt good to have someone to go home to. Anna and Leonida were already gone, as was his biological mother, Alviine, and there were strangers living in the Armses' house. He had no one else. He found his wife in Valga, in a small but clean flat, its air tainted by the stink from the one communal water closet, which was in the neighboring apartment. The room itself had been orderly, his wife attentive in her sense and her hygiene, nodding slowly as he stressed that if anyone asked about his years in Siberia it would be best to remember that he had been convicted for being a counterrevolutionary and for trusting in the third alternative and in the English, that he'd been given ten years for it, for gathering Estonia's own troops after the Germans had left, and for his espionage training on Staffan Island. She could certainly tell that to anyone else who'd been to Siberia, and she should remember her brother's fate.

His wife hadn't asked any more questions. She had probably wanted to be able to walk safely after sunset, had probably understood why it was important to remember that her husband was a real man of Estonia. Those were dangerous times for anyone who had chosen, or was known to have chosen, any side other than Estonia's. The Office, on the other hand, didn't like those who had chosen Estonia. Luckily for Parts, his years in Siberia had hollowed his cheeks into a new shape, and he was hardly likely to run into his old colleagues, who had presumably all been liquidated. It was the beginning of a new, good life. Although the bedroom had never been a place of shared rest for him and his wife, nor of shared passion, they nevertheless learned to share a bed, and their coolness kept the sheets fresh even in the heat of summer. They learned camaraderie, if not quite friendship. Parts hadn't complained about the new apartment or asked why she had moved there from Tallinn. For someone who'd been in Siberia, there was no point in hoping for better, there was no way to get permission to live in the capital. He just had to take things gradually, let time hollow his cheeks still more, let the nosepiece of his glasses press pits between his eyes, construct a new demeanor. He wasn't going to make any more mistakes.

After Parts had lived in Valga in complete seclusion for some time, a stranger struck up a conversation on the way home one day. Parts understood immediately what was happening. His instructions were clear: he was ordered to strike up a friendship with the workers in their combine who had returned to Estonia from Siberia, report to the system on their attitudes and their degree of anti-Sovietism, evaluate their potential for sabotage, and keep notes on their reactions to letters received from abroad. He had accomplished this well, so well that he was considered the right person to start a correspondence in the name of a man who'd once come to his house to visit for the evening. Parts understood that his gift with signatures was already known in the Office. Later on he even heard that the graphics and graphology specialist at the Security Directorate was jealous of him.

BECAUSE OF HIS SKILL, Comrade Parts continued his work with Estonians abroad. He had made a pasteup of a photo of himself with General Laidoner's insignia to inspire confidence and written a skillful account of how Laidoner had personally given it to him as a mark of respect. The Office was satisfied with Parts's creative language and his repertoire of carefully constructed phrases. He knew how to avoid being overly specific or going after the Soviet system. Only the most ridiculously naive Estonian living in the West would believe that he could cross the line into opinions about the homeland or otherwise threaten the social order without the blessing of Postal Control.

In just a couple of weeks he succeeded in getting a response to a letter written according to guidelines and sent to a certain Villem in Stockholm. The two had studied together in Tartu, and Villem was delighted to receive a letter from home. The Office opened a file on Villem, Postal Control expedited Villem's mother's letters to Sweden, and within a month Parts was whisked to Tartu on a marshrutka transport to establish contact with Villem's mother. In two months he'd collected enough evidence of Villem's participation in a spy ring that he was rewarded with a promise that he and his wife could move back to Tallinn. He got a job at the Norma factory and his wife was made a guard at the railway station, with her own chair on the commuter platforms. They finally had the space for a sofa bed, which his wife made up for him every night in the living room. And after all this success, he couldn't get his wife to Porkov's party sober. They couldn't go. They could never go. He would never taste Porkov's beluga.

THE TURNING POINT in their cool, peaceful coexistence had come in the form of Ain-Ervin Mere's trial two years earlier for killing Soviet citizens as head of the Estonian division of the German security police. Parts had been summoned to testify as an eyewitness to the horrors perpetrated by the cancer of fascism and he performed the task well, first studying diligently in the training arranged for witnesses on Maneeži Street and then presenting himself as an expert in the courtroom, deploring the accused, masterfully using everything he'd learned, all the while glad that England had refused to turn Mere over to the Soviet Union, since meeting the major eye to eye would have been uncomfortable. His testimony had been strengthened by the radio coverage, his eyewitness accounts of the atrocities at the concentration camp at Klooga were widely written of, and he'd even been invited to a kindergarten to be presented with flowers—the cameras flashing, the radio gushing about how the staff at the kindergarten wept and the children sang.

The Office was satisfied. His wife wasn't. She had changed radically—she'd started missing days at work early; the smell of liquor had seeped into the wallpaper; her appearance, which she had always taken care with before, had fallen away curl by curl, her skin graying as quickly as the women's hair covered in ash after the bombings. Parts had heard that she smelled of alcohol at the railway station, too, and had once even fallen out of her inspector's chair. On good days she might energetically begin the housework, as she had today with the laundry, but after the first glass she would forget to open the dampers on the stove or absentmindedly let the tub overflow. Parts got into

the habit of checking the dampers several times a day and constantly sniffing for the smell of gas.

Karl Linnas and Ervin Viks's trial for the crimes at the Tartu
camps had added to the problem and made what had been her occasional bouts of pacing a nightly occurrence. He remembered
the time he surprised her reading a copy of Ervin Martinson's
book on the trial, her hands shaking, a trail of tobacco-darkened
spit at the corner of her mouth, a bubble forming with every
agitated breath. He'd snatched the book from her and locked it
in his office cabinet. Her voice had been filled with horror: How
did he know where he'd be sitting at the next trial, how did he
know what all this would lead to, what would happen to them?

SHE MAY HAVE LOST her sense about the Ain-Ervin Mere trial,
but Parts had done the opposite. Testifying at the trial had been
the beginning of a new phase for him—he took hold of what
was offered and turned it all to his own benefit. A career as a
witness to the sadism of the Hitlerists, and as their victim, guaranteed a secure future. He might be asked to testify in other
cases, maybe even abroad. He was necessary. Why couldn't his
wife understand that?

The book only added new dimensions, greater possibilities. At best it could give him access to information that, if used
properly, would guarantee a good life for them, vacations on the
Black Sea, access to restricted shops.

The Linnas and Viks case would be followed by many similar appearances, Parts was sure of that. Cases were already
being prepared elsewhere, in Latvia, Lithuania, Ukraine, Bul-
garia. The clumsy start of the Linnas trial would be put down
as a mistake, and wouldn't be repeated. The *Sotsialisticheskaia
Zakonnost* had reported the outcome of the case in late 1961,

even though the trial didn't begin until after New Year's. Parts found the whole thing laughable, but he was careful not to grin when it was mentioned in public. On the whole the strides made by the Office had been remarkable, with new tools created all the time, the technological department developing rapidly, and the agency apparatus expanding. More books on the subject were needed. Parts was in luck—he happened to hold a position in what was apparently an area of significant growth in the Office's activities.

And if the Office, with moods as changeful as his wife's, was kept satisfied, who knows, there might dawn a day when Comrade Parts would walk nonchalantly into the photographer's and order portraits for a foreign passport, as if it were an everyday occurrence, as if he'd always been a *viezdnoj*, a good Soviet citizen with a foreign passport. And then his colleagues and acquaintances, some of whom he wouldn't even remember ever meeting, would pester him to bring back dirty magazines, or decks of cards with naked women on them. An image of the chubby-cheeked Intourist guide flashed in his mind. He'd heard that she had a Western contact who always remembered to bring her a magazine taped to his stomach. It had been going on for a long time but she always passed her evaluations—the Office needed magazines, too.

Parts's book wouldn't be part of next year's publications, which were to celebrate Tallinn's liberation from the clutches of the thieving fascist conquerors twenty years earlier, but when the twenty-fifth anniversary came, Parts would be one of its notable heroes, the famous author and witness, presented with flowers. Perhaps the crowd at the Tallinn philatelic exhibition would be able to admire his face on a stamp or commemorative envelope. He wouldn't need to constantly keep up his correspondence, labor hour after hour over his letters, both the forged and the genuine, some filled with disinformation, some preemptive, some meant to test the mood of the recipients. His work on repatriated emigrants would be over. The Office would realize that he needed his own office; *Cross & Cockade* would beg him for more articles on Soviet pilots, and so would other Western magazines. His only required correspondence would be with those contacts interested in exchanging ideas with a respected Soviet author, or discussing his specialized field, Soviet pilots. But his cover job at the factory and the chatter of refugees would be a thing of the past, since he would inevitably be tainted in their eyes. He would be a new person. He would have a new life.

The only problem was his wife's nerves. After all these years they were giving way completely, just when he had the support of the Office, just when the future was clear.

ВИЛЕНИН
1963

Tallinn,
Estonian Soviet Socialist Republic,
Soviet Union

THE SAFE HOUSE WAS deserted except for Comrades Porkov and Parts, two desks, a Magnetofon, a few chairs, and a constantly buzzing telephone. Parts himself had gone mute; he was holding in his hands a set of folders containing the list of names from the Klooga camp, and for a moment he wondered if he could hear something humming, was even about to ask the Comrade Captain if he'd brought the headquarters cat with him, until he realized he should keep his mouth shut—the sound was coming from inside him. The green of the wallpaper intensified to such a brightness that it made him squint. Comrade Porkov nodded at the lists and said that they weren't complete—the fascists had taken their archives with them when they left—but the Directorate of State Security had managed to procure an abundance of useful information, as had the excellent work of the special commission investigating fascist crimes.

"Many of the victims have not, of course, been identified, and we would be pleased to be able to complete the list," Porkov said. "Unfortunately, the identities of many of the murderers are also still shrouded in obscurity. Far too many. I'm relying on your help in the matter. Letting such criminals go free is not acceptable to Soviet morality. That's not how we work. You can acquaint yourself with the materials at home."

COMRADE PARTS FELT FEVERISH about the Klooga files all afternoon. They tickled his leg from within his briefcase where it sat on the floor of the factory guard booth. He wanted to take them out, glance at them just a little, but he knew how he would react if he found something. He remained nervous even when colors returned to normal. The sun had never been so high in the sky, the day never so bright. He had to shade his eyes with his hand even inside the booth, trying the whole day to think about something else, to behave as normally as possible, to concentrate on trivial, everyday things—the workers moving through the gates, the waistbands of the women's underwear filled with goods from the factory, the men's bulging breast pockets, the commotion when the inspector arrived, how the cognac offered to her made her blush, how she chuckled at the jokes of the men buzzing around her as she crossed the factory yard. The inspector's visits were always greeted by the handsomest men in the factory. Parts calmly accepted a few chocolate bars and nodded at a driver who left with a load of tin for the inspector's garden. He thought about his wife, who had promised to go buy milk, but part of him knew already that if he didn't pick up the milk himself all he would find in the icebox would be bottles with a centimeter of sour milk at the bottom. He tried to keep his mind on anything but the contents of his briefcase, and on the way home he thought with fear of what he might find there. If he did find something, what would it mean? The milk was forgotten in his nervousness. In the icebox was a row of milk bottles, their aluminum lids shining with past days of the week. Parts emptied the bottles into the sink and, after using the bottle brush, added them to the other ones his wife hadn't brought back to the store that stood leaning in a row against the gas canister rack. He held his breath, closed his eyes for a moment, and sat down. There was no point in getting upset over the milk bottles again. He should focus on what was important—the Klooga lists. He settled for sour cream instead of milk, angrily mixing sugar and store-bought apple compote into it, his spoon clinking, and went into his office. He would go through the Klooga files, and if he didn't find anything inter- esting he would go through the lists from the rest of the camps, one at a time. Porkov had been in such an accommodating mood that it was entirely possible he could obtain information from the other camps. If Parts didn't run across any names that were embarrassing to him, he would get hold of still more lists, any lists, dig up every name and make a thorough investigation of anyone who might know him—were they still alive, and if so, where were they now?

COMRADE PARTS'S INSTINCT was correct. In the list from 1944 he found a familiar name. Just a name, no date of death or indi- cation of transfer to another camp or evacuation to Germany. A name he wished had been someone else's. Anyone else's. He had been searching for any name he recognized, but this was the very name he didn't want to find, a name that felt like if he pronounced it out loud his tongue would be covered in blisters. A name that shouldn't even be on that list. Roland Simson.

His cousin had disappeared, gone his own way almost immediately after the Germans arrived, and Parts hadn't heard anything about him since—no gossip, not the slightest rumor, not even from Auntie Anna, who would have told him if she had any news of him. Parts had assumed that he had either escaped to the West or died before the Soviet troops arrived, so why should Roland of all people have ended up at Klooga—why not someplace else? Worst of all, why had his name turned up in the Klooga prisoners list? Parts feverishly leafed through the papers, cooling his mouth now and then with the sour cream. Three prisoners had mentioned Roland's name, but there was no testimony from Roland himself. A man named Antti remembered the day Roland arrived because it happened to be his own birthday and he'd decided to give his bread to the first prisoner he met. Roland Simson had just been brought in; he had introduced himself in clear Estonian and wanted to behave as if they weren't even at a camp. Antti had asked to have Roland in his work group—the Jews were in weaker shape—and Roland proved himself a hard worker. Cursing birthdays and all other days of celebration, Parts squeezed his hands into fists until the nails sank into his flesh. The pain cleared his mind. Roland's admission date was not long before the German withdrawal. He'd probably been executed at the camp, his body left unrecognizable. Or if he had gotten out alive, he would have been shot in the woods, or later, once the Red Army arrived—but who would he have encountered in the meantime? Who would he have spoken to? How long would he have been in the woods, and with whom? There had to be a file on Roland, some information about his being killed or captured. Parts squeezed his pencil until it broke. He had to find out for certain what happened.

ВИ.ЛЕНИН
1963

Tallinn,
Estonian Soviet Socialist Republic,
Soviet Union

A BOUND NOTEBOOK PEEPED OUT from the middle of the
pile on the reading table at the archive. A diary. Parts recognized the handwriting immediately. The floor seemed to give
way, the corner of the table swayed. He hadn't expected this.
Anything else, but not this. Even his careful mental prepara-
tion for a visit to the archive wasn't sufficient to maintain his
composure—the find was too important. He concentrated for
a moment on stabilizing his breathing and managed to force his
legs to remain where they were, to hold his head straight after
a few instinctive jerks and a panicked twitch in his cheeks, to
make himself turn his face once again to the files in front of
him, although the tabletop and chair had turned to plasticine
that was starting to melt in the surprisingly hot air, he could
feel it bending, almost hear it buckling. He kept repeating in
his mind that it was just an illusion, a trick of his mind, nothing more. He gripped the edge of the table as if it were an

airplane throttle and opened the diary to a random page. The year written at the top of the page hit him in the ribs like a missile.

When the archive guard went to check on a visitor at a reading table farther off, the diary slipped into Parts's shirt as if of its own accord. Parts didn't fully understand what he'd done, and yet he did understand. Stealing a document was a serious act, easily traced if anyone should compare the returned materials to those marked on the column of files released to him, or if anyone went through the list of people who'd been given access to the diary in question. He wouldn't be able to return it—it was too late for regrets. The notebook was against his skin now and he smelled smoke, a direct hit.

AFTER THIS ABDUCTION, Parts tried to behave normally, concentrate on the other materials spread on the reading table, but his skin grew wet with sour sweat against the book, the rustle of papers from the other tables grated in his ears, and the smallest cough or cleared throat made him jump, sure that every noise was a reproach, a sign that his act had been observed, that the twitching muscle in his cheek had betrayed him. His eyes lit on the guard watching from the front of the row of tables. Parts kept his pupils in check, didn't let them dilate, didn't avert his eyes too quickly, he was sure of that, just as he was sure that the guard's face showed no flicker of suspicion. The guard looked back down at the catalogues on the table in front of him—apparently requested materials—as if nothing unusual had happened, and started going through them, expunging the chapters inappropriate for the next scheduled reader.

PARTS HAD ALREADY been given access to particularly dangerous books, marked with two six-pointed stars, and now that he'd gotten his hands on something even hotter, what had he done? He'd gone and risked getting himself in trouble again. It had taken months of drinks with Comrade Porkov to wheedle permission to look at materials from the restricted libraries and archives. It was another reminder of his lowly station. Nevertheless, when the steel door of the archive opened, it was a moment of victory. He'd gotten through it, it opened for him and only him. When he showed his papers to the department manager, he felt privileged. He wasn't just anyone. But at any moment he could become no one. He was risking everything for one notebook.

He tried to concentrate again, made himself stare at drawings of dugouts, sifted carefully through every bandit's flyer. He had to behave as normally as everyone else in the reading room, try to soak up as much information as possible from the materials he'd been granted at the moment because he didn't know if he'd have another opportunity to research these illegal, rather professional-looking newsletters again, didn't know if he'd ever get his hands on them again—didn't know if he'd get caught, and what would happen to him if he did. Most of the issues of the newsletters were just two sides of one page, but some were four or even six pages, written with fervor. Their ardent language was easily recognizable—he remembered his training days on Staffan Island. At the time he had been in on the planning of an elite group whose exploits would include chasing the Red Army out of Estonia. He'd often smiled at the naiveté of youth, though he wasn't smiling now. But he might smile again, he would make sure that he was able to smile at such things again, and in order to do that he had to get out of the archive with his contraband without getting caught. If what he'd stolen had been less important, if some other date had been at the top of the page, he wouldn't have been as nervous. But the date and the author of the diary were dangerous for him, and the cover of the notebook was burning his bare skin, eating its way into the raw flesh of his belly—he was plunging into a high sea with his tail smoking. His index finger glided over the lines of the drawings, balancing along the chimneys, the stoves, the bunks on the walls, the ventilation ducts, and although he tried to keep on track, the blows to his ribs were real and they shoved his finger off course and made him open his collar, the veins of his neck throbbing violently, his heart pounding against the notebook, the area around his navel slippery with sweat, his wings already disappearing into the waves. He could hear the smack of lips as a man at a table behind him put his pipe in his mouth, the scrape of the match against the striking surface, the man standing up, staring straight at him, blowing smoke out of his mouth. Had the man seen anything? Parts couldn't stay there a moment longer. He would have to leave his reading material behind; it was time to jump.

The chair screeched against the wood floor as he stood up. The guard's hand paused in its careful task, his gaze lifted. Parts approached the guard's table and put the borrowed materials down in front of him. His sweaty fingers had left marks on the drawings, but the guard didn't reprimand him. He was a methodical man, his ink making its marks on the columns with excruciating exactness, and Parts braced himself to argue if he was told that a document was missing from the pile. Parts would claim that he hadn't received it, was ready for a full assault, ready to raise his voice, to complain about the negligence of the department, and especially about the woman who had given him the materials, but at that moment the steel door squeaked open and the woman in question walked in. Parts froze. The woman tried to squeeze behind the guard's table to the card cat-alogue; her hip, covered in a bright expanse of chintz, knocked a glass ashtray from the corner of the table, and as it broke on the floor every eye turned toward them. The woman gave a start, the ink left an ugly track on the column of text, the guard snapped at her, the ink bottle tipped over, the guard snatched up a stack of blotting paper, Russian curses echoed, the guard ordered everyone to keep their eyes on their own work, the pile of papers at the edge of the guard's desk fell over, and at that moment Parts drily remarked that he was in a hurry and surely they could check his returns in without his help. Leaving the guard still arguing with the woman, the ink spreading over the careful columns, the ashes floating in the air, Parts snapped up the keys the woman had dropped on the table, unlocked the door, and tossed the keys to the person sitting behind the near-est reading table before stepping outside without anyone taking any notice of him.

ВИ.ЛЕНИН
4 коп.
1963

Tallinn,
Estonian Soviet Socialist Republic,
Soviet Union

COMRADE PARTS PUT his hand on the table next to the diary. All was quiet upstairs—his wife had passed out. The paper of the diary was spotted from damp, its edges worn soft. Parts took a breath, lifted the cover with his thumb, and turned to the first page. The notebook still had the same effect on him, even though he'd gone through it many times now—his pulse accelerated, mice started to scurry up and down his spine. The sentences were tightly packed, some in pencil, some in pale ink, the purple-stained, lined paper punctured by the pressure of a sharp point. Parts could tell from the curve of the letters the emotion they were written with, but there was no mention of the real name of a single person or place. The code names used were strange, too, clearly names invented by the writer—Parts hadn't found them in his searches through illegal documents.

Some journal keepers made complete records of the members of their groups, the locations of their dugouts, all of it—details of alliances, food rations and mealtimes, where provisions and weapons were stashed, an unbelievably stupid record of everything. But not this one—he was exceptional. The diary was labeled as that of an unknown bandit and was originally found in a metal box in a burned-out dugout. Three bodies had been found in the dugout, three bandits of the Armed Resistance League who had been identified, although they were unknown to Parts. The accompanying report concluded that the diary couldn't have belonged to any of them because samples of the dead men's handwriting had been obtained from the Anti-Banditism Combat Department and none matched the writing in the notebook. The only evidence of this particular bandit's existence was the anonymous diary. Only Parts knew that the diary had belonged to Roland Simson.

The entries began in 1945 and the last pages were written in 1950 and '51. It was those last pages that were shocking—not their contents, but the dates themselves. The final entries were made seven years after Soviet control began and the borders were closed. It proved that Roland had still been alive two years after the March deportations, when the bandits' supporters were removed from the country, their lackeys pulled up like weeds until there was no farm left that supported the Forest Brothers, everything collectivized, the insurgency wiped out.

Contrary to what Parts had assumed, Roland hadn't been shot in the back at Klooga, hadn't ended up in an unmarked grave in the cellar of a house burned down by the Germans, hadn't been imprisoned or died of his wounds in the woods. He hadn't escaped the country, hadn't been evacuated. If he had survived in Estonia until 1951 as a free man, then no one else had killed him, either. He was still here.

Parts decided not to panic. He would figure this out, teach himself to know Roland like he knew himself. He would think like Roland. That was the only way he could find his trail. The faster he could understand the writers of illegal journals, the faster he would find the men who'd gone underground, and this man in particular. Because even if a person succeeded in obtaining a new identity, a new name, in building a new history for himself, something from his old life would always turn up. If anyone knew that, Parts did.

The profile formed by the diary didn't quite correspond to the person Parts had known. That man had run into battle unafraid, defiant. The writer of the diary was a much more wary man. Nevertheless, the entries in the notebook were written as if there would be a reader for them in the future. That was what Parts didn't understand. Roland had lived in the valley of death, he had no hope of a return to a normal life, no possibility of survival, so where did he get this wellspring of faith that one day his voice would be heard? Of course, Roland wasn't alone in this. Parts could well remember the fervent obsession of those life stories shoved into bottles in Siberia. Memoirs. "These words are a record of the crimes of the Bolsheviks for generations to come." Sometimes just scraps of paper, many of them buried secretly along with their authors, in unmarked graves. Some of the bottles probably rested in some archive behind seals—just like the diary Parts had cleverly planted for himself, examined only by those with security clearance—and some of them would never be found, never be read. Parts also remembered a colleague who had been brought to Katyn, in Poland, as a child. Softened by liquor, the man had whispered that of course they had understood what was happening to the Poles, and that the Estonians were next. "You should have seen the look on my mother's face." All the Poles had been given vaccinations and then put on a bus, and no one had resisted— they wouldn't give dried provisions to those about to die, would they? They wouldn't vaccinate them? "We Estonians understood all right. The train car we were put in read 'Capacity: Eight Horses.'" But why had the Poles covered the walls of the monastery, converted into a prison, with their names and ranks, when the next person to occupy the cell would just cover them with his own? Was it some instinctive writing mania, a need to leave some kind of mark on the world? Did Roland have the same mania, a deluded notion that the truth always comes out in the end? Yes, Roland did.

Perhaps Roland was like the old Russian who had told Parts about mustard gas tests he'd performed in a special office in Moscow. The man had desperately scratched the chemical formula on a corner of the bunk he and Parts shared at the camp way station, and said that the head of the special office had been particularly interested in the gas's effect on human skin. Curare darts. Ricin. It was clear that the most accurate results would come from human subjects. "I tested on one German soldier four times. It wasn't until the fifth try that they found the fatal dose." Parts hadn't been able to impress the formula into his mind, although he'd understood immediately that the old man's recipes could be excellent barter later on. There were numerous countries that would have been eager to get them, but at the time, business with foreign countries had seemed like a far-off fantasy. It was wiser to leave the Technological Directorate's labs alone—the old man had said he was the only one of the staff there left alive. Maybe that was why he had such a need to pass the information on. Had that been Roland's motivation for keeping the diary—to secure the information before his days ended?

Parts pronounced Roland's name. He was beginning to get used to it. He was going to have to. In the years to come the name would make its way through his mind innumerable times; he would have to let it move through his brain so that it wouldn't burn him like nettles, the way it did now.

There were crosses drawn in the back of the diary. The page was covered with little crosses for the dead, the pen's grooves almost tearing through the paper. No names.

COMRADE PARTS PUT the notebook carefully back on the desk and started leafing through notes he'd made on the bandits' newsletters. Toward the end the news grew more tedious—they were trying to raise morale, that was clear. You could also tell that they were worried about a lack of new blood in the ranks. By the time Stalin died, most of the illegals had already been removed— 662 bandit groups and 336 underground organizations. How many had succeeded in lying low in the forest? Ten? Five? Was Roland still in the forest? Alone, or with someone, or even with a whole group? Or had he accepted amnesty? Many who had been hiding in the woods had done it, but if he had, there would be some record of it. And if he'd been legalized, he would have been interrogated about what happened at Klooga, there would be some mention of his testimony. No, Roland hadn't taken amnesty. Could he have managed to obtain a new identity anyway? The flood of Russian Estonians and Ingrians into the country had given a lot of illegals an easy way to get a temporary passport. Passports were stolen from trains all the time, and for a short while merely reporting that yours was missing and being able to speak rudimentary Russian was enough to be granted a temporary passport—all you had to do was say that you had come from the Leningrad oblast, and that a local person could provide you with a place to stay. The ones who cheated that way had been caught when their passports expired. If Roland was one of them, how would he have gotten new papers? And who would he have talked to over the years, who would he have been in contact with? He would have needed help from someone, he would still need it, whether he was in the woods or living among people.

Parts picked up a pencil and scribbled a few faint words on the blotter: "The last I heard of my cousin he was in Canada or Australia. I would be grateful for any information I can find about him—he's the only family I have left." He would go to the offices of *Kodumaa* tomorrow and place an ad. As long as the Office didn't know he was looking for the author of the diary, he could look for his cousin and people who knew him without worrying, explain that it was his method of arousing sympathy among expatriate Estonians, adding to his trustworthiness in their eyes. Parts had already succeeded in using *Kodumaa* to track down several people and establish confidential contacts. *Kodumaa* was sent to Estonians abroad, and was the only way to get a receptive response in the emigrant community. Ads framed as searches for missing relatives and friends aroused sympathy even among those who viewed the Soviet Union with suspicion. Founding the paper had been a brilliant move on the part of the Office. Parts's job thus far had been to gauge the emigrant mood, the emigrants' homesickness, any loosening of their mistrust, but now the situation had changed. Perhaps he could just suggest directly that he post fabricated ads from long-lost relatives in *Kodumaa,* searches for people whose names were on the lists of Klooga eyewitnesses. Someone must know something, or know someone who knew someone, and they trusted Parts. He'd been to Siberia, he didn't belong to the Party, he had a Laidoner badge.

His only failure had been with Ain-Ervin Mere. When he was questioned about the time Mere served as the leader of Gruppe B of the German security police, he shouldn't have exaggerated the depth of their friendship—but who could have predicted that Mere would refuse to collaborate with the Office? The decision had been surprising, especially when the information submitted by the Directorate of State Security had turned up such unobjectionable material: Mere had served as a Chekist in the National Internal Commissariat before the Germans came. Parts had been told to bring this up when he contacted Mere—or Miller, which was the name Mere was known by in his years in the Internal Commissariat. So when Parts had started working on Mere, he had reminded him in a letter how they'd met at the old mill and playfully called his old friend Ain Miller. Major Mere never answered his letter, which was awfully stupid of him. Parts was absolutely certain that he could have gotten a better result if he'd been allowed to visit the major at home in England, but no, all he could do was write. He wouldn't make such a clumsy mistake again. At Parts's request, his testimony in Ain-Ervin Mere's trial wasn't written up in the pages of *Kodumaa,* although the case was otherwise dealt with in the paper at length—it didn't suit the image he was presenting of himself among the paper's readers abroad; they had no faith in the Soviet courts.

IT WAS A BIT of a miracle that Roland had never been located, all the more so since his information could be clearly seen on the Klooga lists; those who'd been imprisoned at Klooga and survived or evaded the Germans' evacuation were suspected as spies. So Parts wouldn't be the only one looking for Roland, but he had to be the one who found him, or he might find himself serving as a witness in the same courtroom with him. There was a pressing need for Klooga witnesses at the moment, with the Hitlerists under the microscope. If anyone knew that, Parts did. No one would be left untraced. His book was well under way now, and would provide the best possible cover for the task of getting his hands on his cousin.

ВИ.ЛЕНИН
1963

Tallinn,
Estonian Soviet Socialist Republic,
Soviet Union

Mark was a textbook example of the degeneration and fascismization of the Estonians.

PARTS TASTED THE WORDS he'd tapped out. The train rattling the window spoiled his rhythm, and the manuscript, growing page by page next to the typewriter, trembled. The sentence was pithy and sufficiently charged, but it was too cold, it wouldn't stir anyone's feelings. Nightmares—it had to give the reader nightmares. That was why the cannibalism in Ervin Martinson's histories of the fascists had been such a stroke of genius, although Parts hesitated to call Martinson a genius. There wasn't a child in the world whose dreams wouldn't be disturbed by cannibals, and people weren't going to change their opinion about someone if they'd been taught as children to think he was a cannibal. Martinson had, with one word, twisted the wheel of history in the direction the department wanted. With one word! Emotion was stronger than reason, it argued against reason—they'd gone over that at the Office. Parts wiped the pastilaa off his fingers, rolled in a new sheet of paper, and looked at the most recent guide titled "Prohibited Information in Print Publications, Radio, and Television." He checked his word lists. Comrade Porkov had been skeptical when he gave Parts responsibility for the book. The words for arousing negative emotions were in one list, those for positive emotions in another. At first Parts had thought that such a tight rein would spoil any possibility of developing his own voice, of refining its eloquence. But using the lists eventually became second nature to him; the filter was a sensible one.

It was well known that Mark had taken his superior officers as a model in decorating his Christmas tree. He decked it with the gold rings of Soviet citizens who'd come to the camp and never left, and he let his children dance in a circle around the tree and admire it.

Parts cracked his knuckles. He couldn't quite remember where he'd seen a tree decorated like that, or whether he had seen it himself, but the image was so powerful that he had to use it. It would also strengthen negative feelings about Christmas trees in general, which wasn't a bad thing. Had he found the right wording? He screwed up his mouth. Maybe. Maybe he should add some more eyewitness information. A woman forced to witness this grotesque exhibition.

Maria, a woman brought to the Tartu concentration camp, felt fortunate to be chosen as a servant in Mark's household. She was fortunate to avoid a crueler fate, and fortunate to be able to steal scraps of food from the house, but unfortunate in having to serve Christmas dinner while the glow of the Christmas candles lit up

the rings of Soviet citizens who'd been killed. Was her mother's
ring among them? Her father's? That was something she would
never know.

Comrade Parts had been banging on the Optima so furiously that he'd struck holes in the paper, the letter arms had
gotten tied in a knot, and the keys refused to move. The rings
of Soviet citizens? Or should it be Jews? Would the mention
of Jews push the sufferings of the Soviet citizens into the background, diminish the dignity and the sorrow of the Soviet people, perhaps even pose a threat to it? Parts had noticed that in
the Western books he had locked in his cabinet, Jewishness was
distinctly emphasized.

He untangled the letter arms, freed the paper from the roller,
and stood up to read a few lines aloud. The text was already
starting to have some punch. Women. He ought to focus on
women. Women always aroused emotion. Maria was definitely
a good character, she would generate sympathy. Mark wouldn't
be evil enough if there weren't people around him to bring the
evil out, someone whose eyes the reader could look through and
see the Christmas tree, the Christmas dinner. Yes, he needed
Maria's testimony. Or was he crossing a line, making it too sentimental? No, not yet. He didn't dare add any more cannibalism.
There was already so much of it that he'd had to cite Martinson's books over and over. They were among his recommended
references. But in the future his own works might produce a
similar flood of references, adding weight to his reputation, his
credibility, citation by citation. Still, his fingers felt heavy when
he typed Martinson's name.

Parts curled his toes on top of his slippers and broke off a
piece of jelly cake. Martinson's book offered the perfect character for Parts's purposes: Mark—unidentified, without even

a surname, a brute, a war criminal who was never caught. It wasn't even clear if he'd committed his despicable acts under his real Christian name. That's why it was easy to continue the story. He could find testimony about Mark's deeds, but nothing about Mark himself. Parts shook his head and pondered how his colleagues' mistakes had eventually turned to his advantage. He could see from the files that the security organs had used young, inexperienced men, that they had lacked guidance. There had obviously been a shortage of competent officers. During inter-rogations no one had thought to ask for clarifying information or personal details. Many witnesses had talked about people using only first or only last names, making it impossible to trace them. It was only later that someone noticed how flawed the methods had been at the end of the forties. Hardly any of the witnesses were still alive, because merely being arrested had been evidence enough for execution. The fact that Roland's information had been well recorded in the Klooga papers was a fateful irony.

Mark was a muscular man with broad shoulders whose strength shocked all those who found themselves the target of his cruelty. Maria, who spent many evenings shining his shoes, remembered well how he would make calculations of how much iron he would get out of her, how much phosphorus, how much soap. She also testified that he taught his children their sums by counting out how many prisoners could be made to fit in the gray Brandmann chocolate factory truck. The door of the gray truck would slam—

Parts's fingers halted over the keys. The slam he'd heard wasn't from the door of a truck; it came from upstairs. His shoulders tensed. He listened. Silence. But the silence didn't relax his shoulders, it only stiffened his neck more. He rummaged in the drawer for some aspirin, pulled off the wrapper, and unfolded the paper from around the tablets. The sentence he'd broken off wasn't coming back to him. It was gone. The stiffness in his neck radiated pain into the back of his skull. This was no time for a headache. He was about to get up to fetch the Analgin from behind his wife's valerian bottle in the kitchen, but he sat back down and swallowed the aspirin dry. He had work to do. The jelly cake melted the taste of the pills out of his mouth. He lifted his hands to the keyboard, sent his mind back to the powerful, muscular figure of Mark. It was enough, the core of the whole thing. Enough to make the text believable. One word and his book would be in bookstores all over the East, all over the West, all over the world. He'd also tried adding a few lines borrowed from the diary, to lend his book authenticity, but the language was so different, and too vague—the manuscript had to have concrete details. Maybe he could mention the crosses at the back of the diary as crosses Mark drew as a record of the poor creatures he'd murdered. But was his Mark a person who would count his victims?

Martinson was no doubt working on his next book right now, maybe something more about cannibalism, explaining how it was a natural Estonian trait, how the cannibalism of the Estonians in the fascist ranks had broken all bounds and without the liberation brought by the Soviet Union the Estonians would have eaten themselves into extinction. Parts's chest tightened in irritation. He had to come up with something better than Martinson. He couldn't let anyone surpass him. But just as he was catching up to the sentence that he'd broken off, his wife's hard heels struck the floorboards and started knocking around overhead again—first only a few steps from the bed to the chest and back, as if she were practicing before getting up to speed. As if she didn't plan on going back to bed. Parts put his hands on his knees. Auntie Anna had had the same problem back at the beginning of the fifties, in the countryside. Rats running in herds under the floor and behind the walls so that she couldn't sleep. She'd written to him about it when he was in Siberia. That's the way the times were back then—the rat population had exploded. They called them "emergency rats." Now he had a wife like a rat.

Parts closed his eyes, let the sweetness of the cake dull his hearing, and concentrated on his research. The Office would probably be interested in the possibilities offered by someone like Mark, would probably want to cook up a Mark among the Estonians abroad in order to pressure some host country to produce such a war criminal, but Parts would think of some other name for the purpose and add it to his book. He was keeping Mark for himself. Mark was his star, and revealing Mark's identity to the whole world would be his great moment. He would only give the complete information to the Office when the time was right. Not yet. Then the Office could worry about the final details. The real Mark could be anywhere—Canada, the United States, Argentina—or dead and buried. If he was alive, he would hardly have any objection to someone else being blamed for his actions. Of course it was too bad that the someone had to be Roland, but Mark was just such a perfect opportunity. As for Roland's actual deeds, Parts had already chosen the best of them years ago, and made them his own.

PART THREE

We all know that there were women who participated in Fascist terrorism, in spite of their natural sympathies and their power to produce life. Females who sold themselves to Hitlerism were no longer women, they only looked like representatives of the female of the species. They had become representatives of the pillaging conquerors.

—Edgar Parts, *At the Heart of the Hitlerist Occupation*,
  Eesti Raamat Publishing, 1966

Reval,
Estland General Commissariat,
Ostland National Commissariat

JUUDIT WAS SITTING in Café Kultas, sitting and flirting in a way that was not becoming to a woman—especially flirting that way with a stranger. But there she was, cooing, preening, stroking her hair again and again, and Roland, who was trying to walk past her nonchalantly just a stone's throw away, saw a coquettishness that made such a vivid impression on him that he kept bumping into people. Until he saw her coming toward the café from the direction of Karja Street, he hadn't been completely sure that Juudit intended to follow his plan. Once he had spotted her, he turned on his heel, relieved, and disappeared into the bustle of Freedom Square in front of the café so she wouldn't notice him. He hadn't been able to keep his promise to her not to come around and check up on her. Juudit's job was too important; he had to come and he had to stroll around with the other men, glancing at the roof of the Estonian Insurance Company building, shifting his gaze surreptitiously down the side of the building to the windows of the café, his eyes making the same motion over and over.

ACROSS FROM JUUDIT sat a German officer, but it was the wrong one. The right officer was enjoying his coffee on the other side of the room, ruffling through the newspaper and puffing on a pipe. The blank SS insignia on his collar pulsed in the corner of Juudit's eye; her sweaty hands held the arms of her chair, her heart was thumping, and she didn't know what to say. The hot chocolate in front of her steamed, her hand slid down the chair's arm, a bead of sweat appeared on her upper lip, and a wordless space opened up behind her forehead. She no longer missed the building's neon lights and the street lamps, darkened for wartime. She gave off her own light. Her soul had stumbled into powerful motion and she was gripped by a fierce desire to be with this man, the very German sitting in front of her. Her heart was in a reckless state, her cheeks glowing as if she were still a girl, unaware of her desires, the backs of her knees wet with sweat in spite of the fact that her feet, wearing only stockings, felt chilled against the cold floor. There was an ice cellar behind her, a glow like a sweltering summer day in front of her, hot and cold taking turns, uncontrollable.

She could still get up, leave him with the tongs in his hand, offering her a cookie, and find a way to nab the German Roland had chosen, to charm him, wrap her soft arm around his neck. But she'd already turned to this man, the wrong man, met his gaze, and, worse yet, in the man's answering smile Roland and his plan and Rosalie in her unmarked grave and everything that had happened in the past few years was forgotten. She'd forgotten the bombs and the bodies lying in the streets, the beetles and flies descending on them, the desperate trading in tins of lard, her marriage and its respectability. She'd even forgotten that she was in her stocking feet, that her shoes had just been stolen, the only ones she had, no longer remembered the gang of thugs who'd pushed her down in front of the Kunstihoone Gallery and yanked her shoes off. She'd forgotten the pain, the embarrassment, the tears of anger and vexation, as soon as the officer had reached out his hand to help her up and taken her into the warm café and she'd made the fateful mistake of looking into his eyes.

"You must let me see you home, miss. You can't walk outdoors in your stockings. Do be so kind, Fräulein. Or if you would grant me the honor of stopping by my place, I can ask my maid to fetch you some shoes. I live quite close by, on Roosikrantsi Street, on the other side of Freiheitsplatz."

WHILE JUUDIT WAS FALLING in love in Café Kultas, Roland was dodging snorting horses' tramping hooves, soldiers of the Wehrmacht, and graceful mademoiselles clutching handbags. He made his way around the movie posters that he couldn't bring into focus at the Gloria Palace; the cafeteria with its display window that made his stomach growl, where the servers flourished their scissors over customers' food coupons; the street vendors, errand boys, steaming piles of horse manure, and straight city backs; and past the suspicious gaze of the porter at the Hotel Palace. As dusk fell among mere shapes, among his own thoughts, the cars with cold blue eyes, he stumbled into a young woman who let out a screech, and all the while Juudit was on her way toward love.

JUUDIT GAVE THE MAID her coat and gloves. She took the rags from her feet herself—indignity had its limits. She was shown directly into the drawing room, although she tried to resist, and her feet left wet smudges on the patterned parquet floor. She reddened, more from embarrassment than from the chill, and as the German left to look for something to warm her up, she picked the rags up off the carpet and shoved them under the armchair. The man had wrapped the dishcloths around her feet, with the help of the waitress at the Kultas, and tied a piece of packing twine around them, paying the café for them, in spite of Juudit's protestations. She was mortified by the repairs in the toes of her stockings, which stood out even in the dim light of the café, every single stitch. The reinforced toes hadn't shown at all under the wrappings, but here in the drawing room the chandelier was mercilessly revealing as Juudit tried to curl her feet up and hide them. In a flash a basin of steaming water appeared before her, and next to it some mustard plaster, towels, and slippers with feather tassels, which stirred in a draft of air, on the toes. A handwarmer and a hot water bottle were placed on the sofa. The gramophone played Liszt. Juudit didn't ask how the German valet was going to conjure up the promised shoes. Her lips were numb, though the room was warm, and she hardly dared to peep at the man as he came back carrying a crystal carafe and glasses. She shut her eyes and impressed his face into her mind; it wouldn't be right to forget such beauty. A tremulous pulse throbbed against the handkerchief in her shirt cuff, the handkerchief's monogrammed *J* rubbing against her skin—a *J* without a surname. The man set the tray on a low table, poured some wine into the glasses, and turned his back so she could take off her stockings. Juudit understood the gesture but didn't know how to respond. She picked up the glass and drank the wine like water, greedily, to help her remember how to be a woman. In her marriage bed all of her attempts to behave like a woman had ended in shame; she didn't want to remember those moments, so she drank more wine, brazenly poured for herself from the carafe and drank. The man turned his head a little, hearing the clink; his sideways glance locked on Juudit's startled eyes, and his eyes were no braver than hers, no more elegant than Juudit's frozen hand reaching to take hold of the top of her stocking.

WHEN HE GOT OUT of bed in the morning, Hellmuth carefully covered Juudit with a goosedown quilt, gently tucking it around her feet, but Juudit threw off the cover and let the soft air of the room caress her skin. She lowered her feet onto the carpet, pointing her toes like she was putting them into a bath; she stretched her arms, bent her neck, the air pouring over her skin like new milk. The fuel shortage had made her greedy for warmth. But she wasn't ashamed of it, of walking around naked on the thick carpet, of being alone in a room with a man she'd met only yesterday. The aroma of real coffee drifted into her nostrils, though she still smelled of liquor. They had drunk recklessly, for the pleasure of it. Or maybe they did it to cover the awkwardness of what they saw in each other.

The clatter of Russian prisoners of war in their wooden shoes could be heard outside. Hellmuth put Bruckner on the record player and asked her to come with him to the Estonia Theater that evening.

Juudit climbed back into the bed and pulled the cover over her legs.

"I can't."

"Why not, Fräulein?"

"Frau."

Hellmuth was handsome in his uniform, beautiful to look at. He went to the mirror to put his Ritterkreuz on his collar.

"I would like to," she added.

"Then why can't you, my lovely Frau?"

"Someone I know might see me," she whispered.

"I'm asking you."

Hellmuth came and stood beside her, snapped open his cigarette case, and lit a cigarette, staring at his hands in such a way that she could tell he was as afraid of saying the wrong thing as she was.

"Pardon me, but may I have one, too?" Juudit asked.

"Of course. Forgive me. I can see I've been in Berlin too long."

"What do you mean?"

"You look so young. In Germany smoking is forbidden for anyone under twenty-five."

"Why?"

"They probably imagine it affects reproduction."

Juudit blushed.

Hellmuth grinned. "I didn't object to being transferred to Ostland, because I thought that at least I would be allowed to smoke in my office. The Reichsführer has forbidden smoking at work, as well, but I'm hoping that he can't keep his eye on me when I'm this far away. Smoking is of course forbidden in government offices. There's a permanent campaign against passive smoking."

"Passive smoking?"

"Nonsmokers' being subjected to others' tobacco smoke."

"That sounds crazy," Juudit said, then was embarrassed again. "I don't mean to judge."

"The Reichsführer just wants the best possible fertility; he's worried about the degeneration of the race, which is something I, too, should fight in every way I can."

———

HELLMUTH LIT another cigarette and put it to Juudit's lips, and Juudit didn't know what made her more dizzy, the cigarette or the gesture with which he offered it. She didn't want this morning to ever end. Her head was still filled with the dew of night, her curls heavy with it, and when he looked into her eyes she could feel that all the while, under the tinkle of talk, their hearts were moving toward each other, and the idea of doing anything to stop that movement was impossible.

"There are more and more restrictions all the time, so we should get as much joy as we can while it's still possible. Smoking is already prohibited in theaters in Riga; soon it might be in Estonia, too, although no one is enforcing these rules yet. But I have to go. Duty calls. Will I see you tonight at the Estonia? It might be our last chance to enjoy a cigarette together as patrons of the arts."

He winked and there were sparks of something in his eye— and in those sparks, promises.

Reval, Estland General Commissariat, Ostland National Commissariat

THE GERMAN I'd chosen left Café Kultas alone. I watched his officer's cap receding, his short cape flapping, and I hurried inside. I didn't see Juudit anywhere. When I asked the young waitresses if they'd seen a lady fitting Juudit's description, they looked at me suspiciously and shook their heads. For the next few days I made one phone call after another to her apartment on Valge Laeva Street. She didn't answer. I was starting to worry. Finally I asked Richard, our contact in the B4 section of the political police, to search for a woman named Juudit Parts and learned that she had been courted by a German, someone I'd never heard of, but an SS-Hauptsturmführer, no less. I digested this news, swallowed my disappointment, then found out the Jerry's address. I relished the idea of sending my men after Juudit, frightening her. I would jump in front of her when she least expected it, show her I knew her comings and goings, the exact time she'd stepped out with her Jerry to the Nord or the casino. I imagined the look of shock on her face, how her head would sink into her fox collar, how her mouth, painted with lipstick and deceit, would disappear into the fur. It eased the stinging inside me. But I didn't live out my fantasy because from what I could learn about him, he was a better catch than the German I'd chosen, and I didn't want anyone in our ring to pay extra attention to Juudit. It was safer not to mention her name again. I would follow her myself, and when I'd gotten a good grip on her I wouldn't hesitate to squeeze as hard as I could, to make it clear that she had no choice but to cooperate if she didn't want her husband to know about her exploits, or the German to hear about her deception. I would never leave her in peace.

Reval, Estland General Commissariat, Ostland National Commissariat

Roland managed to find a room on Roosikrantsi so he could stalk Juudit whenever he could get away from his work at the harbor. He'd secured the job with papers surreptitiously obtained by Richard in the B4 office, and his days at the harbor were long. He left for work before Juudit was probably even awake, and came back to his building late at night. He received no replies to the notes he slipped under the door of the apartment on Valge Laeva—she rarely even went there, had moved to a different world whose doors were closed to Roland—and weeks went by before he saw her again, her scarf flapping as an Opel Olympia picked her up at her door. All Roland could do as the car and the boisterous group that packed itself inside sped away was stare helplessly after it and make a mental note of the names of the people leaving the building: General Commissar Litzmann and the ubiquitous, bleating Hjalmar Mäe. Once he caught a glimpse of Commander Sandberger himself coming out of the place. Juudit's German had important guests, and many of them came and went after dark, some even using the servants' entrance. The background information on these men that Richard had pilfered from B4 wasn't pretty.

GERDA'S GIGGLE COULD be heard from the Opel all the way upstairs. Juudit, holding Hellmuth's hand, sat down beside her, and they drove straight into the liquid sunset. After they'd enjoyed a bottle of champagne and the ladies' coiffures had been dampened by a summer rain, they'd decided to move on from the Shore Club to the lively tables at Du Nord. Hellmuth thought Du Nord had a better cook, and better Riesling. Juudit was so grateful for Gerda, who didn't judge her, and in whose company she could show how much in love she really was. When they were sitting alone together on the divan in the Du Nord powder room putting on lipstick, Gerda turned to Juudit and said, "I assume you've taken precautions?"

Juudit turned red.

"I didn't think so. It's no wonder Hellmuth fell for you. Innocence like yours is rare in Berlin, take it from me. A woman's best friend is her pessary—everything else is snake oil. I know a doctor where you can get one," she whispered. "It'll cost you, but I'm sure that won't be a problem. Trust me, it's completely discreet, and then you won't have to worry."

Gerda wrote the doctor's address on the back of a calling card and the greatest worry for a married woman with a lover was lifted. Juudit's sigh of relief made Gerda laugh, and they giggled on each other's shoulder there on the divan until Juudit started to hiccup and Gerda's eyeliner smeared and they had to pull themselves together. The world looked so different now that Juudit could talk to Gerda about almost anything. When

Juudit whispered that she was afraid of what her husband would think if he knew his wife was going around in public on the arm of a stranger, Gerda had just snorted. She thought Juudit would be crazy to leave Hellmuth, was sure that Hellmuth would marry her because after all even Reichsminister Rosenberg had had an Estonian wife, the ballerina Hilda Leesmann. When Juudit pointed out that the Reichsminister's career had advanced much more quickly once Hilda was carried off by tuberculosis and he'd switched to the German Hedwig, Gerda would hear none of it. Even when Juudit remembered that the Reichsminister was a Baltic German, not from Germany proper like Hellmuth, and a wife from the eastern outposts surely wouldn't be wise for a real German SS officer, Gerda had just laughed at her arguments, and she laughed at them again as they sat on the divan.

"Listen, you silly thing. It's just a matter of making arrangements. I've been watching you two. My Walter looks at other women even when I'm right beside him, but Hellmuth never does. Walter says Hellmuth has a wonderful future, that he has a head for all kinds of strategies that I don't understand. When the war's over, he'll be transferred to Berlin with medals on his chest and you'll be parading around all the salons as his lady. You've chosen well. Your German is flawless, and you look like a regular Fräulein. That chin! And your nose!" Gerda bopped her lightly on the nose, and Juudit's worried brow smoothed. "You didn't go to the German school for nothing. I'll bet you were at the top of your class. My dear, let's go get ourselves a cocktail. Away with sorrow!"

Gerda took hold of Juudit's hand and squeezed. She made everything sound so simple, and maybe everything *was* simple, at least for the moment, here on the divan at Du Nord. Hellmuth had taken her to a whole new world where there was no place for the troubles of her old life. Yesterday Mr. and Mrs. Paalberg had exchanged a glance as Juudit was coming toward them on Liivalaia. Mrs. Paalberg had raised an eyebrow disdainfully and then they had turned to look in the bakery window, and Juudit had thought about how Gerda would have treated such a meeting, had just tossed her head and lifted her face from the street toward the sun, and once she did that she was in a good, even boisterous, mood again. Gerda hated the snobbery that women in twice-turned coats had toward her. She didn't need people like them, or anybody else. Gerda was right. Now Juudit was watching a movie in their screening room on Roosikrantsi, which she liked because in a movie theater she might have run into someone she knew, someone she no longer had anything in common with. She also thought it was wonderful to invite Gerda over to watch *Liebe ist zollfrei* in her own private cinema. She no longer took part in complaining about having to walk everywhere or clucking about the infrequent public transport. She had the Opel Olympia and a chauffeur at her disposal. And she didn't know what she would do if someone she knew sneered at Hitler or the Germans within earshot of Hellmuth—the Germans couldn't understand Estonian, and people used it for a laugh. The Germans were much more easygoing than the Russians. Just recently Juudit had seen a boy pull a face at a German soldier and the soldier hadn't cared in the least. She couldn't imagine that happening under the Soviet authorities. Nevertheless, she didn't let herself get drawn into anything like that when she was with Hellmuth. It wouldn't be right, after all he'd done for her. He'd even promised to look for information about her brother Johan.

Gerda's company lightened her spirits, and a few cocktails lightened them more, but as they were walking back to the dining room, she still looked around. She'd grown used to doing this from the very first evening, though she rarely ran into anyone she knew in the places that Germans frequented—least of all Roland, the one thing she couldn't talk about with Gerda.

AS JUUDIT LIFTED her drink to her lips over the white tablecloth at Du Nord, Roland was pretending to read a sign on Roosi-krantsi Street that had Vacant Rooms painted in large letters at the top. He knew every posted notice fluttering in the wind. From the doors of the nearby hospital came a drifting odor of carbolic acid, waiting, and frustration. He even knew the foot-steps and voices of the nurses and ambulance men hurrying inside, the staff in the German commissaries, the clerks march-ing to the supply room. Although his landlady was almost deaf and blind with age and took no notice of him, there were always Germans tramping down the street, and as the sound of every step quickly became familiar to him, he assumed that the sound of his own would soon be familiar to others, so he'd decided to change lodgings. He would move to the attic of a villa on Merivälja Square. He had to be cautious, living underground, and he'd had enough of watching the guests and outings of Juudit's German. From the reports he'd received from their contact at B4, there could be only one conclusion: the Germans were as twisted as the Bolsheviks, who had sucked the country dry and done it all aboveboard, according to Soviet law. When the Soviet forces had left the Kuressaare castle, Richard had been among the first to witness the piles of bodies, the women with their breasts cut off, their corpses full of needles. The walls of the Kawe factory cellar had been painted with blood. And the same thing was going to happen, just as much within the law as before. The Germans would do whatever they had to in order to keep Rosalie's case from becoming public, if only to create the illusion of legality. Roland was beginning to be certain that he was about to witness the same kinds of acts that the Bolsheviks had perpetrated, and his hands shook as he wrote about it that evening. A messenger would take the letter to Sweden:

SS-Sturmbannführer Sandberger and his puppet leader Mäe believe that Germany has to regain the trust of the Estonians. The Jews who fled here from Germany and elsewhere during Estonian independence have done so much counterpropaganda that the pogroms that worked beautifully in Lithuania and Latvia couldn't possibly get the same result here. Sandberger sensed this immediately and thus understood that the Sonder command had to be kept as invisible as possible, and that no illegal violence should be tolerated. This method and their emphasis on obedience to the law has shown Sandberger's wisdom and psychological insight. Any measures taken will be in strict accordance with German law.

Reval, Estland General Commissariat, Ostland National Commissariat

I REMEMBER WHEN the Shore Club opened. Those were long, white nights. They sold cocktails until three in the morning, can you imagine?"

Juudit had arrived. Her talk reminded me that she was different from Rosalie, from a different world. She'd spent her youth lapping up cocktails and circling buffet tables, twitching to the beat of swing tunes.

We sat silent for a moment and listened to the music from the Pirita Shore Club and I hid my relief. It had been a lot of work to arrange for the short time off and there was a line of men ready to take my job at the harbor. I'd been sure that she would miss the meeting again and I hoped I wouldn't be disappointed like I had been so many times before. Too many times.

"Do you miss the countryside?" she asked.

I didn't answer. I didn't know what she was getting at. The cobblestones of the city didn't suit me any better than they would my horse, and she knew that. But I tried to behave, to tamp down the anger seething inside me from all the nights I'd tailed her with no results. When I'd finally seen her coming and she was alone, relief and fury battled within me. The glass eyes of her silver fox wrap had been as unfeeling as her own, eyes that had forgotten Rosalie, but even so I managed to control my emotions. I shouldn't frighten her too much—just enough. We didn't have a single contact in Juudit's position, and in spite of everything I trusted her more than any of the Germans' other tarts.

"Where are you staying these days?" Juudit asked.

"It's best that you don't know."

"Right. Many of the Merivälja villas are still empty, I've heard."

I looked at the people walking on the shore, a dog running after a ball, women in bathing suits, their legs so shiny-wet that my eyes hurt, couples strolling down to the water arm in arm, wiping waffle crumbs from each other's mouths. Their happiness rippled with the waves, piercing my chest. I was incapable of further small talk.

"Have you found anything out?"

My question made Juudit flinch, although I'd asked the same thing every time we'd met, and her mouth snapped shut. I squeezed my hand into a fist.

"Why do you even come here if you don't have anything to tell me?"

"I could have stayed away, you know," she answered, and scooted farther down the bench.

I understood instantly that I'd said the wrong thing. The hope that always sprang up when I saw her had disappeared again, and in trotted those same thoughts that tortured me every night, rattling their bits between their teeth even as I awoke.

Juudit looked at my fist, slid all the way to the end of the bench, and looked at the water as if there were something of interest to see there. I shuddered. Juudit was like everyone else. She wouldn't hear a bad word about the Germans, not now that the sharp edge from poorer times was disappearing from her cheekbones. Even if I'd told her what I knew, she would have called me a liar. After the victory at Sevastopol there was no doubt that Germany would succeed, and although the Germans were the only ones who could save us from a new Bolshevik terror, our forces believed in Churchill and the Atlantic Charter—the return of independence when the war was over, the promise that territorial changes would not be made against the wishes of the citizens. Our couriers were constantly bringing material to Finland and Sweden—my reports among them—and we were getting newspaper clippings and news analysis from around the world. There was no indication that the Germans would abide by our wishes in spite of their public pronouncements. But so many wanted to believe them, including Juudit, who'd gotten a taste of cream.

"I just keep house there," Juudit said. "I don't hear about anything important from the staff. Besides, he doesn't investigate crimes, only sabotage, and his office only has jurisdiction over Tallinn. I'm sure he doesn't even have access to information pertaining to the rest of the country. Don't you understand? I'm no use to you."

I'd heard the same explanation so many times, the same lousy excuses, even though I'd stressed that any information at all could lead to Rosalie's murderer, even the smallest petty crime. Time after time she denied the rumors, the bullying and misconduct. I didn't believe the Jerries adhered strictly to rules and discipline, and her dogged insistence that they did made me screw my mouth up tight, hoping she wasn't as bad at lying to her German. I could understand her choice of a lover. Her marriage situation wasn't a normal one. But I couldn't understand having to remind her about Rosalie.

SHE WAS CLEARLY getting ready to go, raising her padded shoulders and prying at the Bakelite clasp on her sweater until her fingertips turned white. She did have news—suddenly I was sure of it. The realization helped me control my feelings. I kept my voice steady: "Here's a phone number. If your German leaves town, place a call to this number and say that the weather is good. I want to come and look at his office. Any small scrap of information could help our cause."

Juudit didn't take the paper from me. I shoved it into her purse. She laid a wadded handkerchief down beside me and stared out at the sea.

"Roland, you have to leave the city immediately."

She spoke quickly, her gaze fixed on the water. The Feldgendarmerie knew that there were fugitives and draft dodgers at the harbor. They were going to use that as a pretense to get into the factories there and search for someone behind a recent attack. Hellmuth Hertz had learned that there were such men hiding among the dockworkers.

"The target was Alfred Rosenberg, his train, when it arrived at the station. It wasn't you, was it?" she said, her mouth snapping shut.

I looked at her. She was serious.

"You have to leave," she said. "Rosalie would have wanted you to. Take this money."

She got up, leaving the handkerchief bundle on the bench, and marched away. That's what she had to tell me? That's why she'd come? I was disappointed, but at the same time suddenly alert. I hadn't heard about a failed assassination attempt, but if Juudit had been serious when she asked if I was involved, someone else might be wondering the same thing, and the plot would no doubt lead the Germans to tighten their security protocols. I wouldn't be going to the harbor in the mornings anymore.

Although papers were often inspected on the tram, I got on the next one to save some time—I had to get back to my room and pack in a hurry. Up until that point my new documents had worked perfectly and the altered birth date had never been noticed. I kept them in my breast pocket, where I used to keep Rosalie's picture, and as I rode the jam-packed, rattling tram I realized that my hand hadn't reached to touch it in a long time. Although I'd shredded the photo long ago, for the first time I felt that it was really gone and I'd never get it back again, not even in my imagination. In place of Rosalie's face were forged identity papers, and in my ears the echo of Juudit's retreating high heels. Her steps made the wrong sound as she left—real leather soles and the clack of metal heels—and her hips made her skirt swirl against her legs. I had almost thrown the wad of money after her. For a moment I regretted that I hadn't used the opportunity to hurt her. I hadn't told her what Richard had learned at B4: her brother Johan had been taken to the Kawe factory cellar by the Bolsheviks, and although the jail was supposed to be a temporary housing facility, his trail ended there. There was no information about his wife. I hadn't told her because I'm bad at consoling women. And because Juudit was extremely volatile. If she didn't want to work with me when I returned to Tallinn, then I could let her know what Richard had seen when he walked into that cellar, Johan's last known location. The cellar was empty, but the walls were stained with blood. This wouldn't turn Juudit against the Germans—quite the opposite—but maybe it would take some of the champagne bubbles out of her head and make her wonder why the Germans hadn't informed Johan's family of his fate. Maybe it would remind her of the importance of what we were doing. I needed weapons like that, even despicable ones, because it wouldn't be easy to find another source like her. Juudit warmed in the company of those men, which was a reason to keep an eye on her. I knew that she wanted to stay with her Jerry; I could see that she'd fallen in love with him, that she was walking on rose petals. That was her weakness. I had to learn to use it.

JUUDIT'S HEAD WAS lowered as she went up the stairs. Roland's painful questions had stripped away what little honor she'd once had. Didn't he understand that not everyone could find love through honorable means? As she stepped onto the soft carpet of Hellmuth's entryway, her head was already held high, and she handed her hat and her shopping to the maid as if she'd been raised that way, with servants to meet her when she came home. She marched to the buffet cabinet to squeeze some lemon, lit a cigarette to go with her cocktail, and burned the phone number Roland had given her while she was at it. The world was different now and Juudit had a different future, a better life than she'd ever had before, and she wasn't going to let Roland, who'd lost everything, ruin it. No, Roland wasn't going to pull her down with him, take away what she'd managed to achieve—she had waited so long for someone to love her, someone to want her completely, someone she suited, a man like Hellmuth, waited all her life for a chance to be sick with love from one day and night to the next, to taste milk and honey under her tongue instead of sulphur and rust. Hellmuth wasn't even bothered by her marriage. Juudit had told him just what kind of marriage it was, how it wasn't a union at all. And he hadn't left her, just caressed her ear, and when his tongue found some sugar there from her beauty scrub the night before, he told her she was the sweetest girl in the Empire.

Hellmuth didn't torment her with constant demands to tell him what the Estonians were saying about the Germans. They had conversations, not interrogations, and Hellmuth respected her opinions, even on political subjects. That morning the two of them had pondered the reasons why the Propagandastaffel's photography exhibitions hadn't attracted as many visitors as expected. The empty galleries had been embarrassing. She said it was hardly fitting to the prestige of the Reich to organize exhibitions that didn't draw an audience. It might give the impression that the people didn't support the Germans!

Hellmuth laughed. "You're clever," he said. "But the Propagandastaffel's projects are part of the Wehrmacht. The military always messes things up. But perhaps these matters are a bit boring for you, my love."

Juudit had shaken her head vehemently. The more Hellmuth listened to her opinions, the more responsibility he gave her, the more fervently she loved him. And he did give her responsibility: she'd become his secretary, a job that involved translating, interpreting, and stenography, as well as giving presentations on Estonian folk traditions and religion to visiting scholars from Berlin and arranging séances for the officers who wanted them. Because of his busy schedule, Hellmuth left certain visitors entirely in her care, and Juudit managed them easily—she simply contacted Mrs. Vaik, who arranged sittings with Lydia Bartels. Hellmuth thanked her vociferously, said she was positively Germanic in her efficiency, and gave her a hatpin with agate roses as a gift. He trusted her, and she could never betray that trust; she worked ever more diligently, organized parties ever more masterfully, pored over German women's magazines

that Gerda recommended, even retrieved the *Housewife's Handbook* from home and studied the instructions for seating charts
and place settings. She tried to train the maid to fold the napkins
better, searched for the best staff for dinner parties. With the
help of the cook she created a recipe for squab that was unri-
valed, happily shared it with anyone who asked, and enjoyed
every moment, because by taking great care in all these domestic matters she was finally living the life that she'd prepared
for through her whole girlhood, she was making use of her
education and her social skills, and she was busy—she didn't
have time for Roland. That's why she had invented the story of
assassins hiding among the dockworkers. She'd learned to lie
better than some might have thought—her marriage had taught
her that.

Juudit made sure that the maid was in the kitchen—she
could hear the girl giggling with the handyman—and went
into the bedroom. She pulled open the closet, her head defiantly thrown back and her spine ramrod straight. The felt boots
in the back of the closet were made with good leather, their
soles and seams carefully greased, their surface polished with a
wool cloth. Used with galoshes they would get her through any
kind of weather. When Leonida had sent two pairs, Juudit had
thought she would set one aside for Roland, but his demands
had grown even darker and more threatening than the man himself. In the morning she would throw them to the soldiers in the
street. No. Why wait? She opened the window and tossed them
out in a great arc. They would make someone a very good pair
of boots—she'd had enough. Soon Hellmuth would be home,
and they would go out with Gerda and Walter, and they would
have fun, more fun than she'd had in years, and in the meantime she would have one more sidecar, and style her hair into
gentle waves, and she wouldn't feel the slightest bit guilty. Just

one drink and then she could darken her eyelashes with mascara without any fear of it running.

After her third drink Juudit was ready to sit at her vanity table and pick up her hand mirror, but her hair refused to obey her and she threw the curling iron down on the table. Her gown for the evening—tulle and violet—was on a hanger, and in the dresser drawer lay a new one for the following evening, crêpe de chine, tucked inside tissue paper. But her mood hadn't lightened, and it was because of the mice. Or rather their absence. She had set traps in the corners of every room and every closet, but the traps were still empty. Sometimes she woke up at night, imagining she heard a squeak, and she was always wrong. The mice never failed to come to warn of the death of a relative, so Juudit was certain her husband was still alive. The last time the mice had warned her was when Rosalie died, although at the time she had hoped it was a portent of her liberation.

Reval, Estland General Commissariat, Ostland National Commissariat

WHEN THE TRUCK full of foresters left Tallinn in the morning, I intended to slip in among them. Before leaving I'd packed up all my things in the attic of the Merivälja villa. The house was deserted, which made it perfect, but I felt uneasy there, like I always did in places where life had vanished. The Germans have eaten all the doves from here, too; you no longer hear their cooing behind the barn. Stray cats have taken over the rooms and verandas, making a racket. I spent the last night in the barn just to be safe. At the front door of the house I noticed that the board I'd set up as a trap had been moved. Carefully moved, but moved nevertheless. It may have been only a cat, but I loaded my Walther and listened. I crept across the veranda, across the drawing room. I could see that someone had stumbled into the sheet-covered armchair. As I climbed the stairs, I stepped over the squeaky steps. I stood next to the attic door, opened it a crack, and almost shot Richard, who was waiting inside.

"How did you know where to find me?"

I was holding my pistol against his temple. Richard was speechless with shock and could only manage to stutter that he was alone. He knew the password. I lowered the gun.

"I was ordered to come here," Richard said. "I have to leave the country."

"Judging by the trail you left, you wouldn't have noticed if you were followed."

"Two officials of the Internal Directorate have disappeared," he said. "They're starting to give me funny looks. You have to help. I brought forged travel permits for you."

I quickly gathered up my things and told him to follow me. There was no time to lose—I was certain that he had been tailed. We would leave over the roof.

THE MAIL GIRL FOUND me some German armor and a couple of bottles of cartridges from a stash in the forest. I asked her to take care of Richard while I arranged a place for him on a ship or motorboat. Richard put a folder on the table and said he'd taken as many B4 files as he could. I gave him the money Juudit had given me. As I opened the folder he put the money in his pocket and warned me that I wouldn't like what it said.

"It's a political police report, all originals."

"Dorpat is a surprisingly European city in spite of the misfortunes of recent years. According to Reichsminister Rosenberg, the Baltic countries have a European character. Unfortunately, the Reichsminister's excellent racial theories are unknown here, since the Bolsheviks have kept the country isolated from the civilized world.

"The measures we recommend are to attempt to apply the

research findings of the Reich's new Historical Institute to Estland, and perhaps it would be advisable to establish a separate Referentur here. Otherwise the Estonians won't understand how important the Jewish question is. During Estland's independence the Jews had cultural autonomy. For that reason it would be wise to investigate how much damage was done to Estland under conditions in which there were no restrictions on Jews, and how much the treachery peculiar to the Jews has advanced in such a social environment. The criminalization of anti-Semitism in 1933 was doubtless the result of Jewish machinations, from which we can deduce that the government is very weak or the Estonian race of particularly low intelligence. The race, however, is quite hybridized, so this characteristic would be surprising. It's also possible that the government has degenerated to an exceptional extent or that Jews have even taken part in government. Research is needed into how such a negligent regime has held together at all. Perhaps it would be best to make Estland the largest reserve for Jews in Reichskommissariat Ostland. On the other hand, Commander Sandberger has stressed that pogroms would not be suitable for Estland because of the country's unusually pro-Jewish history. The country has been saved from complete destruction by the influence of its citizens of German heritage. There is also an unusually small number of Jews, much fewer than in Latvia or Lithuania. Perhaps they know how to disguise themselves well enough that the original population takes no notice of them.

"We have chosen individuals with Germanic characteristics as local contacts. The Baltic Germans sent back to Estland by the Reich have found many suitable individuals.

"A parallel line is extremely important in the rest of Reichskommissariat Ostland as well, absolutely essential for the final solution."

I put down the folder and asked the mail girl for something to drink. Richard opened up his tobacco pouch and rolled a cigarette for each of us. The mail girl started to cry.

"Read the last pages," Richard said. "Where they talk about 'operations.' They're talking about the deportations in June."

"The Estonians behaved like Jews, all marching obediently onto trucks and trains. There were no unfortunate incidents. The women and children cried, that was all. Giving them permission to bring their belongings calmed them, just as it had the Jews."

I put the papers down again. The mail girl came and sat with us. Her wet eyes were as round as on a bombing night. I thought about my father on the train. I couldn't think any further than that.

"Who wrote these?" I asked.

"Your cousin."

"Edgar?"

"He goes by Eggert Fürst. He showed up in our department and I promised him I wouldn't tell anyone his former name. He claimed he had remarried and taken his wife's name, but it sounded like a lie. Supposedly his first wife was an adventuress who had left him. He said something about bills of exchange."

"You didn't tell him about our activities?"

Richard looked offended. "Of course not."

I believed him, but I knew how clever Edgar could be.

"What does he do besides typing up reports to Berlin?"

"I don't know. He gets along well with the German officers. His German is fluent. Behaves almost like a real Aryan."

I mentally cursed the attack on Rosenberg's train. All of our plans were at risk now, and I was slinking away like a dog.

I continued reading. The Germans were gratified that police forces had been assembled so quickly in spite of the fact that the Soviets had liquidated the police department over the summer. They saw the Russians' operations as a great help in softening the Estonians—no one wanted to take any notice of the traffic to the way-station camps, let alone the full railcars. No one wanted to be in those cars.

"But why do the Germans compare Estonians to Jews? Are they planning deportations in Germany?" I asked. "Or here? Have they already done something to the Jews like what the Bolsheviks did to us? Who's learning from whom? What the hell are they up to?"

"Something terrible," the mail girl whispered. I remembered that her fiancé, Alfons, was Jewish. Alfons had offered Jews fleeing Germany a place to stay here, but refused to go to the Soviet Union when the Germans were advancing on the country. His father had been deported; he had no illusions about the Soviet Union. I looked at the mail girl.

"We're all going to be killed," she said.

Her words were brittle and certain. I felt dizzy. I could see Edgar's shining smile.

Reval, Estland General Commissariat, Ostland National Commissariat

Edgar couldn't sleep. He got up to mix himself a glass of sugar water and drank it all at once. In the morning he was going to meet SS-Untersturmführer Mentzel at security police headquarters. Mentzel wanted to hear how he had been doing since his transfer to Tallinn, and Edgar had to make a good impression. He was nervous. Mentzel's visit was coming at just the right time: the Estonian security training in Germany had ended and the trainees had been greeted in Tallinn with such celebration that it had robbed Edgar of his peace of mind, clawed worry lines in his brow. If the country filled up with specialists trained in Germany, would they advance more quickly than he had? Would there no longer be any use for his skills in important operations? Would he no longer be needed?

He checked his suit again; it was freshly bought, newly fitted with a stiff lining. He had brushed it twice that evening. Its former owner's left shoulder had been lower than the right, and Edgar had had to stuff the right shoulder with cotton, but the two sides still didn't match. It would have to do—his older suit had been mended too many times. If the meeting with Mentzel went well, perhaps he could take it to a better tailor, or even get some wool on the black market for a new suit, double-breasted.

SS-UNTERSTURMFÜHRER MENTZEL began the meeting with thank-yous: the information Edgar had provided had proved reliable, unlike that of many others, and his reports were unusually professional. Edgar began to breathe more easily, but he also smelled eau de cologne. In his effort to make a good impression he had managed to spill the entire bottle on his new suit. Dabbing it with a damp cloth hadn't helped, and there had been no time to air the suit out. To keep the cloud of cologne from filling the entire office, he tried to move as little as possible, after scooting his chair surreptitiously farther from his German interlocutor. When Mentzel didn't seem to notice anything unusual, Edgar took courage. Perhaps Mentzel was just showing German refinement, or perhaps Edgar's nervousness simply made him imagine that the cologne was stronger than it was.

"What are your impressions of the political police B4 section, Herr Fürst? Tell me your candid feelings," Mentzel said encouragingly.

"The headache there is caused by so many troubling cases of local informers making accusations against each other, Herr SS-Untersturmführer. Accusing anyone at all of Bolshevism, secret nests of communists seen where there aren't any, three different versions of the same sabotage story. The motive seems to be pure envy, resentment, revenge, anything the minds of a lower order can be led to," Edgar said. "Once there was even a denunciation of someone in the employ of our Referentur. When cases like these are given attention, it's hard to concentrate on matters essential to our progress. And uneconomical, in my opinion."

Mentzel listened carefully, leaning slightly forward, and the nervous tingling in the soles of Edgar's feet disappeared, a gust of confidence splashing over him as unexpectedly as the contents of the bottle of cologne that morning, but in a good way. It made the pads sit on his shoulders as if he'd had the suit custom tailored just for him, and a feeling of expertise straightened his back.

"The situation has to be gotten under control or we'll begin to look completely ridiculous. This is not how Germany operates. And Germany will not be taken advantage of!" Mentzel shouted. "Cognac?" he asked. "It's Latvian. It tastes a bit like gasoline, unfortunately. Another lamentable problem is the question of why so few Estonians have registered for our voluntary armed forces. We were expecting much greater enthusiasm."

Mentzel stressed that he didn't want "correct" answers—all he wanted was the truth. Edgar swirled the cognac in his glass with a small motion of his wrist and watched the swirling liquid with great concentration. An irritating gust of cologne had circled the room as he reached for the glass, and his feeling of confidence had fractured. While he was talking he hadn't noticed the smell. Mentzel's encouraging attitude had helped. Or had he just imagined it? He hesitated. He had to play his cards right, but he didn't know which cards were right and which were wrong. After B4 had been moved to Tõnismägi, into the same office as the German security police, he'd watched sourly as the others advanced their careers from one post to the next, took up challenges, hurried out in their parade uniforms covered in more and more valuable stripes, while he wasted his skills on spiteful, simpleminded gossips and their accusations.

Edgar screwed up his courage. "There are rumors among the public that after the war the Estonians will be relocated beyond Peipsi or to Karelia, Herr SS-Untersturmführer. These rumors cause the people to doubt whether the German army is the right choice for an Estonian. The June deportations have made Estonians sensitive to anything that involves leaving their homes or their country."

Mentzel raised his eyebrows and rose from his chair. His shoulders tightened, the cognac shook in his glass, his stripes trembled.

"This is absolutely confidential. It's possible that relocation will affect the Baltic Jews, and perhaps also the coastal Swedes, but the Estonians? Under no circumstances. Is gratitude a concept entirely unknown to the Estonians?"

"I am certain that there is no limit to the gratitude of the Estonians when it comes to the Reich's liberation of our country. The general mood is very calm, no one is planning to bomb Wehrmacht transportation, or offer any other resistance—with the exception of a few random Bolsheviks. But the food shortages make people rather nervous. There might be more recruits if the men could carry the Estonian colors."

"I'll see what I can do about it. Is there still talk of a Greater Finland?"

"Hardly at all. I'm not concerned about that."

The meeting ended. Edgar got up and caught another whiff of eau de cologne.

"I've recommended you to one of my colleagues. You'll receive further details later. He's looking for a reliable perspective on the situation from a local's point of view. You can feel free to present your own opinions, Herr Fürst."

IT WAS a relieved man filled with optimism who stepped out of headquarters. It made Edgar smile to think of how hopeless he'd felt when the train carrying the new batch of security police arrived—the train windows hanging loose, some of the cars piled with birch branches. On the platform he'd cursed the fact that he hadn't tried to join earlier, hadn't followed someone other than Roland. He should have been among the handsome young men coming home, listening to the speeches of senior representatives of the German security forces at the railway station, the friendly words of SS-Obersturmführer Störtz and SS-Obersturmführer Kerl, the stirring oratory of Director Angelus.

His worry had been increased by the fact that men who had trained on Staffan Island were designated as Finland volunteers, so the ban against granting the iron cross to fighters from Estonia and other conquered countries of the eastern regions didn't apply to them—they were so highly valued that there was a desire to skirt regulations so that they could receive the Ritterkreuz. And they did receive it. He felt a bitter envy when he heard that anyone with an iron cross around his neck was allowed into exclusive places, even Estonians. If he hadn't gone with Roland, he might have a cross around his neck, too. But the game wasn't lost yet; the meeting he'd just left proved that. Maybe one day his photos would be sold throughout the Third Reich, or at least in Reichskommissariat Ostland, and children would mix up paste to put his picture in their scrapbooks. Anything was possible. Edgar hadn't seen his cousin since that awkward episode when Roland had driven him out of Leonida's cabin, and the rift between them suited him fine. The damaging halt in the arc of his career that Roland had caused seemed to resolve itself. It was all behind him now—the days wasted sitting around the cabin, that tantrum about Rosalie, the utter madness that had burned in Roland's eyes, his stubborn nagging about Edgar's wife. His marriage was none of Roland's business.

Reval, Estland General Commissariat, Ostland National Commissariat

ALTHOUGH HELLMUTH HAD URGED Juudit to stay home on the fifth of October and warned her about the threat of a terrorist attack, Gerda stopped by and persuaded her to come along to see off the legionnaires.

"Terrorist attack? Pshaw. The boys should have the image of Estonian beauties in their eyes when they go off to war, not just weeping mothers. It's our duty to go to the station!" She looked on as Juudit gave herself a beauty treatment, carefully mixing one part ammonia and two parts hydrogen peroxide with her fingers and dabbing it on her scalp with a cotton ball. Gerda thought Juudit ought to let a hairdresser lighten her hair—she would get much better results.

"Admit it—the only reason you're dressing up is for the boys. But you don't have to do all that yourself anymore. Sometimes I think you don't realize that," Gerda said reproachfully. "Let this be the last time! I heard that some girls are bringing provisions for the legionnaires. I figured I'd just paint my fingernails."

Juudit laughed. There was no resisting Gerda, and in the morning they ran to stand in front of the Gustav Adolf *Gymnasium* for the best view of the procession as it marched toward Town Hall Square. The road and courtyard were covered in flowers; people were following the band, the crowd growing. Girls in folk costumes swarmed around the legionnaires and pinned the flowers of the homeland to the men's chests. Estonian flags waved madly, German flags hung limp until someone sent down an order and they were lifted higher. Town Hall Square buzzed and hummed; herds of little children hardly breathed as they stared at the rows of volunteers, their erect posture, their shorn heads. Gerda dragged Juudit after her, the crowd treading on their feet, and they managed to hear, if not see, SA-Obergruppenführer Litzmann's arrival. Juudit stood on tiptoe, Hjalmar Mäe puffed behind Litzmann, and was that Security Police Commander Sandberger, with white lapels spread across his chest like a seagull's wings, or was it SS-Oberführer Möller? Gerda waved with her free hand. Photographers swarmed around Litzmann, lunging forward and back looking for the best angle and dashing spent flashbulbs— flashbulbs they'd been given in profligate abundance—onto the cobblestones. Flags bloomed over the square—white, blue, black, red. The roar of the crowd made one dizzy. Juudit lowered herself onto her heels and swung her just-bleached locks, the hair at her temples already starting to curl again. There was no one she knew among those departing, not even Gerda's relatives. So what was she doing here? Gerda had said this was a moment to experience, when Estonians could fight for their freedom. "They finally have their own legion, Juudit. Do you understand how long we've waited for this? The fate of Estonia depends on how much of a stake the people have in the fight against Bolshevism. Can't you see that?"

Juudit lifted her hand, into which Gerda had shoved a small blue, black, and white Estonian flag, the shouting grew more intense, and soon the reason for the cheers was passing by the spot where they stood: Petty Officer Eerik Hurme, with an iron cross on his chest alongside his medals from the Finnish Winter War. Juudit already knew what it would say in tomorrow's paper. The march of the legionnaires would be described as resolute, the parents proud; they would remember to mention the Estonian flag many times, always together with the German flag, and there might be a picture of Litzmann, with his hooked nose trembling fervently, shaking the hand of Petty Officer Hurme. Juudit knew that Hellmuth was receiving reports of low morale and annoyance caused by the requirement that mobilized soldiers sign a paper stating that they were providing their service voluntarily. The reports expressed concern that this mood was spreading, as were rumors that boys were fleeing conscription. Juudit watched as these genuine volunteers marched past, then suddenly saw a familiar profile a short distance away. It was a man, watching the crowd. She covered her mouth with her hand. The dark head appeared again, a little farther away. He turned—she'd been wrong, her mind was playing tricks on her—but then the head flashed into view again, just a meter away from the man who had turned, the one she'd mistaken for him. She combed the crowd with her eyes, but it was no use, and crossing the square was impossible. Maybe she was just seeing things. Maybe she had seen a dead man. The dead have three months to stay and say goodbye to the living. The crowd was so thick that she was pressed against Gerda's side. The speeches had to be heard to the end, although she was feeling faint, and she had to sing the German national anthem, and follow Gerda across Harju Street and Toompuiestee to the train station. Hellmuth was there somewhere, on the trail of Bolshevik saboteurs. The indifferently equipped legionnaires had already formed rows on the station platform. Juudit searched in vain for Roland or someone who looked like Roland.

"They've written 'Victory or Death' on the railcars," Gerda shouted.

Then the singing began— *"Saa vabaks Eesti meri, saa vabaks Eesti pind"*—and the train lurched into motion, the anthem unwavering. Tears rolled down Juudit's cheeks and she felt as if she were suffocating.

ONLY A FEW MONTHS EARLIER, in Hellmuth's office, they had been going through telegrams from Litzmann and the Reichsführer. The maid was serving coffee to the group when Juudit came back from shopping with a box of pastries from Kagge's in her hand, heard the clink of spoons, and hurried in to offer the men a treat to go with their hot drinks. She'd just had time to hear the bleat of Hjalmar Mäe's trembling voice:

"We have to promise that the training will take place here. And that they will only be used to fight the Soviets, not the West, under any circumstances."

Then Hellmuth's secretary at headquarters got sick and Juudit was called in. She had taken shorthand the whole day, followed Hellmuth from one meeting to the next, filled notebook after notebook with discussions of how the Estonians thought they were being given shoddy treatment in the German army. A separate legion joined to the elite forces, the Waffen-SS, could change the situation completely, stop the continuous drain of fighting-age men escaping to Finland. Juudit wrote, her pen flying, and she understood that Germany must be desperate, so desperate that the Germans were even trying to trick Estonians into joining up—when only fifty to seventy percent of Estonians possessed the racial characteristics and general health to qualify for the Waffen-SS. When she left to write up her notes in longhand, a German came in with a letter and stayed to talk with Hellmuth in a lowered voice: The Führer had felt faint when someone had suggested arming the Ukrainians. He would never put weapons in the hands of such untrustworthy people, such wildmen!

When she got home, Juudit immediately made a cocktail, and then she cried. She was only fifty to seventy percent good enough for a German. Her racial characteristics and health were clearly good enough from the waist down, but not from the waist up. That's what Roland would say if he knew. He would say that she'd never be as good as a one-hundred-percent Fräulein. Didn't she realize what kind of career Hellmuth's friends back home had in store for him, his relatives' plans for him, regardless of who or what he wanted? How did she know they didn't already have a suitable wife lined up, someone thoroughly German, a woman who wasn't divorced, wasn't from the conquered eastern territories, someone whose hair fell in soft waves and didn't turn wild and kinky when it rained? With her second sidecar Juudit cried some more, for the desperate fate of Germany, and with her third she pressed a cool spoon against her eyes to ease the swelling and tried to calm herself before Hellmuth came home.

She wasn't called to headquarters again. It didn't bother her at all, though she'd hoped at one time to become Hellmuth's real secretary, someone with real status at headquarters. She would have liked to join the throng of secretaries, interpreters, and typists hurrying to Tõnismägi in the mornings; she would have been happy even to be in the last row of teletype operators if only it brought her closer to Hellmuth's everyday life.

Now she was content to stay home and translate tedious reports on distillery safety, on the activities of the Kawe and Brandmann chocolate factories, and articles from Estonian-language newspapers. She was content because she didn't want to know any more than she had to. Gerda was lucky. Gerda didn't know shorthand.

Reval, Estland General Commissariat, Ostland National Commissariat

Edgar's legs felt weak as he gave his hat and overcoat to the coat-check girl. Why were they meeting here? Why not on a park bench, at a coffee shop, or at Tõnismägi? Was it to underline his position, to taunt him with the forbidden delicacies carried out from the kitchen, to place him in unfamiliar territory? The intoxicating aromas of restaurants and shops that were exclusively for Germans carried out into the streets. He had often yearned for them, and this restaurant was no exception. Officers flocked up the stairs and into the dining room, bustling waiters wove among the uniforms over the creaking floor, the smell of roasted meat sizzled from the kitchen, and the gleam of utensils punctuated the tang of polished brass. Glasses rang like bells, bottles were slipped into ice buckets, sherry cobblers were handed round to the cocottes, and everyone was happy.

He didn't see SS-Untersturmführer Mentzel, but Edgar

must have been recognized, because someone beckoned from a table in the center of the room before the maitre d' had time to lead him across the parquet. SS-Haupsturmführer Hertz. Edgar recognized the stripes, and raised his arm in greeting. The SS-Haupsturmführer stood and answered the salute lazily. SS-Haupsturmführer Hertz was a handsome man. Too handsome.

"A pleasure to meet you, Herr Fürst."

"Likewise, Herr SS-Haupsturmführer!"

"Untersturmführer Mentzel recommends you highly. Unfortunately, he had to leave Reval unexpectedly. He asked me to send his greetings. I understand you studied in Dorpat?"

Edgar nodded. He could feel the blush spreading all the way to his fingertips.

"I've heard a great deal of praise for the theater there. Do you recommend it?"

"I recommend it warmly, and the opera as well, Herr SS-Haupsturmführer! They know Puccini so well at the Vanemuine that it would meet even your standards, sir. I understand that musicians come from as far away as Stuttgart to perform there."

Edgar's voice was firm. He commended himself on his cultural knowledge, although it seemed an odd start to the conversation. The determined hack of a meat cleaver from the kitchen was distracting. Yet another waiter hurried past with dishes under silver cloches; the mouths of the Germans at the next table bled red wine. Edgar was thirsty. His tongue felt swollen, as if he hadn't had water in days. Beneath his growling stomach he felt a tingle he hadn't felt in ages. He didn't know if he wanted it to stay or if he wanted to be rid of it.

"Many thanks, Herr Fürst. I haven't yet had a chance to get to know Dorpat's cultural offerings, but I shall attempt to correct the situation at the first opportunity. But to our business.

What is your opinion about changing the street names to German? The Internal Directorate is against it, thinks the Estonians won't like Adolf Hitler Street. And how was Reichsmarschall Göring's speech received among the public?"

The Haupsturmführer slipped in the change of subject carelessly, his sentence ending with a sort of smile that wrinkled the skin around his eyes. He reminded Edgar of Ernst Udet, the flying ace's flying ace—the likeness was especially apparent in the shape of the nose, and there was something in the lips that reminded Edgar of Udet's portrait on his favorite postcard. But Ernst was very young in that picture; this man had seen more of life. Edgar turned his right cheek toward the Haupsturmführer—this showed his nose at the best angle.

"Reichsmarschall Göring's Thanksgiving speech was a bit problematic, particularly with the food shortages. You will recall that he said—"

The Haupsturmführer furrowed his brow. "Yes, yes. That we must feed Germans first, and only then provide for others."

"One could perhaps present a cautious assessment that the result was a small but noticeable decline in Germany's popularity. Doctor Veski's activities have also aroused concern."

"Who is Doctor Veski?" the Haupsturmführer asked.

Another plate of croquettes whisked past. The growling of Edgar's stomach had ceased, the fire below had increased. Edgar raised his eyebrows slightly, to make his eyes brighter, and held them there. He could see from the reflection in a knife that his skin was gleaming as if he'd spread pomade on it with a spatula, and every schnapps was adding another layer.

"Doctor Veski is a philologist at Dorpat University. It's said that he's creating a precise map of the eastern territories. And that he's creating it because the Estonians are going to be transplanted to Russia. There is talk that all the Russian villages on his map already have Estonian names."

Edgar heard his own voice and knew that his words made sense, but they were fragments of a conversation he'd prepared in advance, and he wasn't sure if he would be able to answer questions that diverged from his preset course. His eyes wandered, unable to avoid the Ritterkreuz the Haupsturmführer was wearing, forcing him to tear them from it continually.

"Is that so? It's rather surprising, in fact quite incomprehensible. What is feeding such rumors, and who is spreading them? I can assure you that such plans would not be in the interests of the Reich."

"Of course not, Herr Haupsturmführer!"

"You are better acquainted with events in the country than others are, Herr Fürst. Much better acquainted. You have the whole picture."

Haupsturmführer Hertz's face flashed another smile. Edgar was disconcerted. He raised a hand to his burning cheek, brushed by that smile.

"And what about anti-German activity?"

"For all practical purposes, there is none."

"I've read your reports. Exceptional. Thanks have come from Berlin. I'm certain that you are just the person for a particular task. I hope you can continue your work in Gruppe B Abteilung B4, but in a slightly new direction. You've never met Gruppenleiter Ain-Ervin Mere personally? I'm sure you'll get the chance at some point. He reports directly to me. Your task will be to keep me apprised of internal morale at the Abteilung and any internal threats. We've learned that a spy from the underground organizations has succeeded in infiltrating some very confidential operations, and I want to know what the situation is in Gruppe B."

As Edgar left the restaurant and went into the street, the schnapps he'd poured into his empty stomach started to come back up. He hurried around a corner, found a courtyard tunnel, and waited for his stomach to calm. His cologne hadn't caused any problems this time—he had remembered to keep the bottle well away from his clothes—but he should have known to eat something before the meeting. He knew he was trying too hard. Every meeting was spoiled by some mishap. But it wasn't only the schnapps; it was the man who had been sitting across from him. The moment their legs brushed in passing under the table, Edgar decided that he was going to make himself indispensable to SS-Hauptsturmführer Hertz. Hertz would depend on him, and Edgar would see him again, soon.

Vaivara, Estland General Commissariat, Ostland National Commissariat

As the Opel drove out of Tallinn, Juudit tried to hum "Das macht die Berliner Luft," but Hellmuth just looked out the window with one arm absentmindedly around her shoulders and the other extended stiffly over the open ashtray, his hand holding a cigarette rather than the top of her stocking. Juudit's voice faded out. Once again they weren't going to sing happy tunes like they always used to do, not a single rousing march. Hellmuth didn't take out the little Estonian–German phrase book to practice useful expressions, the one with the stanzas from Marie Under that Juudit had written on the cover; he didn't whisper in her ear, in Estonian, "your mouth in my mouth." The lines rushing by between the telephone poles changed to barbed wire. Hellmuth rolled down the window, threw his cigarette butt into the wind, and turned his face toward the breeze as if there wasn't enough air in the Opel. She could feel his tension as he sat beside her, looking her in the eye at regular intervals—too regular, as if he did it consciously, to keep her from noticing his furrowed brow.

The men from the petroleum company Baltische Öl had been coming and going secretly on Roosikrantsi Street for some time, and tense words had crept under the bedroom door and into Juudit's ears: Germany's most important job in the wartime economy of the former Baltic countries was to extract petrochemicals—the supreme leader of the Reich wasn't going to haggle over it. That was why the Opel Olympia was rushing to Vaivara and its potential oil production, with the nervous Juudit on board. Maybe it all started with Stalingrad. The continual retreat on the eastern front. Nervousness had begun to creep in among Hellmuth's friends, and Juudit didn't dare to think about what it might mean. She closed it away again and again and tried to be lively company while Hellmuth sighed about how the officer corps had become a hodgepodge of new replacements.

At first Juudit had thought it a good sign that the Germans were building apartments for the labor force and repairing the factories demolished in the Bolsheviks' retreat. Surely they wouldn't have been willing to put such an emphasis on local production unless they were convinced that the Bolsheviks would never advance that far. So why was Hellmuth worried? The news was full of propaganda. Gerda would have said that politics won't put a dress on a woman's back, that she shouldn't get mixed up in it. Gerda was right. The acrid smell of exhaust made Juudit's temples tight. Everything was too complicated. She didn't understand, and she lamented how the intimacy between her and Hellmuth had dwindled to their time in the bedroom, superseded by these military concerns.

WHEN THEY ARRIVED in Vaivara, Hellmuth left Juudit behind to watch as he hurried to discuss important matters with the men, clicking his heels in greeting. She went to look for a good spot for what might be the summer's last chance to sunbathe. She put on her sunglasses, took off her shoes and rolled down her stockings, and lifted the hem of her skirt, but not too high, for the sake of propriety, and because she could already sense the autumn in the cool breeze. She felt a shiver for other reasons, too, though not enough to get her Pervitin out of her handbag. She'd started carrying it with her after the bombings in February. Apparently the army wanted to get rid of its supply and Hellmuth had it by the case. He had been right—the Pervitin helped. It dissolved her anxiety like the bombs melted the snow. She remembered the black earth, unnatural for February, the lines of evacuees along the highway, the sleighs packed with people leaving the city, and how on the night before the bombing she had seen her first drunken German soldier. She snapped her purse open. She didn't notice the ruins anymore; her eyes passed them by as if they were dust on furniture. She was numb to everything—except her husband. Her bright red toenails shining in the sunlight brought to mind again her husband's rebuke about them; his auntie Anna supposedly didn't approve of nail polish. Now they could gobble up the light as free and as red as Leni Riefenstahl's. Riefenstahl's painted toenails were famous, and she always took two photographers with her when she traveled, to take pictures of her and her clothes.

"WHAT WOULD YOU say to that? A few chickens, a cow, a simple life in the country? With you."

Juudit wasn't sure she'd understood him right. The Opel bounced over potholes in the road, knocking her elbow against the armrest and making her yelp in surprise and pain. When they'd left to make the trip home at sunset, Hellmuth had been silent as he got into the backseat of the car, and he'd remained silent for a long time. He hadn't even taken Juudit's hand, or kissed her. Had he really said something about the possibility of staying here after the war? Here? In the countryside?

"A lot of officers are planning to do the same. Don't you want to live in the country, sweetheart?"

At first she had thought he was talking about going back to Germany without her. But he would stay. She wouldn't lose him. Next her thoughts flew to an image of life in a village like Taara—the smell of rye; the girls carrying their milk cans to the horse carts; herself, living with a German even though she was still married; the stares; the clots of spit flying at her neck every time she turned her back. It wouldn't matter if Hellmuth bought them an estate instead of a farm; she didn't want to be a concubine at a manor house. SS officers' requests to marry went to the state security headquarters for processing and she was sure she wouldn't pass the screening. Even if they got permission, such a marriage would ruin Hellmuth's career—she had no business in Berlin. Maybe that was why he was talking about moving to the countryside. But his words meant something else, too: Germany would prevail, the Bolsheviks would not return. Otherwise he wouldn't be planning a future here.

"I've written to a few of my friends and recommended the Estonian countryside to them. You've been a wonderful guide to life in the provinces. The soil seems fertile, good for growing— what else could you need? We could have our own paradise out in the country."

"But after the war I'm sure you'll have tremendous opportunities to do anything you want, anyplace you want," Juudit protested.

"I thought you wanted to stay here."

"You've never asked about the future before."

Hellmuth opened his cigarette case and lit one. "Do you want to go to Germany, then?"

"You've never asked about that, either."

"I didn't dare to."

The words soothed her. She had panicked for no reason. He wasn't far along with his plans. He hadn't yet looked at land or houses. Maybe she wouldn't have to explain to him that Estonians looked at mistresses differently, wouldn't have to put her shame into words. Germans seemed to be so much more tolerant—a companion or a secretary with a swelling belly didn't cause alarm. Women were just sent on vacation, to some German city where the time could apparently be passed more pleasantly and safely and the food was better. That's what happened to a woman who had gone to the same seamstress as Juudit, and another who had gone to the same hairdresser. Gerda had eventually packed her bags, too, but at least she'd promised to write. Gerda could tell her what it would be like living in Germany. Maybe she could visit Gerda before making her final decision. In Germany she wouldn't have to deal with any acquaintances from her old life. Maybe once she was there she wouldn't care if she spent the rest of her days as a secret lover. Hellmuth could marry a wife acceptable to his family and the Reich. Juudit could bear even that, as long as they were together.

"I'll go wherever you want to go," she whispered.

Reval, Estland General Commissariat, Ostland National Commissariat

Edgar glanced at his pocket watch. He was on time. The fabric of his pocket had become stretched from the repetition of this impatient gesture; he spent every day counting the hours until his next meeting. Every crumb of information he'd managed to get was doubly exciting because every matter to report felt like a personal gift to SS-Hauptsturmführer Hertz. Hertz was satisfied with him, he could tell. He might even be invited to spend an evening at the theater at some point. He'd already prepared himself for that possibility by ordering a new suit from his tailor, instructing him that it should look like it came straight from Berlin.

The buzz in the restaurant was the same as always: the Allgemeine-SS in black, the Wehrmacht in gray, long-legged, as always. Seeing veterans of the eastern front was like a needle in the eye. Edgar made himself look away from their eagles and swastikas. The stories of Stalingrad were unsuitable for women and children, and for Edgar.

Hauptsturmführer Hertz waved and stood up.

"Nice to see you again, Herr Fürst. Waitress! I recommend the squab. Absolutely delicious. Bring some of that excellent Riesling, too."

As he sat down at the white tablecloth, Edgar tried as usual not to stare at the man's Ritterkreuz and remembered to keep his eyebrows elegantly raised. Just enough to make his gaze appear open. Not overdoing it. Right cheek toward Hertz. The morning had passed in nervousness, the warm towel he'd put over his face before shaving had been too hot and he had lost his styptic—it had been a mistake to sharpen his razor. He was behaving like a young man barely out of his teens preparing for his first date with the one his heart had chosen—he was that excited—repeating phrases he might need to use, his voice trembling. This thought made his moaning skin burn even more and the glow didn't cool when he went outdoors. Luckily the restaurant was dim. Edgar noticed how the adventuresses who passed their table sized Hertz up, and he noticed with satisfaction that Hertz paid them no attention whatsoever. He was polite to the ladies, but his gaze never wandered to their knees, let alone their hips. So the powder mark on his otherwise spotless collar was all the more surprising.

"You've done excellent work," Hertz said. "I can't thank you enough. And now I have a new and interesting task for you. As I'm sure you understand, a greater workforce is needed here, and they've decided to send it."

The dishes brought to the table calmed Edgar's galloping thoughts, and he wet his lips with the wine but didn't swallow. He didn't dare to ask for something else to drink, though his mouth felt so dry he could hardly get his meat down. He cleared his throat. He had to concentrate on work; he couldn't afford to lose Hertz's trust.

"There aren't enough men," the Hauptsturmführer said.

"Industry isn't getting up to speed. The Bolsheviks' scorched-earth tactics did unbelievable damage—but I don't need to tell you that. We need new manufacturing facilities and new housing for the workers. The previous labor camps were under the purview of Reich security forces, but the work camp they're establishing now will be under the economics side of the SS. We're counting on them to get better results because, to be quite honest, the performance of the labor camps hasn't quite been what we'd hoped. We'll be working directly under the appointed Inspekteur der Konzentrationslager, SS-Gruppenführer Glücks, who answers directly to Reichsführer Himmler. In other words, I've been transferred, and now I'm gathering up responsible staff for this important project. I went last week to get to know the area where the new camp will be built, and I can tell you there will be plenty of work. The roads are in deplorable condition—I have a renewed appreciation for my driver's mechanical skills. SS-Hauptsturmführer Hans Aumeier, who's been named commandant of Vaivara, has ten years' experience on the economics end, so I assume he'll be guiding camp efficiency to a new level. We're in discussion on the administrative arrangements at the moment. We'll be working together with Baltische Öl petroleum company and the construction administration's Einsatzgruppe Russland-Nord, and I need a reliable man on board, someone who understands the native mood."

Reval, Estland General Commissariat, Ostland National Commissariat

JUST AS JUUDIT turned onto Roosikrantsi, Roland, wearing a German military jacket, stepped out from a courtyard passageway in front of her and politely raised his hat. Juudit froze. She thought about running away—was there time to get to the door, to get inside? It was only a few dozen meters. Roland's fixed stare had startled the maid, who was carrying the shopping—Juudit noticed her uncertain movement.

"You can go in, Maria," Juudit said.

The girl slipped through the gate; Juudit forced a polite smile and nodded to a passing neighbor and the manager of the German commissary. Roland took her by the arm and steered her away from the building.

"Let's go for a walk," he said.

They walked arm in arm. Roland's stride was relaxed. His voice wasn't.

"I need your mother's apartment."

Juudit didn't answer. If she shouted loudly, she could get away from him for good. No more imagining she'd seen him in a crowd, no more being startled by his sudden appearances, no more wondering if Hellmuth would ever find out. They were out in public. There was a patrol officer just a scream away. Juudit opened her mouth, but no sound came out. Her eyes flew from one passerby to the next. She went over how she would introduce him if they passed someone she knew. Alternatives flew through her mind in a flock, but every sentence she prepared struck up against the glass of Roland's stare. He held her arm tightly, forcing her to walk at a steady pace as she struggled against him.

"There are fewer refugee transports to Finland as the days get shorter," he said. "But there's a severe housing shortage, so it's hard for people underground to find a place to stay. Everyone's afraid, everyone's asking for papers."

"Talk more softly," Juudit whispered.

"Even you're afraid. Are you thinking in German now?"

"No."

"The apartment on Valge Laeva Street is next to the park, which is good. The park offers shelter and the Bolsheviks destroyed the warehouses next door, so it's easy to get to. You don't need the apartment, and others do," he said. "Have you heard from your brother, by the way? Can't your Aryan manage to solve even that?"

Juudit opened her mouth again, then shut it. Hellmuth had told her that it was best to wait until the war was over. Then they would have a better chance of finding out Johan's fate. He had taken her in his arms and the empathy in his touch had made her cry. She didn't want to talk about Johan with Roland. His voice was cold. Her throat tightened, but she wouldn't cry in front of him. They turned into Lühike Jalg Street and started to climb the stairs to Toompea. She could slip under the railing, run down the cobblestones. There was a crowd of people on the stairs—maybe Roland wouldn't be able to run after her quickly enough, and she could yell, and that would be the end of it. But she just said, "I can't get involved in something like that."

"Nothing's being asked of you."

Roland took Juudit's purse from her numb hand, looked through it, and took out the keys. They'd reached Kohtu Street. On the lookout platform were yet more German officers, some with binoculars, and photographers and reporters filming the borders of Ostland. Roland started to steer Juudit away. On the Patkuli stairs he took her hand, holding it like a newborn chick.

THE CLOCK DIDN'T SEEM to have moved at all. Its pace either slowed to nothing or sped up. In any case, it was always wrong. Tomorrow was the day Juudit would go to the apartment on Valge Laeva to complete the task Roland had given her. She paced around the office, unable to work although a pile of translating was waiting next to the typewriter. The sentences got all tangled every time she tried. It was a lucky thing Hellmuth was busy so she could be left alone, jumping whenever a car backfired or an ambulance sped by or a shadow moved in a corner, trying to calm herself by walking around although every circuit of the room made her feel more like an animal in a trap. Hellmuth wasn't dreaming of country life anymore; he was thinking about Berlin, talking about his childhood there, the places Juudit must see, until at last his brow would crumple like paper.

"Maybe someplace else, then, someplace where we wouldn't see the war," he said.

Hellmuth was serious about her but Juudit was the one risking everything. She could lose all this—the smoking table that he had cleared off to make a place for her typewriter, his office, the Estonian newspapers the maid piled on his desk. He often just stopped in at headquarters and spent the rest of the day in his office at home; he preferred to listen to Juudit rather than to the office interpreters, so she translated the newspapers for him. Those were the days she liked the best, and she could lose them. Being able to send her mother Estonian newspapers. The newspapers were running out of paper to print on in spite of the fact that the mills were operating at full capacity. But the Germans had enough of everything, and so did she. She could keep scrubbing her face with sugar. But not without Hellmuth. Juudit continued pacing. She wasn't going to get any work done today. Her skin felt raw. Her stockings were tormenting her. Her legs itched as if they were covered in layers of wool like the ones she wore in the summer as a child to protect against snakes. She took off her garter and rolled her stocking down. The beginning of a varicose vein on her right calf always made her think of her friend whose father had been executed by the Bolsheviks, his remains dug up from Pikk Street. She could still remember the smell of the girl's mother, her sweaty powder, her groan as she took off the rubberized stockings she used for varicose veins. Her skin was red. And those veins. Juudit couldn't afford to have varicose veins, couldn't afford to lose Hellmuth's interest, his fingers that crept up her legs in the darkness of the Estonia Theater. Hellmuth's worries had grown with his transfer. He had a longer trip to the offices in the economic division and missed working in his own area of expertise. There was a hollowness in his touch now, and this worried Juudit more and more each day, frightened her into taking greater care of her beauty. Her life depended on Hellmuth's feelings for her. Without them she had nothing.

A noise from outside made her start, although there was always noise when the children in the morning session came home from school. The clock only read noon, but she already craved a drink. The itch was unbearable. Tomorrow would come soon. Thirty hours from now she would go to meet the refugees. What if she ruined everything, if she didn't know how to act and made a stupid mistake? What if there was some-one she knew among the refugees? What if she just didn't go? Roland could find someone else to do it. How could he be sure the coast guard schedules he'd obtained were accurate? How did he know the fishermen in the ring were trustworthy, or how long they could fool the inspectors, or whether they would have enough saws and other forestry equipment to cover the refugees hiding in the trucks? And what if the fishermen started blackmailing them? Where would they get the money? Where exactly were the trucks and the fuel coming from? Juudit didn't want to know. Why hadn't she resisted earlier? What had kept her lips sealed? Stalingrad, Tunisia, Rostov, or the fact that citizens of the occupied eastern regions were being drafted into the German forces? If she had confided in Gerda, *she* might have had a solution, might have told her to use her womanly wiles, to steer Roland, not let him steer her. But Juudit wasn't Gerda, she didn't have Gerda's instinctive ability to melt even the most hardened opponent with her charm. Juudit missed Gerda, missed her advice. She hadn't received a single letter from her, though she'd promised to write.

Tomorrow Hellmuth wouldn't notice if Juudit slipped out after curfew because in the morning the whole group except for Juudit was going to Vilnius for a few days. But now the clock that had felt so slow started to rush. She usually couldn't predict when Hellmuth would be home early and when he wouldn't. She had to get ready. Hellmuth would be back, and the heels of guests' shoes would be clattering over the floor. The cook was already whipping the eggs, the maid setting the table. She should be preparing to charm her guests. Nerves show immediately in a woman's skin, that's what Gerda would have said, and Juudit couldn't afford to let them show. She started by lathering up her shaving soap. She'd learned from Gerda that you can only get really smooth legs with a razor, not with hydrogen sulfide, which stank in any case. The tan on Juudit's legs was weak, pale. She ought to do something about that. After her bath she sprinkled salicylic powder under her arms and put the can back on the shelf next to the black pen she'd used to use to draw seams along the backs of her legs in her stockingless days. Her darkened elbows showed in the mirror like storm clouds. She picked up the hand mirror and tried to see how bad they were. She should have the maid bring more lemons. Other than that, her transformation from dove soft to scaly snake didn't show. Or was she just fooling herself?

EDGAR TOOK A MOMENT to breathe as he stood at SS-Hauptsturmführer Hertz's door. He could see the soft light of the entryway through the green glass transom. He straightened his shoulders. The tailor had done his work well, and made sure the badge on his sleeve was straight. *OT-Bauführer*. Because of the shortages he would have to make do with a sleeve badge and his employee ID booklet, but what did it matter? He had plenty of reasons to be pleased. He'd waited for this invitation for a long time. Once he was through this door, the whole Empire would be open to him. Men from Baltische Öl and the Goldfeld company would arrive; so would the Einsatzgruppe Russland-Nord, whose activities he'd already researched. When the Germans had retreated from the Caucasus and lost access to the

Caspian Sea, their gaze had turned to Estonia. Edgar understood immediately what it meant. They were out of oil. They
would never surrender Estonia. Petrochemicals were the future.
Baltische Öl's interests would be prioritized, and although he
had never researched the subject, he would start now.

The maid took Edgar's coat and hat. There was already
a cheerful atmosphere in the room, the Führer's portrait on
the wall slightly askew. Hauptsturmführer Hertz gave him
a warm welcome, led him to a room full of guests, and left
to look for his girlfriend, who was still in her dressing room.
SS-Sturmbannführer Aumeier came over to continue a conversation he and Edgar had begun earlier in the day about a trip
to Vilnius and Riga. It seemed an intriguing device had been
invented in Lithuania to make processing easier, and they would
see it at work at the Paneriai camp. Perhaps something similar
could be used in Estland. Edgar told him the system of delega-
tion was progressing well with the police patrols as well as Third
Battalion Major Koort. Regulations said that staff members had
to maintain a two-meter distance from the inmates; they still
needed to discuss logistics. The Sturmbannführer nodded—it
was a familiar situation: the SS-Wirtschafter wanted to keep
close tabs on certain key sectors.

The door to the drawing room was open, and at first Edgar
was too focused on fitting in to realize why the voice of the
woman talking with the Hauptsturmführer in the hallway
sounded familiar. Then he knew: there was no mistaking that
voice, even over the cheerful chatter of the other guests. Edgar
glanced at the windows. No, he shouldn't even think it—but
the center window was a large double door. It must lead to a
balcony.

He squeezed his way to a corner of the balcony, pressed
his back against the stucco, and held tight to the railing with

his right hand. The hem of the curtains licked at his shoes from between the doors. He could hear the click of high heels in the drawing room, the squeak of the floor, and that easily recognizable female laugh. There was no way to jump—the apartment was too high up. The guests were going to the table. Edgar heard Sturmbannführer Aumeier mention his name and say something about his needing some fresh air. When the maid came to summon the woman to the phone, Edgar saw his chance. As her footsteps retreated, he slipped back inside, exchanged a few quick words with his host, walked calmly across the carpet, then quickened his steps and found the water closet just as Juudit walked past him into the drawing room. There was a door from the water closet into a hallway, and another from the hallway directly to the entryway, where he found his hat and coat. He whispered to the cook that he'd had a sudden bout of queasiness and had to leave, asked her to convey his apologies to the hosts for his sudden departure. Later he sent word that they could send a car for him when the rest of the guests were ready for the trip. He felt well enough to travel.

WHEN STURMBANNFÜHRER AUMEIER'S DRIVER pulled into Roosikrantsi early the next morning, Edgar drew the brim of his hat over his eyes, just in case. After the car came to a stop, the others got out to stretch their legs, but Edgar stayed in the back seat, saying he still felt weak and wanted to nap a little. Between his turned-up collar and his hat brim he saw the maid—the same one who had taken his coat the evening before—dash out to the street and almost collide with the handyman, who was wielding a broom on the steps. The ordinariness of the morning calmed him. The blackout curtains were raised, the smell of fresh-baked bread wafted from the bakery, the horses with their heavy carts clopped toward the commissary, and finally SS-Haupsturmführer Hertz came out, stopped to buy some nuts from a boy who was selling them, came over to say hello to Edgar and the other travelers good-naturedly, and got into his own car. The next moment the door flew open and Juudit ran out in a flowered housecoat that fluttered in the morning wind, and the breeze blew her to Hertz's Opel Olympia, where she slid into the back seat, and he lifted his hands to her shoulders and caressed her sleep-tussled hair, her ears, with great tenderness. The sight of it blinded Edgar for a moment, flowed through him like he'd accidentally swallowed lye and there was nothing he could do about it, though it ate through him like deadly poison, because in that touch was all the love in the world, everything gentle and precious. The SS-Haupsturmführer was behaving like this right there in front of everyone—the joking boys, the junk sellers, the street sweepers—letting this woman run out into the street to say goodbye, even though the wind pressed her nightgown against her legs, the silk went sliding off her shoulders, and he repaid this exhibition by caressing her ear. Such a measure of impropriety, such a display of intimacy, belonged between the sheets, in the boudoir. Such a gesture was too good to waste on a tart. Edgar had seen how men were with war brides, but this was different. This was a display of something most people have just once in their lives, and many never have at all.

The scene replayed in Edgar's mind again and again—the woman running to the car, getting in, the man raising his hands to her shoulders, stroking her hair and touching her ears. The movements wouldn't stop repeating, the man's expression of happiness, of having forgotten everything else, Juudit's smile that made the cobblestones sparkle with love, the light on their faces. Edgar couldn't avoid thinking of the two of them in bed, although he didn't want to know anything about that, Hertz's hands touching Juudit's earlobes, her face, Hertz kissing her eyebrows, her nose. There was nothing exceptional about Juudit's earlobes. Juudit was a simple girl. Beauty was not among her greatest gifts. And she was married. What right did such an insignificant female have to touch the Hauptsturmführer so obscenely, to traipse into drawing rooms that Edgar didn't dare to enter? What right did she have to walk into the Germans' world, just like that, without earning it? A woman gets into a car, the light comes on for a few private moments, darkens the day in the street, becomes a lighthouse in a black sea, and the two people inside don't even notice it, because they don't see the world around them, they don't need it, they illuminate each other. The man touches the woman's ears. The light comes on. Their light.

When he'd worked through these thoughts, Edgar realized that Juudit could be made use of in the beds of the Germans. That time would come. But before that happened, he would go deeper into the job he'd been given, take production inventories, visit his auntie Anna, make discreet inquiries as to what she knew about Juudit's activities. He had no desire to live in Tallinn now. The muddy camp at Vaivara was his only alternative—he wouldn't run into Juudit there. For the first time in his life, he hated his wife.

PART FOUR

Fascist agents of Germany were cleverly sent to Estonia even before the country was occupied by Hitlerist forces. One of these agents was Mark, whose fiancée absorbed her suitor's teachings. According to eyewitness reports, Soviet prisoners often saw this woman washing a military coat and shirt, belonging to Mark, that was red with blood. She claimed that Mark had simply been dressing birds for dinner. "It was clear to me, however, that Mark took part in the execution of Soviets," witness M. Afanasyev says. For the nationalists, murder became an everyday occurrence. After every bloodbath, the murderers arranged drinking parties or orgies, which Mark's bride also took part in, shaking the plucked-out fingernails of Soviet citizens from her skirts.

—Edgar Parts, *At the Heart of the Hitlerist Occupation*,
   Eesti Raamat Publishing, 1966

ВИЛЕНИН
1963

Tallinn, Estonian SSR,
Soviet Union

H IS WIFE SHOVED the shopping bags piled on the table
toward Parts as if she were expecting praise for buying
groceries. The viscose lace at the hem of her slip quivered; blue
smoke filled the room. Parts put his own purchases on the floor,
opened the window, and pushed the rustling hopflower vines
aside, keeping his motions steady, though he'd been startled
by his wife's unexpected appearance in the kitchen. What was
going on? What did she want this time? When she had on several occasions expressed a desire for more fashionable towels,
he hadn't objected. He'd bought new Chinese terry cloth to
replace the linen ones and fought to find Polish toothpaste to
put alongside the tooth powder. He'd stood in line for a permit
to buy a Snaigė refrigerator, then gone to the back of the requi-
site three more lines before finally managing to cut to the front
to get the next-to-last refrigerator available that day. All of it
was his responsibility, because when it came to creature com-

forts his wife's job at the railway station was useless. If Parts should happen to want some drier frankfurters, he had to find them himself, making acquaintances at the combine who could get frankfurters before they were even sold to the shops, where they added water to increase the weight. It was useless to dream of fricadelle soup until he had a friend at the meat combine— the ground meat at the grocer's was adulterated, sometimes with rat. All this took time from his work, but he did it anyway, for his own comfort and to keep his wife's fits at bay. How much thinner did he have to stretch himself?

His wife pushed the shopping bags another centimeter toward him, but he didn't give them a glance. A cold dinner would have to suffice. He wasn't going to start frying cutlets today, or look at her purchases. He wanted some time in peace, before she started making more demands.

Surprisingly, she opened her mouth, her breath sour, and started explaining that she had spent the afternoon with Kersti, who also worked at the railway station, and that they had gone to such and such a shop, but it had been closed for inventory, and after who knows how many places closed for inventory they'd ended up at a place where a friend of Kersti's worked, where there was a buzz at the back door, and they'd gotten oranges. She continued poking through the shopping bags and a cake box fell on the floor. Fresh pastilaa, she said, from Kalevi's. His favorite jelly cakes.

Was it a car she wanted? A Moskvitch cost five thousand rubles. An impossible sum, an impossibly long line for a purchase permit, and he hadn't received his advance yet.

"And then we went to see Kersti's new apartment, in a highrise. The kitchen is a little box. At least we have space to sit and eat, and to cook. She doesn't, although otherwise the apartment's very big and stylish."

"That's as it should be," Parts said. "People can eat in the communal dining room. Who really needs a big kitchen?"

Conversation.

Their first in months.

She looked at him and reminded him that they were at home and it was just the two of them. Parts concentrated on arranging leftover pigs' feet on a plate, careful not to touch his wife's shopping bags, not picking the cake box up from the floor. He swallowed his disgust at her thick toenails poking in the air, swallowed the question of how her childless friend had acquired her new apartment—did she have a lover? His chances for an uninterrupted evening were dwindling. Maybe he should give her the brown envelope from the Office now—money always calms women down. Her breath smelled like a pharmacy. That was nothing new. But as he walked past her, he noticed a slight smell of dry shampoo, and her hair did have an unusual lightness about it. As if she wanted to impress on him that she was in her right mind.

"Why are you talking to me?" Parts said, emphasizing every word.

She flinched, her bluster peeled away, and fell silent. The ash on her cigarette grew, the coffee cup shook in her hand, and Parts closed his eyes, didn't say anything. There were only a few unbroken cups left in the coffee service, which had, after all, been a gift from Auntie Anna. He remembered what had happened the last time. His wife had laughed, said it didn't matter, they didn't need a whole setting, since they never had any guests.

"They were so happy with the new apartment. It's no wonder. Everybody's getting on with their lives and careers, starting families, happy families, but for us this could be our last day in Tallinn. You behave as if you don't even realize that."

Parts looked his wife in the eye for the first time in years. Her once beautifully open eyes had been swallowed by flesh. Pity stepped into the kitchen and scraped the scales from Parts's irritated words. His voice softened.

"I don't intend to ever go back to Siberia. Never," he said.

She turned on the radio.

"Are you sure? I listened to the Ain-Ervin Mere trial on the radio, and all the programs about it. I went to the Officers' House, too, and watched the beginning of the performance outside. You people no doubt knew exactly who was there, but I put on a scarf and sunglasses. Look for me in your photos—I'm sure you'll have plenty of them."

Parts sat down. The radio blared and his wife lowered her voice so that he had to read her lips to understand what she was saying.

"Why in the world did you go there?" he asked. "Mere wasn't even there. He's in England, and they'll never extradite him."

"I had to. So I would know what it was like. What it sounded like, what it looked like."

She lit a new cigarette—the old one was still smoking in the ashtray. The shout of the radio made the smoke and ash dance.

"For heaven's sake, it was just a show trial! Ain-Ervin Mere wouldn't agree to keep working with us, that's all!"

"So he made a mistake. Are you sure you won't?"

Parts was taken by surprise, and hissed, "Mere was an important agent. I've never been a man of any significance. They don't arrange theater like that for little people."

"What if they're looking for just those kinds of people, as a warning to others? You've already been convicted once of counterrevolutionary activities. Or do you think that testifying in the trial made you a hero for all time?"

Her elbow shoved the grocery bags again. An orange fell out

of one. It rolled into the hallway. Parts wondered if he should tell her more about the book project. No. She would enjoy the rewards once it was written, but there was no need to tell her what the Office's plans were, or the part the book would play. He poured himself a cup of the grain coffee she'd made and sat down at the table. She slid the ashtray back and forth. Ashes flew into his cup. He swallowed the surly words that rose to his throat.

"I don't want to be next," she said. Parts twisted the radio knob louder. "We got some new girls at work. One of them immediately had to leave. They didn't tell us why, but Kersti knew that her father was in the German army. I wait every day for the time when they come for me. I've been waiting ever since the Russians returned. I know they'll come."

PARTS WOULD WAIT one more moment before he began to type. He would wait for his wife to empty her bottle, and while he waited he would suck on the bones of the pigs' feet. He wiped his fingers, unlocked the cabinet, and took out the journal. Could his wife know what Roland had really been up to after the rift between them? Anna and Leonida had passed on in the years when Parts was in Siberia, but had Roland been in contact with them, the careful Roland? Mothers always know something. The phonograph in the living room started playing Bruckner. The weak feeling brought on by his wife's rare exchange of words with him was spreading. He lowered his fingers to the keyboard and pursed his lips. He could still go back to her, pick up the orange that had rolled into the hallway, peel it for her, take her hand, ask her to tell him everything she remembered, say to her: Let's rescue each other. Just this once let's blow on the same coal. There wasn't much time. She could help him find Roland. She might remember details that he didn't, might be able to guess things he couldn't, places Roland might have gone, people he might have contacted. He could show her the journal. She might recognize the handwriting, too, or even the people mentioned. What if she held the key to his questions about Roland? This could be the right moment. Maybe she was frightened enough, finally ready after all these years. Why else would she bring it up, tell him she'd gone to watch Mere's trial? Was it a sign that her pride had finally crumbled? Had her desperation destroyed it, or was it the realization that no one but Parts could protect her future? Why couldn't he take that small step, take her by the hand? Why couldn't he trust her even that much, this one time?

ВИЛЕНИН
1963

Tallinn, Estonian SSR, Soviet Union

In 1943 Mark thought of a way to make some money. Because some of the Hitlerist crowd understood that Fascist Germany would lose, many of them already had a backup plan—to make it to the West, where they could sabotage the opposition to the Third Reich and continue to spread Hitlerism. With the help of some fishermen friends, Mark started assisting these good-for-nothings with their insidious plan to escape to the naively welcoming West. Because he'd been a celebrated athlete during the days of bourgeois Fascism in Estonia, his face was well known and he was admired, so it was easy for him to make contacts. He asked to be transferred from Tartu to Tallinn. He had already proved his ability in the Hitlerist intelligence service, so the Tallinn Fascists welcomed him. He found an apartment where he could conduct Fascists to wait for transport by boat. The apartment belonged to his fiancée's mother, a woman who had betrayed her people with a Fascist officer—

Parts lowered his wrists to the table and wiped his damp neck with his handkerchief. His wife's heels had started up again, like a pounding rain, but the text was nevertheless flowing well. Word choice was tough, though. Lover? Fascist female? He shouldn't use the word "whore," it was too strong—in poor taste, in fact. A woman in an intimate relationship with an SS officer? A fascist Estonian woman in an intimate relationship with an SS officer? A woman who adored Hitler and was in a filthy relationship with an SS officer? A Hitlerist bride? An occupation bride? Or would "Hitler-loving war bride" be the most elegant choice?

Parts thought about his wife's nature, her friends in her younger years, his deceased mother-in-law, and tried to find the precise phrase. His wife would no doubt have been able to think of something. He remembered the childish hope that had kept him alive until he returned from Siberia—the hope that their shared past in a country that was becoming something new would form a foundation for their union, that they would understand each other in a way no one else could. They were starting from a good place. His wife hadn't divorced him, although many others had divorced while their spouses were in Siberia. He hadn't received a single letter from her, but she had sent packages—as many as were allowed. His store of hope had a strong foundation, and during the Ain-Ervin Mere testimony he had even wondered whether he ought to bring her with him on the kindergarten visits. She could have given presentations on her husband, the heroic witness, thanked the Red Army for saving his life; they could have posed for photos with the children, she holding a bouquet of carnations. Maybe the Office would have seized on that idea if they'd had children of their own, or maybe the Office had been conscious of his wife's past, and didn't think she was appropriate for kindergartners. It was for the best. Her breakdown had been quite sudden.

Parts considered himself experienced enough to understand the primitive instincts that sometimes possessed his wife, and he had once suggested to her that she could find a companion, get a bit of contact with younger men. It would have had a calming effect, given her other channels for her drives and emotions, at least allowed him to work in peace, but she had reacted by shutting down. This upset him. Contrary to what she imagined, he knew from experience how helpful it could be to act on these cravings, how it made a difficult life more bearable, if not exactly delightful. At the camps he'd quickly learned how the law of the jungle asserted itself in that world—the animal instincts. Some of the other boys were let into the criminals' barracks because they had beautiful faces; Parts had to demonstrate his unusual skills to be let in, but once he was accepted, life became manageable. No one dared to come and get him there, to take him to the woods or the mines, and he'd set up an exchange with the doctor for Vaseline, since, like the criminals, the doctor, too, needed a forger. But he'd put those crazy times behind him now, drowned those memories out of his mind like unwanted kittens thrown in the river; the sweaty clutches on his neck had faded into the lost longings of the past.

Parts had discussed his wife's situation with a doctor, who said his suspicions were probably correct. An empty womb had almost certainly caused her unstable condition—she might be infertile. He recommended seeing a specialist. Parts hadn't dared to suggest that to her, although according to the doctor, barrenness could be a cause of personality disorder. If she'd had a child she might have had something else to focus on during the trial, and her collapse might have been at least partly averted. Besides, they could have given a child a good life; the house would have made the child an eligible prospect, as would Parts's respected position. He certainly wouldn't have minded having a little fellow around. He'd even done what he could to effect such an outcome with several attempts at conjugal activity, until he'd retreated to the sofa bed, and finally dragged the sofa into his office. It was rough going, presenting himself as a normal family man without having any offspring, and communicating with the Office staff would have been easier if they could have socialized with other families; in fact, it would have made his job go much more smoothly if he had a child he could show the world. He should talk to the Office about it. He'd heard from one recruit who had been turned when the Office arranged an adoption for him in only a week.

He'd given up his walks along the Pirita because of the children. There were always too many laughing toddlers, the irritating hum of tops, paths blocked by baby carriages and children taking their first wobbly steps. Once he saw a father flying a kite with his son, the kite a perfect hourglass against the blue sky. Parts lifted his face to the breeze and slowed his steps. He would have liked to have a son to tell stories to, stories like how Alexander Fyodorovich Avdeev had shot down the celebrated Walter Nowotny over Saaremaa. Alexander had been a handsome man, like all pilots, and his plane, a Polikarpov I-153, was like a beautiful seagull, but its gull's wings were poor ones and the Polikarpov was discontinued. His son's eyes would go wide with wonder, he would want to hear more, and Parts would tell him about the time he flew a Polikarpov and the plane had gone into a steep nosedive. His son would hold his breath with excitement, and Parts would recount how he might have crashed into the ground if he hadn't kept a cool head and pressed the side rudder with his foot to shift the spin in the opposite direction, how the spinning stopped but his head reeled, making him feel like the plane was still spinning, which was perfectly ordinary, a challenge for any pilot. That's what he would have said, and then he would have patted the boy on the shoulder and promised that they could go later and buy some airplane stickers and asked: Shall we fly the kite some more? And the boy would nod, and then they would look up together and see how the kite had risen.

The clop of his wife's heels on the stairs shot the kite down. Parts opened his eyes and saw, instead of a blue sky, the curling yellow wallpaper of his office, the dark-brown cabinet, the lacquered surface that he wiped fingerprints from with the edge of his handkerchief whenever he saw them. In the cabinet he had several files of stickers that he'd picked up from the stationery section of a department store. They had airplanes on them.

THE TYPEWRITER'S PAPER RACK was bent under the weight of his head; the letter arms were stuck together. Comrade Parts rubbed drying slobber from his cheek. The pendulum of the grandfather clock swung the wee hours. A proper wife would have come to wake her husband, not left him sleeping in such an uncomfortable position. Comrade Parts slid his chair back, went to lock the office door and open the sofa bed—he wasn't going to get any more work done tonight. Maybe the kite boy would appear in his dreams. He could tell him about when he met Lenin, how he'd been hanging on his mother's arm but he still remembered Lenin's fixed gaze and how Lenin had told his mother, This boy will be a pilot, he has a pilot's keen vision. As the sofa bed sprang open, it occurred to him that he was so alone that he was seeking company in his dreams. He sat down on the stack of bedding, his tiredness gone. The moon hung in the round window like a glove button fastened with a button-hook, and he pulled the curtains over the glass, made sure there was no gap between them, freed the torn paper from the type-writer roll, tidied up his desk a little, and opened the journal to the page that made him smile, the page that comforted him. The first time he'd read the journal, he had been disappointed because nothing in it seemed to refer to him. He had also been afraid that something would—or, if not afraid, at least trou-bled by unpleasant possibilities. Then he'd read it again. "We don't have enough skilled forgers. We're missing the Master, who knew how to carve flawlessly correct seals. I know there are people with such skills, but not among our group." It had taken him a while to understand this, and smile. They needed him. The Master. He was the Master. He scrawled the word on the blotter. His pen stopped. He'd written it with a capital letter because it was capitalized in the journal. He squeezed his eyes shut and opened them again, flipped through the journal pages at random, not finding what he was looking for. An idea lit up his mind. He'd been so blind.

At first Roland's blunt sentences had annoyed him. He'd been sure there was nothing to be gotten out of them. No names, no places. Just dull reports about the weather and the wonderful sunrises, the sobriety of the movement, condemna-tions of drinking, in fervent phrases. But he'd let the rambling descriptions fool him. Roland had tricked him. The journal was about real people, real places. He would read it again, line by line, listing every capitalized word and studying each one of them as if it had a secret meaning. As if it were a name.

After ten pages he felt his concentration slipping again—the pages went on and on about the difficulty of obtaining paper and printer's ink, about how the poorly mixed ink smudged eas-ily. The expensive paper was so spoiled by the ink that their newsletter was illegible in places, and Roland had been in a rage. Parts decided to take notes on the most useful passages about the precautions the bandits had taken. When the men came in secret to eat in people's homes, they used a common plate so that if they had to leave suddenly there would be less to clean up and they wouldn't have to worry whether someone had remembered to take the extra dishes off the table. A good example of the craftiness of the fascists. The authentic details made Parts's fingers fly again, dashing off line after line—from the kerosene lamps that smoked up the dugouts to the holes in the bottoms of their shoes to the Chekists' sweeps through the forest, turning over every large stone searching for dugouts, to their difficulties with repairing a radio and their joy at acquiring a mimeograph machine. Reflections on how difficult it was to find a good writer for their newsletter, plans to form a separate press division, and another vivid example of fascist cunning that Martinson had doubtless never used: a sleeper agent who had infiltrated the Forest Brothers had been discovered when he asked Roland a simple question about the score of some very recent sporting event—if Roland had known yesterday's sports scores, it would have been clear from his answer that their radio couldn't be more than a day's travel from their camp. No one who was really in the resistance would have asked such a question. Parts read furiously, making note of the occasional capitalized words, his fingers feverishly tracing the well-reasoned analyses of the foreign news, pages about waiting for a war that never came, the war to free Estonia, sentences stinging with bitterness, pages that raged about the March deportations and the collectivization that came afterward.

The vines lashed the window, and Parts closed the journal. He'd found what he was looking for: "But my Heart is safe, which gives me great comfort. My Heart didn't flee to Sweden like a rat, or end up in Siberia. Many others ended up there, including the man who caged my Heart at the church." As he had with "Master," Roland had capitalized "Heart." "I've lost my relatives, but my Heart is still with me, and my family hasn't betrayed me. The future is not lost." Parts had read these sentences before, but he hadn't realized that they were the key to the text: "my Heart," capitalized. It was a code name, probably that of a woman. The first entry about this Heart was as early as 1945. The first about Siberia was in 1950—after the March deportations. Desperation had clearly overtaken Roland, and no wonder; the elimination of banditism had been the first priority of the new minister of security, and he'd done a good job of it. The mention of the church must mean that Roland was talking about this Heart's spouse, but there was no hint in the journal of when the husband had been taken to Siberia. Maybe he was arrested in the early Soviet days, or maybe not until the mass deportations. Roland clearly had feared for the woman's safety: the trains that left in the spring of 1949 were filled mainly with women, children, and the elderly, many of them people whose families had already been taken away, or relatives or supporters of the men hiding in the forest.

Parts went to the kitchen to get some lard from the cutlet he'd fried the night before and spread it on a slice of bread. The Armed Resistance League had for all practical purposes been liquidated, their supporters taken away in the deportations, their ranks shrunken to nearly nothing. Anyone could be a Chekist sleeper agent, and still Roland wrote about the future. Why did he distinguish between his relatives and his family? Who were the ones he considered relatives and who family? Did "family" refer to his forest comrades?

It didn't matter. What did matter was the Heart, the woman whose husband had been sent to Siberia. A woman still living inside the country, who had to be followed, who apparently knew more about Roland than anyone else. Would the Office allow him to search the lists of those sent to Siberia for someone whose wife had remained in Estonia? Not likely. How would he justify such a request? Would Comrade Porkov give him the information as a personal favor? How had the Heart avoided the camps? Had she been with Roland in the forest? "I've lost my relatives, but my Heart is still with me." Did Roland have an intimate relationship with a married woman? What kind of woman was she? A bandit leader's lover, a camp cook for the Forest Brothers, or perhaps just someone who had given them aid? Did she live in the forest? Had she participated in armed resistance? The Armed Resistance League wasn't mentioned in the journal, but the bodies found in the dugout had been those of active members. Would careful Roland have shared all this information with this Heart? Should Parts try to find her not only because she might lead him to Roland but also because she might know everything Roland knew? Was Parts ready to take that risk? A lot of pilots who were shot down never saw their attackers until it was too late. He couldn't make the same mistake. Parts bit his tongue until he tasted blood. He remembered how protective of Rosalie Roland had been. Had he been the same way with the Heart? Or had loneliness driven him to desperation, made him talk? And above all: Was Roland's Heart a threat to Parts? If his own marriage had been different, Parts would have talked to his wife about this; it was just the kind of puzzle her brain was good at.

Parts would never be as careless as he'd been when it came to Ervin Viks. It had been a great shock to walk into the Special Operations office at the Tartu camp and see Ervin Viks behind the desk, signing papers, standing up to greet them. Parts's career had been on the rise, he'd been touring the manufactur-

ing facilities with the Germans, and suddenly a former colleague
from his days in the Soviets' Internal Affairs Commissariat had
materialized in front of him. Viks's eyes had latched on to him,
the recognition uniting them more strongly than any bed could
unite two lovers. For an imperceptible moment Viks had made
a gesture that spoke volumes—had moved his hand across his
Adam's apple, like he was cutting his throat. The captain accompanying Parts had picked up some papers from the desk, read a
bit from them, and Viks had offered to show him around Special Operations, but they had a busy schedule. They'd walked
out of the office, leaving its odor of vodka behind them, and as
they crossed the yard Parts had been afraid the whole time that
one of the prisoners would recognize him and shout his name.
He should have investigated Viks before. Viks was the only one
left who knew that Parts had worked for the Internal Affairs
Commissariat before the Germans came. Viks had obviously
already purged his own past—the fact that Viks had overlooked
him had to be a mistake, a blind spot. Or maybe Viks had just
assumed he'd already been taken care of. But Parts had been in
error, too. How could he not have remembered Viks? He knew
the man's kill tally. Viks was one of those men whose professional skill, whose ability to kill, would always be needed. It had
carried him into the Referentur B4 leadership. Later on, Parts
wondered whether he should try to get close to Viks or stay out
of his range. Viks had a high rank. He couldn't get rid of Viks
easily, but Viks could get rid of him. All he could do was hope
that Viks had become so busy that he didn't have time to chase
down subordinates. Besides, Viks was doing him a favor at the
Tartu camp, in a way—he'd sent thousands who had worked for
or with the Internal Affairs Commissariat to their destruction.
Toadies, informants, yes-men, Bolsheviks. Viks had cleared the
sky for both of them.

Parts decided to be bold and present his request to Comrade Porkov. He needed a list of the deportees whose wives had remained in Estonia. It would be a sizable task, but that was where he would find what he was looking for, and it could be the information that led to a breakthrough.

ВИЛЕНИН
1963

Tallinn, Estonian SSR, Soviet Union

COMRADE PARTS KEPT the journal in a drawer with a false bottom, in a hidden compartment that was originally reserved for photo albums. He'd placed a tiny piece of string between the false bottom and the side of the drawer, and so far he had always found it in place. Roland was just as careful with his Heart in his journal, purposely hidden from outsiders. In fact, Roland had been more careful, had even destroyed his photograph of Rosalie, but World War I Flying Ace Ernst Udet still looked intently out at Parts from the postcard in the photo album. Parts grabbed the album and headed toward the flames of the stove, but the sound of clacking heels from above cut his motion short, the album still cradled in his arms. In his mind, he'd shared all of his thoughts with Ernst, and Ernst had always understood, known how to advise him about evasive maneuvers and tactics, which were as important to Parts as they had been to Ernst in his air battles. Everyone needs a person like that, some-one who understands—even Roland. Had this Heart filled the space left by Rosalie? Had his cousin shared his memories with her, laid his head on her breast and told her everything weighing on his soul, even the things that would horrify her, make her more afraid? The heels clacked again, like a kick in his ear. His eyes leapt to the ceiling, which creaked, whined like a kicked dog as the legs of the bed scraped the floor above. Parts got up from his desk again, locked the album in the drawer again, put the string back in its place, and started pacing around the room. His legs were drawn to the same clacking route traced overhead, and when he noticed this he stopped. His wife might be trying to drive him crazy, but she wouldn't succeed. He sat down with the journal again. He still didn't know how to justify the request for materials to the Office, how to explain why he needed the list. Such an unusual request demanded an unusually strong justification. What would Ernst have done? Ernst had been blamed for the downfall of the Luftwaffe, but it hadn't been his fault. He'd had an ache in his neck that could be cured only by hanging a Ritterkreuz around it. His problem was a pilot's greed for fame, for glory.

Parts squinted, cracked his knuckles, and now that the noise upstairs had quieted, built a story claiming that he remembered a certain anti-Soviet individual who had worked as an assistant to Karl Linnas and would no doubt be of interest to the Office—a woman whose husband he'd met when he was in the camp—and how he'd been surprised that her husband had been taken there and not she, since she was the one active in the resistance. He couldn't quite remember the woman's name, but he was sure he would recognize it if he went through a list. It was a weak story, he realized that. Linnas's appeal shouldn't be underestimated, however, or the fact that Comrade Porkov couldn't resist an opportunity to shine, a chance to prove his effectiveness. Porkov's vanity would be Parts's weapon.

Parts had similar weaknesses; he knew that. He had ap-

proached the journal too arrogantly, thought Roland was simpler than he was. That was why the central clue had eluded him.
It wouldn't happen again. He picked up the journal, although
he had it nearly memorized by now, knew every word of the
two-page explanation of the Russians' skill with bacteriologi-
cal warfare and the Americans' worry over it. There had to be
more, he was certain of that. More than just the Master and the
Heart. Someone in the Office would know how to interpret
the codes better than Parts could, but he couldn't give up the
journal yet. He continued to 1950, where Roland deduced that
both sides feared each other. "No one's talking about Estonia.
Estonia has dropped off the map like an unidentified body on
the battlefield." When it became clear that the men who joined
the destruction battalions were freed from the rules of engagement, there was a bitterness in his words. "The winner doesn't
have to negotiate. That's why the communists have no need to
negotiate with us." Nothing about his family or friends. "The
rats are abandoning ship, heading to Sweden. Our boat is leak-
ing and I'm not sure I can keep it from sinking." More remi-
niscences about the triumphant mood of those first years spent
in the forest, descriptions of the forming of divisions, clearly
referring to regional divisions of the Armed Resistance League.
Those lines in the journal were sure, satisfied. He'd traveled
around the country, met key people in each division. He'd had a
broad network. Where were those men now? Who were they?

Parts wondered once again at how well Roland's plain language sat in a written text. Things that had annoyed him in
Roland's speech had a certain beauty in them, almost a clumsy
poetry, on the page. "Eight dead, ours. Seven yesterday. How
many tomorrow? Lack of new blood is wearing us out, exhaust-
ing us." And again the mention of the Heart. The word was
smudged, right at the bottom of the page. Roland's Heart had

been able to calm the hot blood stirred up among the men by an Austrian radio commentary. The commentator had been certain that the war to free Estonia would never come. "When liberation finally arrives, everyone will suddenly be a patriot. How many new heroes will we have then? But when our fatherland is in danger, those same people grovel and go with the flow, dance for cheap baubles, lick the boots of the traitors, hunting down our brothers for nothing more than the right to buy in a restricted shop."

Parts decided to refresh himself with a sprat sandwich and padded into the kitchen. In the hallway his foot struck a mousetrap his wife had set. There was a wad of handkerchiefs on the floor, including some stolen from his shelf. He kicked them farther down the hallway, then changed his mind and used a towel to pick them up and throw them in the trash. As he made his sandwich, his mind grew clearer. Parts didn't believe Roland had any interest in poetry. At least not so much that he would write it by the page except for some specific reason. Parts remembered a passage in the journal about a poem on the meaning of art, something titled "Dog Ear." Roland said Dog Ear was too individualistic, no use to the movement, disloyal. He questioned Dog Ear's purpose, then started to bad-mouth all the poets in the country. Parts remembered the passage clearly: "Creatures of little talent who call themselves poets. They use their melodious language to swim right in with the Soviet writers, join their circles, where the most minuscule merit can get you something to put on your bread, can buy you a good life. I have nothing but contempt for that. My Heart curbs my hand. Dog Ear isn't worth it." And there it was. Roland had misled him again. Dog Ear wasn't a poem, it was a poet. Roland doubted Dog Ear's loyalty because Dog Ear was a person, not some random line of poetry.

If Dog Ear had turned legal later, he might be easy to find, might know something about this Heart. Maybe he could add Dog Ear's name to the list he'd requested from Porkov. His flimsy justifications for requesting them wouldn't be made any weaker by adding one more name. But he couldn't make it a habit.

Parts mixed himself a glass of sugar water and picked up his sprat sandwich. The milk was spoiled again.

PART FIVE

Known as one of Linnas's henchmen, Mark earned a reputation for cruelty at the Tartu camp. But who exactly was Mark? None of the eyewitnesses or survivors of Mark's horrible treatment knew his last name. Perhaps we ought to define Mark, to learn something about his background. He was an ordinary farmer until he got caught up in Fascist ideology and started attending Fascist meetings. He found a bride who shared his opinions. They felt a particularly strong hatred toward Communism.

—Edgar Parts, *At the Heart of the Hitlerist Occupation*, Eesti Raamat Publishing, 1966

Reval, Estland General Commissariat, Ostland National Commissariat

There were only a few hours left. The adults sat awake on bundles made with sheets and pillowcases, the children slept in the iron beds. Or pretended to sleep. There was no sleep in their breathing; one eye shone brightly open and clamped shut as soon as it met my gaze. I noticed Juudit watching the refugees. I was watching her. Juudit crouched down near an older woman and their whispers tickled my ear as if they were full of secrets, though Juudit would hardly be sharing her personal affairs here, among strangers. She went to help a man with sores on his back. He had taken off his shirt in front of the stove, and she was spreading sulphuric acid on his skin with a goose feather. The smell stung my nostrils. The crowded room was already charged with tension, sighs echoing through it like breaths in an empty bottle, but Juudit's soothing hands reassured me. She seemed to have found the right words for these panicked souls, to know what to say so none of them would lose their heads when it came time to get into the trucks. I couldn't have chosen a better person to receive them. The others had been doubtful when I announced that I'd found an apartment to use as a gathering point and a new person to be there to meet the refugees, telling them her name was Linda. I'd sworn that she was trustworthy, and hadn't said anything about her relationship with a German. I also hoped that the deeper she was involved in the operation, the more likely she was to keep her mouth shut about it. She had started to let crumbs of useful information slip out, and her opinion about everything connected to the Germans seemed to be starting to falter.

This was a particularly restless group of refugees. Hjalmar Mäe's speech had aroused something like hope. According to Mäe, the mobilization would be the first step toward sovereignty. I could see uncertainty in the refugees' eyes, a desire to believe his words. It never ceased to amaze me how gullible people could be. Or desperate. But the numbers of those who didn't trust in a German victory or the Reich's promises of Estonian independence and autonomy were growing day by day. No one wanted to stay and wait for another slaughter. They were sure the Bolsheviks were coming. The pastors were talking about the return of a godless state.

In the coming year we would provide transport to a lot of men seeking to avoid serving in the German army—there were already some in the group, recognizable by their posture. They were brave boys with burning eyes, ready for battle as soon as the boat reached Finnish waters. I secretly hoped that they would form our Estonian corps, the seeds of a new Estonian army, once Germany withdrew. Then we could use the situation to our advantage like we had in 1918, when the Germans left and we struck back at the Reds and won our independence. Captain Talpak was already in Finland organizing the unit. My faith in him was great, and I invoked his name when the boys asked about Estonia's having its own army. The captain had refused to cooperate with the Jerries and many were following his example. Before he fled the country, Richard had written references for our boys, which allowed them to avoid the front and be sent instead to Riga for the Wehrmacht's military intelligence radio training and then return to our forces. The first few had already done that and were just waiting for the moment to spring into action.

Just a few more hours and it would be time. Juudit tiptoed shyly over to me. I made ample room for her. She sat an arm's length away, took the paperossi I offered, and lit it on my outstretched match. A curl was stuck to her cheek. The shadows of her trembling eyelashes showed her anxiety. I noticed that the blue, black, and white enamel ring was back on her left hand.

"What should we do with the pigs?" she whispered in my ear. A drop of spit struck my earlobe. I wiped it away. I could feel the warmth of her body and it felt like a German's warmth. I didn't like it. "The pastor's family refuses to leave them behind."

"Tell them they've been stolen."

She nodded. Arranging these transports was getting more expensive all the time; prices were rising and gougers were playing the market with people's panic. Those without money ended up finding their own means of escape, or staying. But that wasn't enough. Even among the refugees some ugly things went on. There was limited space in the boats, and there were plenty of people like this pastor. Most of them had the sense to slaughter their animals before leaving and pack the meat to bring along, but this pastor apparently thought he could get a better price for a live pig in Sweden.

"You keep watch here," I said, getting to my feet. I could

take the pigs to the cellar to wait for someone to come and get them.

"Watch over what? I'll come with you."

In the dark hallway, she put her hand on my shoulder.

I shook it off. Her voice tightened. "I know you have a problem with me, but don't we have more important things to think about?"

"You're just like the others."

"What's that supposed to mean?"

"Fixing up a nice little future for yourself," I said with unnecessary gruffness.

"Roland, I still think in Estonian."

We started down the stairs carefully, holding on to the railing. There was no moon; it was a perfect night for a transport.

"Germany isn't going to disappear," Juudit said.

There was mockery in my snorting breath—she could hear it.

"And I'm not even getting paid for this," she said, "unlike that weasel Aleksander Kreek, charging a fortune to smuggle people out, and who knows who else. You, for instance."

"I'm not doing this for the money," I snapped.

She stopped, and started to laugh. The laugh spread up and down the stairs and burned up the oxygen until I couldn't get a breath. Did she think I was collecting money for myself, so that I could escape across the sea? Was she just teasing me because I taunted her about her German?

The railing shook as Juudit leaned on it, and I had to let go. The stairs groaned under the weight of her uncontrollable giggles. A door downstairs opened and closed. Someone had peeked out into the hallway. I grabbed Juudit by the shoulder and shook her. The smell of her Baltic baron, his heat, his sickening stench, came out of her gaping mouth, and I had to put one hand over my nose, the other hand squeezing her arm until her delicate elbow popped. She didn't stop, her laughter jerking through my body, mocking my powerlessness. I had to keep her quiet, but I didn't know what to do, feeling her close to me, like a little bird in my hand.

"Are you trying to get us caught? Do you know what they would do to you? Is that what you want? Is that what you're hoping for?"

I tried to listen with one ear for the downstairs neighbor or any noise from outside. Maybe someone had already called the police, maybe we should empty the apartment, but there were still hours to go before the truck arrived. I fumbled for my Walther and my shaky balance faltered. Juudit was limp, not even trying to get loose. We fell onto the landing. Her light body was on top of me, my hand still clutching her arm. Her open mouth closed over mine, her breasts pouring out of her blouse. It was so silent that I could hear the change in her odor, salty as sea stones, her tongue like a slippery tail swimming into my mouth. My body betrayed me, my hand let go of her arm and moved to her hips, and then the thing happened that shouldn't have happened.

WHEN WE GOT OUTSIDE, I adjusted my clothes several times. Juudit washed her hands in the freezing water of the rain barrel. We didn't look at each other.

"Do you think the neighbor will call the police?"

"The neighbor?"

"Your neighbor came to the door."

Juudit may have flinched. "No. She knows my mother. I'll go talk to her once we're back inside."

"Should we pay her off?"

"Roland, she's a friend of my mother's!"

"These days you have to pay even your friends. There are all kinds of people coming and going, and I assume your mother doesn't know anything about what's going on."

"Roland!"

"Pay her something!"

"I can give her some ration stamps. I'll tell her I don't need them."

I took hold of her wet hand and pressed it to my lips, which still tasted of the pure sweetness of her mouth. Her skin smelled like autumn, like raindrops on a ripe apple. I fought back a sudden desire to bite her hand. Where had the smell of her German gone? She smelled like my land, like she was born in my land, like she would molder in my land, my land's own bride, and suddenly I needed to ask her forgiveness for how hard I'd been on her, so many times. The stars sifted through the clouds into her eyes, and her eyes were like forest doves bathed in milk. Darkness covered my awkwardness; I didn't open my mouth. Tender feelings didn't fit the time.

I put my hand on her neck and wrapped a curled wisp of her hair around my finger. Her neck was soft, like peacetime.

Reval, Estland General Commissariat, Ostland National Commissariat

Edgar glanced at SS-Hauptsturmführer Hertz sitting beside him. Hertz leaned against the Opel's headrest, his graceful, manly legs spread. He looked tired of traveling; he was constantly checking his watch, clearly wanting to get where they were going and back to Tallinn as soon as possible. It was a bad sign. Edgar had prepared himself well for the visit. Up-to-date figures waited in his portfolio, neatly arranged. He'd organized a tour to present the progress at the Vaivara manufacturing facility. And there were other matters that needed to be resolved. He'd made arrangements ahead of time with SS-Obersturmführer von Bodmann regarding which things to emphasize. He should talk about prisoners of war—without them it would be tough for Vaivara to succeed. The next prisoner convoy list was once again full of Jewish names. This was a manufacturing camp, administered by the Organisation Todt military engineers—Jews weren't under their jurisdiction. But there was nothing Edgar could do about it unless the others agreed to discuss the matter. They had to find a solution, to get Hauptsturmführer Hertz to listen to Bodmann. He was the head physician of the camp, after all. But Edgar's mind kept coming back to Hertz and Juudit's relationship. In this same car, the man's hand had lifted to touch Juudit's ear; Juudit's hand had perhaps been on this door handle, her handbag on that cushion. On this very seat, Juudit had bent toward her lover, nestled against him, pressed her cheek to his collar insignia, the hem of her skirt perhaps revealing her knees, where the man had perhaps put his hand, Juudit calling him by his first name.

The Hauptsturmführer's collar wasn't smudged with powder this time, his uniform braid didn't smell of a woman who'd rubbed up against it. He would return to Germany or tire of his war bride before long, like they all did. But the gesture of his hand when he'd brushed Juudit's ear still troubled Edgar. The city was swimming with finer ladies, but Juudit had managed to catch a man who could slurp up oysters in Berlin while meting out death sentences in Ostland, a man whose accuracy with a Parabellum would no doubt be just as amazing. She'd caught a man fit for someone better than her. The situation was problematic.

Edgar leaned against the car window, which banged his forehead with every bump. It felt pleasant, shook his thoughts into place, shoved the brain-corroding obsession to the back of his mind. He had never been this close to Hertz— SS-Hauptsturmführer Hertz. The driver's neck was sturdy; his voice was ringing as he hummed and sang. Juudit hardly would have discussed her marriage, but how would Hertz feel if he knew her husband was Mr. Fürst? He would hate him, that went without saying, and it was exactly what Edgar didn't want.

"Bauführer Fürst, I heard that you've had some problems with food smuggling—some of the Todt men bringing food for the prisoners."

"It's true, Herr SS-Hauptsturmführer. We're trying to break the chain. On the other hand, the subversive activity can be kept to a minimum if—"

"We can't allow any exceptions. Why are they doing it?"

Edgar concentrated on staring at the collar insignia. He didn't want his words to come out wrong. It wasn't clear what kind of answer Hertz wanted—something to reinforce his own opinion, something in opposition to it, or something else. The memory of Juudit's gesture brushed Edgar's temple again and he wished he knew what kinds of conversations she had with Hertz. Was she an honest lover, or did she tell him what he wanted to hear?

Edgar coughed. "These people are an unusual case, a disgrace to the race. But it's possible they were attempting to bring food to the camp for Estonians only, not for Jews."

"According to the reports, local people were giving them food as well when they were sent to work outside the camp. Where did such sympathies come from?"

"Outliers, Herr SS-Hauptsturmführer. I'm sure they mean to feed only the prisoners of war. They know that the Jews led the destruction battalions here in 1941. The State Commissariat for Internal Affairs and the Bolshevik Party were led by Jews, we all know that. The politruks and the commissars were all Jews. Not to mention Trotsky, Zinovyev, Radek, Litvinov. The leaders' Jewish backgrounds are well known! When the Soviet Union occupied Estonia, the country was flooded with Jews. They were particularly active in the political reorganization, Herr SS-Hauptsturmführer!"

Hellmuth Hertz opened his mouth and breathed in, as if he

were going to comment on the tone of Edgar's defense. But then he didn't. Edgar decided to take a risk.

"Of course the situation is affected by the fact that some Estonians knew people in the destruction battalions, and those people weren't Jews."

"I'm sure there were non-Jews among them, but the most important ones, the ones who made the decisions—"

"Were Jews. I know." Finishing Hertz's sentence was cheeky, but Hertz didn't seem to notice. He just took out a silver flask and two schnapps glasses. The sudden brotherly gesture delighted Edgar, and the heat of the cognac dispersed the doubts he'd felt in formulating his answers. He couldn't be completely sure whether Untersturmführer Mentzel had kept quiet about his activities during the Soviet days, although he'd given his word. The irony was that Edgar's experience during his years with the Commissariat for Internal Affairs had proved abundantly practical in his work at Vaivara, which was why he dared to assure the Germans that the labor transports would go without a hitch. And they did. He'd had many stimulating discussions on the subject with Bodmann, who had an interest in psychology. People were too afraid of trains. Every car was a reminder that if the Germans withdrew, the next trains would take Estonians straight to Siberia. Some daredevil might bring some bread and water if a Jew managed to tear open a window and thrust a mug out, but Edgar didn't report those incidents, even to Bodmann. Some risks were necessary for the sake of productivity. But what if Hertz's comments about the destruction battalions were meant as a hint? He of all people knew that the talk of Jews in the Soviet army was greatly exaggerated, but did saying so make Edgar questionable? Or was he worrying about nothing—was he just infected by the Germans' worried mood? All around him, faces were growing taut and shrunken, day by day, like mushrooms drying in the oven.

_____

SS-HAUPTSTURMFÜHRER HERTZ carefully lowered his shined boots onto the muddy ground of the camp, his nose wrinkling slightly. Edgar glanced at the guards, among them many Russians, which was good—they wouldn't recognize him. SS-Obersturmführer von Bodmann stepped into the administration barracks as soon as Hertz and Edgar arrived. Greetings, the clicking of heels. Bodmann and Edgar exchanged a glance—they would get right down to business as soon as the formalities were over. Bodmann and Edgar had been on a first-name basis ever since Bodmann realized that they shared the same concerns about what was needed for the camp's success. Sometimes it seemed as if they were the only ones who cared if it succeeded. The labor force was weak and a typhus epidemic had taken a heavy toll; a saboteur had even collected lice from the infected in a matchbox and purposely spread the infection. Bodmann had sent repeated requests for clothing and medicine, but to no avail. If Edgar saw locals giving food to the prisoners, he looked the other way, since there was no danger of being charged for dereliction of duty. The German engineers who had been stationed there with their families, on the other hand, were amazingly strict. An engineer's wife had beaten the Jewish cleaning woman senseless for nothing more than swiping the key to the bread box. With Bodmann he could at least discuss the food problem—with the engineers he clearly couldn't.

"Every prisoner should bring in two cubic meters of shale per day, and from that we can extract a liter of oil in two hours." Bodmann's voice was raised. "Do you understand how the Reich suffers if even one worker provides inadequate input? And it's happening too often. The prisoners of war are physically stronger, but the Jews from the Vilnius ghetto are in such a weakened condition that I need more supplies to get them in working shape. Bauführer Fürst, please explain the situation."

"The business owners don't want Jews. Even if it is a question of just a few thousand, compared to tens of thousands of prisoners of war, delegating the labor is challenging. The prisoners of war are so much more desirable, the results are so much better when we can use able-bodied workers."

"Exactly. Hauptsturmführer Hertz, we've repeatedly inquired about what to do with the elderly—has anyone read our reports? Why should whole families be sent from Vilnius? In some families there are no physically capable men at all," Bodmann said.

"Send them somewhere else," Hertz barked. Edgar noted a slight lack of respect in his tone. Bodmann was the SS-Obersturmführer, after all, and the leader of the camp.

"Out of Estland, you mean?" Edgar asked.

"Out of sight, wherever you like!"

"Thank you. That's exactly what I wanted to know. We haven't received any confirmation for such an action in spite of our requests and Mineralöl-Kommando Estland has promised us more laborers. We need usable workers."

Edgar decided to shift the conversation to the improvements they'd made to the camp:

"We've installed a water main so that water doesn't have to be carried in from outside anymore. The Jews were making contact with the locals when they went to fetch water, and even when we made the trips early in the morning it was still impossible to avoid these encounters. But that's no longer a problem."

A heavy silence settled over the room. Bodmann shook his head imperceptibly.

"Perhaps we'll show you our methods later," Edgar said. "Gentlemen, I've ordered a simple meal. Shall we go to the table?" There was a muttered affirmative.

A shot could be heard outside. Then silence. SS-

Unterscharführer Karl Theiner was probably making his usual rounds, after his work at the infirmary was done. The vein along Hertz's nose twitched and he stood up from the table, his glass untouched.

When they stepped outside, they saw a line of trembling, naked prisoners, white and dry as leather. Their hands tried to cover their genitals. Judging by the wheezing and jerking, the prisoner who was shot wasn't dead yet, but his teeth were already gone and the artist had arrived with his pad to record the event.

All Edgar could make out on Unterscharführer Theiner's shapeless face was his open mouth. He was quite certain that the Unterscharführer had an erection, and that after this titillating experience he had a long night of pleasure ahead of him. Oil wasn't the Unterscharführer's primary area of interest. This had already caused problems.

Hauptsturmführer Hertz drew back. His lighter clinked as he lit a gold-tipped cigarette. The sound of the artist's lead on the pad and the flutter of sketch paper came to them over the coughs and wheezes. Edgar could hear Hertz mumbling something to himself. It sounded like he said power is unbecoming to anyone.

Reval, Estland General Commissariat, Ostland National Commissariat

J UUDIT HAD JUST come in and put her fur stole on the rack in the hallway of her childhood home when there was a knock on the door. The knock was wrong. With her heart pounding in her chest, she opened the stove; retrieved the Mauser, wrapped in a cloth, from behind the stacked wood; laid her coat over the hall stool, with the gun underneath; and threw her silver fox muff on top of it. The knock came again, impatient. Juudit looked at herself in the trumeau mirror. Her lipstick was fine, as were the waves in her hair. Maybe she should flee. But there weren't many alternatives—the window was too high up. Maybe her moment had arrived. Or maybe someone had just forgotten the code—those things happened. People forgot crucial things when their nerves failed them. When she took hold of the doorknob, there was no feeling in her hand.

An unknown man was standing in the hallway. His overcoat was made of good fabric, the cut fashionable. He lifted his hat.

"Good day, ma'am."

"Yes?"

"It's unpleasant standing in the hallway. Could we talk inside?"

"I'm in a bit of a hurry."

The man stepped closer. Juudit didn't move. Her hand squeezed the doorknob. The man bent toward her.

"I want to go to Finland," he whispered. "I'll pay whatever you ask."

"I don't understand what you're talking about."

"Three thousand German marks? Four thousand? Six? Gold?"

"I must ask you to leave. I can't help you," Juudit said. The words came easily, her posture straightened. She would be all right.

"A friend of yours told me to come here."

"A friend of mine? I don't believe we have any mutual friends."

The man smiled. "Ten thousand?"

"I'm going to call the police."

She pulled the door closed. Her hands began to tremble. She could hear the man's footsteps descending the stairs. The clock on the wall was approaching eight. The first family would be coming soon, and they'd been discovered. She had to remain calm, take a few Pervitin, think. Maybe she should just run away. There was still time to escape. Every noise from the street or the hallway made her jump, and yet she stayed where she was. What was she worried about? What did she care what the look on Roland's face would be if she didn't open the door? What would it matter if every person coming here was caught—all of them, one by one? She could still save herself, still warn Roland, even, but the refugees were already headed to her apartment and she didn't know where to divert them. Roland would know, but Roland wasn't here. She picked up her handbag and coat, hid the Mauser underneath her coat, and opened the door. The hallway was quiet; nothing lurked there but the smell of fat frying in a neighbor's pan. She crept down the stairs, careful of the squeaking steps, and went out the back door to the courtyard and behind the shed, where she knew Roland would come, by the same route the refugees would take, through the ruins of the bomb-swallowed buildings. She would wait, melt into the wall of the shed and wait. Maybe the man had been watching her for a long time. Maybe they wouldn't be caught—the apartment looked empty, and she hadn't admitted anything to the man. He might just be investigating, wanting to find out the escape route. Maybe they wouldn't plan an ambush until they knew for sure. If the man at the door was from the police, and if he knew who she was, the same information might fall into Hellmuth's hands at any moment—but this was no time to think of Hellmuth. Of being discovered. She should think about what she was going to do, how to get through this. The answer was clear. She wouldn't let any more people use this apartment for a way station. She would wash the whole house with lye, even the wallpaper, put water on to boil, scrub the black streaks off the basin with borax, rub the copper until she'd polished away all the low suggestions the refugees had made to her, refugees like the man who tried to use a gold watch to buy space reserved for others and give it to his own family. When she was done, she wouldn't remember those people anymore, people willing to leave behind their mother, their mother-in-law, their grandmother, just to bring along more junk, or a horse. Next summer she would gather goatsbeard from the woods and spread it over the floor the way she and Rosalie used to do. The air would be fresh, the floor clean, the scent of the plants would chase away the smell of strangers. That's what she would do once she got through this.

She found a bench next to the woodshed and sat down. Her knees knocked together like a mousetrap. Roland would arrive at any moment. But the first to come through the ruins wasn't Roland, it was a man with two children. She could tell from a distance that they were refugees; their gait was careless, they imagined the darkness hid them. She stopped them. They had the password. She told them the way to the apartment, gave them the keys. There was nothing else she could do. The next family came an hour later: another pastor afraid of the Soviets, and his young bride. No children, just small plywood suitcases. Even in the darkness she could see the tears in the woman's eyes, the man starting at the slightest sound, flinching at shadows. They were followed by a group of boys. Two of them were already on the army's books, but they'd deserted. Juudit couldn't risk lighting a cigarette, for fear the burning end would be seen. She pulled her hat down over her fair hair. The day before, she'd arranged juniper branches on the table. The juniper berries had crosses on them for protection, like rowan berries and bird cherries. Next to them she'd laid a Bible and a print of Jesus on the cross—they would try anything these days, she and the refugees. Why had she agreed to this? Why had she let Roland's wasted life ruin her own? Why had she allowed him to manipulate her, not used her elbows like Gerda did? Why put everything she'd achieved at risk, the milk and honey under her tongue, Hellmuth, Berlin, the cook, the maid, the chauffeur, the Opel, the silk lingerie, the leather-soled shoes, the bread without sawdust? Roland could never offer her that, not any part of it; all he could offer was danger. And what if he was right, what if she was trying to hedge her bets? Was she? Didn't she believe Germany would win? Had she ever believed it? Had the people who'd come through her mother's apartment ever believed it? Had she believed the German promises of Estonian independence, even after she'd heard what they said over their glasses of cognac: Nine hundred thousand people can't make it as an independent country, surely even they understand that.

Juudit got another Pervitin from her purse. It kept the scratch of the mice out of her ears. Roland was late. She didn't dare to think what she would do if he didn't show up. That wasn't an option. Roland had to come, and he would know what to do, although she knew he doubted the ability of his people to act. Many of them had joined for the adventure, as if they didn't understand the stakes at all. Roland's words when he talked of it were full of spit and contempt. No, she wouldn't think about such things right now. Later.

JUUDIT SENSED THAT Roland was near before she saw him. He'd grown familiar with this night trek, his eyes were at their keenest in the dark. Juudit was learning the same skill. When his hand came to rest on her shoulder, she didn't even flinch.

"Why aren't you inside?"

"I was waiting for you. Something happened," she whispered. She told him. The fine hairs on her arms stood up like a bird's down in freezing weather. Roland was so close. He took off his hat and rubbed his hair. She could almost feel the rough dampness of it. For a fleeting moment she remembered how his hair had tickled her neck on the landing, but this wasn't the time to think about that. If Roland would just tell her that everything was under control, she would believe him. He put his hat back on and said:

"We have to stop using the apartment. You're freed from

this job after tonight. Give me the Mauser, the one you hid in the stove."

He was calm, much calmer than Juudit had imagined he would be. As if he'd expected this. Maybe it was an everyday occurrence for him.

"What if . . . ," Juudit began, her voice weak. The soothing words she'd hoped for didn't come.

"I can't hear you. Is your purse full? Give me the gun."

Juudit shook her head. Roland smiled, turned away, and walked toward the back door. Juudit ran after him, grabbed his shoulder. Roland shook her off.

"Let's not go inside. Let's leave."

"We have to arrange the transport."

The words struck her in the chest, pressing down on her.

With every step Roland wanted to turn around, order her to run away, as fast as she could, but he didn't. Being exposed made the courtyard feel like a lamp warehouse display window, and still he behaved as if Juudit didn't matter, as if the situation was normal. This might be his last chance to tell her what was hidden in his heart, the restless feeling that he didn't dare to name, that had started on the landing when Juudit had come too close, a restlessness unbefitting a soldier. The stairs were painted white to make them easier to use in the dark, but Roland stumbled anyway, had to wipe his knees, and, secretly, his eyes. He could still turn around, wrap his arms around his dove-eyed girl, and she wouldn't resist, he knew that. They could run away together. But his hand didn't reach for her, it reached to give the secret knock on the door.

JUUDIT'S NAME SURPRISED HIM, when it came up. Edgar stared at Aleksander Kreek, a celebrated athlete and his former colleague in the political police B4 section, as they sat in the Kalevi sports club in comfortable chairs, the glass of beer Kreek had bought on the table in front of him. Edgar tried to hide his reaction, to behave as if the name meant nothing to him. Kreek had always been a grasping man, and he would ask for something if he noticed Edgar's interest. Edgar's collaboration with Kreek had gone well ever since they were in the B4 in Tallinn, and although Edgar was consumed by his work at the camp, he still managed to come into Tallinn now and then to meet his old contacts, including Kreek. Kreek had been worth the money he'd invested in him in the past, and he still was. Edgar shifted the conversation to other subjects to throw Kreek off, asked about what was happening at the sports club. Since the Germans came, the club had moved back to the space the Bolsheviks had taken from them on Gonsiori Street, and Kreek showed him around enthusiastically. Everything was just as it used to be. Had Edgar really not been back to see it? As Edgar followed him around acting interested, he thought feverishly of ways to get as much useful information as possible, remembering to praise Kreek's athletic career, his impressive shot-putting. It didn't stop the man from asking for gold. He wouldn't lift a finger for marks. Kreek led Edgar to the street door.

"The apartment I was talking about—it's the smugglers' new way station. I sent a man to check on it yesterday, and a woman he recognized opened the door. He'd seen her at the Estonia Theater with some German officers. All those girls look the same, but my man's wife went to school with this one, and she wondered at her fine clothes and said they ought to go up and say hello. When his wife approached the woman, she turned her back on her. His wife was very upset about it. Interesting, don't you think?"

"HOW MUCH?"

"Right to business, eh?" Kreek laughed. Edgar could tell the man was about to leave.

"I don't pay for useless information. Give me an address. Names."

"My man could only remember her first name—Juudit."

Edgar slipped a bundle into Kreek's coat pocket. Kreek left the room and returned a moment later.

"The address is Valge Laeva 5-2."

Edgar's own mother-in-law's apartment. The one Juudit lived in before her German. Auntie Anna had told him about it, that Juudit had moved there, before Johan was taken away. Edgar tried to remain calm—Kreek might get the idea of making more demands if he realized how valuable the information he'd just sold really was. It was time to act. If Kreek knew about it, someone else almost certainly did, too. The situation had changed. There was no longer time to wait for the right moment, the moment when he could use Juudit's relationship with Hertz. But he had an opportunity to use Juudit in other ways—if the smugglers were exposed carefully, with his help, it would be seen as his accomplishment. To make that happen, he needed someone Juudit would talk to, someone she trusted at least a little. Someone Edgar could trust, too. Auntie Anna. And Leonida.

Reval & Taara Village,
Estland General Commissariat,
Ostland National Commissariat

WHEN JUUDIT FINALLY WENT to get her mail from the apartment, now emptied of refugees, there were letters waiting for her from Anna and Aunt Leonida. The letters had a tense tone. Leonida didn't understand why she hadn't seen Juudit in such a long time, and Anna wondered whether Juudit had abandoned them completely. She must come and visit. Aksel was butchering a pig for Christmas; they were going to make headcheese. They missed her tremendously. Because the farm could get young people from the cities to do the haying and potato digging for their required community service, Juudit had stopped going to the countryside, pleading that she was too busy at work. Her excuses had been completely believable. Anna's and Leonida's weren't. She checked to make sure there was nothing left in the apartment that would indicate the owner was involved in underground activities, and made a decision. She wanted to know what this was all about. And taking some time for herself, away from Hellmuth's eyes, wasn't a bad idea. Her time of the month had come when it was supposed to, and she hadn't heard from Roland or seen him. All of that was over and her life had returned to its usual course, or at least as calm a course as was possible with Germany in this prickly situation. But still it would be good to be away from the city for a little while. Juudit didn't know how the last refugee transport had gone, and she didn't want to know. She had saved herself, that was the most important thing. Her luck might not be as good next time. The fear that had gripped her during that last transport was unlike any she'd ever known—bright as a floodlight—and she didn't intend to experience it again. She had kept the Mauser, however, and hidden it on the same shelf where she'd once hidden the boots meant for Roland.

She decided to give her mother's apartment a thorough disinfection. There was a shortage of cleaning chemicals, but Hellmuth could help take care of that.

JUUDIT HAD PREPARED HERSELF for innuendos about her scandalous life, had assumed that rumors must have finally reached the farm. But there was no indication that anyone at the Armses' place had anything against her except that she'd been away so long. She was ordered straight to the table, where lung cutlets were waiting. The petrol she'd brought as a gift elicited a flood of gratitude. Anna and Leonida continued their work and refused her help—she ought to rest after her long journey. The granite stone was heated on the stove and Leonida opened the newly butchered pig's stomach while Anna participated in her usual unhelpful way, bustling around behind her. Along with the pig, they offered up village gossip: the rats had killed their best mouser, a high-ranking officer had summoned Lydia

Bartels to Berlin, Mrs. Vaik was living at the Bartelses' place alone now. Neither Anna nor Leonida seemed concerned about their children, though they did mention that Roland's gelding was all right—Aksel said he always went to the barn when the sky started to rumble.

The two women were talking around something, circling it like hungry crows. The air in the kitchen was heavy with people who were absent, dense with prattle about the "war of nerves." There might be an ultimatum made to Germany and its allies at the conference in Tehran, they said, and Leonida added something about how it was all a bluff, a propaganda war aimed at Germany:

"Of course we know that every one of these announcements is just another Bolshevik attempt to cover their own weaknesses and difficulties. We just have to remember that. You have to be prepared to defend against psychological bombs, too. Isn't that right, Juudit?"

JUUDIT FLINCHED, nodded. They hadn't mentioned her husband once. They hadn't hinted at her bad reputation. Leonida groaned as she lifted the stone into the pig stomach. There was a hiss and a sputter, steam rose as the hot stone rolled inside it and cleaned it. The kitchen was filled with the smell of scorched meat. Juudit remembered her first visit to the Armses' farm after she'd heard about Rosalie's fate. She'd left Tallinn immediately and found the kitchen at rest, as if on a sickbed, none of the work done except for the fire lighted in the stove, Leonida fumbling for the handkerchief in her sleeve without ever managing to get it out, leaving it bulging there like a tumor. Now Rosalie's spirit had faded from the house; everything connected with her had been gathered up and Leonida had to turn the intestines and wash and salt the stomach alone, make the sausage alone, without Rosalie. Juudit still didn't fully grasp that Leonida would never have her daughter back, Juudit would never have her cousin back, as if Rosalie had never been a part of this family, as if Roland had never been engaged to Leonida's daughter. The house had never felt so strange, and Juudit had never felt so strongly that she didn't belong here.

It was just as impossible to understand why she herself didn't say a word about Rosalie, why she joined the ranks of the silent. Maybe there was nothing to say. Maybe life was so fragile and meaningless that there was no need to add to their troubles. There was headcheese to be made, lard to be rendered; there were intestines to be salted for next year's sausage—so much work to do, all to maintain the fragile lives of others. When she'd been waiting for Tallinn to be destroyed, and hoping for her own destruction, she hadn't understood this, but now she did, ever since the refugee incident. She had too much to lose. Maybe Leonida and Anna did, too. The thought made her look at them with new eyes. Was the extra money they made from the sale of the lard reason enough to keep silent?

The stone in the stomach had stopped hissing. Leonida and Anna had been watching her the whole evening, she was well aware of that.

"Juudit, there's something I wanted to talk to you about."

IT WASN'T UNTIL she got home to Roosikrantsi Street that Juudit's tightly stitched patience failed her. With trembling hands she mixed a sidecar that sloshed over the edge of the glass, and the parquet floor rocked like the deck of a ship. Had Anna gone crazy? And what had happened to the sensible Leonida? Their demands were unreasonable, worse than Roland's.

After the third sidecar, her head started to clear, but she couldn't sit still. She opened the kitchen cupboards, glad that she had given the cook time off. She'd found a note from Hellmuth on the table: due to urgent business he had to travel, would return in a week. So she had time to calm down, to think about what to do. She finally found some eggs, checked to make sure the bowl was clean, cracked them, mixed in some sugar, and started to whip them. She whipped her way into the bedroom, took a gramophone disk from the dress box in the wardrobe, started the Boswell Sisters playing, and whipped. Paul Whiteman was next in line. She whipped until it started to get dark, time for the blackout blinds. The eggs turned shiny and stiff. She wrote in the top of them, like she had as a girl. The man she would marry. Then she realized she hadn't written *H*, for Hellmuth, in the pale yellow surface; she'd written a *D*, for Deutsch.

She fetched a spoon, sat down next to the gramophone, and ate the whole bowlful. Her access to a pantry full of eggs could disappear at any moment. After the last refugee transport she'd resolved to never again put herself in a position that threatened her quality of life. But how could she have known that a new threat was waiting around the corner? She snapped open her purse and took out her tube of Pervitin. Two tablets. It helped a little. Not enough. Her mind was whirring like Anna's spinning wheel. Where had Anna and Leonida got the idea to start organizing refugee routes? Weren't they afraid for themselves anymore, for the farm? Leonida obviously didn't understand Juudit's work, her position; she had seemed sincerely puzzled when she saw Juudit's reaction to her suggestion, when Juudit said, "How can you be planning such a thing? After all the Germans have done for Estonia!"

"We have to get these people out of the country."

"What does that have to do with me? Besides, it's winter," she had protested.

"They can go over the ice. We have to save them if we can."

Anna's thin skin had been splotched with excitement, and her shrill voice had joined in with Leonida's lower pitch. "You're a part of this family. Can't you be helpful for once? Have you forgotten my uncle? He killed himself the moment the Russians' first planes appeared in our skies, because he'd seen the Russian revolution. Have you forgotten what we experienced during Bolshevik times? The communists will kill us all!"

Juudit had left after a loud exchange of words, without saying goodbye, without taking her package of headcheese. Did they really think that she, who worked for the Germans, would be so easy to convince? It was too much of a coincidence that these old women would choose that moment to suggest refugee aid to Juudit. If Leonida knew, then the whole country knew. This was too small a place for secrets. Only Rosalie remained a secret.

When she'd dashed out of Leonida's house, Aksel had caught up to her quickly with his horse, insisting that she get in the sleigh. She had stomped her felt boots for a moment, squeezed her fists inside her muff, then relented. Aksel wasn't conciliatory, didn't demand that she come back; he just set off to take her to the train station, patted her shoulder clumsily, and said she should forgive Leonida.

"She's not the same woman she used to be. Sorrow has few words."

The only change Juudit had noticed in Leonida was a heart grown colder, but she didn't want to argue with Aksel.

"And Anna is terrified of the Russians coming. She can hardly sleep, stays up all night listening to the sky. That's how it is."

Aksel had already turned away, ready to leave. "Our only daughter," he said as he climbed into the sleigh and disappeared in a puff of snow.

Juudit snapped an icicle from the eaves of the station and bit it as she went looking for the station office. She found a telephone there and placed a call to Hellmuth's chauffeur, who had dropped her off at the station earlier to wait for Aksel and gone ahead to the hotel. It would have been too complicated to explain why a secretary had an Opel and a chauffeur at her disposal.

She'd spent the night at the hotel before returning to Tallinn. On the way home she'd asked the chauffeur to stop at the cemetery. The grave had no marker. As if Rosalie had never existed. Juudit didn't know what she had come for, but she was sure of one thing—she would no longer have anything to do with Anna or Leonida. All of a sudden she understood those people who would rather bring their possessions onto the boat than their families.

Reval,
Estland General Commissariat,
Ostland National Commissariat

THIS WAS the second day in a row that Juudit had let Roland into the Roosikrantsi apartment before Hellmuth got home, and she didn't know how to explain it to herself; lately she wasn't sure who she was more afraid of, or why. There were too many Germans coming and going—the military commissary and court were right nearby—and yet she let Roland come to the apartment. Yesterday he'd been dressed as a chimney sweep, today as a delivery boy from Weizenberg's grocery. The precautions he took did nothing to calm Juudit as she kept watch in the entryway. She listened in turn to the sounds from the hallway and Roland working in the office, but who else could she turn to? There was no one else she could talk to about Anna and Leonida's intentions, no one else who could help her, or even advise her, no one she could trust in these matters even a little. Roland's attitude had once again surprised her. He insisted that the whole thing was a coincidence and then immediately used her moment of weakness to demand that she let him into the Roosikrantsi apartment. Roland was so naive. Contrary to what he imagined, Estonia would never need witnesses to the destruction wrought by the Germans; there would be no war reparations, because Germany wasn't going to lose. Or had she let Roland in because she herself no longer believed in a German victory? Or was the real reason Hellmuth's comment before he went to Riga, that perhaps a life in the South Estonian countryside wasn't for them after all? Maybe there was no place in Estonia for them. Hellmuth had thought that Berlin would always be open to them, but who could feel welcome in a place where there was war? Juudit agreed completely. She wanted to get away from it. With Hellmuth, and quickly.

She'd thought about it for many nights and days, thought about Berlin or some other metropolis where no one would know she had divorced, or rather left, her husband. Her relatives, acquaintances, Roland, everyone here could talk about it and she wouldn't care in the least. But it was a long way to Berlin. It was a long way to anywhere. Was Hellmuth really willing to settle someplace other than Germany, someplace where no one would look askance at a German from the Reich attached to an Estonian woman? Like Commandant Drohsin at Ereda and that Jewish woman, Inge Syltenová. Juudit had seen the report in Hellmuth's office. They had fallen in love, the commandant had escaped, and friends at the prison had dug a tunnel for Inge. They were caught attempting to reach Scandinavia and they committed double suicide. But of course Juudit and Hellmuth weren't in the same situation. As she got up to put out her cigarette, Juudit wondered if she dared ask Hellmuth whether they had any money other than ostmarks. Did they have enough Reichsmarks? It would be better yet if they had gold. Or even silver. Something. She ought to have accepted the gold watches from the refugees. Why had she been so childishly honorable about that? If Hellmuth wasn't willing to go someplace other than Germany, he wouldn't have been talking about places without war—there was no other way to interpret it. So why was she risking their future by letting Roland into Hellmuth's office, when the cook or the maid might come back from the market at any moment?

The office door slammed. Roland's steps creaked across the parquet floor of the drawing room.

"I hope you left everything in its place," Juudit said.

Roland didn't answer, just went to the servants' entrance, shoving his notes into his breast pocket. On the threshold he stopped and turned to look at Juudit, who stood swaying between the mirrored drawing room doors.

"Come here."

Juudit's eyelashes pressed her gaze down to the pattern of parquet. Too much mascara. That's all it was. It was such a long way to the door; Roland was so far away. She held on to the doorjamb, put her right foot over the threshold, then her left, held on to the kitchen table, the sink, and finally stood in front of him, wobbling like a gelatin.

"There was one other thing," Roland said. His field jacket smelled of questionable lodgings, smoke, a coat that hadn't been taken off to sleep. "The Feldgendarmerie intercepted three trucks. They were all full of refugees. Two of the trucks were organized by Kreek."

"Kreek?"

"I'm sure you remember him. The shot-putter. Two of his fishermen are members of our ring. Kreek charges the refugees three thousand marks and gives twenty percent to the truck driver. The money's collected from the refugees before they get in the truck. They don't have to pay the fishermen if the cargo never arrives. Kreek has to be stopped. Should have been stopped a long time ago. You could do it—Juudit, don't look so frightened."

"How?"

"Tell your German about it."

Juudit stumbled backward. "You can't ask me to do something like that. How would I explain how I got the information?"

"Just tell him that you've heard rumors about someone who's organizing refugee transports by sea. He can take care of the rest."

"But they'll be killed."

Roland came up very close to her. His eyes were hidden under his hat brim—he'd left his hat on when he came inside. "What do you think happens to the ones who fall into the hands of the Feldgendarmerie?"

Juudit wrapped her arms around herself in a lonely woman's embrace. The handkerchief in her shirt cuff throbbed against her wrist.

"Don't fret about Anna and Leonida. I already told you, forget what they said."

"How?"

"Trust me, it's just a coincidence that they mentioned their idea to you. Old women talking nonsense."

She didn't believe him. It couldn't be a coincidence. He just wanted to keep her calm. She squeezed her arms tight. Maybe the whole situation was so desperate that Roland was secretly planning an escape. Maybe all of them knew deep down what was going to happen, so there would be no point in telling Roland about the conversations Hellmuth had with the other officers in the evenings: ". . . Wouldn't it change the Führer's opinion if we had to leave Finland? . . . Ostland must not be surrendered, Ostland must not be surrendered, that's all they keep repeating in Berlin. . . . For Sweden's sake, of course. So that Sweden can hold its line, and the Führer probably also has the idea that we have friends in Finland, people who won't tolerate a new regime, who need our support. . . . It's crazy! All for the sake of Sweden and Baltische Öl. We can't take another hit. We can't defend ourselves. . . ." Once, after too many cognacs, Hellmuth had curled up next to her and said he suspected they couldn't fight off the Bolsheviks much longer. "But you can't talk about this, you understand? With anyone. Think of the hysteria it would cause if the Estonians thought we couldn't hold our own against the Bolsheviks. . . ." And Juudit had nodded. Of course, she said.

Instead she presented a demand to Roland before she'd even had time to think it through:

"I'll expose Kreek and the others on one condition: that Hellmuth and I are given places on a boat when the time comes. I'll pay all the costs."

She was immediately horrified by her own words. What had she said? She hadn't talked about any such plans with Hellmuth. Was she hoping Roland would refuse, ask her to come with him instead? Why didn't she explain? Why didn't she tell him that she was afraid of Anna's stupid scheme?

Roland's cheeks twitched. But he didn't ask why Hellmuth wanted to leave, didn't ask why Juudit was willing to leave behind not just Tallinn but also Berlin, didn't ask if she and Hellmuth had already planned this. He didn't ask anything. He said:

"Fine."

1944

GROSSDEUTSCHES REICH

Reval, Estland General Commissariat, Ostland National Commissariat

THE APARTMENT WAS SILENT. Juudit sensed Hellmuth as soon as she stepped inside the front door, but the apartment was silent, the hall was still, the kitchen mute, the air motionless, the servants sent away. The moment had arrived, she knew it at once. The floor in the hallway sighed as if with regret; the drawing room curtains were pulled tightly shut, their pleats fossilized; the leaves of the ficus were grayish. Juudit put her silver fox on the trumeau. It slipped off and fell curled up on the floor. She took off her coat. It resisted. The sleeves wanted to go back out into the hallway; her overshoes didn't want to come off, and when they did come off they flew toward the door, their toes pointing out toward the stairway. She could still dash out, down to the street, but maybe there was already a car waiting there. Maybe there was a row of men waiting for her. Maybe the whole building was surrounded. Juudit's breath caught in her throat, the sound of it echoing in the drawing room. Her mouth had dried up, felt like it was about to crack at the corners. Her light shoes thudded like furniture ready for moving. She could still try, still run. There was still time. But instead she stepped over the threshold into the bedroom. She'd already guessed that Hellmuth would be sitting in the armchair, the table beside him with its lace cloth, on the cloth the Parabellum. He was wearing his greatcoat; his hat was thrown on the bed, and next to it Juudit's Mauser. The hot air burned Juudit's cheeks. Hellmuth's skin was white, his forehead dry. Juudit took off her hat with trembling hands, held the hatpin in her fist. It was so hot, her underslip was bruised with sweat, which would soon spread to her dress as well.

"You can leave if you want to."

Hellmuth's voice was matter-of-fact. The kind of voice he might use as he stepped into headquarters, the voice he must have used every day at Tõnismägi, but never when talking to her, not until now.

"I'll let you go."

Juudit took a step into the room.

"No one will come after you."

Juudit took another step.

"You have to leave right now."

Hellmuth's hand lay on the lace tablecloth. Beside it gleamed the Parabellum, well polished, ready.

"I don't want to leave like that," Juudit heard her voice say, somewhere far away.

"At this very moment the whole ring is being arrested. I won't insult you with explanations. I'm sure you understand."

She took one more step. She reached a hand toward the dressing table and fumbled for the cigarette case and lighter. The flame leapt up. *Roland!* Had Roland been arrested, too?

"Can I sit down?"

Hellmuth didn't answer. Juudit sat down. Roland was already lost. That must be how it was. A broken spring pressed against her leg. She would never fix this chair. She would never again dress in front of this table to spend an evening at the Estonia. The hatpin sweated in one hand, the cigarette trembled in the other.

"I was given a job. I was supposed to get to know another person, not you," Juudit said. "At Café Kultas. I was supposed to strike up a relationship with this other person. It was something that my friend's fiancé thought of, not me. But then you were there."

The ash from the cigarette fell to the floor. Juudit pressed the calfskin sole of her shoe on it, then slipped her shoes off her feet and took off the bracelet Hellmuth had given her and dropped it on the dressing table. It shone like thirty pieces of silver.

"I didn't dare tell you. And I didn't want to not meet you."

"They must have been very pleased with you. Excellent work. Congratulations."

Juudit got up and started taking off her dress.

"What are you doing?" Hellmuth said.

"This is yours." She folded the dress carefully and laid it next to the bracelet. The splotches of sweat had spread from her sides to her back and hips. "I understand what this could mean for you," she said.

"Are you listening to me? They're coming to get you right now, at any moment. You have to leave."

"But if I'm the only one who isn't arrested, the others will suspect I'm a traitor."

"That's not my concern. The prisoners won't know who was arrested. They were picked up separately."

"Do you think they'll believe you had nothing to do with this? That you didn't know? Hellmuth?"

"Don't say my name."

Hellmuth looked past her. His hand was raised, his palm toward her as she tried in vain to catch his eye. He got up, took two quick steps, grabbed her by the arm, and started to push her toward the door. She resisted, wrapped her foot around the leg of the chair, clung to the door frame. Her hatpin fell on the floor. Hellmuth shoved her against the doorjamb, toward the front door, still not looking at her.

"Come with me," Juudit whispered. "Come with me away from here, away from everything."

Hellmuth didn't answer, just pulled as she struggled, and Juudit's feet caught on the drawing room chairs and tables and the chairs fell over, the rug buckled, the folds of the fossilized curtains fell apart, the vase fell to the floor, the ficus fell, everything fell, Juudit fell, Hellmuth fell with her, their bodies fell together and their tears carried them away.

Vaivara, Estland General Commissariat, Ostland National Commissariat

NARVA CAMP WAS the first to be evacuated; two days later, Auvere and Putki, then Viivikonna. The prisoners were all sent to Vaivara. Because of the lack of space the Vaivara children and the sick barracks were moved to Ereda, and the Viivikonna command center to Saka. Edgar ran from place to place, cursed the weather and the scarcity of the provisions, received evacuees staggering from their long journey on foot, directed the Wehrmacht trucks that brought the prisoners who were too exhausted to walk, organized more men to take care of the horses carrying the sick, sent some of those in a weakened condition to the civilian hospital, refusing to pause, to return to that desperate moment when his work detail was ordered to prepare to receive the evacuees from Narva camp. The Germans kept stubbornly repeating that this was just a temporary measure, but who could believe that? The production facilities they'd built were probably already being demolished. It was only a matter of time before the front collapsed.

When Edgar's courier brought his monthly order of Manon tobacco straight from the Laferme factory, Bodmann came to pick up his share and shook his head—these evacuation plans weren't realistic. The prisoners would never be able to walk all the way to Riga. Why did they ask his opinion and then not listen to it. Edgar lay awake at night considering his options. The opportunities the camp offered in the cigarette business would soon be lost. He hadn't been to Tallinn in months. The operation to eliminate the refugee transport ring had been successful but he didn't even know who had been arrested. What had been a very simple plan in the beginning had proved complicated, although Auntie Anna had understood immediately that the saboteurs and army deserters who had wormed their way into the packs of refugees had to be caught or they would weaken Germany. Anna and Leonida had done their best and hadn't revealed the true purpose of the extremely confidential plan. Juudit, on the other hand, had behaved contrary to expectations. She got angry and left, cut off contact completely. Edgar had made a mistake when he imagined that he knew his wife's way of thinking and acting. He wouldn't make that mistake again. In the end he thought of a solution. He sent two women pretending to be refugees, with children in tow, to the place on Roosikrantsi. They rang the doorbell when Juudit was at home and she had no choice but to let them in, then take them to the way station. Edgar had sent his man to report the address of the refugee way station to SS-Hauptsturmführer Hertz. He didn't mention Juudit's name. Hertz had promised to take care of the matter, after which he never contacted Edgar or came to Vaivara. He'd been transferred. The liquidation of the ring hadn't brought Edgar the recognition he'd hoped for and his mind was plagued with forebodings—not only was all the work he'd done at Vaivara a waste of time, he had also apparently gone to a lot of trouble for nothing in his other operations as well. Now his hands were tied.

———

IN MAY the Führer ordered a halt to all evacuations. The front was stable. Immediately afterward there was an order to begin construction of a new production facility. The news would have been encouraging if Edgar's tobacco courier hadn't told him the rest—the fighters from Tartu, who were in the thick of it, were certain that the Germans were preparing to evacuate children and women by force and send the men to the camps. Tallinn was in complete chaos. The highways were crowded with people fleeing from the city to the countryside and other people trying to make it into the city to get to the harbor. The Germans, however, were sending out propaganda supporting legal means of escape—you could go to Germany, although no one seemed to be interested in heading in that direction. The Reichsführer had pardoned all draft dodgers and any Estonians who'd fought with the Finnish forces if they returned to fight against the Bolsheviks and clear their traitorous records. Amid all this, Edgar was stuck in the Vaivara mud, but a new opportunity arose when the men from B4 came to make an inspection and told him about the problems at the Klooga camp. The laborers were already evacuated from Klooga, and because the trains were full they hadn't been allowed to take any luggage with them, and there were heaps of their belongings on the ground that the guards were picking through like crows. The local people had seen the abandoned piles of clothes and now there was a rumor spreading that the evacuees were being drowned by the boatful, so these men had been sent to investigate what was happening at the other camps. Edgar was ordered to show them around Vaivara to prove that they didn't have any such problems. That was when a new plan formed in his mind. Bodmann had said that Klooga had the best conditions and the highest-quality results of any camp in Estonia—the laborers were housed in stone buildings, and the food portions were sensible because food distribution was done through the Waffen-SS's Truppen-wirtschaftslager. The work was also cleaner—manufacturing depth charges and lumber. The most attractive aspect of Klooga, though, was that it was closer to the evacuation points in Tallinn and Saaremaa, and farther from Narva and the Soviet border. Edgar decided he had to get there. While he was giving the B4 men the tour, he offered them some tobacco and told them about his career in B4, making clear that he would happily continue working at the camp, but . . . He gestured at his surroundings and received knowing nods in response. They promised to get back to him. An evacuation order interrupted the tour. The order was canceled two hours later. The following weeks were equally chaotic: the commandant making telephone calls all night, one day's instructions retracted the next, workers sometimes ordered to the harbor, sometimes to their normal work in oil production, sometimes ordered to evacuate, and Edgar finally sent to Klooga. He left his entire stash of Manon tobacco to Bodmann out of sheer relief.

Klooga, Estland General Commissariat, Ostland National Commissariat

A MACHINE GUN HAD APPEARED next to the barracks. Roll call.

SS-Untersturmführer Werle strutted to the front.

The prisoners were to be evacuated to Germany.

SS-Hauptscharführer Dalman started calling out men who were physically strong to prepare for evacuation.

Another roll call.

I was used to the constant control and roll calls, but something was different this time. I recognized a few Estonians among the prisoners. Most of them were Latvian and Lithuanian Jews. I waited for my own name. It hadn't come yet. It would soon, I was sure. Just as sure as I'd been when I got into the truck at Paterei that I was being taken away for execution. But I was alive; I'd been brought here. I peered around, looking for other Estonians from the same transport, not daring to turn my head, but I saw only three. Alfons, the mail girl's fiancé, was still next to me. He'd been brought from Patarei, too. He'd deserted from the German army and gotten caught. My name would be called soon. I was sure it would.

They had added new guards to the camp the day before.

Work was interrupted. We weren't sent to our posts, and no workers came from outside the camp, not even the Finn who sometimes gave us a little bread. Connections between the prison camps were good. Messages were hidden among the cargo sent from one camp to another. I'd even found a list of names marked with where the prisoners were from and where they'd been sent. I asked about Juudit. I'd asked about her in Patarei, too. No one had heard anything, not even our trusted Estonian guard. Maybe she'd paid her way in gold onto some ship, posing as a German. I hoped she had. Or that she'd been shot immediately.

We were given soup at lunch. It was good, a little better than usual, and it calmed the other prisoners, but not me. The Untersturmführer walked past me talking in a loud voice, almost yelling, telling the cook to leave some soup for the three hundred who'd been taken to the woods. Said they would need it after a hard day's work.

The prisoners were ordered to line up again. Standing made me dizzy, although I'd just eaten.

The gates of the camp were clogged with trucks.

We weren't going to get out of this alive.

The afternoon advanced. Six men were chosen from the rows of prisoners. Two oil barrels were rolled onto a truck. The guards ordered us to sit in front of the barracks. They were restless, pale. One of them was so nervous that he couldn't get his paperossi lit and just threw it on the ground, from where it was immediately snatched up. The guards looked more frightened than the prisoners.

The next fifty were ordered to the front of the lines. The evacuation would be done in groups of fifty, at most a hundred at a time. Up to that point they had called only for Jews. Alfons whispered that the Estonians would soon have work to do—they would kill the Jews first, the Estonians afterward. The Germans were leaving to escort the prisoners. That was when Alfons made his move. The cook stumbled as he walked past us. The guards turned to look. The cook whimpered and rubbed his ankle. We were ordered to carry the cook and push the soup cart. The kitchen was deserted, but the cook was suddenly lying on the floor with a broken neck. The guard was still at the door, looking out at the yard. Alfons made a signal. Suddenly we were out the kitchen window, in another window, going up stairs to an attic, and from there onto a roof.

There was a bustle at the gates. We tried to be as invisible as possible. It wasn't difficult, we had become very thin. The guard in the kitchen doorway dashed back and forth and yelled for assistance. They were searching the kitchen, opening and closing cupboard doors.

Alfons whispered, "They'll give up soon enough. Looking for missing prisoners would arouse attention, make people restless. They're supposed to act calm."

He was right. The guards left the kitchen, and the cook's body, and went back outside. I watched them march across the yard. Suddenly I spotted a familiar profile among them, and almost fell off the roof, but managed to keep my composure and my balance.

"Have you ever seen that man here before? Working as a guard or anything?"

"That one?" Alfons said. "I'm not sure."

The prisoners were being driven toward the women's barracks. I could see the camp barber and shoemaker. Circulating among the troops was an unmistakable figure. That bouncing walk, unlike any other.

I was too far away to see his expression clearly, but I could tell that my cousin was not overcome by panic like the guards, not to mention the prisoners. His pulse may have been racing from excitement, but not from fear.

He held his head high.

Fighting had never suited him.

Evidently this did.

Reval, Estland General Commissariat, Ostland National Commissariat

Edgar knocked on the SS-Hauptsturmführer's door again, harder this time. The sound echoed through the corridor. He listened. The building was still. The only sound was a dog's bark downstairs. There wasn't a German to be found in the Roosikrantsi neighborhood these days. The commissary doors had been torn open, the shops had been emptied, the patients had disappeared from the hospital. Edgar took a lock pick from his pocket. He'd made it himself, and it had proved very useful. The lock clicked open. The apartment was deserted, the servants gone. The living room was a mess. A dried-up ficus lay among fragments of its broken pot, the soil strewn around the room. The carpet was crumpled, the curtain torn half off its rod. Edgar glanced quickly into each room. The office cabinets were open, the drawers empty. In the bedroom he could smell Juudit's perfume. A few dresses still hung in the wardrobe. The dressing table drawers gaped open. Empty. Kitchen cupboards, empty. Edgar checked the windows. Aside from some cracks, they were intact. There was just dust on the bureau and windowsills, no ash from a bombing. The potting soil was dry as a bone, on the cocktail cart there were glasses whose contents had evaporated, and on the smoking table an April issue of *Revaler Zeitung*. Edgar found a bottle of juice in the cold pantry, opened it greedily, and sat down to think. The chaos of the apartment wasn't from the Germans' departure. It happened longer ago than that. If Juudit was arrested, she hardly would have been allowed to pack. Had the servants emptied the apartment after she left? But why such a mess? What was the hurry? The dining chairs were gone. There were signs of more haste than in other Germans' homes he'd seen. Had there been a fight? Was the mess the aftermath of the arrest, or something else? Had Hertz kept Juudit's part in the ring secret, or delayed its discovery so that the spotlight wouldn't be shone on him? Had Hertz himself been in trouble? Perhaps Juudit and her lover both were already on their way to Germany.

When Edgar had finally gotten away from Klooga and made it to Tallinn, the city had already been emptied of Germans. His stomach had started to gnaw at him, but he didn't let desperation get the better of him, didn't allow himself to break down, even though he guessed that all the ships had already sailed. An Opel Blitz full of harried Germans had pulled into Klooga the morning before the camp liquidation and disappeared the moment it was over. He should have escaped then, or spent the night with the guards who'd run away from the camp, instead of waiting for permission to get in the truck that brought the last of them to the harbor. But it was too late for regret. Everyone was gone. The Germans' medical stores and clinics were empty, the army barber and shoemaker vanished, nothing left of the Soldatenheim but the sign, the washbasin built into the floor of the laundry on Vene Road. The Estonian flag was flying from the pole at Pikk Hermann. He had stopped to stare at it. A kid running down the street had told him that Admiral Pitka's men were meeting to defend Estonia's new government. "And Captain Talpak is here, too! All the good men of Estonia are arming themselves! The Russians will never get in here again!"

He was too late. He would never get to Danzig. This was confirmed when he reached the harbor.

THERE WAS no time to think it all through. He got up too quickly from the table and his head spun from the hunger and the vomit from the camp that clung to his boots. The smell hadn't hit him until now. After wiping them with a dampened towel, he went into the bathroom to freshen up, without looking in the mirror. He knew himself well enough to realize that he now had the same look on his face as the other people who'd been in the truck that brought him to Tallinn. When the truck broke down, the others had turned their back on the harbor, the German army, the Germans' orders. They started walking toward home. Edgar headed toward the harbor.

Water still came out of the bathtub faucet and he allowed himself a quick wash, tried to shake the sleepless fog out of his brain, and went into the office. He didn't find any valuables, no gold, no silverware. All that was left of the desk accessories were a few ink stains on a blotter. He should have acted sooner, made Juudit tell him where things were hidden, where the most important papers were, the gold and other valuables, should have arranged a time to clean out the apartment while the refugee ring was being arrested, but he'd been optimistic, naive. Too late again, even when it came to this. But this was no time to stagnate. He fetched pillowcases from the bedroom and started to fill them with the papers that were left. For a brief moment he wondered whether the Germans had left these files on purpose, and if they had, whether the files might be fakes. Could it really be that the apartment of a Hauptsturmführer working for the Sicherheitsdienst hadn't been searched and purged, or that Hertz himself wouldn't have taken confidential papers with him? Edgar couldn't believe the Germans would be that careless when it came to their documents, but it didn't matter. Papers were papers, whether they had been left there on purpose or not, and if the haul was too skimpy he could add a bit of juicy information of his own to the files. He stuffed unused forms, empty envelopes, and blank paper into the pillowcase for good measure. He found a couple of rubber stamps, too. After a moment's thought, he packed up all the office supplies that had been left behind, including the typewriter, ribbons for it, and some unopened bottles of ink at the bottom of the desk drawer. Among the reports were some he recognized, lovingly composed by him—these he burned, along with Eggert Fürst's identification papers, his OT-Bauführer armband, and his evacuation permit, which had a short time ago given him such great happiness. He closed the stove door with his right hand. First he would hide the treasure he'd found. He had to manage it even though the pillowcases were heavy, had to get back to Klooga quickly, so he could look through the piles of clothing for something that fit and let the Bolsheviks find him there, Edgar Parts, a prisoner made to witness horrors, but rescued in the nick of time by the Red Army.

Klooga, Estonian SSR, Soviet Union

THE CAMP WAS DESERTED, even of Germans.

We heaved ourselves along the rooftop and back into the attic. In it were creatures reduced to skeletons, horrified looks glued to their faces. I tried to pull one of them to his feet but he pushed away from me screaming, couldn't understand what I was saying, and I couldn't understand the language he was speaking. I repeated that the Germans were gone. I worked out the German words—*keine Deutsche, keine Deutsche, kein mehr*—not really knowing German, not wanting that language coming out of my mouth, but still trying to make it clear that the Jerries had left. The words didn't get through. His screams were filled with animal terror. He was empty of humanity, the remains of a human. There was something menacing about all of those men. I was afraid to turn my back on them. Alfons started slowly backing toward the door. I followed his example and we got to the stairway and bolted outside.

The camp gates were open. There was no one to be seen. We took off at a run. I was weak, my running more like dragging. I tensed my muscles to clear my thoughts. Hunger hadn't yet started to eat my brain. The Germans might still come back. No one from the attic had followed us.

When we got through the gate, we headed for the woods. I put my hand over my mouth, covered my nostrils with my fingers. Those who had tried to escape had been shot in the back. Their corpses lay strewn among the trees. Alfons and I couldn't look at each other, or to the side, or to where the heat was coming from. Charred trunks, pale, recently felled trees, and what was between them. The arms poking up, the legs, the shoed and shoeless soles of feet. I focused my eyes far ahead. I would look for the first farm I could find, change my clothes, ask for food. Surely someone would help us. We would say that the Germans had left. I kept going forward. I would never think about what I'd left behind. This was the moment we had waited for, prepared for. The Germans were gone and the Russians still hadn't arrived to take over. We wouldn't let them make it this far.

PART SIX

In the imperialist West the cruel voice of the
nationalist retributionists is yammering ever
louder, the cesspools they've created in New York,
Toronto, London, Stockholm, and Gothenburg are
seething like ants' nests. We must remember that
the emigrant "committees" or "councils" that have
sprung up in these cesspools are always nests of
destruction, filled with spies. The traitor's palette
of the nationalists is never-ending! The enemy
never sleeps, never forgets! It continues its work
of destruction and that's why the new generation
must be vigilant. Since the bankruptcy of Hitlerist Germany a new generation has arisen that has
only heard of those strange days in textbooks and
the talk of those who lived through that time. Soon
there will be no eyewitnesses left, no more books
witnessing that sadism. The next generation must
nevertheless remember that this so-called free
world is where nationalist Fascist murderers walk
free, and New York echoes with their trumpets!

—Edgar Parts, *At the Heart of the Hitlerist Occupation*,
   Eesti Raamat Publishing, 1966

Tallinn, Estonian SSR,
Soviet Union

THE MOSCOW SALAD WAS EATEN, the small pot of coffee drunk. Comrade Parts would order another directly, although it wouldn't help his frustration. He had been sitting in Café Moskva for hours and there was still no sign of the Target. The whelp was late, and Parts didn't know when he'd be able to go home. Maybe not until the café closed its doors. Parts blinked, trying to stay awake. His new assignment was a respectable one, but it had been a shock at first.

Parts had stared at the photo of the Target on the desk at the safe house—sideburns, pimples, the self-satisfied look of youth, a face that life had hardly yet touched. He couldn't understand what was happening. He still didn't understand. A job had been allotted to him in an operation whose purpose was, from what he could tell, to survey the anti-Soviet activities of students. His new priority was to keep an eye on a twenty-one-year-old pup who was part of this group—who he met, where, and when.

Parts had permission to continue his writing, but only so long as it didn't interfere with his new duties.

When he'd stepped out into the street after being given the assignment, the cobblestones under his feet had felt slippery in spite of the dry weather, and he had the vague nausea that portended a migraine. His relationship with Porkov had become one of trust, the manuscript was coming along well, and no sign of dissatisfaction had marred their relationship. The three-year deadline for his book hadn't even run out. But he wasn't going to answer to Porkov anymore—he'd been given a new supervisor. His last meeting with Porkov had been completely normal. If someone had finally noticed the stolen notebook, why hadn't they come looking for it? Had he made some other mistake? Was the Café Moskva assignment meant as a reprimand? Or had Porkov himself been transferred due to some infraction? Parts's new assignment made no sense. The Office had its own men for surveillance, and he wasn't an expert at this, not with the brief training he had received. He was known as a handwriting specialist. Why then did the Office think this job was appropriate for him?

Next to the information on the Target was a list of materials to be returned to the Office, including Porkov's most recent version of "Prohibited Information in Print Publications, Radio, and Television." Parts wondered if they would let him have the revised list when it came out, whether they would consider it unnecessary for him now. Although he'd read the directive and knew it inside and out, he hadn't liked the demeaning tone of the order to return it. It was a reminder of who was in charge. At least he was allowed to keep the typewriter at home.

His colleague in the corner of the dining room ordered some tea. Parts averted his eyes—he was ashamed for the man. There was a popular joke going around town: You can tell a spy by the way he closes one eye when he drinks his coffee—because Russians are used to drinking tea from a glass with a spoon sticking out. The joke had made Parts laugh, but not anymore. He could tell his colleague was an Office man from a mile away. He just sat and stared, the table empty in front of him. Maybe it was some new method the Office was using, a way to make people conscious of the all-seeing gaze of the authorities. Parts didn't believe in such methods. He believed in naturalness and invisibility, which was why he had first tried to strike up a flirtation with some silly secretary or clerk at the factory. Women always offered a believable excuse for hanging out in cafés. Flirting with women was time-consuming and expensive, however, and Parts had ended up choosing a simpler alternative—he would pose as a teacher grading papers, or perhaps as a writer. Having papers in front of him would also make it possible to take notes on the events of the evening, which would make it easier to provide cleanly written reports. He'd resolutely shaken off the humiliation of the new assignment the moment he gave his coat to the hat-check girl, and as he went up the stairs to the dining room he'd found an erect bearing to accompany the swinging of his briefcase. People came to a café for enjoyment, so he had to look like he was enjoying himself.

THE SITUATION WAS CAST in a more interesting light by the fact that along with the new post he had also finally been officially assigned to his publisher, Eesti Raamat, and an editor as well. Comrade Porkov had never taken care of the matter in spite of his promises, even though he was to get half the advance. Parts's new supervisor hadn't shown the slightest interest in the money, and with it Parts had finally been able to give up his post at the Norma factory guard booth. But the time freed up from his day job was spent tailing half-grown students instead of writing.

His visit to the publisher had been peculiar—the publishing director had peeped at him nervously, and kept glancing at the door. You could almost hear the padding steps of the Glavlit censors in the hallway. Parts himself had already spotted one—he recognized him by his vacant, nonchalant expression. The publisher had sat behind his desk restlessly tugging at his collar. Fear for his job was chomping at the skin of his neck. The open surveillance the man had to endure offered enough amusement to slightly ease Parts's depression about his new assignment. No one had asked him anything about the manuscript, an envelope full of bills was silently shoved at him, and in the hallway he'd been stared at as if he were a man in the good graces of people in important places. The sweet touch of power had brushed his cheeks. He'd almost felt the admiring sigh of the Glavlit man on his skin. Maybe there was no reason to feel caught short, maybe he'd misunderstood the whole situation, maybe the Office simply considered him so multitalented that they were giving him an opportunity to shine in yet another area. In any case, getting out of the factory was certainly a plus, as was his publishing contract.

OVER THE COURSE of the evening, however, Parts's erect bearing started to wilt. There was no sign of the Target; nothing seemed to be happening. He laid his manuscript between the pot of coffee and the plate of chocolate truffles and started drawing sentence diagrams. At the Target's regular table a couple of girls were discussing whether their travel permit to Saaremaa would be approved before their father, who lived there, celebrated his birthday. A flock of tech students who were friends of the girls flooded in from the stairway. The whole table ordered fifty grams of cognac and some coffee. Parts's colleague watched the girls with hard eyes. But their faces were unknown to Parts— he hadn't seen them in the photos he'd been shown at the safe house. The group made a restless movement. There was expectation in the air, a spirit of uneasiness; no one seemed absorbed in the conversation. One of the students was fiddling with her student ID card, another kept straightening her student cap and touching the brim. But the cognac interested all of them, as did the Valeri cookies. Then Parts noticed that one of the tech girls was wearing long pants. He wrinkled his nose and flipped through his papers, twirling his pencil, but always keeping his eye on the group, his colleague's motionlessness, and the general goings-on in the dining room. Two men who'd settled in at the next table poured full glasses of Lõunamaine from a carafe and the drink increased the younger man's coquetry; he nibbled on a caraway cracker, offered to share it with the older man, accomplished this by means of a complicated operation that involved first halving the cracker and then transporting it to his own mouth and from his mouth to the waiting lips of his companion. The older man lit a cigarette, the matchstick flaring up, the flame shining in his eyes. Parts could see the movements of their feet by the slight fluttering of the tablecloth. From the drift of the younger man's legs toward the older man's, Parts could guess how both men's nostrils quivered suddenly, how they looked at each other, their gazes already wrapped in bedsheets. Parts squinted. All this activity had so captured his attention that he hadn't noticed the Target coming into the dining room. Did he come in alone? How long had he been standing in the middle of Café Moskva? Parts stole a glance at the group at the table, looking for new faces, trying to notice if anyone was missing. His colleague in the corner was looking straight at him, a smile trembling at the corners of his mouth, mockery twinkling in his eyes. Parts turned his glance back to the Target's table, then to the dining room again. This wasn't possible. The Target had disappeared.

Tallinn, Estonian SSR,
Soviet Union

Rein's voice carried from the kitchen to the ears of Evelin, who was waiting in the living room. She tried to listen, but the noise of the radio and the record player they'd turned on when they came in swallowed up what he was saying. So this was it, the house where Rein went, without telling her why, or who he was meeting. This was the house where Rein had never brought her before. Evelin was excited and sat stiffly in her chair, although she was alone and no one was watching what she did, monitoring whether she was sitting like a lady. There was a crystal bowl of cat's tongue cookies on the coffee table and a grandfather clock ticked, chiming every fifteen minutes, the pendulum swinging; the blinds were rippling in a draft of air. The cream had curdled in her coffee and she didn't know where to pour the coffee out. Maybe Rein just wanted to protect her and that's why he hadn't told her about all of this. Or maybe he just wanted to have a secret, something a little more important, or maybe he didn't trust her enough yet. Or maybe he'd brought her here because he wanted to reassure her, so she wouldn't feel lonely. The rest of Evelin's classmates had left for Tartu when the banking student group was moved there. Evelin hadn't wanted to go, she wanted to stay with Rein. The decision to apply for a transfer had been an impulsive one. She wasn't going to become a bank manager, like she'd thought—she was going to be an engineer. The Soviet Union needed engineers, they were the strong legs that the whole society stood on. If Evelin had known that she would be sitting around here doing nothing, she could have brought along her lecture notes or some other equally sleep-inducing reading, like Saarepera's "Description of Annual and Quarterly Industrial Typology and Production Calculation Methodology." Now all she could do was suck on currants and munch on cookies.

In her first year of study Evelin had dropped in at Café Moskva a few times and immediately noticed Rein and the group that gathered around him. How could she not notice him? Or the girls in his group? She never would have believed that Rein could be interested in her, a country girl with two sweaters, one skirt, and one dress, ignorant of all the things that Rein knew all about, surrounded by girls who changed their dresses, shirts, and pants every day, always wearing something different. Pants! Evelin's mother had promised that she could get a new dress from the sale of the next calf, but that wouldn't be for some time. When she was younger, she couldn't have imagined how difficult student life could be when you only had one dress hanging in your closet. Everything had been easy in high school, you just starched your collar and took good care of your one dress, and you were fine. No one else here seemed to miss their old school uniform.

Evelin was thirsty, but she didn't dare to leave the living room. The coffee that had been waiting for her on the table was already cold when they arrived. The table setting showed a woman's hand, though there was no one in the house but the man in spectacles who had opened the door. Maybe Rein only came when the man was here alone. You could see the owner's good taste in the stylish furnishings. The bookshelf was full of only books from the black market or straight from the press. Evelin admired the cabinets that reached all the way to the ceiling and dreamed of having a setup like that in her own home, the home she and Rein would share. There would be cognac in the liquor cabinet, the linens would be organized on shelves, and she would polish the cabinet doors every day—there wouldn't be a single smudge on them, and their surfaces would shine and make the room look bigger. She and Rein would drink Aroom every morning after she had put away the sofa bed, pounded the cushions in place, and folded the blankets to hide away during the daytime, and there would be enough coffee for guests, coffee with nothing else mixed in. They would have cactuses on the windowsill. Rein would turn on the Magnetofon and put on some electric guitar music his friends had recorded, and as the tape started to play he would pull her next to him on the divan. She would finally have sheets of her own.

Before Rein had agreed to take her to this secret house, Evelin had hinted that she suspected he had another girl. The accusation had flown out of her mouth easily, without her thinking about it. All those well-dressed girls at Café Moskva troubled her. She was particularly uneasy about the white-legged art student who slept on the bunk above her in the room they shared with two other girls. Every time Evelin sneaked Rein into her room, the top-bunk girl would already be in bed, and she would stick her leg, chest, or thigh out from under the covers, her hair flowing over the edge of the bed. Rein's eyes would fasten on the girl's leg or breast poking out, shining in the dark like a white moon, and the girl would move her arm in her sleep, plumping up the breast a bit, just waiting for his open mouth, for a drop of drool. That's why Evelin didn't want to bring Rein to her dorm, because it was full of girls running around in their slips, giggling in the kitchen in their nightgowns, and because the top-bunk girl always went to bed early when Rein was coming over and waited for him to tiptoe into the room. Evelin had only invited him there after he'd pestered her for a long time. She had fried him some potatoes in the kitchen, a large portion, using a good dollop of the fat she'd saved in a cup, and Rein made the dorm monitor laugh and forget to enforce the ten o'clock rule. Evelin didn't even want to go to his dorm. Last year the boys had decorated the walls with bedbugs on pins. It would be even more uncomfortable there. And anyway, Rein never asked her.

THEY HAD COME into the bespectacled man's house through the back door. They'd made their way there by a meandering path between apartment houses, onto a big road, and into a thicket, Rein pulling her along through the bushes and across the backyard of another house. When they arrived, Rein had pulled a few twigs out of her hair and patted her on her tousled head. Her stockings were still intact, and her heart was light. Rein knocked a rhythm on the gray door, and while they waited for it to open Evelin watched the neighbors. A woman was carrying heavy water pails on her shoulders, gauze diapers fluttering on the clothesline behind her like winding sheets. The woman emptied the buckets into a tub and went back to get

more water. Farther off someone was sharpening a scythe. Evelin remembered a girl who had been thrown out of the dorms
and how the roommate with the white legs had laughed, saying
that only stupid girls got into *that* kind of trouble. Evelin didn't
want to be among the stupid; she didn't want to be ruined, to
sully herself, even if Rein claimed that such a thing couldn't
ruin you. It certainly could, Evelin knew that, and it made her
nervous every time they met. She couldn't explain interrupting
her studies to her parents. Their permit to raise calves, along
with her stipend, ensured that they would have enough money
for her studies, but it meant that her mother had to take care of
the calves on top of her kolkhoz work. She was slaving away
so Evelin could go to school, and Rein was constantly pushing her into a situation that could put her studies in danger,
sneaking his hands in where she didn't want them. Whenever
he managed to stay over in the girls' dorm and jammed himself
into Evelin's bunk, he would nuzzle against her breasts and his
hand would reach for her abdomen and Evelin would shut her
eyes tight, force the top-bunk girl's breasts out of her mind,
and shove Rein's hand aside, holding it away from her, and
to keep from thinking about whether he was angry she would
think about the summer exams, partly for his sake, too, since he
was going to have trouble passing. Rein just didn't have time
to study, he had so many other things, more important things,
to do.

SHE HEARD Rein's voice now from nearby, his laugh sounding like the kind that comes out of men's mouths when they've
thought long and hard and come to a satisfying decision. There
was a tinge of relief in it, too long a laugh to be lighthearted,
too hard, like Rein's laugh often was. He was still laughing as

he led Evelin to the back door again, and they left through the same jungle they had come through before. Rein tugged off his coat, wrapped it around her legs, lifted her in his arms for the sake of her stockings, and carried her to the road. It wasn't until they got to the bus stop that Evelin noticed a cloth bag dangling from his hand.

"Did that man give you something?"

"Books," Rein said.

"What books?"

"You wouldn't want to read them."

Evelin didn't ask any more questions because Rein didn't like nagging women. He was in a good mood now, stroked her collarbone, whispered in her ear: You see? There's nothing bad going on here. His lips were so close to her lips that she could feel his kiss, and stepped back.

"Everyone can see us."

"So?"

She turned her head away and his lips touched her ear, his breath gusting into it, and her ear became a shell, like the one she'd saved from the hitchhiking trip she took to the Caucasus, and she wrapped her arms around herself like a creature in its shell so that he had to move an elbow's length away.

In spite of his carefree mood, Rein was tense; his hands were hotter than the sweaty bus they boarded, and it wasn't because of her skirt hem, although she had shortened it more than she'd intended. She turned her back to him to fend off his squeezes, which had become a real nuisance.

In the packed bus she managed to slide her hand into Rein's bag and she felt photo paper, a large stack of it. She slipped her hand out. Rein breathed on her neck.

———

THAT EVENING BEFORE going back to the dorm, Evelin shoved her hands into her coat pocket, surprised by her boldness. She had secretly worked one of the photos out of Rein's bag. It was just text—a photo of a page of a book. The words were in a foreign language.

Tallinn, Estonian SSR,
Soviet Union

THE GIRL IN LONG PANTS sitting at the Target's otherwise empty table waved her leg again. Another girl sat down at the table and started writing on small rectangular slips of paper. An unpleasant tension spread into Comrade Parts's temples. Here he was, a capable man, and his job was to watch little girls making crib sheets. On his way to the café he had seen his colleague slip into the entrance of the Palace Hotel. At this moment the man was probably enjoying champagne in international company, shoveling slices of white bread covered in black caviar into his mouth. Why hadn't Parts been invited? Had someone commented on his work? Was the Office dissatisfied with him? Had officialdom really judged him better suited to this kind of assignment, spying on petty tarts and hooligans? Parts simply couldn't believe that. He knew how to behave enough like a Westerner to qualify for the international environment at the Palace. There must be some other reason. His wife's behavior might have attracted attention. Perhaps she was seen as a problem and the security committee thought it wisest not to give him a more visible role. The idea wasn't out of the question. He was no longer invited to meetings with the high-ranking personnel at the Pagari. The evening soirées had dried up, too. Parts sighed. The sigh rustled his papers. The darkness of the café tired his eyes. He couldn't help but blush when thoughts of his wife bubbled into his mind—that time when he was out with her and ran into Albert Keis, the head of the Estonian News Agency, and she started talking about the school art collection. At first Parts had no inkling, had just let the conversation continue until his brain registered that she was praising the works of the young Alfred Rosenberg on the walls of the Peter the Great Secondary School. Parts had coughed, something suddenly stuck in his throat.

Albert Keis's eyebrows had shot up, the whites of his eyes visible on all four sides. "What exactly are you talking about?" he said.

"The works of the young Alfred Rosenberg. He shows signs of great talent, an impressive use of line."

Luckily Parts had been able to pull himself together and rescue the situation by pretending indignation. Indeed, he, too, had heard that Rosenberg's works were still hanging there. Why hadn't anyone taken the initiative about it? He managed to work himself up to such a gale that it blew his wife's mistake, her ecstatic expression of admiration, into the background. The new iron they'd bought to replace their broken one weighed heavy in the shopping bag and Parts felt like leaving it on the street right where he stood. People buzzed around them, the windows of the department store glared, Keis continued to stare at them with his fish eyes, Parts's voice rose, passersby gawked, and the hand carrying the new iron went numb. His wife had turned to look at a display window as if she had nothing to do with the whole situation.

Later Parts heard that there had indeed been works by Rosenberg found at Tallinn Middle School Number 2, formerly the Peter the Great Secondary School, and they'd been quietly removed. His wife had tried to explain that she'd done him a service. After all, she was the one who told them about the shocking circumstance, and revealing it could only benefit him. But Parts remembered the words she'd used—"talented," "impressive," "a real artist." What if Keis reported the incident to the Office?

PARTS ORDERED a Moscow salad, a pot of coffee, and three truffles. By the time the waitress returned with a tray, his colleague had arrived and slid into the same corner where he'd been the evening before. There was a hint of a sneer on the man's face, and it couldn't be for anyone but him. Parts tried to hide his embarrassment by tapping his pile of papers against the tabletop, and when he'd gotten them in order he laid them out, touching his breast pocket in passing. His passport was there, as always. He recognized the compulsiveness of the gesture and tried to keep his hand under control when it rose again toward his pocket, diverting it to fiddle with his white collar. The pressers at the Kiire laundry combine did their jobs well enough, but since he'd gotten his advance, Parts had started to dream of a servant. The communal laundry never got things really clean. The Martinsons no doubt had a servant, and probably a washing machine, too. It was so easy for people like Martinson to underline their status with a thing like that, just mention the washing machine in passing, how it made life so much easier, and then of course we have Maria, or Anna, or Juuli, to come in and clean and do the washing for three rubles a day. Soon Parts would have a girl to come in, too, and she could iron the handkerchiefs, which they had piles of from his wife's bad spells. He would just have to explain the reasons for the change to his wife and not back down.

Parts didn't like irons. The coal iron that they had used when they'd lived in Valga had pleased him even less than it did his wife, but for different reasons. Its red glow had been a vivid reminder of Patarei prison, where he'd been taken after the Germans withdrew. He had heard yells from the next room. They had a man named Alfons there, a Jew who had survived the Germans and was thus in the eyes of the Soviets clearly a German spy. Listening to his shouts, Parts had resolved to get out of there alive. The fact that they had dug up his spy training at Staffan Island still smarted. They had once again succeeded in showing their superiority, and he had failed. For years afterward the glow of the iron still carried the reek of burning flesh, the smell of humiliation. His store of German documents had rescued him from being ironed alive, but he would have gladly shared the information he had with the Russians anyway. He was a sensible man—there was no need to threaten him. Let them use the iron on unimportant people.

After he'd soothed himself with truffles, Parts started to sort through his papers, taking notes as he went and not letting his thoughts wander the way they had the last time. His conjectures about his wife would have to be pondered elsewhere; he didn't want his worry to show, wanted to keep a cheerful expression, although a doubt had lingered in a corner of his mind after he'd gotten the list of wives left behind by men sent to Siberia. His weakly justified and confused explanation had been accepted; he could see Porkov's glare even here in the Moskva, his hand reaching all the way to the Kremlin. Porkov had promised him information about Dog Ear, too, but before the matter could be settled their working relationship had been terminated. At first Parts hadn't found anything useful in the lists, no one he could have pegged as Roland's Heart. He'd immediately eliminated women too geographically remote from Roland's home area; he didn't believe Roland could have found his way into a relationship with someone he didn't know who lived far away, and the sketches in the journal had made reference to the fact that Roland hadn't been away from his home province for long. Roland would only trust a woman he had some existing connection with. There had been only one familiar name on the list, but it was an improbable one. Parts's wife.

For the past two years Parts had been going through the list over and over, and he kept returning to his own wife's name. He had begun to look at her with new eyes, searching for some hint in her behavior, some crack that he could use to make her open up and speak, something that would make him certain, some means of bringing out the truth. His suspicions were supported by the fact that he didn't know exactly what she had been doing while he was away. She hadn't gone to Auntie Anna's funeral, but she had been to visit her while she was still alive. Auntie Anna had written to him and said that for once his wife had made herself useful, picking berries and mushrooms and making preserves as Leonida's and Aksel's strength diminished, managing to get carbolic acid for the fruit trees and berry bushes in exchange for some lard and spraying the plants the way Roland had taught her so there would be enough unblemished fruit to take to market. She had dusted the flowers in the yard, too. She'd even gone to the woods to cut firewood and spent most of her nights in the barn or the shed, sometimes staying at Leonida's old cabin, which the kolkhoz had never found any use for. That had been wise, though. There were plenty of witnesses to her relationship with the German, times were tough, and her husband was in Siberia. But still. What if her sudden yearning for the countryside and frequent trips to Auntie Anna's house were actually connected to Roland? What if she had gone out with her berry basket straight into Roland's arms? What if Roland had spilled the secrets of his soul into a pillow he shared with Parts's wife?

Out of the corner of his eye Parts could see the leg of the girl in pants. He took slow bites of his salad, looking for the canned peas and breaking them one by one with his teeth, now and then wiping mayonnaise from the side of his mouth with his napkin. Maybe he'd lost his touch. He'd always had a natural instinct for which direction to take, but now he felt at a loss; the research for his manuscript kept running into dead ends, obstacles, or his wife's eyes, like a wall of silicate brick, and he didn't understand why the Office had put him in this situation. He also felt a little rusty in the field, in spite of his training. The previous evening he had panicked, once he was sure that the Target really had vanished and wasn't just in the men's room. He'd gathered up his papers and hurried out to the street to listen for a moment, then gone straight to the Target's dorm building. He'd felt like a dog that had lost the trail of his prey, and gave up, the moon reflecting mockingly from the dark eyes of the dorm windows. That afternoon he had waited hopefully in an appropriately unobtrusive corner near the Target's lecture hall, but in vain. The sideburned youth had been missing from the flood of students there, clearly a different crowd from the group that gathered at the Moskva. These were ordinary students. They lacked the perceptible excitement, the trembling agitation that reached its zenith when someone in the group made some point or other. Secret lectures, that's what they were doing. It was no wonder that regular studies didn't interest the boy. He was interested in the Molotov-Ribbentrop Pact, and what life was like in Finland and the West. Among the lecturers were probably those who'd traveled to the West, journalists or athletes who'd slipped through the Office's sieve, gotten permission to travel, and repaid the privilege with this. Was it envy that bit into Parts's flesh like a swarm of horseflies? Or was it just the stuffy air in the café?

He had to get some results, get his career back on track. He had to sweep away his uncertainty, remember his own skills, how magical things could happen if you said them out loud or wrote them down on paper. The first time he'd witnessed that kind of miracle was in the *gymnasium*. There had been money missing from the teacher's overcoat pocket and he'd been told to stand in the corner of the classroom until he was ready to confess. At the end of the school day the teacher had gathered up his books and said that he could spend the night there if he didn't want to open his mouth, it was clear he was the culprit—while the others were outside for recess he had stayed behind because it was his turn to clean the blackboards. Young Parts had denied he was guilty, and as he let the words flow from his lips he'd felt a march beat in his pulse, a rumble in his ears, but no sour smell of fear came from his skin. His armpits were dry, his breathing as sedate as when he was at church, even though unbelief weighed like lead in the pit of his stomach. There was no way to get out of this, no way at all. The teacher would have to be crazy to believe him. But the teacher did believe him, and his belief had grown as Parts talked on, in a sure voice with no trace of a pubescent squeak, the steady voice of a man speaking the truth, and said that it had to have been his seatmate, who needed money because he hadn't done his homework and had to pay someone else to do it. He had seen him come into the classroom while he was cleaning the blackboards. Parts had to hide his smile as he closed the *gymnasium* door behind him.

Once he got around the corner he let it spread over his face, and it was still there as he passed the boys playing Boer War, and as he went through the park and past the cobbler's shop all the way to his own block, still warming his face that evening as he pressed his head against his feather pillow, under which was hidden the stolen money his seatmate had given him for writing his report.

THE TARGET ARRIVED with his friends at 5:40 p.m. and ordered a pot of black coffee and a Moscow roll, as usual. Parts was alert.

"We've prepared for the questions about the Twentieth Party Congress, the Twenty-First Party Congress, and the Twenty-Second Party Congress."

"Make me a crib sheet, too."

"Make it yourself." The girl laughed, giving the Target a playful slap.

Parts's pencil was smoking—he'd gotten everything down. The pianist hadn't started playing yet and the café was nearly empty. He could hear their conversation beautifully.

The girl in the pants got up and toddled past to the ladies' room. Parts wiped his mouth irritably and just then noticed the Target waving to a man who'd come in from the stairs. The man had a thick scarf wrapped around his neck, but Parts recognized him. Mägi, the radio journalist. Mägi sat down at the table and leaned toward the others, and the whispering commenced. The girl in pants returned and hurried to the table when she saw who had arrived. Parts managed to lip-read a few phrases, made out "St. George's Night Uprising," and put it in his notes, all the while ostensibly flipping through his papers. He was sure there must be microphones already installed in the students' regular table, but he didn't let that weaken his vigilance, even though it made him nothing more than a backup recorder in case of technical failure. It was raining outside. Customers coming in shook the drops from their hats. Parts wasted a worried thought on the photographer who must be outside taking pictures of people coming and going from the Moskva and no doubt longed for some warm broth and a pirozhki. He fiddled with his collar and tried to perk up, twisted the wrapping off a truffle, bit the truffle in half, and set down the rest. His colleague was sitting in his usual place. Maybe he wasn't here to watch Parts's Target. Maybe he was watching someone else. The mere thought of spending endless evenings in the Café Moskva felt like a weight on Parts's temples. The students were young and overconfident, so the project wouldn't take long in any case, but Parts decided to speed it to its conclusion. These hooligans were going to make a mistake, going to be emboldened further and abandon caution. Parts was starting to feel sure of that. They could easily be scooped up right where they sat, and he, a specialist, could get back to his normal work and buy the whitest, highest-quality paper for the final draft of his manuscript. When it came to his book, there was no time to lose.

He was certain it would be easy to make a contact in the Target's dormitory, someone who could report about any telegrams or letters the Target received and their contents. The security committee hadn't yet given Parts permission to enlist contacts, but he could think of irrefutable justifications why they should. The Office never turned down a perfect informant. He would also have to justify why it should be he who performed the *verbovka*. And of course even if the Office did give the task to someone else, Parts could take a risk, approach the contact himself and make it clear that no one else in the organization was to know about their meeting. A contact wasn't likely to question Parts's authority. Aside from the one time he failed in recruiting Miller, these things were usually easy and inexpensive, which never ceased to amaze him. In the best cases a *verbovka agenta* could succeed with just a few rubles or some trivial favor. Some, however, wanted proper payment—trips, or school assignments for their children, or a better job—which was understandable. In fact, Parts felt a certain respect for those people. Who wouldn't want to be a guide for Intourist? Who wouldn't want his children to pass their exams, even if they weren't loaded with brains? Who wouldn't want to go to the front of the line for an apartment or a car, a safe post for a son in the military to ensure he came back alive, or books that you couldn't get even under the counter? But the ones who worked for free, who reported on their neighbors' or coworkers' activities for no pay—who did they think they were pleasing? And why? Meanwhile the peace movement in the West seemed to be a constant source of new and productive informants, without any of the problems they had here. The enthusiasm of those informants was dumbfounding. You didn't even have to pay them. Why? Their ideological-political recruitment came cheap, but Parts still found it difficult to understand the psychology of such people. He relied more on compromising information to motivate his informants. There were also those who got pleasure from prying into the affairs of others, and those motivated by envy. Parts considered such sources unreliable. But recruits who didn't seize on the opportunity for self-promotion that their services offered, those he couldn't begin to understand. Were they the kind of people who had already achieved communism in their personal lives and no longer needed money or other rewards? Degenerates. That's what they were. You weren't supposed to say that out loud, but communist theory would do well to recognize the realities of the biological degeneration of certain citizens, which had nothing to do with remnant conflicts of a degenerate class society.

The Target was unfortunately one of those people who

probably couldn't be recruited successfully. He already had the attention he wanted. The skirts couldn't take their eyes off him. No one talked over him when he opened his mouth. No need to become an informant to feel important. He had a good place at the university, stylish clothes, and was so young that the practicalities of everyday life—waiting lists for apartments, opportunities for future children—didn't yet worry him. His parents obviously had the money and the means to take care of such matters. Nevertheless, he clearly wanted to play the hero, and people like that always caused problems. The easiest people to recruit were the most colorless members of a group: the girl no one asked to dance, the boy whose name no one remembered, the woman who ordered the same thing everyone else did, the man who was more moth than butterfly. A girl whose built-in fear just needed a little nudge. Parts had noticed many potential informants among the group gathered around the Target.

Tallinn, Estonian SSR,
Soviet Union

EVELIN STACKED the layers of cookies, quark, and jam on
the dish and held back her tears. Rein had been demanding to know why she hadn't introduced him to her parents, and
she couldn't tell him the real reason. She would have cried if
she'd been alone, but the kitchen was full of angry voices. The
boys from tech had come in drunk the night before and pried
the locks off the food pantry again—the girls' precious sausage
and less precious canned vegetables had disappeared into their
greedy mouths. There was nothing left on Evelin's shelves but
a jar of jam. She would have to get by on that and the cookies until her next stipend. But it wasn't hunger she was worried about. She was worried about Rein. Lora swept past with
her skirts flapping and poured a dribble of milk into a glass to
wash her face with. These girls didn't have the same kinds of
problems as Evelin did. They had conquered the back rows
of movie theaters, sighing with their suitors. Evelin seemed to

be the only one who tried to concentrate on what was happening on the screen, although Rein was always pushing his hand up her skirt to the edge of her stockings and she was always pushing it away again. Someday soon he would grow tired of it, leave in the middle of the film, force people to get up, and they would stare at Evelin, friends nudging each other, greedy eyes fastening on Rein, and when he swept through the doors of the theater he would be swept out of Evelin's life. The girls made a racket, their slippers padding over the linoleum, every flash of a slip under a dress hem reminding her that she ought to let Rein take hers off, she really ought to. Not so long ago everything had been fine, she had been excited about the new place to live, they'd gotten rid of the lice, and Rein was wonderful. But after a few dates, just holding hands wasn't enough for him anymore. And then came the other demands. He wanted to meet his future in-laws. But she didn't want Rein to see the pitchfork handles and barn mucking, the landscape of the kolkhoz, the poverty. Her father would insist that Rein drink with him, they would get drunk, anything at all could happen. Rein was from the city, from an educated family. His mother never went out without a hat. Evelin carried the cookie cake to the cupboard to set and retreated to her room to do her mending and think of a solution, but the tears blurred the run in the stocking and when the white-legged girl walked into the room, Evelin jumped up, threw down her darning hook, and ran out. She was just the person Evelin didn't want to see. There was no place to find a moment's peace. Evelin stood at the street door and sniffled. Walking out didn't seem like a good idea anymore. Mustamägi was dim and deserted, and she didn't want to walk on the busier street with its traffic. The high fence of the neighboring building closed off the darkness beyond; during the daytime they kept prisoners working there out of view.

In the hallway some boys passed her carrying a Magnetofon and one of the girls shouted after them to record some electric guitar. Carelessly. She shouted it so carelessly—"Bring us some dance music"—lifting her foot so that her bare leg flashed from under the hem of her coatdress. One of the reels fell out of someone's hand and rolled down the hallway and Alan dashed after it, toward the leg, glancing at Evelin as he passed, Alan whose sweaty hand had once made a wet stain on the back of her Bemberg dress. An electric guitar. Alan had told her he planned to build one for himself. Would Alan have been a better choice than Rein? Would he have made the same demands? They couldn't all be like Rein. Evelin turned away suddenly and went back to her room, where the white-legged art student was teasing her hair with a comb and some furniture polish.

Rein must already be at the Moskva. He had said he was going there after their conversation. Or fight. If it was a fight. Maybe it was. If Evelin brought Rein home to her parents, maybe Rein would bring her to the Moskva. No. Maybe she would take off her slip. Or no. Maybe she would bring him home. Then Rein could know that she was serious and wasn't just toying with him, like he said she was. Or maybe the slip. Evelin thought again about the girl who'd left the dorms crying, how everyone had nodded knowingly. Suspended. One of *those* girls. No, she wouldn't take off her slip. Rein had laughed when she said she didn't believe that everybody did it. That couldn't be true. The white-legged girl from the top bunk, maybe. An art student, naturally. Girls who studied pedagogy were like that, too. And what if she were a brilliant conversationalist, like the girls at the Moskva? Would Rein focus on other things when he was with her, besides her underwear? Possibly. The coming summer worried her. Rein would be in town, first as an intern, then on the beach, sunbathing with his friends from the café, nibbling

on smoked eels. After her practicum, and on weekends during her internship, Evelin would be working on the farm. She
would be spraying DDT on the cabbages and swinging a pitchfork while Rein was having fun. Rein would have two whole
months to find someone else's underwear to take off.

If she didn't come up with a solution to this problem, she
would lose Rein, and that was something she couldn't bear. She
knew how it would be. She would go back to the life she'd lived
before Rein. Rein had changed everything. When she'd started
going out with him, the other girls treated her differently,
invited her along with them, asked her to join their lunch table,
sat beside her in lecture. No one gave her that look anymore at
the dances, that pointed look at her dress that was always the
same dress.

Tallinn, Estonian SSR, Soviet Union

COMRADE PARTS'S WIFE was rubbing Orto cream into her cracked elbows with slow, circling motions. She was obviously expecting him. Parts put his shopping bags down on the kitchen floor and started getting out the ingredients for a sprat sandwich, taking no notice of her until she squeezed some more cream into her hand and asked why he wasn't home in the evenings anymore. The question didn't bode well. He had managed to calm her for several sweet months with his publishing contract, napoleon cake and champagne, plus three bottles of Beliy Aist cognac, and gas delivered to the house. She had interpreted these things as a sign of the Office's favor. Then her spells had started again. Parts couldn't avoid answering her if he wanted to write in peace. He explained that he'd been given a new assignment that required him to work in the evenings.

"Does it have to do with the book?"

"Not exactly. In a certain sense it does," Parts said.

"In a certain sense?"

She seemed to understand instantly that the new assignment was a demotion, her eyebrows lifting derisively. Parts added that his writing required other kinds of activities in order to get the best results, that after sitting at his desk all day he needed fresh air, needed to walk a bit. Juudit snorted, her upper lip curling. He could see her teeth, the lipstick smeared on them. Her disdain was paralyzing. The radio snapped on, its shout fluttering the curtains and his wife's hair as she leaned forward and whispered, "Has anyone read your manuscript? Is it possible they don't appreciate its excellence? That they have perhaps realized that you can't write a book? You promised me you could ensure that we would have no reason to worry."

She straightened her back, stared at the tube of cream, squeezed it, let the cream squirt out of the cracked metal tube and drip onto the table. Parts stared at the shiny stain and wished for a spike in arms production so there would be a shortage of glycerine and there wouldn't be enough for lotion and his wife would stop torturing him with it. She touched the skin of her elbow, her brow wrinkled. The cream continued to flow from the tube. Parts grabbed the tube and threw it in the slop bucket. His wife's hand froze, her breath catching. Parts left the kitchen. Behind him he could hear her starting to smash the porcelain. Soon the last of Auntie Anna's set would be in pieces. His failed patience would cost him his last memory of his aunt. A serious mistake. There had been a kernel of truth in his wife's words, and he had admitted as much by reacting too strongly, revealed himself in a humiliating way. He couldn't let that happen again. He should have changed the subject immediately to her neglect of the home and how it was affecting his work, how his ambition had crumbled when he came into the building and caught a whiff of scorched milk, no doubt from the neighbors next door making macaroni with milk for their kids. It was that smell of a living family that had torn painfully at him when he opened his own door to stuffy air and a cold apartment. But he'd quelled his rising anger and fortified his blood with a swallow of Hematogen. Then he went into the kitchen and his self-control failed him. His wife's words still stung:

"What if this is a sign? What if the Office doesn't care about your book anymore? Maybe it means that we're next. What if this demotion is the first step in a case against you?"

A PASSING TRAIN RATTLED the windows and Parts waited for the noise to stop before beginning his work. He would have liked to live in some other neighborhood, but he had no choice, and at least the whole house belonged to them. It was far better than the nine square meters normally allotted per person. Living in a single-family dwelling could be a bragging point— it had been arranged with the help of the Office, cognac, and truffles. A friend of his wife's had written to certify that she was expecting twins, and Parts had remembered an elderly couple, distant relatives already frail, who wanted to move in. No one ever asked about the twins, or about the old couple. He had thought he'd get used to the trains, but he'd been wrong.

Contrary to what his wife believed, the Office had looked at his manuscript, and they thought he had the right approach. But as far as Parts knew, none of his colleagues who were working on the subject of the Hitlerists had been saddled with assignments like his café duties. They were sitting in offices at the Office, or in the special archives, or were employees of magazines, or full-time workers for the Office, publicly praised, some of them even invited to Moscow—all of them publishing works on the subject as fast as they could. There was nothing very different about the work they produced, yet their conditions of employment were different. Comrade Barkov was already the head of research for the Estonian SSR government security committee, and word had it that he was writing a thesis on the Estonian bourgeois nationalists' transition to fascism. He no doubt had help from a wife who did his filing, typed clean copies for him, and made sure he was free to concentrate on what was essential. Or maybe he had a secretary. Or several. It was the same with Ervin Martinson. How else could he be so prolific? A pile of papers covered in corrections and exclamation points, demanding immediate attention, waited on Parts's desk. The Office was full of typists, but somehow they couldn't spare one for Parts's manuscript. His old doubts returned. Maybe the Office felt that his past was an obstacle to public recognition after all. Maybe he wouldn't be showered with flowers in a couple of years, maybe he'd be sent to scour the countryside marking the places foreigners weren't allowed to see, or hunting down closet scribblers, or, worse yet, working as a restroom attendant, listening to what people talked about in the toilet. Maybe they would take his typewriter away.

Could it be because of his wife's background, or her present condition? Seeing to her pharmaceutical needs required planning. He'd been forced to take responsibility for stocking the medicine cabinet, since she was hardly capable of using the tactic of rotating pharmacies. Picking up the same prescription from the same place would attract unwanted attention. People would start to talk, and the talk would find its way to the Office. It was just the sort of material the Office collected—they wrote down a target's prescriptions, drugstore purchases, doctors' visits, liquor expenditures, and used all of it to build a profile of untrustworthiness, potential weaknesses, to create ways of ensuring a worker's loyalty, or to make him behave in a way beneficial to the Office.

He had never seriously thought of sending his wife to the asylum at Paldiski 52, but maybe the time was approaching when it would be worth considering. Her problematic background was a credible, even probable, reason for his professional difficulties. Divorce wasn't an option because leaving a sick wife would be a deplorable, immoral thing to do, but if she were sent to an institution for the good of her health, Parts could go on with his life as normal, perhaps even earn some sympathy. The Office would most likely support such a decision. Parts knew how to present the idea to them. He remembered a Russian woman at the Norma factory who had brought her elderly mother-in-law to Tallinn from Russia. The old woman had stopped speaking Russian, wanted to speak only in French. The whole family had been in a fluster, and they locked the old woman in her bedroom. No one would have known about it if the woman hadn't managed to escape. The story had amused Parts at the time because the woman's husband was a well-known Party member. He taught communist theory at the university and was always reminding people that the ruble would soon collapse because money was a capitalist invention, and suddenly he had a woman living in his home who muttered in French and longed for her friend the Countess Maria Serafina and praised his wife's resemblance to the late Tzarina. At least that's what they thought she was talking about—no one in the family could speak French. The mother-in-law was sent to Paldiski 52. The story wasn't funny to Parts anymore. He could see the signs of the fragility of the mind, its inexorable fallibility, every day in his own home. Everyone had his breaking point, and if nothing else destroyed the mind, time would. It would take you back to moments you didn't want to return to, chasing after countesses and tzarinas, to memories of Lilya Brik driving the first automobile in Moscow, or the wood-gas cars in Siberia, how you had to throw stick after stick of birch in the burner, how the generator would sputter, memories of wood being chopped, fat burning, and flesh, the smell. The frailty of the mind could carry you back to memories of a fire that revealed skulls and femurs, memories that should be forgotten, that you have forgotten, until your spirit is beaten down, and it brings them back and makes them true again, the fire and smoke, the crackle, the woodpile and the smell and the gunshots and the cries of anguish and the past becoming reality again, as if it were happening now. He might shout out his memories in public, too, in the middle of the day, while waiting in a long line, and step into that same dark place where all those he imagined he'd cleared out of his path for ever and ever had stepped long ago, the very same darkness. He couldn't let that happen, not to him, and not to his wife.

AT TIMES Parts was sure he was about to make a breakthrough, absolutely certain that his wife was the Heart mentioned in Roland's diary. At those moments he dreamed of a day when he would present his wife with the evidence of her anti-Soviet activity during his time in Siberia. He imagined the scene, enjoyed the fantasy. He would be calm and polite—perhaps standing under the orange lamp in the living room, his back straight, his voice firm and low, presenting his facts with careful exactitude. The expression on her face would break open like an eggshell with his very first irrefutable statement, and by the time he finished she would be lying on the carpet like a stillborn calf he'd dragged forth with his own hands, the rope still in his grasp.

IN HIS HOPE for such a moment Parts had even traveled to the Armses' old house in Taara Village. The landscape there had been strange and familiar at the same time. He could smell the hogs on the kolkhoz from inside the bus. Ash trees still lined the avenue to the manor house. There was a smell of smoke in the air—they were burning winter hay near the apple orchard, and piles of leaves farther off. He saw the swoop of a goshawk between the trees. The chickens had been let out and were dashing around the yard, some basking in the sunshine. He noticed that the yard at the Armses' house didn't have a rooster. Feed was too precious to waste on useless mouths. The Office had probably already gotten word of a new joke going around: The new farming system was so strict it wouldn't even grant a hen her rooster.

DISTANT RELATIVES OF LEONIDA'S had moved into the house and were standoffish with strangers. When they all sat down to dumpling soup, the mood was a little lighter, and Parts mentioned in passing the times his wife had come to help on the farm. He spoke confidently, as if he knew what he was talking about. His wife's name wasn't familiar to them, but then he got the idea to ask about the photos from Anna's funeral, which had to be among the possessions Leonida left in the house. Just as he'd suspected, Roland wasn't in the photos. Funerals, weddings, and birthdays were always closely watched and had been the downfall of many forest men, who couldn't all stay away from important family occasions. Roland was an exception. The idea that at Auntie Anna's funeral her children were nowhere to be seen brought tears to Parts's eyes. It was a wrong that couldn't be righted. He didn't let the others see how upset he was, and got up to leave. As he left the farm, he stopped by the still house. It, too, was occupied by several people, who directed him to the stable to speak to the head agronomist. Parts found the man at the kolkhoz office in the former manor house and told his story again, said he just happened to be in the area and was looking for someone who had known his aunt before she passed away, someone he could talk with about her last moments. The agronomist remembered the former tenants of the still house, and remembered that one of the women was now living in the new silicate house with her daughter, who worked as the kolkhoz bookkeeper. When Parts went to knock on the woman's door, she was distrustful. It wasn't until he started talking about his years in Siberia that the woman mentioned Rosalie, and said that she'd wondered about Rosalie's fiancé, who had fled to Sweden but never sent his old mother a package, adding that of course that was how things were in those days. Parts couldn't get anything else out of her, just that same story Anna and Leonida had made up to hide Roland's whereabouts, or because they wanted to believe it.

Parts also went to Valga, looking for old neighbors and orchestrating chance encounters at the market. Over a glass of beer he steered the conversation to the past and lamented that he hadn't been able to find his dear cousin, who had often visited his wife at home while Parts was away in Siberia. The neighbor in question had tried to bring to mind Parts's wife's guests. After wrinkling his brow for a bit, he apologized. He didn't remember the cousin, or any visitors at all. From what he'd heard, Juudit had preferred to keep to herself. Parts believed him, and squashed his feeling of frustration like a cockroach. He'd wasted a lot of time for nothing. It was time to get out of this backwater and back to his real job, and behave like a professional.

He did, however, continue to study his wife, analyzing over and over the impression he'd had of her right after he came back from Siberia, going over the Valga years in his mind, the couch springs, the mousetraps in the corners in every room, the cries from the neighbors' baby, the intimate noises that had carried through the walls and kept her awake at night, the set of her hands as she lit the stove or washed the milk bottles to take them to the store. He remembered the original owner of the house, the wife of a man who ran a bus company, her submissive demeanor, her old-fashioned dresses, how his wife had always apologized for disturbing her whenever they happened to be in the kitchen at the same time, to show she understood that she was a guest in the woman's home, acknowledging that they were the only Estonians in the house. But he didn't remember her doing anything suspicious. She hadn't cared about picking up the mail herself, she was never called to the phone, had never met with anyone or had visitors, had always stayed at home.

She had been silent about the days of German rule, except for a brief episode when Parts had found out the fate of Hellmuth Hertz. It was a few months after he returned to Estonia. Parts found his wife at home with a bottle of vodka and a candle lit. When he asked what the occasion for celebration was, she announced that it was her German lover's birthday. Parts asked whatever happened to her German, and she answered that he'd been shot on the beach like a dog. She said it as if it were self-evident, as if she assumed that Parts knew all about her adventures, and Parts behaved as if he did know, including the part about when they were caught trying to escape, how she had shot at the Germans who were after them, but missed, was such a bad shot that she hadn't been able to save him. She started laughing, poured the contents of her glass down her throat, shook her head. She would have liked to kill every one of them she could hit. Parts thought back to the movement of the German's hand when he caressed her ear. He didn't feel anything anymore when he thought about it, just longing, and he got up and left, walked through the night and came back in the morning. When his wife woke up, she didn't seem to remember their conversation of the night before. They never talked about the German again. Afterward, of course, he had wondered if she'd been a bit too mild, considering that she had lost her lover and her new life, but perhaps time had done its work. After all, Parts didn't cry about Danzig anymore. He'd managed to move on. But what about Roland? Had time cooled the memories in his mind, too? Parts remembered well how when the hammer and sickle was hoisted up the flagpole at Pikk Hermann on September 22, 1944, the flag that was taken down wasn't Hitler's—it was Estonia's own flag. Five days of independence. Five days of freedom. Parts had seen the flag himself, although in his manuscript he naturally didn't mention it, because the Soviet Union had liberated Estonia from the Hitlerists. Had Roland seen that same sight, and if he had, had he been able to let go of it?

The noises from upstairs interrupted his thoughts again. Maybe the Office didn't realize how willing Parts was to send his wife someplace where she wouldn't be a danger to anyone. But no. The Office must know his situation. They must have had his home under surveillance. They probably still did. Every single word he and his wife exchanged was likely recorded, everything, including the time she suddenly threw a jar of sour cream and hit him right in the head. Parts had cleaned up the mess. He closed his eyes. What if his wife had been recruited to spy on him?

Parts opened his eyes, went into the bathroom, took one more gulp of Hematogen, and splashed water on his face, patting it dry and plucking the bits of terry cloth from his cheeks. He looked tired; his hairline was receding. He picked up his wife's mascara, spit on the brush as he had seen her do, and dabbed it on his temples. Then he rinsed away the dandruff that floated down into the sink and looked at the result in the mirror. The mascara freshened up his appearance. The scar on his cheek that his wife had given him was fading quickly. There was no reason to feel down, even if he hadn't yet had a breakthrough in her case as he had hoped. Sometimes you just had to accept that you'd come to a dead end. Sometimes your suspicions were groundless. Maybe he didn't need to lock his office door before going to sleep. On the way back to his desk he stopped to look at the mousetrap in the corner of the entryway. If his wife didn't have anyone to worry about, why did she always check those traps—she who was usually so careless about household chores?

Tallinn, Estonian SSR,
Soviet Union

THE SMOKE OVER the table was so thick that Evelin couldn't make out the faces of the people introducing themselves. One with too much beard, three girls wearing pants, one with overgrown bangs. She forgot all their names immediately and before she had time to even sit down she was already involved in a conversation. The Lithuanians had their own man in the Kremlin who knew a lot, knew how to go along with the authorities, but not too much. We should follow Lithuania's example. They didn't have hordes of Russians coming into their country like Estonia did. What had they done right? Poles were pouring into Lithuania. Just Poles. Imagine!

"We didn't kill enough Russians, that's why. There's not a Russian left who would dare go to Lithuania."

"And all those new factories—they only accept Lithuanians, no Russians. Why can't we do that?"

"If we act like Lithuania, the situation might change. Get all the young people into the Party, like they did there."

"Just like in Lithuania."

"That's the only way to fix our own country. There's no other way."

"No other way." A sigh went around the table. "No other way."

Evelin kept quiet; she didn't have anything to say. Rein's fingers had let go of hers. They fluttered over the table in rhythm with the excited talk. A few hours earlier he had pressed his lips against her hand on Victory Square and blown air between their palms, said that was where their shared heart was, where it would always be warm and loving. His good mood blew through Evelin's hair like the summer wind at Pirita Beach and he smoothed her curls and they laughed and Rein invited her to Café Moskva to meet some of his friends. Evelin had looked at the glass door of the café just a stone's throw away. She would be spending an evening there. All because she had told him that she'd written to her mother and said that Rein would be coming to visit after exams. He had stopped in his tracks, and at that moment Evelin was sure she'd made the right decision. Nothing could go wrong from now on. After this she would never have to reassure Rein that she loved him, that she was serious, not toying with his feelings, not teasing him, would always be his. Rein would start telling her the things he told his friends, about the books recorded on microfilm that the man in the spectacles developed for him in the darkroom at the gray house. She would find time to arrange things at home for Rein's visit. She had to. Maybe during haying her father wouldn't have time to drink. Her grandmother could be sent to visit relatives. Her mother was sure to understand that it wasn't good for a young couple to be apart all summer. Now Evelin was in Café Moskva in her best blouse but she didn't know what to say although she was trying feverishly to think of something, anything. The talk around the table was strange. She didn't like the way they whispered, spoke in lowered voices. She felt a tightening in her throat and tugged Rein's sleeve. She wanted to go home.

"But why? The night's just started."

"I don't feel well."

"Not from the cognac, I hope."

"I just don't. Sorry."

Rein walked her to the stairs and she glanced out of the corner of her eye at a man they had been talking about at the table. KGB. Naturally. Good God. These people were crazy. Her Rein was crazy, too. She should have known, should have guessed from all the precautions he took, all his secrecy. As she walked past the KGB man's table he tapped his stack of papers, not looking at her as his hand brushed the tablecloth and dropped a crumpled truffle wrapper onto the floor. Evelin could see the dandruff on his forehead, the sharp part in his hair, his shiny nose, his pores, a little scar on his cheek, and she felt weak and squeezed Rein's hand. It was dry. Rein wasn't worried. He was used to being watched by the KGB every evening. Lunatics. Evelin pictured her mother's horrified expression if she'd known what kind of company her daughter was keeping.

COMRADE PARTS COULD STILL feel sleep pressing against his eyes and he decided to go to the men's room to wash his face while the Target sent his pasty fiancée home with a pat. He would have plenty of time. It would take the Target a while to placate her. Parts had never seen the girl in the café before, but the Target's behavior showed that this was the kind of girl he could introduce to his parents, the kind he could marry. She was different from the other girls at the café: dressed up for the evening, careful of her clothes, like a girl from a poor family who knows she won't get another dress until next year. Her demeanor was slightly tense, her face watchful, her expectations high. Parts was certain that the Target wouldn't take the time to walk her all the way home, even though he should, even though most girls would be terribly hurt by such neglect, but she was one of those girlfriends who were always ready to forgive, and the Target was one of those young men who were well aware of the bottomlessness of that forgiveness. Couples like them rarely offered any surprises. They were always the same. It was just a matter of time before the Target managed to enlist her into his foolishness.

Just as Parts was pushing the men's room door open and inhaling deeply so he could hold his breath as long as possible from the toilet stench, his ears caught something. Two of the boys in the Target's circle were arguing in a corner of the leaky, slippery room. Their talk cut off when he walked in, but he had already heard the word and the phrase that followed it, and although something lurched inside him, he walked over to the sink like any man would, turned on the tap, waited for the water to bubble into the basin, wet his hands, patted his face, and went into one of the stalls. He closed the door and leaned against it. The lock was broken. The young men left. Dog Ear. He knew he'd heard it. One of them had clearly said that Dog Ear's new collection of poems had already been sent to the West and had garnered a lot of interest.

Parts stared at the graffiti on the stall wall, the curve of the letters, the obscenities and counterrevolutionary quips. Some of the handwriting was easy to recognize. It made him feel sorry for his colleagues who had to hunt down the culprits. He wasn't one of them and he never would be. That fear had faded in a moment. He knew he was on the right track again. He stepped out of the stall, rinsed his hands, and threw a ruble to the wash-room attendant, making a mental note of her face but unable to tell if she was someone who might work with him. Maybe. Could Dog Ear be so stupid that he always used the same name? Or was this Dog Ear an imitator of the original? Even if he was, an imitator would have to know something about his predecessor. Parts would figure it out. As he walked back into the dining room, he was already smiling, and every step had a little more bounce in it. He should never have lost faith that scum will pile up in one place all on its own.

Tallinn, Estonian SSR, Soviet Union

THE WASHROOM ATTENDANT WAS no use to him. She was a religious old lady and apparently a sincere one, or she wouldn't have been assigned to watch over the lavatory. But Parts had better luck at the student apartments. He met his new informant at Glehn Park, not far from the dorms. The informant arrived limping, complaining of an injured leg. Parts barely managed to listen civilly to her, tried to get her to hurry up and spit it out. She had proven herself surprisingly capable and patriotic, so there was no reason to pretend friendship anymore. In addition to collecting mail, she had copied the Target's telegrams in neat black letters. Parts thanked her effusively, promising to return the bundle in a week as he slipped it into his briefcase, leaving her to rest her shaky legs with the Russians spending the day among the shady shrubbery, unwrapping the newspaper from their boiled eggs and chomping on their onion tops, the students studying for exams, the couples making love in the ruins of Glehn Castle. The Office never would have shown him copies of the letters the Target received—or at most would have given him selected excerpts, typewritten—unless they'd wanted him to start up a correspondence in the Target's name, and he wasn't going to get that kind of assignment, at least for the time being. There were a few letters from the fiancée in the bundle, but Parts didn't dare to hope that any of them would mention Dog Ear. He didn't believe she knew very much, but even a few pages would be enough for a handwriting sample, and maybe something else of use would turn up. Then he could forge letters as evidence or lure Dog Ear out of hiding.

AS HE CAME IN his own front door, he stumbled over a pile of his wife's shoes. His wife's footwear bulged where her corns were and although she could manage with sandals in the summer, in the winter she needed boots, and it was impossible to find any. She would rub her aching feet in the entryway and nag him about it, demanding to know when they were going to get access to the restricted shops—in the next life?—making snide remarks about how in spite of his big talk the only new development she could see was the downward trend of his career; he couldn't even get them any rat-free ground meat. Parts untangled his slippers from a sandal and threw it in the corner. She was right. The situation had to be remedied before it was too late. If nothing else worked, he could buy some bismuth salt and put it in the Target's letters. If he remembered correctly, American spies used something similar. The lab at the Office would find it and increase their surveillance.

PARTS WENT INTO the kitchen, lit the stove, and waited for the water to boil, closing his ears to the clomping sounds upstairs.

There was nothing particularly interesting in the telegrams. The Target's fiancée just told him of her daily routine. The informant had also made a list of visitors and random notes about what she felt was suspicious activity—unusual clothing, for example. Those were completely useless, too. Nothing about Dog Ear. Parts flipped through the addresses on the envelopes. Evelin Kask, Tooru Village. The handwriting was round and even, the pen tip pressed on the paper just right, not too hard, the ink not smudged anywhere, the letters standing narrow within the words. A nice girl's handwriting. He steamed open the envelope. Childish, random observations and descriptions: "I studied hard for the exams and everyone here is waiting for the results, even my neighbor Liisa. My mother wants to send you her own birthday card, but I ought to warn you about my grandma—she's peculiar. She's sitting across the table from me now and asking a lot of questions about you." There were roses on the birthday card. Parts flicked it across the table. The letter was full of longing and prattle and Parts didn't believe that even a foolish girl like her would bore her boyfriend with such tedious descriptions of the countryside and trivial village news. It had to be a secret code, and to break it he would need a lot more correspondence. Something was up, but what? And what did it have to do with Dog Ear? If he did find Dog Ear before the Office did, and it was the same Dog Ear as in the diary, would he be able to squeeze any information out of him about the identity of the Heart?

THE WATER IN THE KETTLE had boiled away. Parts turned out the light and went to the window. The dead trees outside had melted motionless into the dark. He was in dangerous waters. Opening the letters wasn't his job. He wasn't supposed to know the whole picture—just his own small part—he wasn't supposed to go out of bounds. Maybe they were writing a report on him right now, pasting new pictures onto cardboard, recording his personal information, his file bulging; maybe they were considering the best tools to use based on the descriptions in that file, Postal Control already activated, of course, and home surveillance. He remembered the hair he'd left between his papers, how it had disappeared while he was out. Maybe he was wrong to suspect his wife. Perhaps it was just his imagination. He turned on the light and reached for the sprat sandwich, then set it down again. The can of sprats had been opened yesterday. He got an unopened can from the pantry, and a fresh loaf of bread, bought today, from the bread box. No more mistakes.

He went back to the material his informant had given him, trying again to find repeated words, signs of a code. Frustration was unavoidable, the stupid girl's stupid words might be just stupid words. He bit off a sprat's head and sucked on it for a moment, deep in thought. Just as he was starting to feel angry, his eye fell on the piece of blotting paper he'd found in the envelope, folded over some dried flowers. There was writing on it in rose-colored ink. A name. Dolores Vaik. For a moment Parts thought he was dreaming. But he was awake. He snapped up the card. The sender's name was Marta Kask. Parts heard his own heavy sigh from far away. Spit collected in his mouth. Dolores Vaik's daughter's name was Marta. He slowly put the piece of blotting paper, the birthday card, and the envelope down in front of him, and formed the connections, very slowly, in his mind: The Target's fiancée was in the country, at her parents' house. She'd written the letter from the country, used a piece of blotting paper that another woman, Dolores Vaik, or someone who'd written "Dolores Vaik," had used. It was most likely Vaik herself. Judging from Evelin Kask's letter, Dolores Vaik lived at Marta Kask's house. Mrs. Vaik's daughter's name was

Marta. And Marta Kask's daughter seemed to be the Target's fiancée. Had the Office purposely placed the Target's fiancée in his path? Was that what this was all about? Had they done it because they knew that he knew Marta and Mrs. Vaik? Too complicated. That couldn't be it. It was too improbable. How would the Office know they were acquaintances of his, and if they did, why would they care? And yet there was some sense in it. Mrs. Vaik had stayed in Estonia when Lydia Bartels left with the Germans. She'd worked as a veterinarian's reception- ist and she'd participated in illegal activities—Parts knew that. She must have been observed at some point, particularly since she had a contact in Germany, or because of the illegals and emigrants, or because she knew too many people compromised by antigovernment activities. But why would the Office feed Parts the close relative of such a person? Was it about Parts himself? Were they trying some new, preemptive method on him? Remarkable. Really remarkable.

Parts remembered Marta Kask well. When Mrs. Vaik was widowed, she and Marta had supported themselves by helping Lydia Bartels with her sessions. Parts had often sat in Bartels's kitchen waiting for Germans who had insisted on coming to one of her séances. Marta had offered him and the driver something to eat, the Germans had winked at her as they left, and she'd flicked her wheat-colored hair and fended off their approaches. There was continual traffic at those sessions—Bartels had been the favorite of the spiritism enthusiasts among the officers.

Parts hardly noticed the renewed stomping upstairs. He tried to think of counterarguments, tried to find reasons why the connection was a coincidence. He had to get more informa- tion about Mrs. Vaik and Marta, more recent information. That was where the answer would be. He tried to calm his imagina- tion. This was no time for fantasies.

Karl Andrusson. The ads Parts had placed in *Kodumaa* had borne fruit. He had recently received a letter from Karl, in an envelope with Canadian stamps on it. Karl had expressed his gratitude that Mrs. Vaik had taken such good care of his foot. If it weren't for her, his flying career would have been over.

Parts threw open his box of letters and took out the Canadian bundle. Karl always stuck a lot of stamps on the envelope because he knew how valuable they were in philatelic circles.

Comrade Parts dipped his pen in the inkwell.

Tooru Village, Estonian SSR,
Soviet Union

EVELIN'S FATHER LAY on the autumn grass, drooling from the side of his mouth. He had a pistol in his pants pocket. Evelin knew that. She let him be and stepped over the timber of the threshold onto the covered porch. He wouldn't use the gun, not really. The dog, who had waited for her at the bus stop, slipped past her feet into the kitchen. Her mother hurried to greet her, her grandmother followed, warmth steamed from the kitchen, and she was inside, suddenly inside, and grain coffee was rushed to the table, and fresh sweet rolls, and the coal hook clattered, and the aroma of manna pudding reached her over all the other smells as her mother took it out of the oven and pressed her for news. Evelin led the conversation to village happenings. She didn't want her mother to ask about Rein. Luckily her mother got carried away talking about their neighbor Liisa, who had received a letter from her son in Australia, although she'd been sure he was dead, hadn't heard anything from him in twenty years, and then she gets a letter! He sent her a chiffon scarf with it and said he would send more, he knew you could get good money for them here, and they were easy to send, and Liisa was so proud, dizzy with happiness, had been talking about it for weeks, saying My son is alive, as if it couldn't be true, as if it were all a dream. Evelin pretended to listen, let her mother ramble, her grandmother carding wool, Evelin putting in a noise now and then, thinking all the while about Rein and tugging on the curls at the back of her neck. Her mother, father, and grandparents all had straight hair. Her father's was straight as a horse's mane. Why did she have to end up with curly hair? The girl with the white legs had hair that was pale and soft. Evelin was sure Rein liked that look better.

After the evening at the Moskva they'd hardly seen each other. Rein had told her she was a coward, teased her at first for how alarmed she'd been, then reassured her that there was nothing to be afraid of, everything was all right. But it wasn't. Rein hadn't invited her again to the café or the house where the man with the spectacles lived. The visit to her parents' house had been postponed, he had so much to do. It had been a relief. When she'd come back to town at the beginning of autumn, the bustle of activity at the Moskva had diminished, it was almost like it had never happened, and Rein hadn't forgotten her over the summer. He'd taken her out to the movies and dancing right away. But he smelled like vodka and smoked eel from the night before. She could tell what company he'd been keeping and she couldn't refuse when he started to prod her again about when he could come and meet her parents. Maybe at Christmas—which would mean preparing herself for it all over again. The old terror came back. How could she bring Rein here?

"We're beating the flax tomorrow," her mother said. "Liisa said she would give us a hand. Come help me with your father. We should get him indoors."

"Let him lie there. Are they paying him in liquor again? Has the roof been fixed yet?"

"Don't start, Evelin."

Soon they would have the Christmas butchering to do, and in the meantime all the autumn chores. There weren't enough working-age men in the village. Her father did it all, got paid in good old Estonian vodka, and stayed well into the night at the Party boss's wife's house, always working on something that needed fixing, whenever her husband was out. He always came home drunk. Her father would get Rein drinking, and then what would happen? She could already hear the excruciating dinners they would have—Dad drunk, Mom prattling on about calves and flax and Evelin's favorite lamb from childhood, about how she had always wanted to watch as the water started to bubble around the flax when they soaked it in the lake. Evelin glanced at her grandmother carding in the corner. Where would they put her while Rein was visiting? They couldn't send her away at Christmastime. Evelin had heard her father talking about how her grandmother shouldn't travel anymore, and for once Evelin agreed with him. If her parents came to Tallinn and met Rein, maybe he would stop pestering her about coming here. But they couldn't leave the animals and the house unattended—the village was full of thieves. Would Rein be satisfied if only her mother came, so her father could take care of the calves and chickens while she was away? Evelin would bring it up as soon as there was an opportune moment. But she didn't want to talk about Rein right now. What if someone found out what he was involved in? If he got thrown out of the university, he would end up in the army and be gone for years. Did he even realize that? How could he be so reckless? So selfish? How would they ever have their own sheets, their cactuses on the windowsill, their cabinet polished to a shine? What if he was involved with something that could end him up in prison? She couldn't see herself waiting for him outside the walls of the Patarei, or running to buy him bottles of Vana Tallinn, sending it to wherever the army posted him. She remembered a classmate who'd come home in a zinc box after he failed his exams twice and didn't go to the commission interview and then was sent into the army. Rein was crazy, playing a crazy game.

Evelin had made the wrong choice. She should have paid more attention to that Polish tech student who wanted a wife from Estonia and said so outright. He studied hard, but he wasn't like Rein, who refused to call Victory Square Victory Square because he didn't want to use the name the communists gave it. Or she should have gone out with that Siberian boy during her first year. He had asked her to the dance, but she didn't go, she had her eye on the upperclassmen just like the other freshman girls, thinking they were wiser, thinking he was immature, the way he would always say in the middle of a nice evening that he just wanted to go to sleep between clean, white sheets, nothing more. Clean, white sheets were enough for him, but not for Evelin, and now look where her greed had gotten her.

Her mother coughed and held her side. It was getting better, her cough, the too-deep wheeze of her breathing. Evelin said she would do all the barn work that weekend, but her mother said no, her studies were more important, and her father thought so, too. Nothing was more important than Evelin getting out of the kolkhoz, and once the flax was retted she was going to make Evelin a new sweater that would be good to read in, would keep her warm even in the winter. She would leave the sleeves long and wide like Evelin had asked her to, although Evelin hadn't told her why she wanted them that way—to hide her cheat sheets. The summer exams had gone well, even the orals. Her scores in Party History and Industrial Intensification and Efficiency were high. She'd had a chance to look through all eighty of the professor's questions and had made crib sheets for herself and Rein. Sometimes she'd gone to the countryside to study and when she got back to town she sat in Glehn Park day after day cramming for the tests. The park was plagued by exhibitionists and rowdy gangs of kids and couples necking. She wasn't the only one they were bothering—other lone women had gathered on the bench next to the artificial pond to read and bask in the sun. She'd gotten to know one of them, a woman who'd once given her half of the orange in her lunch. The woman had even helped drill her on Marx. It was more fun that way; it kept her alert. She'd also given Evelin tips about hairdressers who were particularly good at blow-drying curly hair, laughed and said she was no stranger to untamable hair. But eventually her presence had become oppressive. She was too curious for a complete stranger. Evelin stopped studying in Glehn Park and never tried the hairdresser the woman recommended, though she'd seen how Rein stared at the white-legged girl's flowing tresses.

After the summer exams Evelin crammed for fall-term chemistry and physics to ease herself into the change of subjects. Office technology and touch-typing went well, but you didn't get a grade in your study book for those. Next came more exams in Party History, Problems in Economic Analysis, and Problems in Analytical Methodology. She needed to find a good place to study for the exams in January, and was already worried about it. The library put her to sleep, it was too noisy in the dorms, and she couldn't go outside in the winter. Maybe she should switch to a more interesting subject. Highways? Surveying? Social sciences were out—no more Marx for her. She had other options, but Rein was more of a worry. He didn't care if there wasn't a place to study. Passing calculus and programming was no problem. ALGOL programming was easy for him—the final exam consisted of simply solving some task on the computer—but he wasn't going to pass the orals. On the other hand, his parents had money, otherwise he never would have passed his previous courses. He spent the fall planning a student demonstration, and he'd started to talk to Evelin about it, warily.

Tallinn, Estonian SSR,
Soviet Union

IN HIS LETTER to Karl Andrusson, Parts had sent greetings from Mrs. Vaik, saying his wife had "always kept in touch with her." He also mentioned how Mrs. Vaik had been delighted that Karl had used his skills and become a pilot. The reply came unusually quickly, in spite of Postal Control—it only took a few weeks. Parts was so eager to open it that he tore the Canadian stamps, and it didn't even upset him. Karl was happy to hear about Mrs. Vaik and asked Parts to give her his address. The Andrussons' mother had lost contact with Mrs. Vaik when she moved in with her daughter, but she'd heard rumors that her granddaughter was studying to be a bank manager at the university in Tallinn.

Parts had his confirmation—he'd been following Mrs. Vaik's granddaughter the whole time. There was nothing else of importance in Karl's letter, just musings about whether Mrs. Vaik missed her home province as much as he did, though there was an ocean separating him from it and she was at least living in her native country. Parts cursed himself. If he'd had any relationship with his wife, he would have known about this and wouldn't have had to get the news by rowboat from Canada. Karl Andrusson might even have information about Roland, but Parts didn't dare ask—he didn't want to get the Office interested in Roland. Using a false name, though, would arouse Karl's suspicions, make him start asking the wrong questions. Parts popped a piece of pastilaa in his mouth and wiped his hands on his handkerchief. He let the window-rattling train pass and closed his eyes to see the pattern better, not pausing to lament that it hadn't occurred to him to use Karl before. He'd clearly let himself be blinded by his research: a disease of the profession. The more he weighed the matter, the more improbable it seemed that the Office would have trained him and transferred him to surveillance simply by chance. His real Target was, in fact, Kask, or the Kask family, and perhaps the real goal was for Parts to apply preemptive methods to Evelin Kask or her parents, or to try to gain the girl's confidence. Was she really such a significant target? All this trouble for one young girl— what was the larger purpose? He already had plenty of compromising material. It would probably be enough just to hint to her how easy it was to get expelled from the university, what a snap it would be to put her grandmother on a train headed for a cold country. Parts listened to himself. Confusion was one of the Office's methods, and they had confused him, he had to admit it. If he started using the girl to hunt for Dog Ear, he had to be careful not to alert the Office. But perhaps he would take the risk and switch his interest from the Target to the girl. Just for a little while. Would anyone notice?

THE END OF the Moskva Café operation was approaching and it lightened Comrade Parts's mood as he melted along behind Evelin Kask when she came out of class. He looked at her with new eyes, greedily, catching her scent. A good, old-fashioned chase, though she behaved as she always had. Parts adjusted his steps to the cobblestones along Toompea, his coat dissolving into the walls, sensing his own invisibility. The length of the girl's skirt was more modest than the others', and she had on white Marat summer gloves that patted and tugged at her hair every third step. Her metal heels slipped on the stones and rose clumsily onto the bus, wobbling a little as she got off at a stop near the dorms. Parts kept a sufficient distance as she went into a building, letting her reach the second floor before he followed. He dug some empty pen cartridges out of his money pouch and let the line grow a bit before he got into it himself. The woman sitting behind the counter was focused intently on her work. She removed the balls from the ends of the pens, pushed each cartridge into the machine, turned the crank, handed back the filled cartridge, and took the kopeks. The line whispered and murmured, moved forward. He didn't see any of the students from the café. Suddenly the girl's face tensed and she held the bag she was carrying a little farther from her body, her arm straight. A tech student came up and said hello to her, but left quickly. Parts looked around, saw the boy go out the door with the girl's bag in his hand, and slipped out of the line, letting the boy gain a little distance and walk between the tall buildings alone, past a gigantic Dove of Peace mural to a bus stop. Parts waited for a while before joining the group of people at the stop, got on the bus last, and exited last. When the boy left the road to push his way into the bushes, Parts almost tripped over his own feet and understood his mistake—he'd lost the Target several times on this same road, but had blamed his own fatigue and overcautiousness. Only now did he realize that it hadn't been an accident. Those skillful disappearances were a sign that the Target knew someone was following him. The Target was simply better at evasion than this boy was. This boy wasn't careful at all; his steps were noisy, he swore as he stumbled among the thistles. Parts saw him slip into the back door of a gray house and made a note of the time. He'd already guessed that the bespectacled man who let the boy into the house was conducting illegal activities.

A child was spinning a top next to a sandbox that smelled of the neighborhood cats. The child was happy to take a ruble from him and tell him the name of the poet who lived in the house.

Parts went to the library to acquaint himself with the man's poetry. He'd published poems in praise of the rising of the workers at just the right time and in just the same tone that Roland had cursed in the works of Dog Ear years ago. Of course, it could be a coincidence, but how many poets could there be who were mixed up in illegal dealings and used the same code name?

Tallinn, Estonian SSR,
Soviet Union

THE FOLLOWING EVENING, Comrade Parts dozed over coffee, truffles, and a Moscow salad in the Café Moskva. His vigilance was taxed by the late working hours and by his attempts to familiarize himself with poetry. When his chin dropped onto his chest, he straightened up and looked around. The Target's circle was joined by a group of art students in violet caps, though some were bareheaded, and one girl wore a too-short skirt and held her hand tight against her legs as she walked, either to pull the hem down or simply to prevent it from creeping up any farther. The cornflower-blue skirt was topped with a white blouse—he should remember to mention the nationalist colors in his report.

THE VIOLET CAPS WERE followed by a small, dark man with hair that straggled like an unkempt woman's and a beard that hid his features. Parts recognized him—a tasteless painter of anti-Soviet works. The Office had no doubt been alerted to the man's activities long ago. His appearance alone, with its nod to capitalist fashion, exuded imperialism. The café's limp-wristed pianist played his usual tunes, the long-haired painter flirted with the girls. Then one of the girls gave a little cry of surprise that cut through the smoke like a sharp brushstroke and woke Parts from his torpor. His eyes flew open. What was that tune? Had it come out of his own head? Out of his mouth? Was he dreaming? The music still had a jazzy beat. The girls had fallen silent. A smoker at the next table forgot to flick the ash from her cigarette and it fell onto the table. The Target stood up. Parts furtively looked around. The group of students had turned toward the pianist. The woman at the next table was beaming, her hand lifted to touch the shoulder of her companion, her mouth silently moving. *Saa vabaks Eesti meri, saa vabaks Eesti pind.* Parts blinked. The music changed to a march rhythm that flowed through the pianist as he improvised, the stirring cadence slipping away and reappearing again. The woman's lips contin-ued their soundless song, and now the bearded man had stood up and so had the twittering girls on his arms, and soon the entire group was on its feet. Parts could hear himself gasp. He looked at his colleague at the table in the corner. He, too, was standing, his posture stiff, as if ready to leap, his gaze alert, sweeping over the dining room, meeting Parts's eyes for a moment, and at that moment the march slowed and the bearded man and the Target opened their mouths. *Jään sull' truuiks surmani, mul kõige armsam oled sa.* . . . Parts's colleague swept across the room like a wind, slammed the lid shut over the piano keys, stopped in front of the bearded man's gaping mouth and, waving his arms, said something to him, and then, just as windily, left the café. His coattails brushed Parts in passing, his face splotched, his eyes slits. After he'd stomped out of the room and down the stairs, the pianist opened the piano and began playing his regular evening repertoire. The bearded man's friends dashed to the top of the stairwell, their foreheads shining with sweat, their frenzied whispers echoing. They didn't look around as they went, and no one looked at them, as if they'd become invisible, yet the whole room rippled like the sea before a storm. Parts had heard a few snatches of words, but he didn't want to believe his ears. Had his colleague really gone up to the bearded man and said, "For God's sake, be quiet! I'm with the KGB!"

IT WAS the same pianist the next day, and the next, and Parts started to wonder if his colleague had even reported the incident. In any case, he didn't come back to the café—another colleague had replaced him. The bearded man stayed away, too. There was already more than enough compromising information on him. The group was obviously planning something, perhaps a student march, in which case Parts's assignment to the Moskva would end before it happened, or right afterward. He would have to hurry if he wanted to confirm his suspicions while the group with all its tentacles was still free and easy to access.

THE POET HIMSELF opened the door. The house was as gray as before, the man's clothes fading into the walls as he adjusted his glasses, his eyes barely visible behind the thick lenses. Parts smiled politely and said:

"Dog Ear."

The moment was undeniably delicious. Parts knew that the man still had a chance. The skills of a good actor, a proper defense, could save him. Parts had seen many liars in his day who could mount a wonderful deflective battle. But the man in front of him wasn't one of them. The expression on the poet's face collapsed like a house whose timbers have rotted away, taken down with one strategic blow of an axe.

"I believe we need to talk. Let's not let your past disturb your present career as a writer." Parts paused for effect. "You ought to think about your young followers. Your writings are not raising the morals of our youth the way they should."

"My wife will be home soon."

"I would be happy to meet her. Shall we continue our conversation inside?"

The poet backed up.

"We'll try of course to make the publishing ban as short as possible, won't we?"

THE POET WAS an easy case. Much easier than Parts had expected. As he left the house, he wondered how the man had kept up his illegal activities as long as he had, right under the Party's nose. He'd been a distinguished Soviet poet for decades, had enjoyed the approval of the propaganda department, Glavlit, and every possible agency, yet he had continued his underground activities. All the while writing poems in praise of the Party. Parts walked briskly to the bus stop. Only then did his weariness hit him, and he had to lower himself into a crouch. The poet cracked easily because Parts had incriminating information. But there was nothing he could use to blackmail his own wife. The poet had let the identity of the Heart drop into Parts's lap like a Junkers bomber that had run out of fuel, but Parts still wasn't sure whether Roland had told the Heart everything, every single thing. Was this why the wall between Parts and his wife was so insurmountable? Had she actually known this entire time about all the reasons he'd had to get rid of Roland? Did it even matter anymore? He was baffled at how little the confirmation had shaken him, and quite admired himself for it. How calm he was. How professional. Maybe he'd always guessed it deep down, but that wasn't important. A pure pleasure that he hadn't felt in years came over him. He was in control of the situation, and it was a feeling he'd almost forgotten. As if he'd snatched an entire flock of birds out of the air and held them in his hands and they'd turned to stone at his touch, frozen in midflight. His typewriter keys were waiting for him at home. So was his wife. The Office could take care of finishing up the case.

Tallinn, Estonian SSR,
Soviet Union

EVERYTHING WENT WRONG. Rein and the three others who'd organized the march had been arrested. Evelin trembled in bed under her blanket. The quiet of the dorm pressed down from the ceiling. The shouts still rang in her head: *The militia! The militia!* She didn't want to leave her room. They were no doubt whispering in the kitchen. She had no news, didn't know where Rein was or what was going to happen, that's what she'd told them. But she did know. Rein would have to give up his studies—everyone understood that, there was no need to whisper about it. Should she go home? Could she? Would the militia go there and get her? Would they evict her from the dorms, from the university? Her mother wouldn't be able to bear it. She couldn't tell her family about this. It was impossible. Would Rein be sent to prison or the army, or both? Or maybe to an insane asylum? Evelin sat up. An insane asylum. Good God. That had happened to the boy who wrote flyers, the one whose typewriter they'd been searching for when they turned all the boys' dorm rooms upside down. Every room, all one thousand beds, all one thousand closets. They didn't find the typewriter, but they found the boy, and he was taken to Paldiski 52, and no one had heard from him since. Rein was crazy. She had been right about that. And being in love with a crazy person was dragging her into his craziness. She'd put her graduation at risk—her graduation dress, her chance to wear a faded cap and carry a worn-out ballpoint pen like the other final-year students, her chance to be an engineer. She and Rein would never see each other again, would never have their own sheets or cactuses on the windowsill or a polished cabinet. She would never again have to wonder whether she should let him take off her slip. She should have let him. She should have gone out with someone from the Party. She should have listened to the girl who told her that Rein was a poor choice, should have thought of herself: *I want to graduate. I want a family. I want a home. I want to get married. I want a good job.* Evelin ran to the closet. There was nothing incriminating in it, she knew that, but they would come soon and they would go through the closets, the beds, the pillows. She threw her belongings into her plywood suitcase, put on her shoes, ran into the hallway and down the stairs, the other girls peeking out of their rooms. She could feel their gaze pricking her skin, her steps echoing in her ears as her feet carried her along the fence toward the bus stop, the fence with the prisoners working behind it. Would Rein be there soon? Would she? She ran faster. Her bag was heavy, but she kept going. Terror carried her to bus number 33, so full of factory workers that there was no place for her, but her panic pushed her through the folding doors, squeezing her in, and stayed with her as the bus pulled away. Evelin leaned against a babushka's white, sheet-draped bundle, like all the other white sacks full of goods bought in Estonia that the Russians carried on their backs, stooped, toward the train station and from there to Siberia, and soon she would be going there, too, that's where they would take her. The grinding of her teeth was the grinding of the tracks, tensing her spine with fear, ready to strike her, to sink its teeth into her flesh, but not yet, not yet, first she would go home. She wanted to see her home before they came, because they would come, they always did. Maybe they were already waiting at her mother's house. Evelin's eyes were dry, though they had been wet like Rein's when she saw the parade of torches in rows descend along Kiek in de Kök. They had squeezed each other's hands. Everything was peaceful and Rein thought of the St. George's Night Uprising in medieval times. That night, too, the torches of the slaves had risen out of the darkness. But it had ended in a bloodbath. She should have remembered that. She should have remembered it when she heard Rein talking about it, not just smiled, as they started marching along the Narva road toward Kadriorg singing *"Saa vabaks Eesti meri, saa vabaks Eesti pind,"* but she had smiled and cheered with the others like an idiot, until she heard the shouts of *Militia!* and a girl in front of her kicked off her high-heeled shoes and took off running toward an alley in her stocking feet and people started pushing back from the front of the march and the torches fell on the ground. *The militia!* someone shouted again, and her hand was loose from Rein's hand and she couldn't see him anywhere and she ran—*militia!*—ran without knowing where she was going, and ended up at the gates of Patkuli, shut for the night, and climbed over the gate and curled up on the stairs waiting for the confusion to die down.

As the bus approached her home, Evelin realized. Everyone would see them coming to arrest her. The whole village would see. She couldn't do that to her parents. She went back to Tallinn.

Tooru Village, Estonian SSR,
Soviet Union

C OMRADE PARTS JOINED the end of the line. Women with
scarves on their heads turned to look at him. He didn't recognize anyone in the village. The whole area was new to him
and he hadn't had time to prepare for the task psychologically.
Everything had happened so quickly. Suddenly he just found
himself riding in a marshrutka on his way to the countryside.
His superiors had given no sign that they knew he had ever
crossed paths with Mrs. Vaik and Marta, but he couldn't think
of any other reason that he of all people was given this assignment. It wasn't his area.

Marta Kask was due in the village for shopping day, like
everyone else. Amid the bustle—men carrying bread for the
cows in sacks on their bent backs, loads of empty milk bottles
strapped on bicycles—he recognized Marta easily.

"Marta? Is that really you?"

Marta jumped, her eyes widening as though he'd thrown a

stone in a lake, and at that moment his uncertainty vanished. The woman didn't understand the value of the information she had, he was sure of it. She didn't realize that she had material that could be bought and sold to save her daughter, knowledge of the time he'd spent in the company of men in Berlin that she could use to blackmail him. For an instant he pitied her, then he got to work, pressing through the crowd to where she stood, marveling at the odds of their meeting, telling her how he was here for only one day, working on Estonian Soviet Socialist Republic Teachers' reform issues.

"They're planning to move all the history teacher training to Moscow, but it'll never work," he said with a laugh and a wink. "I won't let it. We ought to have a cup of coffee together, since we've had the good luck to run into each other after all these years. What do you say?"

He noticed her looking around, looking for someone—but who? She obviously wanted to send word ahead. When a young scamp ran up to her, Parts grabbed a three-ruble note from his pocket and pushed it into his hand.

"A kid ought to be allowed something sweet on shopping day, don't you think? I'm coming to look at your school tomorrow. Go tell your teacher that everything's going to be fine."

The kid disappeared.

"Why such a long face, Marta?" He looked straight into her eyes, registering the movements of her pupils, the way she shifted her weight from one foot to the other and adjusted the angle of her scarf over her temples. "It really is such a coincidence to meet you like this. As an old friend of the family, I ought to tell you that we've been worried about your daughter—Evelin, isn't it?"

"Worried? About Evelin?" Marta said, her voice cracking like the surface of a lake in a sudden freeze.

"Working for the education ministry is a wonderful job. You get a view of the future of the entire fatherland, and we're very concerned about the future of our youth. It's so terribly sad for a young person's life to take the wrong direction. I assume you've heard about the student march?"

Marta flinched at the question, silent for slightly too long, unable to decide whether to confirm or deny.

"Evelin is innocent, of course—but her friends. Her fiancé was arrested."

Marta looked like she would topple over.

"We can talk more about it over coffee," he said, gesturing meaningfully at the people in their vicinity. Marta looked around as if hoping for rescue.

"Perhaps you should make your purchases first, then we can go."

Marta seemed afraid to move. Parts led her to the waiting line. She obeyed like a sheep. The abacus on the counter clacked briskly—still four pigs' feet left, the rustle of wrapping paper, Marta tugging at her scarf, settling it better against her forehead, tucking a wisp of hair underneath, damp, a bead of sweat flowing down her temple like a tear. Parts, smiling politely at the people pushing their way toward the counter, didn't budge from her side. Someone came to tell Marta that her husband had been first in line that morning. Marta nodded. Parts gave her a questioning look.

"Grocery shopping is always left to the women," she said.

He guessed what she meant. Her husband had come to buy liquor and forgotten everything else. The same problem everywhere, in every kolkhoz, no one interested in working on paydays or when the shops had something to sell, even the cows left unmilked. Comrade Parts felt refreshed. The situation was progressing very smoothly.

He helped her put the jars of sour cream in her bag and led her out, her steps wavering as she pushed her leaning bicycle, the bag of bottles clinking, the silicate bricks of the village center breathing cold. The air smelled like snow and frost. The mood was oppressive, Parts cheery. Marta turned her bike into a driveway. Smoke curled from the chimney, there was mooing from the barn. Whitewashed trunks of apple trees lined the garden.

"It's such a mess inside," Marta said. "Maybe . . ."

"That's completely all right, Marta dear."

She glanced in the direction of the sauna. Parts stopped in midstep. He turned and ran toward the sauna. Marta ran after him, clutched at his hand, his coat. He kicked her away, left her shouting behind him, and pushed the sauna door open. Roland was asleep on the bench, his suspenders hanging from the top of his pants, his mouth open. Snoring.

Tallinn, Estonian SSR,
Soviet Union

Roland Simson, previously known as Mark, had become Roland Kask, and was living modestly, attracting no one's attention, in the village of Tooru. His daughter Evelin Kask was studying in Tallinn. Who would have believed that a man pretending to be an exemplary father had just a short time before mercilessly shot infants before their mothers' eyes? Who would have believed that people capable of such despicable acts were spreading their insidious disease to the next generation? Evelin Kask followed in her father's footsteps. She had become an enthusiastic anticommunist and supporter of nationalist imperialism.

COMRADE PARTS LAID his wrists on his knees. The last chapters were starting to come together. Work was like child's play now that he had his days to himself. The photographs for the book had already been chosen. He'd picked one of them to be a portrait of the author in the days of fascism. To their credit, the Red Army had photographed the Klooga camp as soon as they arrived, and among the photos of prisoners shot in the back Parts had found one to call his own. Luckily for him, emaciated people on the verge of death and those already dead bear a strong resemblance to one another.

> *Comrade Parts survived Klooga by pretending to be dead. He was one of the group of brave Soviet prisoners brought from Pata-rei to Klooga to be murdered. He witnessed the horrors. They tried to force him to burn the other Soviet citizens on pyres and he attempted to escape. He was shot in the back and seriously wounded. If the Red Army had liberated Klooga even one day later, he would have perished. Thanks to his resourcefulness he is a living witness opposing the Fascist cancer and telling the truth about it today.*

Was that a good caption, or was the shooting a bit much? What if someone wanted him to prove it? He would think about it some more. There weren't likely to be any more editorial comments from the Office, but he still had to flesh out the details, give them a dash of truth; then the book would be ready for its flight into the world. He had found the finishing touches for the story when he went to acquaint himself with life in Tooru Village, tasted the local color, estimated distances, researched landmarks, trudged to a cairn in the middle of a field where there was an unobstructed view of the Kasks' house. He'd come equipped with galoshes and two pairs of wool socks in case of snakes. And binoculars, good for detailed observations of the life of the house, for watching the two scarf-headed women going about their work.

He wasn't tired at all, even though the previous night had been raucous. The Office meeting had continued late over a meal, followed by one or two bars. It wasn't the sort of thing he was used to, but why not, just once? He had managed to work in hints about the subject of his new project and indirect reminders of the Finnish experiences of his youth, had mentioned that blending in would be easy for him in Finland. As a respected author and research historian he would have a ready-made, entirely believable background, and the academic world wouldn't pose a problem. It was time he started planning his future. Why not the Soviet embassy in Helsinki? The work of a cultural attaché might be pleasant. The reopened ship traffic between Finland and Estonia meant that the Office's resources were stretched to their limits. The authorities had to hurry to acquire new working operatives, people who could be trusted, and there was a danger that they would see him as a suitable candidate for surveillance of Western tourists in Tallinn, for broadening correspondence with Finland, but not for a posting to Finland. He hoped his book would alleviate this problem when it was published. He didn't intend to just watch as the boats left the harbor. He was going to be on one of them.

Or perhaps he could work for the DDR section of the committee for Estonian cultural relations abroad. His German was excellent. Maybe he could get into the German archives to do some research. He might even find something there about a man named Fürst. Up until now the name had never come up, but it might before long, either here or in another country. That might even be fun. Parts decided to look for someone at the head of the Office who had the committee in his purview, someone to whom he could suggest the idea. It would be better if his appointment to Finland or Berlin were someone else's idea. Too much initiative could be dangerous. They would suspect him of wanting to defect.

Just a few pages more, then the climax. The impatient keys of the Optima danced merrily.

The Fascist officers had to hurry because the Red Army was approaching in full force in 1944. In the morning all the prisoners at Klooga were ordered to line up for roll call. To keep the situation under control, SS-Untersturmführer Werle lied and told the prisoners they were going to be evacuated to Germany. Two hours later the Commandant's assistant, SS-Unterscharführer Schwarze, was leading the selection: the three hundred most physically sturdy men were pulled out of the lines. They were told they had been ordered to help with the evacuation. That was also a lie. In truth, the men carried logs to a clearing about a kilometer outside the camp. That afternoon, six more healthy Soviet citizens were chosen from among the prisoners. They were ordered to load a truck with two barrels of either petroleum or oil. The barrels were for the pyres. Mark supervised the building of the pyres.

At the camp, Mark behaved brazenly, as befitted his nature. Mark was the Germans' henchman at Klooga just before the Red Army freed Estonia from Fascist slavery. The Fascists didn't know what to do with the prisoners. There was no time to transfer the camp because the victorious Soviet Army was on its way and most of the prisoners had been so severely mistreated that they didn't have the strength to travel. Boats were waiting at the harbor for the soldiers and officers, but what should they do with the prisoners?

Mark thought of a solution. He suggested the pyres.

The logs were laid on the ground with planks placed on top of them. The logs were of pine and spruce, the planks seventy-five centimeters long. In the middle of each pyre were four planks facing in four different directions. They were supported by a few pieces of wood, and were apparently meant to serve as a kind of chimney. The pyres covered an area of about six by six and a half meters.

At five o'clock in the evening, the sadistic murder of the brave Soviet citizens began. The victims were ordered to lie on the logs with their faces down. Then they were killed with bullets to the backs of their heads. The bodies were in long, tight rows. When a row of bodies was complete, a new row of logs was placed on top of them. The pyres were three or perhaps even four layers high. The place was twenty-seven meters from the forest road, the pyres about three or four meters apart. Eighteen more shattered bodies were found in a radius of five to two hundred meters from the logs. Fragments of bullets were found in the bodies. The dead were later identified by their prisoner numbers.

When the Soviet special commission investigated these atrocities, they also found a burned house nearby, of which nothing remained but the chimneys. In the foundation of the house were found 133 charred bodies, some burned completely to ashes, making identification impossible. Everyone who was there at Klooga on September 19, 1944, is guilty of the mass murder of Soviet citizens and will be given the severest of sentences.

EPILOGUE

Tallinn, Estonian SSR,
Soviet Union

COMRADE PARTS WATCHED his wife from the second-story window. She looked peaceful sitting on the park bench. Her legs weren't even crossed, they were stretched straight in front of her, and her arms were relaxed at her sides. The woman sitting next to her seemed to be smoking, taking long drags with furious motions, but his wife never turned to look at her. Parts could see only the side of her face. Her figure had broadened noticeably. He had never seen her so motionless, like a pillar of salt.

"A remarkable change," he said. "She used to chain-smoke."

"Quite. The insulin shocks have helped," the lead doctor said. "We aren't yet sure of her diagnosis. Asthenic neurasthenia or perhaps psychopathy combined with chronic alcoholism. Or asthenic psychopathy. Or paranoid schizophrenia."

Parts nodded. The last time he'd visited the hospital, the doctor had told him about his wife's nightmares. He hadn't been allowed to see her that time because of the troubling side effects of the medication—her delusions had increased. But the treatment was only in its beginning stages. The doctor felt she was an interesting case; he had never met a patient whose symptoms were so focused on the unspeakable Hitlerists. A more commonly seen symptom was her nurturing instinct toward anyone at any time, though that was more common in women who had suffered the tragic loss of a child. The doctor struck Parts as someone who could spend a long time figuring out his wife's condition. He offered Parts a chair. Parts wanted to leave, but he came away from the window and sat down politely. Perhaps the doctor imagined that as the husband and the closest relative he needed special attention. The doctor seemed sorry that the wife of a man like Parts was being transferred. There were many patients in Paldiski 52 whom no one ever visited.

"Have any more delusions surfaced?" Parts asked.

"For now, no. I hope that the fantasies her mind creates will disappear as the treatment progresses. The illusion of a daughter remains. On her livelier days she talks continuously with her imaginary daughter—asking about her studies, giving her beauty tips, recommending hairdressers for curly hair, things like that. Completely harmless. Unlike her other fantasy figures, her daughter doesn't arouse her aggression. It's more a feeling of pride. She imagines that her daughter is a student at the university."

"Perhaps it's her childlessness that brought on the illness," Comrade Parts said. "She would never agree to see a specialist about it, even when I insisted. Could all of this have been avoided if she had received treatment earlier?"

He let his voice crack ever so slightly, like a man attempting to hide his emotion, although his emotion was mostly relief. Judging by what the doctor said, his wife had finally gone com-

pletely nuts. The doctor hastened to assure him that he had no
reason to reproach himself. These matters were always difficult.

"The interior minister recommends Minsk. That's not such
a long journey," Parts said.

"You have no cause for worry. The new specialist psychi-
atric hospitals are very advanced. Your wife will get the best
possible care."

Parts left a box of Kalevi's chocolates and a string bag full of
oranges on the table for the doctor. He would never ask them to
send his wife home. Since peace had come to his home, Parts's
thinking had become clear, transparent as glass. He had been
much too sentimental, too careful. He should have done this a
long time ago.

THE MORNING WAS particularly clear, the light unusually invig-
orating, and the squirrels in the park gamboled around him as
he left Paldiski 52 savoring the thought that he never had to see
his wife again. This was the end, and the beginning. His steps
grew lighter and lighter. He decided to take a long walk. He felt
like drifting, like a balloon let loose. The first printing of his
book had been eighty thousand copies, and they were already
printing more. They'd only printed twenty thousand copies
of Martinson's piece of trash. Tomorrow would be his day at
the restricted shop. He would buy some ground meat, and in a
month he was going to the DDR, where he knew there had been
a printing of a couple hundred thousand, and then to Finland,
where the book had also been published. He would meet new
people, make new contacts. But today—today was a day off. He
had reason to celebrate, and in this celebratory mood he decided
to explore the new places in the city, ride the new trolley from
the Hippodrome to the Estonia. He bought some Plombir ice

cream and continued walking with it in his hand, not feeling tired, until he noticed that he had walked all the way to Mustamägi. The students coming and going didn't bother him at all anymore. In fact, he felt like he belonged among them, like his life was just beginning, too. The sun slipped out from behind a cloud, the wind blew the sky clean, the silicate walls dazzled, and he had to lift his hand in front of his eyes. At the corner of a hedge a pair of doves took off flying. He turned to look at them, but he couldn't see anything, the sky was too bright. The air had brightened and made the sky as white as a chalked wall, bright as the white of Rosalie's flesh against the whitewashed wall of the barn when she had turned to look at Edgar. So white and angry.

"WHAT ARE YOU up to with those Germans?" she whispered. "I saw you."

"Nothing. Just business."

"You're feeding them communists!"

"I would think that would make you happy. And what about you? What have you been doing there? Does Roland know that his fiancée has been making merry with the Germans late into the night?"

"That's ridiculous. I was just going to the still at Maria's house."

"Then why didn't you tell Roland?"

"What makes you think I didn't? Leonida can't always bring the food to the still. I have younger legs."

"Should I ask him? Should I tell him you got tired of waiting for him to come home?"

"Should I tell your wife that you're back?"

"Go ahead."

"I don't want to hurt her. That's for you to do," Rosalie said. "She's better off without a sick, inadequate husband."

"What are you implying?"

"I saw how you looked at that German you do your business with. I saw it when he was leaving."

"Is looking at a person forbidden in your lunatic mind? How were you looking at him? Your eyes were shining, all right."

"I saw him when he left, coming out from behind the fence. I saw. I know. Do you understand? But Juudit doesn't understand. She doesn't want to understand, can't comprehend it. She's never heard of the kind of sickness you suffer from. But I know there are men like that, men like you. I've thought about it for a long time, by myself. Juudit deserves someone better. I plan to tell her to annul the marriage. She has grounds for it. An abnormal husband, a sickness that makes you unable to perform, unable to have children like a husband should. I've looked it up. It's a disease!"

Rosalie's face creased and wrinkled, the wrinkles turning red, their white edges breaking apart as her hatred struggled out. It wasn't in her nature to have feelings like these. She was a laughing, joyous girl. But no. Her loathing was stronger. It was overwhelming.

ROSALIE'S NECK WAS slender as an alder twig. Like the twigs she would have used a few months later, tied into a broom to sweep the walls before they were whitewashed. Then she would have mixed the limewater, rattling the lime bucket, taken the new horsehair brush that Roland made from the horse's trimmed tail, and pulled the walls toward the light, whiter and whiter toward the light, with fingers thin as cigarette holders, fingers that Roland so loved.

Glossary

Anti-Banditism Combat Department (in Estonian,
Banditismivastase võitluse osakond, or BVVO)

> A unit of the NKVD dedicated to fighting "banditism" (a
> term that encompassed purely criminal activity as well as
> armed anti-Soviet resistance) from 1944 to 1947. In 1947 the
> unit was merged with units fighting political banditry (armed
> anti-Soviet resistance) under the Ministry of Security.

Armed Resistance League (in Estonian, Relvastatud Võitluse
Liit, or RVL)

> An underground organization formed in the Estonian county
> of Läänemaa that fought the Soviet occupation in the late
> 1940s.

Directorate of State Security

> The Estonian branch of the KGB.

Estonian SSR

> The Estonian Soviet Socialist Republic.

Glavlit

> The main government censor of printed materials, televi-
> sion, and radio in the Soviet Union.

KGB (in Russian, Komitet gosudarstvennoy bezopasnosti)

The State Security Committee of the USSR. The KGB was responsible for security and intelligence, with the exception of military intelligence, which was part of the GRU (Glavnoye Razvedyvatel'noye Upravleniye, or Main Intelligence Directorate). The Security Directorate of the Soviet Union went through many name changes: the Cheka (abbreviation of Chrezvychaynaya Komissiya, Emergency Commission, 1917–1922); the GPU (Gosudarstvennoye politicheskoye upravlenie, or State Political Directorate, 1922–1923); OGPU (Obyedinyonnoye gosudarstvennoye politicheskoye upravleniye, or Joint State Political Directorate, 1923–1934); GUGB (Glavnoe Upravlenie Gosudarstvennoi Bezopasnosti, or Main Directorate of State Security, 1934–1941; unit of the NKVD, 1941–1943); NKGB (Narodny komissariat gosudarstvennoi bezopasnosti, or People's Commissariat for State Security) and MGB (Ministerstvo Gosudarstvennoi Bezopasnosti, or Ministry for State Security), 1941, 1943–1945, 1945–1953; MVD (Ministerstvo Vnutrennikh Del, or Ministry of the Interior of the Russian Federation, 1953–1954); and KGB (Komitet gosudarstvennoy bezopasnosti, or State Security Committee, 1954–1991).

People's Commissariat of Internal Affairs (in Russian, Narodnyy Komissariat Vnutrennikh Del, or NKVD)

Soviet commissariat that included the police, secret police, firefighters, border guards, archives, and other functions (1922–1923, 1934–1954). The Russian NKVD became the NKVD of the Soviet Union in 1934. The MVD (Ministry of the Interior) was founded as its successor organization in 1946. There were no people's commissariats following the war—their functions were taken over by the ministries. The MVD continued the commissariat's activities, although certain of its functions were given to the KGB when it was established in 1954.

Staffan Island

An island off the southern coast of Finland near Espoo where the Erna units of Estonian fighters received Finnish military training in 1941 for intelligence gathering and guerrilla warfare in Soviet-occupied Estonia.

GERMAN NATIONAL SOCIALIST OCCUPATION OF ESTONIA (1941–1944)

Baltische Öl

Baltische Öl G.m.b.H. (Gesellschaft mit beschränkter Haftung), a German petroleum company operating in Estonia.

Dorpat

The German name for Tartu, Estonia.

Feldgendarmerie

The Wehrmacht military police.

Gruppe B

A division of the Estonian department of the German security police. The security authority was divided into the German sector (Gruppe A) and the Estonian sector (Gruppe B). The Estonian political police were known as Abteilung B IV (Department B4).

Legionnaires / Estonian SS Legion

The Estonian SS Legion was part of the Waffen-SS from 1942 to 1943. The legion wasn't given the strength that had been planned for and didn't participate as a force in battle. In 1943 the legion was replaced by the Estnische SS-Freiwilligen Brigade, which conscripted Estonian men born between 1919 and 1924. Forced-labor conscripts were given a choice between labor and the brigade.

Omakaitse

An armed domestic security force made up of Estonians. The Omakaitse was first established in 1917 to protect public and private property during a time when society couldn't offer security. The first Soviet occupation abolished the organization. On June 22, 1941, members of the Forest Brothers who had fled Soviet conscription refounded the organization and participated actively in the Summer War (July 22, 1941–October 21, 1941). Following the Germans' victory parade, the Omakaitse's weapons were confiscated and the organization was disbanded. Omakaitse was formed again in August of that same year, this time under the authority of the German occupation. In 1943 Omakaitse became compulsory service for men aged seventeen to forty-five, and in 1944 for men aged seventeen to sixty who were not subject to general conscription.

Organisation Todt

The Third Reich's construction and engineering corps, composed of civilian and military labor. The Todts were responsible for large construction sites both in Germany and in occupied and conquered areas, and they used slave labor.

Ostland

The Reichskommissariat Ostland was the German occupation authority for the parts of Estonia, Latvia, Lithuania, Belarus, and Northern Poland that fell outside of combat areas from 1941 to 1944.

Reich Security Forces

The Reichssicherheitshauptamt. The Third Reich's main security agency from 1939 to 1945 under the authority of the SS. The Reichssicherheitshauptamt included the Gestapo (secret police), the Sicherheitsdienst (SS intelligence service), and the Kriminalpolizei (criminal police).

Reval

The German name for Tallinn, Estonia.

Sicherheitsdienst

German for Security Service. The SS's intelligence service.

SS

Schutzstaffeln der NSDAP. The military arm of the National Socialist Party.

SS-Wirtschafter

An officer of the SS-Wirtschafts-Verwaltungshauptamt, the SS's economic and governmental authority.

Todt

See Organisation Todt, on *page 366.*

Waffen-SS

A wing of the SS military forces.

Wehrmacht

The German National Socialist Army (1935–1945).

Available From

Vintage Books

ALL THE BIRDS, SINGING

By Evie Wyld

From one of *Granta*'s Best Young British Novelists, an emotionally powerful, award-winning novel about an outsider haunted by an inescapable past. Jake Whyte has retreated to a remote farmhouse on a craggy British island, a place of ceaseless rains and battering winds, with only her collie and a flock of sheep as companions. But something—or someone—has begun picking off her sheep one by one. There are foxes in the woods, a strange man wandering the island, and rumors of a mysterious beast prowling at night. And there is Jake's relentless past—one she tried to escape thousands of miles away and years ago, concealed in stubborn silence and isolation and the scars that stripe her back. With exceptional artistry, *All the Birds, Singing* plumbs a life of fierce struggle and survival, sounding depths of unexpected beauty and hard-won redemption.

Fiction

THE AFTERMATH

By Rhidian Brook

Set in post-war Germany, the international bestseller *The Aftermath* is a stunning emotional thriller about our fiercest loyalties and our deepest desires. In the bitter winter of 1946, Rachael Morgan arrives with her only remaining son, Edmund, in the ruins of Hamburg. Here she is reunited with her husband, Lewis, a British colonel charged with rebuilding the shattered city. But as they set off for their new home, Rachael is stunned to discover that Lewis has made an extraordinary decision: they will be sharing the grand house with its previous owners, a German widower and his troubled daughter. In this charged atmosphere, enmity and grief give way to passion and betrayal.

Fiction

THE LIGHT IN THE RUINS

By Chris Bohjalian

1943: Tucked away in the idyllic hills of Tuscany, the Rosatis, an Italian family of noble lineage, believe that the walls of their ancient villa will keep them safe from the war raging across Europe. But when two soldiers—a German and an Italian—arrive at their doorstep asking to see an ancient Etruscan burial site, the Rosatis' bucolic tranquility is shattered. 1955: Serafina Bettini, an investigator with the Florence Police Department, has successfully hidden her tragic scars from WWII, at least until she's assigned to a gruesome new case—a serial killer who is targeting the remaining members of the Rosati family one by one. Soon, she will find herself digging into past secrets that will reveal a breathtaking story of moral paradox, human frailty, and the mysterious ways of the heart.

Fiction

VINTAGE BOOKS
Available wherever books are sold.
www.vintagebooks.com

Printed in the United States
by Baker & Taylor Publisher Services